WIZARDEX I

THE NORTH COUNTRY

Michael Perry

Thank you for reading. If you enjoy this book, please leave a review or connect with the author via: https://ello.co/doctoredgar

ISBN: 978-0692810552

TABLE OF CONTENTS

~SPECIAL THANKS~

There are a long list of entities that I wish to thank for helping me finally get this thing off the ground and while I'll be unable to list all of them here, you know who you are. So, with that, thanks goes to (in no particular order): My wife, my two dogs, my younger brother (for all the late night coffee trips), Denny's (for providing the late night coffee), G2 Pilot pens, snazzy leather notebooks, Spotify (in particular - Genesis, The Knife, The Cranberries, Iron Maiden, Clark, Onra, Living Colour, Metallica, Megadeth, Disturbed, Grimes, KING, Ingrid Michaelson, The Jetzons, Rush, Kylie Minogue, Echosmith, Sally Shapiro, Flying Lotus, Yeah Yeah Yeahs, Pretty Girls Make Graves, Waterproof Blonde, ABBA, Little Dragon, Lone, Shigeto, Bat For Lashes, Ryuichi Sakamoto and many, many more…), video games (in particular – Skyrim, Kirby's Adventure, Super C, Mega Man 2, The Guardian Legend, The Blue Marlin, Little Nemo – The Dream Master, Dragon Valor, Dragon Force, Jade Cocoon, Brigandine (Dryst…you badass) and many, many more…), Kiromitsu Mushanliaki, cartoons (in particular – Dragon Ball Z, Teenage Mutant Ninja Turtles (original series), Pokémon, Bump In The Night and many, many more…), Hugh Laurie (for always making me laugh), David Ellefson (for expressing interest in my first two chapters), Robert Powell (for being such a good narrator as well as making a good Jesus; speaking of…), Jesus Christ, John Cena (for never giving up), Vince McMahon, Triple H (for the brutal workout outlined in his book), Hulk Hogan (for being immortal), CM Punk (for giving me an excuse to shout, "IT'S CLOBBERING TIME!"), Frank Zappa (I thought he was a man, but he only was a muffin), pizza, cheesesteaks, Philadelphia (for providing the pizza and cheesesteaks), Pronoun, J.R.R. Tolkien and last, but not least – Steven Brust, my favorite fantasy author of all time.

~PROLOGUE~

"You elves cook a good brisket." Stated the man as he chomped into his meat, letting the drippings run down his beard.

After a few moments of smacking his lips, he spoke again.

"The boar is fair, as well."

He reached for the center of the table, where sat an ornate, silver plate with a whole ham rested on top of it, and dragged it towards him. Using his fingers, he pried a piece of bone from it, stuck it in his mouth, and began to suckle the marrow.

"Mmm." He said, as he giggled in delight.

Finished with the bone, he spat it out of his mouth onto the marble floor, next to him. Without much thought, he clasped a giant goblet with both of his hands and poured the mixture contained therein – a light, elven wine, into his mouth, allowing the excess to drizzle down his face and onto his hairy chest that was exposed by his open, brown robe.

Having finished his wine, he slammed the goblet down on the table – a thick piece of furniture made of mahogany with a dark finish, with a thud that resonated throughout the room.

"Cheese." He said, almost forgetting that his present company was sitting at the head of the table, some five feet away from him, surrounded by foodstuffs.

The one at the head of the table snapped his fingers at the request, which summoned a servant who was standing some distance away from the table, attempting not to impose himself and to ignore the fact that the, "guest of honor", as his lordship described him, had deplorable manners.

The servant, dressed in a black button down with a red bowtie, a suit that was in stark contrast to the pureness of the floor, scurried toward the table. Upon the table laid a large tray with assorted cheeses which were already cut and ready to eat. He hefted the tray and carefully brought it towards the guest.

When the servant arrived near to where the guest had seated himself, the guest eyeballed him, then eyeballed the tray, as if he were suddenly suspicious of both elf and dairy. Finally, he smiled, waved his hand over the tray, and said, "All of them."

"I beg pardon?" Asked the servant.

Annoyed, the guest pointed downwards at the table and said, insistently, "Just put it down, there!"

The servant, doing as was asked of him, placed the tray in front of the guest and returned to his prior position as the one he just served began to stuff his face.

The one at the head of the table, who was also an elf, placed his elbow on the table and his forehead in his hand.

The guest, taking a moment to break from his indulgence, turned toward the elf and spoke.

"Don't you want some?"

The elf lifted his head so that his eyes were just above his hand and simply responded, "No", before he restored his forehead to its former place of rest.

"Sure, you do." The guest said in a voice that the elf would have interpreted as being soothing, had he known better.

The guest laughed, slightly.

"Sure, you do." He repeated as he studied a piece of cheese before popping it into his mouth.

The elf at the head of the table glared at the guest and did his best to hold back his disgust.

"I hope that you're enjoying yourself." He said with much effort.

The guest deigned not to respond and simply concentrated on his act of gluttony. The elf cleared his throat and spoke, again.

"Your master well knows what it is that I want."

The guest stopped chewing for a moment, as if in thought, then he smiled, ripped a leg off of a roasted turkey nearby, and pointed it at the elf.

"Do you see this turkey, your majesty?" He said, spitting out the word, "majesty" as if he bit into something sour.

The elf raised an eyebrow and responded, "Yes".

"It was alive once, yes?"

"Yes."

"And you had it butchered, yes?"

"Correct."

"You eat it when you hunger, and it lends you its strength, yes?"

"Yes."

"Then, my dear monarch, what's the difference?"

"I don't understand."

"You kill one to benefit the whole," said the guest, waving his arms into the air, "after all, where would your kingdom be if the great king were to starve?"

He took a bite out of the meat before continuing.

"So, you sacrifice one to benefit many. Now, all my master is asking for is for you to do the same thing, again."

"We're not talking about wild game, here."

"Come, now, great king. What is one city in comparison to the rest of your kingdom, hm?"

The guest chuckled as he picked at the fowl with his fingers.

"Your people are starving." He said with a mouthful.

"I needn't be reminded of that, especially given your current circumstances."

The guest laughed a deep, belly laugh, allowing food to spew forth from his mouth.

"Then come take it from me, then!" He exclaimed, loudly, before chewing some more. He swallowed.

"But you wouldn't do that, now would you?"

"Oh?" Asked the elf as he sat up straight.

"Why, pray tell, wouldn't I?"

"Because you aim to please!" He declared, laughing and throwing the remainder of his turkey leg onto the floor.

"You see that meat on the floor, king?"

The elf looked down at it, shook his head, and said, "Yes".

"If your people so want to rid themselves of hunger, then they shall come crawling unto me like dogs and I might let them have this scrap that I've cast onto the ground."

The guest took in some more wine and wiped his face with the sleeve of his robe.

"Much like you did, remember?"

The elf stared down at the table while his guest chortled.

"I said, 'come here, boy!' and you came running to me like a mongrel." The guest said as he continued to laugh at the elf. He then proceeded to stick his tongue out and make panting noises while wiggling his rear end into the seat of his chair.

"Woof, woof!" He barked.

"That's enough, damn it!" Cried the elf.

"Fine, then." Stated the guest, nonchalantly, as he continued with his meal.

After a few moments passed, the elf finally broke the silence.

"Tell him that he can have the city, but nothing else, until I have completed my conquest."

The guest gave the elf a look of surprise and then a smile.

"That's a good elf. Bide for a moment."

The guest closed his eyes for a brief period of time. The elf couldn't see what was going on, exactly, but it appeared as if his guest were concentrating on something. Before he could look further, the guest suddenly opened his eyes, returned his attention to the elf, and spoke.

"It is done."

"Do you mean he knows?"

"Yes."

"But, how?"

The guest put a finger up to his mouth and said, "Shh. Nevermind the details. Just know that he knows and that he agrees to the terms we discussed."

The elf was very curious as to how his guest could have made contact with his superior in such a manner, but decided to let it go.

"I'm supposed to give you this." Stated the guest as he pulled out a rolled up scroll from his open robe and tossed it in the elf's general direction.

"What's this?" Asked the elf as he stood up and reached over the table to grab the scroll before returning to his seat.

"Instructions."

"Instructions?"

"Yes. Just do everything that scroll tells you to do and you will win your little, 'conquest'."

"So, now your lord is a master strategist, as well?"

The guest chuckled, "Who needs strategy when deception is so much...cleaner?"

The elf nodded and placed the scroll in the left, side pocket of his jacket.

The guest grabbed a napkin, wiped his mouth, stood up and threw the napkin haphazardly onto the table before he spoke.

"It's been a pleasure."

The elf stood up, as well, and said, "The pleasure has been all mine."

The guest smiled and said, "One more thing."

"Yes?"

"On my way in, I saw a young elf, with fine, curly, blonde hair and the most beautiful, auburn eyes. I believe that she was a member of your guard."

"What of her?"

"I wonder what she smells like? Oh, how I would love to smell her hair. I'm willing to bet you that she smells quite like lilies."

The elf didn't respond and let the guest continue.

"You'd like to find out, wouldn't you?"

Again, the elf chose not to respond. This time, however, his guest walked up to him and placed a hand upon his shoulder before he continued.

"I want you to fuck her. Hard. Do you understand?"

The elf dropped his head and stared hard at the ground.

"Will you do this for me?"

The elf continued to stare at the floor.

"Hey," said the guest, placing his hand upon the elf's chin and tilting his head up until their eyes locked, "will you do this for me?"

The elf chewed his lip and whispered, "Yes".

"Good elf." Replied the guest as he gently smacked the elf across his cheek, twice.

The guest turned to walk up the steps that he took to arrive at the banquet hall while the elf turned his back toward him and thought. A moment later, the elf turned back toward his guest to say something, but stopped short when he saw that his guest was nowhere to be found. The elf whirled back toward the table where his guest had feasted to find it empty, the chairs undisturbed, the floor clean as ever. He started to make an inquiry of his servant as to the events that just took place, but his servant was also not present in the room.

The king sighed and took a seat at the empty, banquet table.

Pondering for a moment, he called for his guard. Shortly thereafter, a young, female elf dressed in a skull cap and armed with a long spear came running into the room. As was pointed out to him earlier, she was quite fair. She hustled down the steps, shaking her chainmail, stood in front of the king and saluted.

"How may I be of service, my liege?"

The king stared at her for a moment and shook his head. He then took her hand and said, "Follow me."

~CHAPTER ONE – THE ELVEN CITY~

After a quarter century, had our search finally come to fruition? We poured over the ancient texts, with sweat upon our brows and cracks on our fingertips, searching for the clue. Searching…for an answer. Finally, we found it. Not the answer, no, but the clue. Finally, we traced it down. We looked at each other, not speaking a word. But we knew what we were saying. We knew what had to be done. We rolled up the scroll and departed.

Dearest Rudgaf – Lord of Red,

The eastern elven city of Behnon has been besieged and reduced to cinders! I desperately need your wisdom regarding this matter. I urge you to, as quickly as you find possible, investigate this horrifying tragedy. Thank you for your time, which I know to be precious.

Warm Regards,

Moldof – King of the Northern Dwarves

Rudgaf refolded the fiery, red piece of paper, whose color he found to be a bit too ironic, and put it back into the pocket of his cloak.

Burned to cinders?

Rudgaf rubbed his beard at the thought.

How?

Rudgaf wiped the sweat from his brow. The fire in the corner was roaring as the Moon rose to clinch control of the sky. The inn keeper added more logs to the fire to keep it piping hot for all of the travelers that were bound to, and were, coming in to lodge at the inn. Rudgaf, being wise, made sure to show up early to claim his room and bed. After all, no wizard really ever enjoyed making a bed of dirt and rocks. In fact, he reckoned, no one really ever enjoyed making a bed of dirt and rocks. No, he thought, save that for the dead.

"More herbal tea, Lord?"

"Certainly!"

What a gracious host. It's a wonder that I have not been here before!

The Lord of Red sipped his tea.

The tea, hmm! Each sip reminds me of my former home. Why, I can still remember sitting on the fence in my father's orchard, munching on apples. I remember…lying in the fields as the breeze flew through my hair – the remainder of it tickling my nose with the smell of lilies and lilacs. How long has it been, now? Oh, about four hundred and thirty years, I'd reckon. I'm old! Yet, I still feel young. That's all that matters in the end.

Rudgaf pondered for a moment.

How I do miss those wild flowers! I enjoy the North along with my companions, yet I do miss the wild flowers. Not much is ever seen growing around there…that is, unless you count Barlow's forest.

Reminiscing about an ancient home got the red wizard to thinking about other memories. His eyes brightened as he remembered something that he brought along with him in the pocket of his cloak. He reached his hand in his pocket and pulled out a drawing that he had made nearly fifty years ago with his own hands. The drawing, quite lifelike in appearance from centuries of practice, was of his friend, Mika. Holding it up to best catch the light coming from the roaring fireplace, he studied it. Mika, longtime resident of Behnon and friends with Rudgaf for nearly as long, was middle aged in the drawing – around one hundred years of age or so. Yet, he still had a youthful, childish look about him with big, bright blue eyes that one could tell concentrated with utmost difficulty to keep still while the artist completed his work, but badly wanted to go running off on another adventure.

Mika…I wonder how you're doing, old friend?

Rudgaf continued to sip his tea while studying the picture. Mika had brown hair, then, which the red wizard was convinced would now be grey or, perhaps, silver – as some elves, but not many, grew.

It seems like yesterday that you got me out of that bind, Mika. You were the only one that believed that I didn't murder the governor's mistress. I'll never forget you.

The wizard promptly returned the drawing to its former place of residence and then ripped off a chunk of the brown, barley loaf that the inn keeper put on the table but a few moments ago.

Hot!

He shook his fingers and took a ceremoniously large bite.

And the honey barley loaf! Most excellent! Now, this is an inn that serves a fine bread…and this is a wizard that appreciates a fine bread! My mother used to make a bread as fine as this. Yes, I remember how my father used to make me grind the wheat for the bread. I hated every moment of it, but her bread…it was more than enough to compensate for a lost afternoon and anything that can compensate for lost time is a treasure, indeed!

Rudgaf continued to enjoy his bread and, while doing so, took in the scenery with delight.

This is a nice place to sit. From here, I can get a nice view of the skyline through the giant, glass windows. It's a clear night. If the Moon wasn't there, I could star gaze for a while. Pity.

I can also see everyone coming in, and out, of the inn. My back is against the wall, so I can observe every table without having to look behind me. Indeed, I am going to proclaim this as my favorite spot! This inn? The finest I've ever stayed in!

Quickly disposing of the loaf, the wizard stood up in a simultaneous motion of hoisting himself and smacking the crumbs from his white beard onto the oaken table. He peered around the room. It had the look and feel of a log cabin, but it wasn't. Certainly, it had wooden floors, wooden doors, the walls and countertops were comprised of actual logs and all of the furniture was comprised of oak. Certainly, it had the look and feel of a log cabin, but it wasn't a log cabin, not by his estimation.

No one was suspicious looking, which was the second pity of the night. As he peered, he saw dwarves, primarily, which was to be expected in a dwarven mining town. Here and there, Rudgaf noticed some humans and even a few elves, which could be considered suspicious in its own right if not for the fact that they were drinking and merrymaking like all of the rest. Actions such as that, he reckoned, were unbecoming of a person or group of people that had just ransacked a city and laid it to waste.

No, nothing here.

Rudgaf locked eyes with the inn keeper and, taking off his exceedingly large and pointy hat while bowing, thanked him for the food and the drink and all of the generosity. After giving credit where credit was due, Rudgaf turned towards the oaken stairs, felt the fine wood that composed the railing, and climbed up towards his room.

Second on the right.

He then turned the golden door knob, opened the door (which was also made of oak) with a creak and stepped inside, shutting the door behind him.

Drats! I forgot to grab a candle from the inn keeper. No matter, I'll find my way around.

The wizard, looking extremely cumbersome, fumbled his way through the dark of night. After but a few moments, his hand touched a (oak) tabletop. Upon this tabletop, his hands felt a candle holder, but...

Blast! No candle!

He fumbled around some more as his hands were about to come upon a (stone!) fireplace. However, before his eager hands could grasp and feel the very salvation that the wizard longed for, his head decided it was time to take a turn at the "feeling" game as it collided with a (oak) support beam.

Oof!

Rubbing his head and nursing this terrible wound, the wizard turned around and found that his hands were, yet again, beaten to the punch by his toes as it collided with the (oak) foot of his bed.

Ouch!

The wizard had half a mind to jump up and grab his foot, but in order to spare his poor noggin the trouble of taking another turn at the little game he had started, he decided to sit down on, what most certainly was, his bed.

Leave the washing for the morrow!

With that thought he proceeded to toss his hat, cloak, and boots onto the floor. It was a bit nippy in the room, but he didn't feel like trying to fumble for the fireplace in the dark, so he decided that he was going to sleep with his tunic, shirt, and pants still on his person.

Rudgaf whirred around on his bottom, forcing his head to collide with the head of the bed and his feet to collide with the foot of the bed.

Ouch! Dang blasted dwarven beds!

Finally, he was able to situate himself into a comfortable, yet somewhat awkward position with his head and back placed carefully against the head of the bed, with a pillow in between, and his feet slightly dangling off of the foot of the bed. With this, the wizard closed his eyes to join the Sun and the blue of the sky in rest. Yet, Rudgaf couldn't help but wonder, as the night passed, who was responsible for destroying the elven city? Indeed, King Moldof and his letter weighed heavily upon the wizard's mind.

War...Oh, my mind. The world will not allow peace so please, mind, allow an old fool to have peace for the remainder of the night.

With that, the Lord of Red dozed off.

Rudgaf rose with the Sun, as was his custom. Now that he could see the contents of the room clearly, thanks to the light of day shining in through the window next to his bed, he noticed a wash bucket near to his left foot, which planted itself on the floor in the middle of the night. No sooner did he rise out of bed and lay hold of the wash bucket when there came a knock at his door. Upon crossing the room and opening the door, he was greeted by the sight of a smiling dwarf who provided Rudgaf with steamed towels and hot water for the wash bucket, which Rudgaf accepted with glee. Saying not a word, because not a word needed to be said, the inn keeper closed the door and went off doing whatever it is that dwarven inn keepers do.

Do I perform magic? No! True magic lies in the inn keeper's smile.

Sparing you the details of washing, since I'm sure that we've all done it before and know the process by heart, the wizard finished up and replaced his boots, and his flame red cloak and hat, and eagerly went down the stairs for some breakfast.

If breakfast is as half as good as dinner, I'm in for a real treat!

Upon arriving to the dining area, the wizard noticed that it was surprisingly empty. He was the first, and only one up. How the inn keeper knew exactly what time the wizard awoke was beyond comprehension. Rudgaf would have inquired, but he thought better of it.

Let the inn keeper have his secrets and the tricks of his trade.

Rudgaf sat down at his "favorite" table and, without even asking or having a moment for a thought, the inn keeper came around with a hearty breakfast. Presented to Rudgaf was a large bowl of oatmeal with slices of freshly picked apple. With it came herbal tea, barley rolls, and some lemon muffins – all freshly prepared that morning. Again, without even a moment for a thought, the wizard helped himself, all the while the inn keeper smiled and stayed out of the business of the wizard and his breaking of the fast.

The wizard finished, smacked his beard, leaned back in his chair and rubbed his belly.

Most excellent!

Truly, the Lord of Red was pleased.

After having but only a moment to contemplate his pleasure, the inn keeper came up to Rudgaf to try to buy his attention. The wizard locked eyes with him.

"How was it, Lord?" Inquired the smiling inn keeper.

Rudgaf smacked his beard some more and said, "Most excellent! It has been ages since I have had the pleasure to indulge myself in such fine cookery!"

The inn keeper blushed a bit and replied, "'tis but all a humble inn keeper can offer."

The wizard smiled and stood up. Unfortunately, he thought, he had business of a much more serious nature to attend to and could not tarry any longer. Rudgaf locked eyes with the smiling inn keeper again and gave him the customary wave of the exceedingly large and pointy hat with a bow, which had far more meaning behind it than what appeared.

However, as Rudgaf started to make his way toward the exit of that fine establishment, the inn keeper cleared his throat as if to try to garner the attention of the wizard. He succeeded.

Rudgaf, again locking eyes with the inn keeper, who was no longer smiling, awaited the first move. After a slight pause, the inn keeper girded himself up, and said "I beg your pardon, Lord."

Rudgaf smiled and responded, "Yes, fine inn keeper? What is it?"

The inn keeper stood firm and said, "I hope ye don't mind when me story is through, Lord, but I feel that I've overstepped me place."

"Go on."

"Well, me Lord, and I do beg your pardon if me actions offend ye, but ye had a visitor last night."

The wizard looked puzzled and asked, "For me? Good heavens! Did I, in my nightly sloth, ignore a guest that came to see me but thought better of it, lest said guest disturb me in my bedchamber?"

"No, Lord! Ye have no blame in this. Yer actions were becoming of a fine nobleman. No, Lord, I did not allow him to pass. He looked mighty shifty, if I do say so, meself."

Rudgaf shrugged his shoulders and said with a chuckle, "So would've I, to your estimation, if I hadn't been known as a friend to your people! Tell me, good inn keeper, what did this visitor look like?"

The inn keeper looked up to the ceiling and rubbed his chin, remembering every detail of the shady character that dared to defile his good inn. After a moment, he said, "Well, he had a big, white beard…much like yers! He came in, not bearing a sword as ye did, but a pair of fine daggers. I remember that he also had a grey cloak." The inn keeper shook his head, "Can't remember anything more!"

Rudgaf, a little bewildered and upset that the inn keeper did not inform him of this visitor, asked, "Did he give a name?"

The inn keeper, whose stature had decreased substantially in the mind of the wizard at this point in time, responded, "Why, yes he did! What was it…er…Dan…something or other." At this point, the wizard wanted to interject with a suggestion but the inn keeper stopped him and said, "Nope! I've got it! It's on the tip of me tongue…Dana…Danagan! That's what it was, unless me father was an elf!"

Rudgaf rose himself up in anger and said, "Fool! That was a wizard! You should think yourself fortunate to still be standing!"

"Bu…bu…but," prattled the inn keeper, "he didn't look like either of the other wizards from the North Tower!"

Rudgaf shook his head, "That's because he wasn't from the North Tower. He was from the East Tower."

Before Rudgaf had a moment to think as to why Danagan would be searching for him, or how he even knew where to inquire about him in the first place, he noticed that the inn keeper was having a fit of rage.

"The East Tower? In *my* house?!"

The furious dwarf then proceeded to call forth all of his servants and demanded that the place be cleaned, top to bottom, to rid the fine house of the wizard filth. Shocked, yet understanding, the servants went straight to work. But, before the inn keeper could get to the work of "purification", Rudgaf asked that the inn keeper give him back the sword that he had to check in before he was permitted to stay there. In a huff, the inn keeper did as Rudgaf asked him. With a bow, Rudgaf apologized that Danagan had come to see him that night and insisted that he had not been expecting the visit.

"I know, I know." Said the inn keeper. "Yer a good wizard. Yer always welcome here."

They bowed to each other once more. Rudgaf, of course, flared his hat and, replacing it upon his head, turned and left the inn.

~

Danagan had never sported a beard.

Chalk that up on the long list of odd occurrences that had happened over the past month. Although this business with the supposed Lord of Grey was the freshest piece of business on Rudgaf's mind, there was still also the mysterious attack on the elven city to investigate, on top of Thome's sudden excursion into the west of which he told not a soul much about other than a letter that simply stated, "Gone desert trekking". Why Thome, the Lord of Blue, would want to travel to the west where ne'r a raindrop can be found (of course, this is an exaggeration, but not an extreme one) was rather perplexing. But…Thome has always been rather queer. However, that is a story that shall be addressed later and certainly wasn't at the top of Rudgaf's thought stack. Only one thing was on the wizard's mind.

Danagan had never sported a beard.

Now, granted, it had been several decades since the two (being Rudgaf and Danagan) had crossed paths, but, wizards never age. As a matter of fact, the state of the wizard upon the receiving of his or her power remains constant until that power is forfeited. Rudgaf was nearly sixty years of age when he received his power and, at that time, he was sporting a rather significant beard that has stayed with him to the very day (and, thus, why he has an inherent fear of razors). Danagan, however, was a young man, no more than thirty years of age and, at the time, he was rather clean shaven. Danagan has not the ability to grow a beard, yet the inn keeper swore that he had one.

This, along with the business that had brought the wizard to the east in the beginning, was all fairly troubling. If what the inn keeper said was, indeed, true and not some strange hallucination that he had in the middle of the night, then there was someone impersonating a wizard on the loose. Then again, perhaps Danagan sported some ridiculous disguise so as to not be recognized and immediately ousted from the town (which would have been the least of what the dwarves would have done, had they known that he was a wizard from the East Tower).

Now, what is this business between the East Tower and the dwarves? None of your business, that's what. That is, at least for now.

Unlike the north, which is mountainous, rocky and usually cold, the east is mainly woodlands until one reaches the coast. The eastern elves prefer living in the woodlands (thus, why they do) but that's not to say that all elves enjoy woodlands and moderate climates. The southern elves, for instance, prefer the tropical, jungle climates of the south. Some eastern elves, returning to the former people of discussion, prefer to live directly on the coast with sand, water and rude, pinchy crabs. In fact, not every dwarf prefers the bitter cold, either. The dwarves that the wizard had just lodged with prefer woodlands over mountains even though they are, technically, still considered northern dwarves. Yet, the dark iron dwarves, cousins to the northern dwarves, prefer the sand and heat that accompanies the far west. It's really all up to preference.

Rudgaf walked through the woods gingerly, needing not a map. He had roamed the entire breadth of the continent multiple times in his lifespan, so he knew the area fairly well. Rudgaf had taken the path leading from the Northern Tower heading south across the frozen river of "Haran" which, in the dwarven tongue, simply means "Cold". To Rudgaf, it was simply called "Cold River". After crossing, Rudgaf went through the dwarven mountain pass (which the wizards from the other towers were not allowed to take, making it nearly impossible for any of them to pay a visit, lest they wished to scale the mountain) and followed the road through a chain of ten or more dwarven mining towns, all of which are nameless. The snow can visibly be seen fading away into the woodlands at around the fifth town. The tenth town, which Rudgaf lodged at, is right on the edge of the border between the dwarven Kingdom of Moldof (named Moldof, since the northern dwarves always rename the kingdom based on whomever the king is) and the elven Kingdom of Behun (named after the capital Behun, which literally means "First City". This, in Rudgaf's opinion, speaks volumes about their creativity). The city that Rudgaf was headed towards, Behnon, is far north of Behun and more towards the mountains dividing the northern portion of the continent and the eastern portion (for all intents and purposes, Behnon is the ninth city).

...And, if you were of the mapmaking sort and jotting all of this down, it would be right about here that you would be forced to stop. Why? That is because of Barlow's self-made forest. The story goes that, when the northern wizards were attempting to gain the trust of the northern dwarves, the wizard Barlow, being the Lord of Green, created an expanding, ever green, ever variable forest. At first, it was rather localized to the dwarven capital of Moldof, however, it eventually expanded from the capital, swathing a path all the way into elven territory. The forest was a most impressive feat, and much appreciated by the dwarves because, as previously stated, not much ever grows in the frozen north. The forest, itself, is constantly changing based upon the needs of its inhabitants. It is because of this reason that the northern dwarves are rather well off from an economic standpoint – they use the various woods for building homes, selling, and the fletching of bows. It is also for this reason that the elves were not at all upset with the forest encroaching upon their territory. However, for reasons unknown, the forest stopped expanding around one hundred and fifty eight years ago, encompassing the entire northern dwarven kingdom and the northern tip of the eastern elven kingdom, ending just outside of Behnon. The same mysterious reason, perhaps, could also explain why the forest never expanded across the rest of the northern part of the continent into goblin territory or the area surrounding the North Tower. Perhaps this was Barlow's intention from the start, but he was never open to speaking about it. By-the-by, for those of you paying attention, only the wizards call the forest "Barlow's Forest". The dwarves call the forest, "Ara", meaning, "Miracle". It is also known by other names. In fact, the elves refer to it as, "Miri", which means, "Mystery", whereas the orcs and the goblins simply call it showing off.

The red wizard was more than ready to start his journey through brush, branch, and over rocks and streams. As of that morning, most of his trek towards Behnon had been completed, as the final dwarven mining town was a mere few hours walking distance away from his destination. Rudgaf knew that, as soon as he hit Barlow's Forest, his journey was near completion. Every now and then, he would stop to observe the various types of trees and flowers and fully record them to memory in order to draw them later, a hobby that he had recently picked up only a little over a hundred years ago. As of the trees, Rudgaf encountered a gigantic conifer whose roots must've spread out over a mile in all directions.

The tree was very gnarly and quite old, which Rudgaf appreciated (as he did anything that was older than him). The behemoth conifer contained so much character within it, that Rudgaf wouldn't have been at all surprised if it had started walking and talking at a whim. If Barlow were there, he probably could've made it do just that, but that's enough about him and the conifer for now.

It wasn't long after that Rudgaf came into Barlow's Forest. He, of course, took the time to observe every growing thing that there was to observe because, as stated previously, Barlow's Forest was an ever-variable forest that never stayed the same and was never the same in more than one area. This, being the eastern elven area and given the season, would have had Rudgaf expecting to see all sorts of grapes, if he were but a bit further south. The forest, however, only provided what was needed, so instead he saw fruit trees – apples, primarily. While continuing on his trek, every now and again he knelt down next to a tree to observe the various edible fungi growing throughout the land. Despite all the excitement, the wizard couldn't help but feel a tad bit disappointed at the lack of grapes. He imagined his last trip to Behun where vineyards of grapes stretched out as far as he could see. All kinds of grapes could be seen from small to large. Green grapes, black grapes, and red grapes dazzled the country side. Rudgaf's mouth began to water as he daydreamed of elven jam and the delicacy that they were most noted for – elven wine. It took some time for Rudgaf to snap back to reality as he realized that he didn't have time for such things and, in any case, he was far removed from any elven city that could supply any of those delicacies to him, being that Behnon was separated from any city that could make these things by some distance and, in any case, was supposedly in ruins. Suffice to say, the disappointment left him with his countenance fallen as he journeyed on. Yes, eastern elven wine and jam really are that good.

It was shortly after this that the red wizard finally arrived at his destination. Rather, he stumbled upon it, since he had rightly lost track of what he was doing, what with all of the sights to behold and memories to recall. As Rudgaf was admiring the various flora and fauna of the forest, his attention was caught away by an unexpected surprise, as surprises often are. Rudgaf knelt down and observed a body lying face down in the grass. Our surprise, which appeared to have met some sort of unfortunate fate, was most assuredly dead, as Rudgaf noted by the lack of movement. The body was clad in an iron plate body with chain leggings and rough, leather boots. It wasn't adorned with any sort of headgear or gloves, as Rudgaf could easily observe every black hair on its head and the olive, green skin that was exposed on its hands, neck, and head.

It *stunk*.

Indeed, it wouldn't have been pleasant to the olfactory receptors of any man or beast. It was rather clear, given the smell and the various pestilence that surrounded the body to enjoy a mid-afternoon snack, that the body had been around for a while. Fitting the pieces together, Rudgaf was easily able to deduce that this creature had belonged to whatever camp was responsible for the raid of the city, as the body was found a mere ten yards away from the city gate. Rudgaf stared at the body for the space of a few minutes. A true look of disdain and deep concern was fully flush across the wizard's face. Certainly, the question had already been answered but, being thorough as ever a wizard should be, Rudgaf could not resist turning the body over to expose the face of what he already knew to be...

An orc!

It was at this very moment that the cause of death could also be determined. The throat of the orc was slit from ear to ear, which lead to a fairly painful death involving the orc bleeding out and falling face down – thus explaining the position that Rudgaf found him in.

The Lord of Red couldn't help but wonder, however, at how peculiar the situation was. In particular, the fact remained that the battle that took place at Behnon had happened several weeks ago. However, the pestilence just started arriving at the carcass to feast upon it. The carcass, albeit smelly and slightly decomposed, looked far too fresh to be laid down a few weeks ago. If anything, it was no more than a few days old.

Rudgaf pushed forward until he reached the city gate, which was actually more like a door. The door was constructed of mahogany wood and stood around fifty feet high. It was attached to gear mechanisms, the foremost of these were perched above the actual door and constructed upon the stone archway, built for the cause of opening and closing the door. The door itself served two purposes, to let people in and to keep people out, as contradictory as that statement may seem. The odd thing about it, as Rudgaf noticed immediately, was that there was no sign of a forced break in. The orcs were masters of ballistics. There was neigh a city that they couldn't break into. They would haul herculean sized stones onto catapults to take down the city walls, and construct giant battering rams with which they would use to break down any city gate. However, the door was not destroyed. In fact, it hardly had a scratch on it. The actual walls of the city were also left untouched. Even the archery towers, sitting above the city walls on either side of the door, were unscathed.

Was that orc a sentry, then?

Rudgaf nodded his head. Indeed, the orc must have been slain after the city had been overrun. The strange thing, however, was that there was no sign, at least on the outside, that the city had actually been overtaken. Before jumping to any conclusions about the events of the actual battle and whether or not it took place as was insisted, because it clearly hadn't since the city was still standing, Rudgaf decided to actually step into the city via the door which was left carelessly open. It was almost as if whoever was responsible for overtaking the city were actually *welcoming* him in. Nevertheless, the red wizard was determined to enter and investigate without making so much as a squeak.

Stepping into the city quite gingerly, Rudgaf peered around as he treaded the dirt road that led from the main gate, around the city, and eventually to the office of the governor (named Roland, if any of you cared to know). The city was built in such a way, as all elven cities are, to allow the main road to branch off into every area of the city, be it business, government, or residential. Rudgaf was determined to be as thorough as possible and examine every branch of the city. Whether it took him the better half of the day or even a week was of no matter to him.

The business branch of the city was first in order (a brilliant design and completely intentional as no citizen or visitor was allowed to access any other part of the city without first being tempted to lend a helping hand to the local economy and, likewise, no person was allowed to leave without being tempted in the same said manner). To access it, Rudgaf first walked along the main road and turned a corner, which led him to the market – the base of the branch (yes, each branch of the city was shaped like a literal tree branch). Here were various stalls which allowed Rudgaf to reminisce a bit about coming to the area during more peaceful times to inspect the fine elven wares while biting his lip and still being hung up about the lack of availability of the elven delicacies that were mentioned earlier. Not surprisingly, the area was abandoned. Not a soul was to be found. Surprisingly, however, but not out of the ordinary compared with what had been observed thus far, there were no bodies, no signs of struggle, and no signs of war. Perplexed, all the red wizard could do was venture onward into the main part of the branch.

The wind kicked up the dust underneath Rudgaf's feet and collided with the sign of the blacksmith shop, causing it to swing back and forth, wildly. The Lord of Red surveyed the area, but all that could be seen was an abyss of dust and broken expectations. For all intents and purposes, the branch appeared to be abandoned. Rudgaf decided that, since the wind had already chosen for him, he would investigate the blacksmith shop. However, upon arriving at the door way, he found it to be completely locked up and had no way of entering it without potentially causing unwanted attention. Across the street, he found the alchemy shop in much the same condition, as well as the fletching shop, general goods store, and the house of bards. Picking up the pad lock at the last of these shops and swinging it at the door in frustration, Rudgaf decided to lean his back on the doorway and plump down on his rump. He looked around, further, but after observing much of the same characteristics that he had been observing the entire time since his arrival at the city, he gave a long, drawn out sigh.

I'm not going to end up leaving here empty handed, am I?

Rudgaf took off his hat and leaned his head against the hard, oaken slab that comprised the doorway and attempted to make himself comfortable. After a few moments of contemplation, Rudgaf grew tired of his sword and scabbard disabling him from leaning against the doorway as much as he had wanted to, so he decided to unhook his scabbard and place it across his lap. He tilted his head to his left and fiddled around with the brass button that connected the scabbard to his cloak until it came undone. After accomplishing this, he then titled his head to the right to unhook the brass button connecting the scabbard to his hip in the same said manner. It was at this point that he noticed something out of the ordinary. Taking a break from the purpose of making himself comfortable, Rudgaf observed a tiny speck of something red that was upon the wooden floorboards that were built outside of the door to the shop. The speck would've been hardly noticeable to Rudgaf upon his arrival to the front of the store, but now that he noticed it, it stuck out like a sore thumb. Upon further observation, the Lord of Red noticed that it was dark and dry, despite having been in liquid form at some point in time. Rudgaf shook his head.

Blood.

The red wizard smiled with glee as, perhaps, he would not be forced to leave his investigation empty handed. He stood up, adjusted his sword and scabbard, rehooked it back to his cloak, then replaced his hat. He then carefully inspected areas in close proximity to the spot of blood that he originally observed and, behold, he found another. Then he found another, and another, and still, yet, another. As Rudgaf had hoped, the spots of blood seemed to be forming a trail, leading him in a path while simultaneously becoming larger and more frequent.

Fascinated by the trail, Rudgaf followed it without paying the least bit of attention as to where it was leading him. It wasn't until he nearly collided with a wall that he bothered to take his attention off of the blood to look around and notice that the trail had actually led him behind the building where the discovery had first been made. Right in front of Rudgaf was a broken window. He observed bits of shattered glass on the window sill, and still more glass that was cached in blood.

Curious, and ever observant, Rudgaf peeked his head through the vacant frame that once housed a window to observe the innards of the building. Inside, as expected, the Lord of Red noticed yet more shattered glass and blood. However, it was a tad dark in the room to be able to see much further than a few feet, so Rudgaf decided to step into the building through the obvious vacancy in the wall.

The shattered remains of the aperture crunched under his boots as he entered. The red wizard breathed in the dank air of the dark shop and looked around. It had items that would be expected to be found within a house of bards – guitars, lutes, and various other stringed instruments were strewn about the walls. In the midst of these displays laid the rare elven instrument known as the "Bala-Lin" which, in the elven tongue, translates to, "Miracle String". Indeed, it was a miracle, for so rare were these instruments that observing one, in person, was a miracle in and of itself, let alone being able to actually *build* one. To do so required the most delicate of elven hands, lest the strings, made from the very chin hairs of the rare and exceedingly dangerous red dragons of the western hills, should be torn asunder. The wood for the instrument, made from the "Anak" tree, which cannot be found in Barlow's Forest and can only be found in the jungles of the south, was one of the toughest substances known to creation. If chopping one of the trees down was difficult, you can rest assured that whittling a piece of the wood that was no softer than granite into the shape of the instrument was even more difficult. This particular instrument was even more ornate than usual, as it was covered in gold as its finish and perfectly polished, as Rudgaf was able to notice its shine even in the dim lighting of the shop.

Despite being a sight of pure beauty and wonderment, Rudgaf was troubled and puzzled by its existence. Why the orcs would not steal such a rare and valuable item upon ransacking the city was beyond his comprehension. Selling one of these instruments to a collector would generate enough funds, on average, to feed and outfit the entire orc army for the space of half a year. Yet, there it sat, untouched, unscathed, and unblemished, save for the blood that was splattered all over its glass display case which did not come to Rudgaf's attention until that very moment. The blood was located on the back of the display case and, rather than being in the form of spots and specks, it was rather smeared on. Rudgaf began to walk around to observe the offending side of the display case more thoroughly, but before he could accomplish his goal, his feet collided with a semi-solid object. Looking down, the Lord of Red was able to see the offender who blemished the display case, very much dead and very much on the floor.

The dead orc was laid to rest in a sitting position with his back leaning on the stand that held the display case of the "Miracle String". Rudgaf knelt down and, upon closer examination, he noticed that the body did not protrude any foul odors. On the front of the body, near the orc's midsection, could be found a large gash, most likely placed there by a knife or a dagger, and upon pushing the body forward to expose the backside, Rudgaf noticed two, sizeable stab wounds where two daggers would have perfectly punctured the orc's lungs. Putting the pieces of the puzzle together, the red wizard deduced that the orc was probably defending itself when it suffered a severe slash wound across its belly. The orc either then was forced through the window of the shop, or simply fell through, continued fighting, suffered the mortal stab wounds to the lungs, fell against the display case, and died.

Rudgaf turned his hands around to observe his palms and noted that they were wet with blood. The body of this orc was *very* fresh, being laid in that position no more than a day ago. In fact, it was most likely that it was laid there a mere few hours ago.

The Lord of Red stood up and wiped his hands on a spare cloth that he keeps on his person for just such occasions. After thoroughly cleaning them, he brushed his hand through his beard and contemplated the events thus far. What he had observed up to this point was in stark contrast with what had been reported. Even odder was the lack of elves. Where were they? The city showed no signs of being ransacked as was reported, however, the original inhabitants of the city were nowhere to be found and, instead, they were replaced by two, brutally executed orcs that belonged to a race of people that, frankly, hadn't had any business to do with the eastern elves in hundreds of years.

The red wizard turned around and exited the establishment the same way that he entered. He then walked back around to the front of the building and continued down the pathway, passing by the produce store and the butcher shop, both of which were locked in the same manner as the rest of the buildings. He treaded the dirt road, down a hill, around another corner, and entered the final section of the business branch which was mainly dedicated to entertainment such as restaurants, pubs, theatres, and inns.

Perhaps it was intuition, perhaps it was because it was hot, or perhaps it was because Rudgaf was distracted by a desire to quench his thirst but, he passed by a few closed restaurants as he was immediately drawn towards the pub. The pub could easily be spotted by its sign, featuring a large pint of ale, swinging in the wind. Rudgaf made it the highest priority on his itinerary and headed towards the front door of the building as soon as the sign came in sight.

Contrary to elven wine, which was mainly sweet with a tad tartness to it, and fizzled down the throat of the drinker like spectacular fireworks, dwarven ale was only slightly sweet with bitter undertones and smooth enough to the point that it felt as if you were drinking silk, if such a thing were possible. Both are excellent choices of beverage, in their own ways, however dwarven ale is an acquired taste and not everyone, not even every dwarf, enjoys it. Most of the older dwarves enjoy it very much, and actually prefer it to the taste of elven wine. However, most younger people of every race prefer the sweetness of elven wine except for the orcs and the goblins, who haven't had any of either beverage pass through their lips in hundreds of years. Rudgaf had heard rumors that both the orcs and the goblins have invented their own beverages that are far better than both dwarven ale and elven wine, and even better than each other's. Most people just laugh it off as nonsense whenever an orc or a goblin is so bold as to make such a statement filled with such blatant ignorance. However, Rudgaf did, at one point in time, have the "honor" and the "privilege" of following up on the rumors by trying both of these "miracle" beverages. Suffice to say, it wasn't his cup of tea, or mug of ale, or what have you. Furthermore, as far as the battle between dwarven ale and elven wine is concerned, Rudgaf never dared pick a side and was merely happy to report that he would never decline a sample from either them if ever the opportunity arose for him to indulge in one (or two, or three).

As Rudgaf made a heading towards the pub, he obviously had a mind on dwarven ale since that is the only thing served at elven pubs. The elves considered their wine far too precious and special to be served amongst the common riff raff that frequented these types of establishments (ironically, but of no surprise, the northern dwarves do not serve dwarven ale in their pubs – instead electing to serve elven wine, when they can manage to import it) and, to be quite frank, most of the few that have tried the orc and goblin variations of ale share Rudgaf's opinion and never make a personal request for either of the aforementioned ales at any pub.

Before the Lord of Red got too lost in age old arguments that would, most likely, never be resolved, he arrived at the door to the pub to notice that it was not only unlocked and left open haphazardly, but it also had deep gash wounds in it. Looking down at his feet, Rudgaf noticed a trail of blood that led right into the pub and exposed another dead orc whose body was laid across the bar in a face down position. Undeterred, Rudgaf stepped into the establishment and had a look around. He noticed two more dead orcs – one to his left lying face up at the end of the bar, and one still in its seat, head down on the table staring at Rudgaf, mug in hand. Without even having to look, Rudgaf knew that these three orcs met the fate of a dagger and, sure enough, upon further inspection, all three had been killed by a dagger or a knife much like the previous two that Rudgaf had found earlier in the day.

Amidst the process of checking dead bodies, Rudgaf noticed a dripping sound and rushed over to the other side of the bar to notice that the taps for the ale were leaking, leaving a considerable amount of it on the floor, wetting the wizard's boots. Still hopeful, Rudgaf grabbed a clean pint glass from the shelves behind him, held it up to the spout, and loosed the tap on the barrel of ale. Nothing but a drop. Saddened, he tried it on the barrel directly next to the other and came up short again.

Damn.

Rudgaf threw the glass down in disgust, shattering it without a care. Seeing quite enough, he left the pub, reunited his boots with the dirt road, and headed toward the next branch of the city which was purely dedicated to the town square and buildings pertaining to government functions.

Upon crossing the line between the final part of the business branch and the beginning of the government branch, one may notice some slight changes. Other than the obvious – which is that there are no buildings constructed for the mere purpose of selling goods – the other observation that can be made is that there are no longer any buildings made out of wood and even the road evolves from a simple, dirt pathway into a much more refined road, both of the aforementioned being made of stone (marble and cobblestone, respectively). This change, as strange as it may seem, came from the direct result of expansion and the elven civil war, of which we will not delve into here. Suffice it to say that the elven civil war is the reason behind not only the structural change that Rudgaf was experiencing, but is also the reason behind there being two different elven kingdoms, as mentioned earlier.

Before Rudgaf could take the road to the town square, the main part of the government branch, however, he felt as if a pair of eyes belonging to someone or something were scanning the area, looking for him – seeking him out. Rudgaf carefully surveyed the area himself, but after some time, he found nothing. The red wizard shrugged off the feeling as best as he could, took another step forward, and that's when he heard "it". "It" being the loud, unmistakable, soul piercing screech of which the source thereof could not be mistaken.

Dread eagles! It cannot be so!

The red wizard shot a glance up into the sky and lo, at the top of the clouds flew a band of four eagles, their wings outstretched and eyes gazing upon the earth below them. With great purpose, their wings flapped into the wind, the span of which exceeded forty feet, as their mouths gave way to another loud screech. Rudgaf ducked underneath the roof of the walkway of the nearest building in hopes of remaining hidden and hoping ever the more that he was not seen.

The Lord of Red pondered for a moment as to why the dread eagles could be there in the first place. Originally, these birds were from the southernmost coasts, bred by the birdmen that were also indigenous to the area, and under their complete dominion. However, the dread eagles were liberated after Joem, the Lord of Yellow, ousted the birdmen and wrested control of the region from their nightmarish claws. Since then, the dread eagles, now being a free race, often contract themselves out to other races. As fierce as they are, they are often used as scouts, since their eyesight is so wondrous that they can detect movement on the ground from several miles away where they would stay safe from any ground based attack except from that of the most elite marksmen.

Even more frightful than the dread eagles are the breed of birds that usually accompany them. Some call them the death hawks while others call them the "assassins from the skies". These birds typically come in large packs because of their size. Do not be mistaken, however. Death hawks may be much smaller than their companions, the dread eagles, but they are, by no means, "small". Their wingspans stretch between eight to eleven feet on average. What they don't have in size, however, they compensate for with swiftness and razor sharp claws. With their great agility, lightning fast flight speed and excellent marksmanship, they can swarm the enemy and decimate it in but a few moments. In fact, entire armies have been known to be destroyed by the power of the death hawks. Their abilities, coupled with the scouting ability of the dread eagles, makes the duo one of the most feared aerial assault teams in existence, and one that Rudgaf would certainly like to avoid, if at all possible.

I need to stay out of sight. The red wizard thought. *I had best skirt around the government branch and head for the residential branch, for now.*

So, with that, Rudgaf made his way towards the residential branch, using the roofs of the walkways attached to the buildings as cover, and skirting across any open spaces as quickly as possible. For what appeared to be an old man, the Lord of Red was surprisingly agile, so he had confidence that if he stayed focused, he would not be spotted.

To complete the process, the Lord of Red would have to duck, take two rolls across the road to get to the building on the other side, run around said building, and repeat the process. It wasn't easy, but Rudgaf completed the job with the utmost efficiency.

Duck, roll, roll, skirt around, repeat. The red wizard's cloak had become covered in dirt and filth from the process. His body was bruised and tender from all of the rolling as, every now and then, loose cobblestone poked and prodded at him. Still, the fate that would come from being spotted would have been far worse than what was transpiring here, so Rudgaf pressed on even harder. It took around twenty minutes of this process for Rudgaf to finally have the residential branch within his sights, but with such a threat looming above, it seemed more like twenty hours to the red wizard. Rudgaf skirted around the perimeter of the final building in the government branch. Salvation was close in sight. If he could just make it across this last obstacle, he could lay low and rest for the night in the very home that he was currently staring down and hopefully, come morning, the dread eagles would be gone. In a ducked position, Rudgaf took off his hat and wiped the sweat from his brow. Suffice it to say, it had been a hell of a day. The strange appearance of one calling himself the Lord of Grey, the dead orcs, and the mysteriously abandoned city all seemed as if it happened so long ago and certainly not within the same day, let alone within a mere few hours' time span. All that was on the Lord of Red's mind, and all that had been there for what seemed like an excruciating breadth of time, was not being spotted.

Despite the way that he was feeling, Rudgaf put his fears aside and refocused himself. He replaced his hat upon his brow and licked his lips.

Here it goes!

Agile as ever, the red wizard took two quick rolls across the road (which was made of dirt once more). He did it so quickly, in fact, that he misjudged his distance and ended up slamming his back into the wall, making a loud thud and forcing him to exhale sharply.

It was then that Rudgaf suddenly heard a loud screech in the distance, shortly followed by more loud screeches that seemed to come from different sources.

I've been spotted!

Thinking quickly, Rudgaf elbowed the window next to him, shattering it into thousands of pieces. He then dove in through the now vacant space, crawled his way away from the window, and stayed hidden and out of sight.

The red wizard kept his ears open as much as he could, listening for the screeches of the eagles to pierce the loud "thud, thud" of his own heartbeat. It's not that Rudgaf couldn't defeat the eagles and the hawks if ever he were, indeed, spotted. It's just that, although he had a good chance of emerging victorious, he also had a good chance of not doing so, especially if the noise of the ensuing brawl drew the attention of any orcs that may have still been in the area. A few eagles and hawks is one thing, but an entire orc army is another.

The Lord of Red could still hear the spine tingling screeches of the eagles in the distance. However, they slowly started to become softer. They became softer and softer until the red wizard could barely make them out. By the time Rudgaf could no longer hear their cries, the Sun had set and the day was over.

Odd that they never came closer…something else must have drawn their attention.

Drawing a sigh of relief and now feeling as though it was safe to stand, Rudgaf stood up and, for the first time since his arrival, scanned the room that he was in. It appeared as if he had broken straight into the master bed chamber and had crawled in between a large bookcase and a doorway that lead out to the rest of the house. He noticed the last vestiges of sunlight peer in through the shattered remains of the window that he smashed through, which was over in the left corner of the room. To his left, yet not as far as the window, was a night stand and a bed. As far as master bedchambers are concerned, this one was quite small. Rudgaf suspected that the house was much the same.

Not bothering to inspect the rest of the place, and feeling weary from the events that had transpired that day, Rudgaf decided to turn the sheets on the bed and sleep. He laid down, ever so gently as he was now mindful of the bruising that his body had endured earlier, and covered himself. His entire being became flooded with such a large sense of relief that, for the moment, he decided that he was either too lazy or just simply did not care that his boots and hat were still on his person. Before he had any time at all to change his mind and fix these inconsistencies, he was fast asleep.

~

Rudgaf slowly opened his eyes and revealed the surroundings of a familiar place, but it was not the place in which he rested his head for the night. He observed the ever familiar sight of the high, dome arch above him. He glanced over his feet and saw the ever familiar, stained glass window that he was accustomed to waking up to, allowing bright, orange sunlight to make its presence known to all that were in the room. Gazing around, groggily, he saw a chair next to his bed, and his old nightstand which contained a mirror that reflected the light coming in from the window into the red wizard's eyes. He sat up slightly and covered them with his hand, and then turned his attention back to the chair he had noticed earlier and had thought to be vacant, a thought of which was proven to be false. With the chair now being the fullness of Rudgaf's attention, he noticed that in it sat a young man, no more than forty years of age, in a full, brown cloak. In fact, as Rudgaf traced his body from bottom to top, he noticed that this person was covered in brown from his boots all the way up to the point of his hat. When Rudgaf processed this, and scanned downward from the hat to take a closer look at the young man's face, he noticed a countenance that was vibrant and full of life, staring back at him with a deep, sincere smile.

Good morning, Rudgaf.

Wilfrey! How did I...? How did you...?

Shh! You'll wake the others!

Others?

Of course! They're all here, you know. Joem, and Danagan, and Thome...

And Barlow?

Yes, of course Barlow is here! It would certainly be an empty tower without him.

How did I get here?

Did you ever truly leave?

The Lord of Red laid his head back down upon his pillow and stared at the ceiling.

My heart was never fully in it.

Was anyone's?

I cannot say for certain, Wilfrey. Wasn't yours?

Didn't you know? I didn't leave by my own terms.

Rudgaf quickly turned towards Wilfrey, again.

No...yes...I don't know. I feel like I did know at one point. You must know that the entire point of us leaving was so that you didn't have to...

I know.

Well then, why didn't you stay?

The dwarves forced me out.

The dwarves? I see...I'm sorry, Wilfrey. I completely forgot.

It's ok, Rudgaf - I went desert trekking.

You what?

Did you forget that, too? I traveled westward.

Why can't I remember any of this? I have been pondering your whereabouts for more years than a...

Don't despair, my red friend.

Why do you say that? What happened?

Shh, just be happy we're together. Now is not the time for such things. Later, you will remember, but not now.

Rudgaf looked down at his chest and chewed on his lower lip, trying to think of what to say next.

Why don't you stand and walk with me for a spell?

Alright.

The Lord of Red threw off his sheets, stood up, and nodded his head to the Lord of Brown.

Let us walk.

The stone floor of the tower was cold, as Rudgaf noticed that he was strangely bare foot. Along with Wilfrey, he walked through the stone arch and into the hallway as Wilfrey stayed a step behind in order to close the door to Rudgaf's room. Rudgaf waited until Wilfrey was, once again, able to join him stride for stride before pressing further. As the two wizards walked around the circular hallway, they passed the private quarters of all of the wizards. Rudgaf had a mind to pop in to say hello, but the doors were all shut.

After passing the rooms of all of their companions, the two wizards stepped through the entrance to the spiral staircase and headed down to the main floor, passing the library, training halls, and dining hall on the way down. Not much could be said for the ground floor except that it contained racks for each of the wizard's cloaks and hats, some medium sized windows with potted plants, and a giant, wooden door which lead out into the garden. Rudgaf took a look around, amazed at how untouched the place was after having been abandoned for so many years. His reuniting with his former home and the Lord of Brown warmed Rudgaf's heart.

While contemplating all of these feelings, the red wizard noticed that his brown friend had opened the main doors and was beckoning him to come through and make haste into the garden. Rudgaf collected himself and followed his friend.

The two, old friends walked through the midst of the garden – created by the hands of both Wilfrey and Barlow who both tilled and refreshed the earth and grew the plant life, respectively. It was most beautiful, and contained rare flowers that were prettier than the view of the sunrise from the northern mountains, or the fairest of the southern elves. Amongst these rare flowers grew the bushod flower that could rarely be seen only in the deserts to the west. It had a deep, purple shade and sparkled golden in the sunlight.

Trees and vines also bearing fruit could be seen growing in the garden. The ground was tilled and grew various vegetables, as well. In essence, this was the wizard's food source, and when they all lived here, they lived in a self-made paradise.

Beautiful, isn't it?

Rudgaf turned to face Wilfrey as they continued to walk.

Just the way that I remembered it.

You're smiling.

So are you.

I've missed that smile. Brighter is your smile than all of the embers that you have burned.

I've missed this place.

Did you ever truly leave?

You asked me that earlier.

You never really answered.

My body and mind left, but my heart was never fully committed.

Where your heart is, there your treasure is also.

I beg your pardon?

Wilfrey stared up into the deep blue.

Why do things have to be different?

What do you mean?

Why can't things be the way that they used to be?

You know the answer to that as well as I do.

Silence crept in for a moment as both wizards stared at the ground. Finally, Rudgaf stopped walking, while Wilfrey also halted and looked back at his friend who was staring at him intently.

Why did you do it, Wilfrey?

It was what was best.

"What was best"? How can you say that? It caused us to lose all of this. It caused us to lose...us.

I didn't know the power of the stone.

I'm sorry that I didn't tell you. I truly forgot. You know me...I'm always forgetting things.

I forgive you.

Both wizards stared at the ground once more. After a bit of a pause, Wilfrey walked up to his old friend. He placed his hand upon Rudgaf's chin and lifted it up so that Rudgaf's eyes would lock with his. Wilfrey smiled, and then placed his hand upon the red wizard's shoulder.

Do you really believe that we've lost "us"?

Wilfrey...

Pointing at himself and then back at Rudgaf, Wilfrey said, **This. This can never be broken.**

Are you certain?

Of course! We'll always be brothers, right?

Rudgaf wanted to give Wilfrey a resounding, "yes", but for some reason, he suddenly found himself unable to answer. He tried to open his mouth, but it wouldn't open. Wilfrey just stared at him, blankly.

Rudgaf?

Still unable to answer, the Lord of Red wanted to give the brown wizard a warm embrace, but found that he also couldn't move his body. He was paralyzed where he stood.

Rudgaf!

Now, not only was the red wizard paralyzed, he also started to feel faint. His vision started to blur as his world rocked back and forth like a rickety ship in a storm. Wilfrey seemed to melt before his very eyes as every part of the once lush scenery faded into darkness.

Rudgaf!

~

Rudgaf!

The Lord of Red woke with a start, inhaling quickly while simultaneously getting up in like fashion, which caused an inexplicable pain in his left ribs. The red wizard winced and felt the area with his hand, noticing that, somehow, his ribs had been bandaged up without him being aware of it.

"It was a dream," said Rudgaf, "it was just...a dream."

Rudgaf sat in the position that he thrust himself into for a while, staring blankly at the dawn's early light coming into the room from the window he smashed open the day before.

"Wilfrey..."

After sitting for a few minutes, contemplating his strange dream and how it could have been possible for him to have awoken with bandaged ribs when he obviously hadn't done the job, himself, he noticed a peculiar aroma coming from the door next to his bed. Rudgaf's mouth watered as he lightly wafted the air to take in the deep, savory scent of some recipe that was unknown to him. It smelled like a chicken dish of some sort, but there was only one way to be certain – he had to get up and investigate for himself.

Rudgaf flipped over the sheets and blanket that he had covered himself with the night before, and peered at his bare feet. He wiggled his toes, perplexed.

How did my boots come off? I specifically remember not taking them off.

In fact, that wasn't the only thing missing. He noticed that his cloak was also missing, as was his hat.

Most strange...did I suffer through a bout of sleepwalking?

Slowly, Rudgaf swung his legs around and stood. The floor was quite cold. Despite the discomfort, the red wizard stretched and looked around the room for his missing clothes. He could not, however, locate them. He searched underneath the bed, between the door and the bookcase, and in the closet in the upper right corner of the room that he hadn't noticed was there, earlier. Rudgaf was busy scratching his head in bewilderment when, suddenly, a shocking thought came to him.

My sword!

Indeed, Rudgaf had fallen asleep with his sword at his side and, indeed, it was also missing. Severely annoyed, Rudgaf boldly opened the door of the room in order to make a heading towards the kitchen and have a quick "chat" with the person who was obviously responsible for his missing belongings. So annoyed was Rudgaf that he didn't even stop to think that there could very well be orcs within the house that were responsible for his missing belongings and for the wonderful aromas that, even with their pungency, could not distract Rudgaf from getting to the bottom of this folderol.

Stepping out from the room that he had slept in, he came into a narrow hallway. His room, the hallway, and the entire house appeared to be made of oak (something that was quite desirable for a dwarf, but represented poverty amongst the eastern elves, as oak has always been an extremely common wood within the kingdom). Ahead, Rudgaf noticed that the doorway that led into the next room didn't actually have a door but, instead, had a tanned, deer skin draped over it.

Painfully, Rudgaf stepped towards the covered doorway. His left ribs were really bothering him and he wondered how he could not have noticed the injury the night before. Every step that he had to take bothered him just a little bit more so, by the time he got to the doorway, a visible snarl marked his face.

Arriving at the door way, Rudgaf flung back the draping to reveal a small dining room. He stepped in to observe the area. Within was a small, toy clock hanging on the wall, as well as a dining table and four chairs, all made from oak. To his right he saw an uncovered corridor that, when he peered inside, it appeared to him that it led to the living area. Directly ahead of him, however, was another draped doorway that, to his estimation, must have been the kitchen that housed the thief that took advantage of his nightly sloth.

Slowly approaching the doorway, still with a snarl on his face and still holding his ribs, he pulled back the drape in order to see into the kitchen. It was a basic kitchen with a sink and a pump handle for water, as well as a large pot within a sand pit. The pot was slightly boiling over with something that he couldn't identify, but was certainly the source of the aroma that he had picked up, earlier.

Located next to the pot stood a figure that was making itself busy stirring a large, wooden spoon around inside of it in order to qualm its anger. Upon inspection, Rudgaf noticed that the figure was covered from his feet to his head in grey and black. Everything that the figure wore was grey, from his boots, to his pants, to his cloak, except for his tunic, which was black. A nice touch, Rudgaf thought. After making this observation, the red wizard couldn't help but study the face of, what was sure to be, the thief that he was seeking. What he saw was the face of a young man around thirty years of age. He had a pale complexion and was very clean shaven. His eyes were a piercing blue that stood in stark contrast with the rest of his person, and his black hair sat almost as if it were a mop on the top of his head. He wore no hat.

Before Rudgaf had time to act, the center of his attention turned to look at the red wizard and made a half grin that came off as both cocky and sincere. The young man then spoke.

"How about a bit of eagle?"

Suddenly, Rudgaf felt his snarl turn into a bright smile and the knowledge of all of his pain escaped his mind. Walking briskly, he raced over to the young man and they both laughed as they caught each other up in a warm embrace. They held this pose for a few moments, tightly grasping each other's robes, before finally letting go.

"What're you doing here?" Rudgaf asked, breaking the silence.

"I could ask the same of you!"

Rudgaf shrugged, "King Moldof sent me here to investigate."

"And rightly so. I have a lot to tell you! But, first, let us eat."

Rudgaf looked down at the pot filled with some sort of light brown liquid, and then back up at the young man.

"What is that stuff?"

"As I said before, it's eagle. Dread eagle stew, to be exact." The young man inhaled deeply as he turned his face back to the pot and wafted the aroma straight from the source. "It's definitely ready."

"I'm quite famished. I'd be willing to eat anything at this point."

"That's the spirit! I'll go grab some bowls. You go take a seat at the table and...get comfortable."

"Easier said than done, old friend."

Rudgaf groaned a bit as he slowly made his way over to the dining room while his friend grabbed some bowls and prepared to serve breakfast.

The red wizard made his way over to the dining table and, using the table for support, slowly sat himself down into a chair. He stirred there for a while before his grey friend came in with two, wooden bowls filled with stew and two, wooden spoons. He placed a set of these in front of Rudgaf, then in front of a vacant seat which he ended up taking.

Rudgaf reluctantly took a spoonful of the stuff and tasted it, burning his mouth. The stew was still quite hot. The red wizard opened his mouth and exhaled to attempt to cool the stew that was burning in his mouth in order to swallow it. After he forced it to slide down his throat, he grinned.

"How is it?"

"Not bad," said Rudgaf, eagerly taking another spoonful while making sure to cool it before putting it in his mouth, "not bad at all!"

His friend smiled at the red wizard and then began eating, himself.

After a few more spoonfulls, Rudgaf paused and asked, "How did you manage to get the dread eagle?"

The wizard's friend replied, "They were flying all around here, yesterday."

"I am well aware of that. But, how did one of them end up in my bowl?"

The man grinned, "The Lord of Grey still has some tricks up his sleeve."

Rudgaf found the answer to be acceptable and continued to enjoy his breakfast. Not much was said afterwards until they were finished. They just took the time to enjoy the food and the simple pleasure that was each other's company.

After finishing, Rudgaf wiped the excess stew that had deposited itself on his face with the back of his hand. Danagan did much the same. The two of them then stared at each other.

"Well?" Asked Rudgaf.

"You first." Said Danagan with a smile.

Rudgaf then began to briefly explain everything that had happened to him since receiving the letter from the dwarven king, and everything that he had observed within the city.

"Interesting." Said Danagan, rubbing his chin.

"What do you make of it?"

"Well, the dead orcs were my doing."

"I thought that it might have been you."

"Yeah." Said Danagan as he leaned back in his chair, "They attacked me when I got here. I really had no choice."

"But why?"

"Your guess is as good as mine."

Rudgaf pondered for a moment, and then responded, "Well, I won't be able to even hazard a guess until I hear your side of things."

"Well..." said Danagan as he looked up to the ceiling, "Where do I start?"

"Take your time."

"Well, I can say with certainty that I didn't get a kingly order to investigate the city like you did. I kind of just stumbled upon this situation." Danagan paused, again, "I basically came here to follow up on an extremely lucrative 'job' offer."

Rudgaf raised an eyebrow.

"Oh, don't look at me like that!" Snapped Danagan, "You know as well as I do that I don't take those offers any longer. I have no use for money and no desire to stir up trouble as I once did. No...I was simply *intrigued* by the offer."

Rudgaf shrugged, "What was so intriguing about it?"

"Well, firstly, the offer was from King Nolan, himself!"

"You jest! A bounty? Have the elves ever done that?"

"No. At least, not that I am aware of." Danagan shook his head, "But, no, this was for real. It seems that old King Colibrim has been a thorn in Nolan's side and he wanted him...dealt with."

"King Colibrim? The king of the goblins?!"

"You heard me right. He's offering a sum of two hundred thousand platinums for Colibrim's head, too."

Rudgaf gasped, "Two hundred thousand! Is Nolan out of his mind? What'd he do, empty the elven treasury?"

"Either that," said Danagan, "or his kingdom has somehow managed to procure an exorbitant amount of funds within a very short amount of time."

"Who could have given him that kind of support?"

"I don't know, Rudgaf. Do you think that King Moldof might have lent a hand?"

"Certainly not." Replied Rudgaf, "It just wouldn't make sense. The dwarves and the orcs have gotten along for ages and besides," Rudgaf added, "if the northern dwarves declared war on the goblins, they'd also have to deal with the orc tribes."

"Not exactly an advantageous position to be in."

"Not at all."

Rudgaf rubbed his beard, deep in thought. After a few moments, he spoke, "Embezzlement, perhaps? A treasurer from another kingdom?"

Danagan scratched his chin, "I don't think so. It's too much money to try to hide. We're talking two hundred thousand platinums, here. There are entire kingdoms that don't even make that in a year. And anyway, are we really prepared to flag the king of the elves for a conspiracy?"

Rudgaf stared down at the table and said, "I guess not. I'm just suspicious..."

"Of?"

"Well, you mentioned that the bounty was for the king of the goblins, correct?"

"Yes."

"When was the offer made?"

"Well, let's see..." said Danagan as he cupped his chin with his hand and stared at the ceiling, "the offer was originally made a month ago, but King Nolan increased the bounty from one hundred and twenty thousand platinums to two hundred thousand platinums just two weeks ago."

"Wait..." said Rudgaf, "a *month* ago? You mean to tell me that he had a significant issue with King Colibrim a month ago?"

"Yes."

"And now their orc allies are here, and it appears that they've staged this attack."

Danagan shook his head, "So, you're thinking that King Nolan had prior intelligence that this attack was going to take place."

"Yes," said Rudgaf, "that is what I am thinking. But...why didn't he do anything to defend the city?"

"A staged attack to incite a war?"

"Perhaps. But, then again, here we go with the conspiracies, again."

"That doesn't mean that they're not true, though. I just have a hard time accepting that King Nolan would do such a thing. He's always been a powerful ally."

"Yes, indeed he has." Said Rudgaf.

"Although..."

Rudgaf leaned forward in his chair, "Although?"

"Well, right around the time that I started hearing about the bounty, I found myself in the southern regions visiting the kingdom of the junglies."

"Oh? I have not seen the jungle elves in many a year. How do they fare?"

"As good as ever, I suppose. But, while I was there, I gained a piece of information that was very interesting. I stopped by a local pub for a drink, since it's pretty hot down there."

"Understandable."

"But when I went in and asked for elven wine, they told me that they no longer carried it!"

"What a tragedy!" Gasped Rudgaf.

"Exactly! But even more interesting is the 'why' behind the lack of supply. They told me that King Duhan issued a trade embargo against the eastern elves, and started preventing tourism into that area. They're also closing off their borders. It might be pretty hard to get in there, now, without getting shot at by an archer or two hundred."

"That's news! Were you able to find out why King Duhan would do such a thing?"

"Well…" said Danagan, "I'm not too up on elven affairs, as you well know, I just have other things on my mind. But, from the information that I was able to gather, it is King Duhan's opinion that King Nolan has forgotten the ways of 'nature' or something like that. Like Nolan abuses nature, says Duhan, he also abuses his crown."

Rudgaf pondered for a moment, "Interesting. Perhaps Nolan *is* planning something."

The red wizard chewed on his lip for a moment, deep in thought. He spoke, again, after a short time.

"In any case, I think that King Duhan knows more about this than we do."

"Then that's where I will start." Said Danagan, standing up from his chair. "At least, I'll try. I'm fairly confident that my abilities can get me past their border guards undetected, in the event that they don't just let me in."

Rudgaf nodded, "I'd be prepared for that scenario. King Duhan is a very serious king and does not take kindly to anything that he considers an attempt to undermine his authority."

"Right. Don't worry about me, old friend. I'll be fine."

Danagan turned away from Rudgaf and took a step forward, but then stopped and laughed. "I almost forgot!" He exclaimed as he whirred back around to face Rudgaf. "I bet that you'd like your clothes and sword back."

"Right!" Said Rudgaf. "I had completely forgotten."

"Fear not! I'll get those for you right away."

With that, Danagan walked off in order to retrieve Rudgaf's belongings, leaving the red wizard at the table to ponder everything that had transpired. Was King Nolan really conspiring with an unknown entity in order to start a war with the orcs and goblins? If so, then why? What would he have to gain from it? Rudgaf shifted in his chair uneasily. It was then that he noticed that shifting didn't hurt his ribs this time. He tried it again, and then once more, and neither times resulted in any pain. Rudgaf smiled and stood up. At least, he thought, if there was going to be a fight, he'd be in fit, fighting form.

It didn't take long before Danagan came back with Rudgaf's belongings – his hat, boots, cloak, and sword. Eagerly, Rudgaf placed all of his clothes back on his person, and hooked his sword back to his hip.

"Nice hat." Said Danagan.

Rudgaf smiled as he traced the brim with his thumb and forefinger, "You think so? I quite like it, myself. You should get one."

"No, thanks. It would just get in my way. Besides, you could poke an eye out with that thing!"

The two wizards chuckled for a moment before Danagan spoke again.

"I noticed that your ribs are feeling better."

Rudgaf twisted his torso a few times and said, "Good as new! What'd you do?"

"It's an old elven trick that I picked up decades ago. It works pretty good, if I do say so myself."

Rudgaf smiled deeply, "Thanks, Danagan."

Both of them paused for a slight moment before turning their attention back to more serious matters, again. Danagan then spoke.

"So, where are you headed?"

"Me? I have to head back up north to tell King Moldof of what I've found. I should also pick up Barlow, on my way. More likely than not, we're going to need his help with this."

"Barlow…" said Danagan, "How is he?"

"Aloof." Said Rudgaf, "He has been spending most of his time in his forest as of late."

"Sounds like Barlow."

"Indeed."

"What about Thome?"

"Thome? Oh, he just up and left!"

Danagan laughed, "What a kook. Where to?"

"Of that I'm not quite sure. Barlow and I just woke up in our tower one morning, about two months ago, to find a note on our dining table that simply stated, 'Gone desert trekking.'".

Danagan's eyes widened, "What did the note say?"

"Gone desert trekking." Responded Rudgaf, "Why?"

"I…well, never mind. It's not that important. Remind me to bring it up, later."

Perplexed, Rudgaf simply stated, "Ok."

The two wizards nodded their heads to one another, and headed towards the front door. Danagan placed his hand on the rather plain, bronze door knob and was just about to open the door when Rudgaf interrupted.

"Wait, Danagan."

Danagan turned towards Rudgaf and said, "Yes?"

"I forgot to ask you something earlier."

"What is it?"

"Does this whole attack seem staged to you? When I entered, the front gate was left open quite carelessly. There was no damage to the city walls and no signs of a break in of any sort. There aren't even any elven bodies."

Danagan sighed and looked at the ground while he put his hand on Rudgaf's shoulder, "You're wrong about that."

"About what?"

"The bodies."

"No…"

"I'm sorry. It's something that I grew accustomed to seeing from my previous life so I just assumed that you already knew and had the same reaction to it as I did."

"What'd you do with the bodies?"

"I left them. I thought that the elves would be coming in, soon, to take care of the place. I wanted them to bury the bodies since they can identify them and mark their graves whereas I cannot."

"I understand."

Rudgaf thought for a moment while he stared at the ground, "Where are they?"

"Right in front of the town hall. I don't know how you missed them."

"That's a long story. Another time, I'm afraid."

Danagan gave Rudgaf a long stare and said, "You're going to go pay your respects, aren't you?"

"I have to…" Rudgaf trailed off.

Danagan nodded his head and embraced his fellow wizard. A moment later, he pulled back, smiled at Rudgaf and said, "Stay strong. There are dark times ahead. The world is going to need you."

Now it was Rudgaf's turn to put his hand on Danagan's shoulder as he said, "You be careful. The southern elves are excellent marksmen."

Danagan smiled, "Don't you worry about me, now. You should've seen some of the hairy situations that I've gotten myself out of. Cheating death is my specialty."

"You'll have to tell me about it, sometime."

"Sooner rather than later, old friend."

"And what of your doppelganger?"

Danagan chuckled, "Don't worry about it. If you see him before I do, give him hot feet for me, alright?"

"That'll probably end up being the case," explained Rudgaf, "if he ends up turning out to be who I think he is."

The Lord of Grey raised an eyebrow, "Should I ask?"

Rudgaf shook his head, "No. Well, not until I confirm it, in any case."

"Very well, then. I'll be seeing you."

"Goodbye for now."

They both nodded, walked out the door, and took separate paths as they tread the dusty road.

~

Amidst the dead silence in the heat of the afternoon, Rudgaf found the "clack, clack" of his boots against the cobblestone to be quite unnerving when he finally returned to the government branch. It certainly had not escaped Rudgaf's mind that he could be headed into a trap and he was trying to stay focused and alert even though his mind was filled with sadness of the great city that used to be. He remembered times, fonder times, when the streets of the city were bustling with people of every creed and of every race.

The government branch would be of particular interest this time of year as the elections for officials would be taking place. Heated debates would be held in the town square as opponents from all sides and walks of life would argue their case. A gigantic buzz and excitement would fill the air, a kind of energy that marked the health and livelihood of the entire, eastern elven kingdom.

But now, no more. What Rudgaf saw in its place, he thought he would be mentally prepared for. He honed his mind throughout the entire journey, thinking of the many ways that this scene could have manifested itself. He thought about every situation in which this could have come about. He pondered every possibility of his eyes grasping and tugging at the very horror of it, trying to comprehend and make sense of it all. Rudgaf had tried to prepare himself for this sight since Danagan had laid the bad news on him, but no one could have come fully prepared for this. No one is prepared for death.

Indeed, the mystery of the day had been solved. The missing elves had been found. Before Rudgaf's very eyes laid the bodies of his dead allies, many of whom he had known on a personal level. They had all been brutally executed. Some of them were missing limbs which were haphazardly thrown into the pile, and some were even missing heads. Some elves had various parts of their anatomy bashed in, while others surely died of terrible gash wounds. The Lord of Red closed his eyes, forever locking into his mind the memory of a thousand dead mothers and a thousand dead brothers, reaching up to the sky to form a tower of injustice.

Resisting the obvious stench coming from the heap, Rudgaf knelt down next to the pile as he recognized the body of a former friend.

"Mika!"

The Lord of Red gritted his teeth and attempted to fight back tears. To himself he said, "Your hair is brown. It's still brown after all of these years."

The red wizard tugged at his beard in grief and continued, "Mika...you waxed great in years, but numbers didn't matter with you...you were young. You were still so young."

Recalling the youthful, cheery face from the drawing that he held in his pocket and comparing it to what he now saw – a countenance forever transfixed upon visions of terror - Rudgaf could not bear to look upon his slain friend any longer. He turned his head, stood, turned his back on the pile, and walked away from it in order to try to clear his head. The Lord of Red took off his hat and let it fall to the ground. He then shook his head violently as if he were trying to shake the very thoughts and memories out of his head. Failing to do so, he felt himself jerk as tears started to stream down his face.

Why? Why did this have to happen? Why couldn't I have arrived sooner?

Sadness flooded his very essence like a tidal wave of blood and nightmares as he could no longer resist the urge to slump down to the ground, put his head in his hands, and weep. He soaked his hands with sorrow. His beard sopped up his grief. So filled with woe was Rudgaf that, for the moment, he could no longer focus on the mission of finding out who was responsible for turning the fountains of sparkling water in the town square into a river of tears.

~CHAPTER TWO – DEADLY PROJECTILES~

The first part of our journey led us to the southern swamps. We had to cross these in order to get to the mountains in the arid deserts of the west, where our ultimate prize laid. It was until we were greeted by the mists of noxious water vapor that hung in the dank, dreary air that we thought we were adequately prepared.

When coming face-to-face with the beasts who had the gall to call hell, "home", you realize that you can never be prepared to face death.

"Of course." Said the elven guard, sarcastically, as he checked the taps at the bar to discover that they were empty.

"This shit isn't as good as our shit, anyway." Remarked another guard.

The former replied, "Well, we're a hell of a long way away from that now, aren't we?"

The latter scoffed and continued searching the bodies of the fallen orcs that remained in the room.

The two guards busied themselves until another walked through the doorway. As he stood before the previous, two guards, he cut an impressive figure. He was clad in black armor with golden lace. His breast plate accented the outstanding, physical features that all elves prided themselves on. His helmet bore the insignia of the eastern, elven kingdoms – one circle that encompassed nine. On his left shoulder he bore the insignia of his rank – a single-headed eagle with an arrow pressed between its beak.

"Found anything?" He asked.

The guard next to the bar spoke up, "Nothing here, Captain. Just as the wizard said."

"Fine, fine. What of the bodies in the town square?"

The other guard spoke up, "We incinerated them, just like you asked, sir."

"Good. Now, dispose of the extra orc corpses, as well."

"Sir," said the guard by the bar, "won't that destroy any evidence of the orc invasion?"

The Captain shrugged his shoulders, "It doesn't matter. All we need is one."

Just then, another of the guard appeared at the doorway.

"Captain, he has arrived."

The Captain turned around to face the messenger and nodded his head. They both saluted each other before the messenger made his leave. The Captain then turned around to the other guards.

"You have your orders."

The Captain then saluted the two guards, they returned the favor, and then the Captain made his leave.

After a few moments, the guard that was in charge of inspecting the orc bodies said, "These corpses stink."

The other guard inhaled deeply and said, "This whole thing stinks."

The Sun was in the Captain's eyes as he made his way towards the gate. He needed not shield his eyes, however. The object of his attention that stood at the gates of the once, great city was in stark contrast with the brightness of the setting orb.

He sat on a pale horse that was covered in black armor with linked chain that hung about half way down its legs. The rider was also adorned in black armor that had three, distinct points on each of its shoulder pads. His helmet was black, as well, and had a face mask that concealed his identity, although the Captain knew, very well, who he was. There could be no mistake.

The Captain stopped a few paces in front of the figure's horse and saluted.

"Sir, our investigation is near comple…"

The dark figure cut him off. His voice was harsh and sounded as if he were gagging on a mouthful of bees.

"I care not."

"Then…what brings you here?"

"You have new orders."

"Of course." Replied the Captain. "What does his majesty command?"

"The king wants you to raze the city. Make it look good."

The elf looked shocked and said, "But…why?"

"That is what his majesty commands."

The captain hesitated, then said, "Yes, sir."

The dark figure coughed, harshly. "The wizard…where is he?"

"The Lord of Red? He left shortly after we arrived."

"Damn…send word to the king regarding the matter. I have other matters to tend to."

Without saluting, the dark figure turned his horse around and proceeded to exit the city. Just as he was leaving, however, the Captain spoke up.

"May I ask where you are going, sir?"

The dark figure stopped his horse and responded, "I've caught the scent of another."

"What do you mean?"

The dark figure scoffed, "Someone other than the one in red was here. He needs to be dealt with."

The Captain's superior then yelled something that was intelligible only to his horse who listened and then proceeded to gallop off into the sunset.

~

Rudgaf arrived back at the final, dwarven mining town (or the first, at least from his perspective) with a heavy head. He hadn't paid much attention the entire way back, and just happened to stumble upon the town due to his muscle memory more than anything.

The guard at the front gate, knowing who Rudgaf was, let him through without a word. From the gate, Rudgaf could hear the noise of drinking and merrymaking from his favorite inn, although such things were far from his mind, now. His mission, his reuniting, and his fallen comrades pervaded his thoughts. However, it was thoughts of Wilfrey that pierced his heart. He looked forward to arriving back at the northern tower to meet up with Barlow before he continued his mission. The red wizard had a long way to walk, however. Just thinking about it made his feet ache all the more.

Rudgaf pushed aside the door to the inn once he arrived. As he entered, his spirits were immediately lifted once he was greeted with the familiar fire place, oaken furniture, and the ever, magical inn keeper that had made his stay so fine the last time that he was there. The inn keeper smiled at the wizard, took his sword, and hung it up.

"It's good te have ye back!"

The Lord of Red smiled, "It's good to be back."

"Aye. Say, did ya ever find yer wizard friend that came lookin' for ye the last time ye was here?"

"I'm afraid not."

"Well, if ye ever see him, tell him to stay the hell away from me inn! I was knee deep in lisk dung with the towns folk 'round here. Had te do a fair bit a gum flappin' te get 'em off o' me back!"

"I humbly apologize, fine inn keeper. I assure you that, if I had known that he was going to come here, I would've told him to stay away."

"Aye. Don't worry about it, none. Not your fault, the ways I sees it."

The dwarf then cracked his knuckles and rubbed his beard.

"Anyway, time fer business, eh? Sit wherever ye like while I have me workers feed ye and get a room ready for ye."

Rudgaf took off his hat and bowed while the inn keeper scurried off. The Lord of Red then proceeded to scan the dining room, which was packed full. Of Rudgaf's interest was his "favorite" spot which was, unfortunately, taken.

Drats!

As Rudgaf, in his disappointment, continued to survey the room for a place to rest his sore feet, he noticed that the figure that had occupied his "favorite" spot was making some sort of gesture towards him, as if inviting him to sit with it. Putting his attention fully on the figure, he noticed that it was rather slender and that it was wearing a grey, hooded cloak. Rudgaf couldn't make out any features of note other than the ones already stated, but he did notice that the figure was, indeed, beckoning him.

Odd.

The red wizard shrugged his shoulders, girded himself up, and approached the shady character. As he did so, some of the dwarves stopped what they were doing to observe, as if they couldn't believe that he would have the nerve or even an inkling of a desire to sit with such a person. However, they got over it, quickly, and carried on.

Rudgaf stood in front of the table and stared down at the shadow that laid before him. The figure did nothing but stare up at him, which provided for a semi-awkward moment as Rudgaf gazed into the abyss of the robe wearer's hood. After but a moment, the red wizard made himself comfortable in the opposite seat.

Rudgaf cleared his throat.

"Nice night." He said, sheepishly.

The hooded figure nodded and then, slowly, pulled back the hood of its cloak to reveal the long, black hair and slender face of a young, elven female. Rudgaf raised an eyebrow. She returned his expression with a smile.

"It's a bit hot in here, though." She replied as she brushed her hair away from her face.

Rudgaf nodded his head in agreement as a young dwarf approached and handed cups of tea to both Rudgaf and the elf. Rudgaf raised his cup in thanks, and then quietly sipped as he waited for the elf to state her purpose.

The elf sipped her tea, set the cup down and smiled before she continued.

"The name's Ramona."

"Ah. And I am…"

"Rudgaf. I know."

"You know me by name? Impressive."

"It's a habit."

"I see…" Said Rudgaf as he sipped his tea, again.

"You're probably wondering why I called you over here."

Rudgaf shrugged.

"I guess so."

Ramona stared intently into the wizard's eyes.

"I'll bet."

The conversation was briefly interrupted by the young dwarf, again, as he came over with two loaves of honey, barley loaf. Rudgaf knew better, this time, than to grab it immediately. Ramona didn't seem interested in it at all.

She cleared her throat and continued.

"I'll get right to the point, my dear Rudgaf."

Dear Rudgaf?

"I've been studying up on ancient history and its connection with magic."

Rudgaf rubbed his beard.

"Needless to say, your name came up a lot."

"Did it, now?" Inquired Rudgaf.

"Oh, yes."

"And how, my dear Ramona, did you come across these certain, historical texts which were long thought to be lost?"

Ramona gave Rudgaf a large grin and leaned forward.

"Please, Lord of Red, let me do the asking, for now. I will entertain your questions, later."

"Very well."

"Good. I'll get right to the point – where is the black, lesser stone?"

Rudgaf felt taken aback.

How does she know?

"I don't know, Ramona."

"You must have some idea."

"How is that?"

"Because an inquisitive wizard, such as yourself, would not let such a thing remain unknown. One who stops to smell the daisies and draw the countryside certainly wouldn't allow for such a powerful artifact to simply be…lost."

Rudgaf raised an eyebrow.

"I'm afraid that you have me at a disadvantage. You know so much about me and I'm afraid that I know very little about you."

"I'm not a big fan of changing subjects."

"Very well, then."

"So, my wizard friend, what happened to the stone? Where did it go?"

"If I knew of its whereabouts, being that it is so powerful, don't you think that I would've gone and retrieved it long before you beckoned me to sit with you?"

Ramona laughed.

"You test my knowledge, wizard. Know this – I know of the dangers involved with possessing such a thing. These are dangers that you, nor your friends, were willing to brave."

"You presume too much."

"Do I?"

"Of course. Don't be a fool – no text could fully describe the horrors that such an object can bring about."

Ramona shrugged as the young dwarf came by, yet once more, with two bowls of hot oatmeal with fresh fruit and cinnamon. Ramona looked down at it in disgust.

"Is this all these dwarves ever eat?"

Rudgaf took a spoonful with glee and said, "What do you mean?"

"Where is the substance? Where's the damned meat?"

"Dwarves don't eat meat."

"No wonder they're so short."

Ramona laughed at her own joke while Rudgaf simply shook his head and continued to sup. It wasn't long, however, before Ramona pressed her attack, further.

"So...what happened to it?"

"Happened to what?"

Rudgaf's question agitated the elf a little bit, but she managed to keep her cool.

"The black, lesser stone."

"Ah, that. It's gone."

"Gone? Where?"

"Like I said, I don't know. We cast it into the northern sea. It could be anywhere, now."

"So, you're telling me that there is no way to find it? There is no way to get it back?"

"Listen," said Rudgaf as he leaned forward, "it's lost, forever. Even if you could get it back, you wouldn't want to. You want nothing to do with it. I have studied magic for over four hundred years and I, even I, want no more association with it than I already have."

Rudgaf grabbed a chunk of the honey, barley loaf and leaned back in his chair while he ate. After a pause, he continued.

"It has broken more lives than you could know. No one could tame it. Not even the strongest mind could control its power."

"You mean Mazuun, correct?"

Startled, Rudgaf retorted, "You know too much."

Ramona widened her eyes and said, "Have any memory erasing spells in your repertoire?"

Rudgaf scoffed, "I'm afraid not."

Ramona leaned forward until she was no more than a few inches away from the red wizard's face.

"Good. I doubt it would've worked, anyway."

Rudgaf gazed into the eyes of the elf. They seemed much older than the rest of her. Almost...ancient.

Before Rudgaf had time to ponder his observation, one of the dwarves in the room broke the silence.

"Nowoube a gootime te loosen de skivvies an' jig! Whose wid me?!"

The room erupted with a thunderous, "Aye!".

"Whasong shouwedo?" Asked another.

"How about 'King Narvis' Washtub'?" Piped up another.

"Aye!"

Just then, all the dwarves raised from their seats and formed a horizontal line in front of the bar. They then began to throw their hands up in the air, sloshing the contents of their mugs all over the floor. Each dwarf kicked his legs on cue, some losing a boot or two, as their beards swayed in the wind. All the while, they sang (diction excluded for clarification),

King Narvis had a washtub,
'twas always mighty full.
But not of water or the suds,
'twas filled with goblin's blood!
The rungs that he grasped firmly,
to wash his blood stained clothes,
were made of broken dragon bones,
whom he dealt the clever blows.
Spines of hawks hung in his den
and scalps of birdmen, too.
Yet, the washtub was always feared,
for its liquid made a bitter brew.
When ere the king did battle,
Where'er the war did dwell,
he'd bring the washtub to meet the foe
and they'd quake from head to toe!
Oh, King Narvis and the washtub.
King Narvis had a washtub.
Scrub-a-dub-dub!
Scrub-a-dub-dub!
Oh, King Narvis and the washtub.
King Narvis had a washtub.
Scrub-a-dub-dub!
Scrub-a-dub-dub!
And with his axe,
the orc's a hill-a-dung!
Scrub-a-dub-dub!
Scrub-a-dub-dub!
And we're done!

A volcanic roar erupted in the room as the dwarves shouted in glee and clapped their hands.

"Damn fine singin'! Damn fine!" They said.

Rudgaf, who had been watching the spectacle unfold, refocused his attention on Ramona with a grin.

"I love dwarven, folk songs."

Ramona *spat* on the ground next to her.

"Barbarians."

Rudgaf shrugged, "It is what it is."

Before Ramona had time to respond, another ruckus interrupted their conversation. This time, however, it was caused by one of the dwarven, town guards smashing through the door of the inn and shouting. Startled, everyone turned toward the source of the commotion.

"He's back!" The guard shouted.

"Who's back?" Inquired the crowd.

"The wizard filth! The one in grey!"

It cannot be!

"Kill the bastard!" Yelled the crowd as they bolted toward the door.

"Oh, no." Said Rudgaf as he stood up to follow them. Ramona trailed behind.

Rudgaf grabbed his sword from the corner of the room, buckled it around his waist, and then attempted to make his way through the mob of angry dwarves to investigate the scene taking place outside. "Excuse me", and "Pardon me, good dwarf" were repeated time and time again out of his lips as he attempted to carefully wade his way through the crowd.

Ramona rolled her eyes at the wizard and starting shoving the dwarves aside. Consequently, she was able to step outside before Rudgaf was.

"The market is burning!" She exclaimed as she saw flames and billows of smoke rising from the town market.

"Damnable wizard!" Yelled a dwarf in the crowd.

After much excusing and gentle brushing aside, Rudgaf was finally able to make his way out of the door and next to Ramona. He observed the market burning and looked around to see who was responsible. It was then that he noticed a dwarven merchant crawling his way from the market place toward the crowd. Rudgaf ran up to the dwarf and knelt down. The dwarf coughed and gargled while he spoke.

"A wi...wizard."

"Shh...try to stay calm. What did he look like?"

"Big beard...grey clothes...da...ggers."

Rudgaf shook his head, stood up, and faced the crowd.

"Get some help for him!"

A few dwarves from the crowd ran up to the injured merchant, hoisted him on their shoulders, and carried him away to the town infirmary. Other dwarves started to grab buckets of water from the well in order to squelch the flames of the roaring blaze. While they were doing all of this, the Lord of Red walked up to Ramona.

"What did he say?" Asked Ramona.

"A wizard did it. A wizard in grey."

"Danagan?"

"That's what the 'wizard' would like us to presume."

"I don't understand."

"This wizard is the same wizard that came here looking for me a few days ago. This wizard has a beard. Danagan can't grow a beard."

"Fascinating. I didn't know that."

"I'm glad that I could educate you."

"So…what now?"

"We find him. Hopefully before the dwarves do."

"Not a problem. If he left tracks, I can find him."

Ramona inspected the ground. Even though there were several prints that were left on the dirt road, she could distinguish between them quite well. Rudgaf had always known about the tracking skills of elves – they were natural born hunters. However, Ramona seemed to be in a class of her own, as she scouted the ground and traced steps from the pile-up at the inn, to the embers of the market, out of the city gate, and, eventually, to the copper mine.

The mine was more like a cave than anything. The northern dwarves, upon looking to expand their kingdom into the wooded areas of the continent, were rather fortunate to find this particular mine – it was a cavernous area (as stated before) that branched off into several systems of caves, each rich with copper.

A leftover pickaxe and a lantern were left outside of the cave. Ramona, not taking as much time to observe the perimeter of the mine as Rudgaf, walked over to the lantern, picked it up, and held it in front of the wizard.

"Well?" She asked.

Rudgaf snapped out of his observation, "Oh! Yes, we'll be needing that."

The Lord of Red took the lantern from her, laid his hand upon it, and focused for a moment. Not surprised, but impressed, Ramona observed the lantern as it protruded a light glow that grew into an illuminating radiance. Rudgaf held the lantern up to his face and nodded his head in approval.

"Shall I lead?" Asked Rudgaf.

"If you would be so chivalrous."

Rudgaf smiled and approached the opening of the mine, holding his lantern up to the foramen to expose the hidden contents of the darkness, which had not lost its virginity to the pervasive moonlight. The lantern light lit up the copper in the cave, causing a reflection that flashed into Rudgaf's eyes as the copper returned the favor by glittering with glee.

Rudgaf turned his head and waved forward.

"Let's go."

The Lord of Red led the way into the cave with Ramona trailing, closely behind. The red wizard attempted to hold the lantern closer to the ground than he would've liked in order for Ramona to follow the trail of footprints and other markings that she swore must have belonged to the grey wizard.

They followed the trail that led onwards through the caves as Ramona navigated and Rudgaf provided the guiding light. However, they were forced to halt when they came to a narrow passageway that required more thought than just simply walking through.

"It looks like we're in for a bit of a squeeze." Said Rudgaf.

"No problem," replied Ramona, "I'm not the one who stuffed myself full of dwarf meal."

Rudgaf shrugged as the elf lead the way by squeezing through the narrow passageway until she was through and onto the other side. Rudgaf found a portion of the aperture that was slightly larger than the rest and used it to slide the lantern through to Ramona. He then tightened his belt, straightened his sword, and squeezed through the opening without too much trouble. Once he was through, Ramona handed him the lantern and they continued on their way.

After a long space of time, Ramona spoke.

"I hope that the lantern doesn't run out of oil."

"Don't worry about that. We're not burning any."

"How so?"

"All I need is a medium with which to hold flame. After that, it stays lit until I put it out."

Ramona's eyes widened as she looked at the wizard and said, "How do you do that?"

Rudgaf scoffed, "I'm not at liberty to discuss my functional workings with you at this point in time."

"Whatever, let's just keep going."

After a few moments of pacing further into the cavern, Ramona spoke up again.

"Rudgaf?"

The Lord of Red turned toward his companion, "Yes? What is it?"

"Why do you need a lantern anyway? Can't you just hold the flame out in front of you?"

Rudgaf shook his head, "No. What I am able to produce isn't normal flame."

The elf turned toward the wizard and gave him a quizzical examination, "What do you mean by that?"

The wizard sighed, "Fine, I'll explain it to you. Basically, regular flame is produced by the chemical process of burning. This process produces both light and heat – these are forms of energy. However, I do not have dominion over the light. I only have dominion over the heat."

To demonstrate, the red wizard held his hand out in front of him and formed a fireball to the amazement of the elf who said, "Wow. I knew that you had the ability to do that, but it's another thing entirely to see it in action."

Rudgaf smiled, "I'm glad that you find it to be fascinating. Now – pay attention. Study the flame. Do you notice anything strange?"

The elf stepped closer and peered at the fire carefully. After a moment she said, "I can feel that it is incredibly hot, but it looks extremely dim. I would've expected it to illuminate its surroundings, but it's not doing that. In a way, it kind of looks…cold."

The Lord of Red nodded, "That's because what I hold in my hand isn't truly fire, but is, rather, a flame that produces heat energy, but not light energy."

The wizard extinguished the flame, put his hand back to his side and continued, "If you want to see it illuminate something, you either need a source such as a lantern that can burn, thus creating the chemical process of burning, or you need he who commands the light to shine to come and make my flames produce light. Do you understand?

Ramona nodded, "Yes."

"Good, then let us continue our journey."

They followed the chambers and hallways of what seemed to be a labyrinth by this point, with Ramona shouting, "Here!" and "Over there!" from time to time. Dawn had struck a time ago, unbeknownst to Rudgaf and Ramona, as they followed the trail, navigated through tunnels, and squeezed through crevices. The orange glistening from the copper provided, at one time, a majestic sight to behold. However, as they both stood at what appeared to be a functional impasse, even Rudgaf had grown tired of the scenery.

"The trail ends here…" Said Ramona.

Rudgaf stared up at the ceiling and sighed.

"This is a dead end." He said.

"I can see that."

"Our 'wizard' is not here."

"I can see that as well."

The Lord of Red returned his head to a normal level. It was then that he noticed a faint glow in the corner of the wall. He squinted and held the lantern out further.

"Perhaps there is something that you don't see." He said.

Ramona looked him a look of inquiry as he scooted ahead of her to investigate whatever it was that was causing the glow.

The red wizard came to the location of the sight that he had beheld, knelt down, and discovered a large, brown satchel with a crystalline stone protruding out from one of the pockets. Rudgaf picked up the stone and held it in his hand. He didn't know why, but as he held it, he could feel a chill surround his entire being, accompanied by a strange emptiness that he found to be disturbing. Rudgaf closed his eyes as if compelled to do so and entered a state of deep thought.

What do you want?

He thought as if the stone were pervading his thoughts.

What is this? What do you want with me?

Rudgaf snapped out of his trance as the conversation was abruptly ended. He was overcome with a wave of disappointment, disproval, and rejection – all coming from the very stone that he held in his hand.

Strange.

Ramona spoke up, "Are you alright? What are you holding?"

"I'm not sure."

Ramona looked severely disappointed for some inexplicable reason. Rudgaf took note of it.

"Perhaps there is something else, within this satchel, that will give us a clue as to what this...thing is?" Said Rudgaf.

The red wizard put the strange stone in his pocket for safekeeping and then proceeded to rustle around through the satchel. As his hands fumbled through the darkness of the vessel, he could feel something that felt like parchment. He grabbed hold and pulled out what was, indeed, several pieces of paper. With one hand, he held the newly found treasure in front of him and, with the other, he held the lantern up to it so that he could observe.

The parchment looked old and worn with fringed endings. Rudgaf studied closely and observed a drawing of a naked male form with an 'x' shape on its midsection and an 'o' shape upon its forehead. Beside these body parts was writing – some indiscernible scribble that was written in a language that Rudgaf, to his surprise, was quite unfamiliar with. Four more pieces of parchment did the Lord of Red hold in his hand and, upon inspection of these pieces, he found even more of the same encryption. Rudgaf rolled up the pieces of parchment, stuffed them in his cloak, rubbed his beard, and thought for a moment. After a time, Ramona broke the silence.

"What did you find?"

Rudgaf stood and stared down at the satchel.

"More questions than answers, I'm afraid."

"What was on the parchment?"

"A drawing, accompanied by some text that I cannot interpret."

Rudgaf sighed, briefly.

"I am certain that it has something to do with this stone, however."

The red wizard looked beyond Ramona and stared down the beaten pathway.

"Can you get us back to town?" He asked.

"Oh, please."

Rudgaf lead the way with the lantern as Ramona backtracked their way down the long tunnels, through the narrow passageway, and out of the mine. Rudgaf commanded the lantern to cease its illumination and deposited it back in the exact place that he found it before they both continued on to town. Once there, both Ramona and Rudgaf decided to call it a day and rest awhile at the inn.

It was quite quiet when they entered. The inn keeper stood at the bar, shining his glass mugs with solemn countenance.

Other than the inn keeper, two, somber dwarves sat at a table, together, slowly drinking their prized ale. Rudgaf walked up to their table and sat down next to them.

"I see that you were able to put out the fire in time to save some of the marketplace." Rudgaf said.

The dwarf next to him sniffed, loudly. The dwarf on the other side of the table, not bothering even to raise his head at Rudgaf's existence, stared down into his mug. After a pause, the dwarf next to Rudgaf responded.

"Aye."

"And what of…"

"Lani. 'e di'int make it."

The dwarf sniffed, again.

"Stabbed 'im righ'in de liver. There was a lota blood."

The other dwarf pounded on the table with his fist, tipping over his mug and spilling the rest of his ale.

"Sonuffabitch!" He exclaimed.

The dwarves sat in silence while a young dwarf came around and cleaned up the mess on the table. Rudgaf took the opportunity to nod towards Ramona, who had been watching the scene unfold, and signaled that he was prepared to retire to bed early, since he had not slept the night before. The Lord of Red then sat up and made his way across the dining room, up the stairs, and into the bedchamber hallway. Ramona followed suit.

Rudgaf walked up to the door of his room, put his hand on the doorknob, and spoke.

"Will I be seeing you in the morning?"

"Certainly." Said Ramona.

"I'm going to get some much needed rest. You should rest up, too."

"Actually, I think that I'm going to walk around for a bit. I'm feeling sort of cooped up from all of that time in the mine."

"I see."

A slight pause ensued before they continued.

"Well, then." Said Rudgaf as he turned the knob of the door, opened it and stepped in.

Rudgaf turned around and smiled at Ramona. He then grasped the handle of the door and proceeded to close it. When there was but a small crack of light remaining from the hallway, Ramona placed her hand on the door to stop its current course of motion while she drew closer.

"Good night." She said, softly.

She quickly closed the door before Rudgaf had a chance to respond.

The red wizard turned around, kicked off his boots, hung up his hat and cloak, tucked himself into bed (being mindful of the size of it, this time around) and dreamt.

Rudgaf opened his eyes to find himself standing in a small, dusty room. There wasn't much to it. To his right was a small bed, suitable for barely one person, and to his left was a wooden table, a small, wooden chair, and a bookcase. Rudgaf looked the room up and down when he noticed, some minutes later, that he was holding some sort of a letter in his hands. He looked down to observe it.

The letter was quite old as the parchment was fairly cracked and worn. Although he didn't recall it right away, he knew that he had just been reading it. He continued from where he had paused.

I know that someone will be inquisitive enough to find this letter. *It read. Rudgaf scratched his head and continued reading.*

You must find your brother – the one who will surely have received his power from the black, lesser stone just as you have received yours from one of the others. Your brother may be very dangerous. Do not hesitate to kill him. His power will recede back to the stone from which he received it. You must locate this stone and dispose of it any way that you can. Do not try to draw power from it. Do not let your brothers attempt to draw power from it. I know that this may be difficult, but these are sensitive matters.

Trust no one.

Do not seek me. I go into exile because of my aforementioned failures to stop the betrayer. Perhaps...to the west? I have felt a strange urge to travel there for many weeks, now.

I'll have long been dead by the time that you read this letter, anyway.

Warm regards,

Zaan

Rudgaf nodded his head, rolled up the letter, and put it in his pocket. As if out of instinct, he turned around, got on his hands and knees, and crawled through a crawl space in the room that he, somehow, knew was there. He emerged into a room that the wizards had, primarily, used for storage. He then slid a bookcase, one that he knew he had displaced, back into place over the crawl space.

Walking through the clutter of the room, Rudgaf placed his hand upon a door knob, turned it, and opened the door. He suddenly felt himself displaced from reality and, for a brief period, space and time ceased to exist.

He was slightly dizzy when he recovered. He also, instead of finding himself on the other side of the door that he opened, found himself sitting in a chair at a large, round table.

The Lord of Red observed the room that he was in. It was a large, round room made of stone that he could easily identify as the meeting room on the second floor of the tower. He also made note that he was not alone and, sitting there, he gazed at the colors of brown, blue, green, grey, and yellow, all sitting in chairs that encompassed the table. Rudgaf shook his head in order to bring his vision into focus, and found that these colors were one of the properties of the robes worn by his fellow wizards who were speaking in harsh tones.

The one in brown spoke.

...and Rudgaf never bothered to tell us. Why didn't he tell us something so important? Have we all started keeping secrets amongst ourselves now?

Rudgaf heard himself speak.

I don't know...It just slipped my mind.

How could something like that slip your mind? Replied the one in brown.

Calm down, Wilfrey. You know how forgetful Rudgaf can be. Replied the one in green.

Wilfrey snorted.

I've heard enough from you, today. In any case, what is your excuse? Why didn't you bother to speak up?

I didn't even know about Rudgaf's incident until the stone was disposed of. By that time it was too late. Retorted the one in green.

There was a slight pause before the one in green continued.

And if we're going to be pointing fingers...

Come on, guys. We shouldn't be blaming each other like this. Said Danagan.

I agree. Haven't today's tragedies been enough? Spoke the one in yellow with a tear in his eye.

No. Let me continue... *Said the one in green.*

What? You don't agree with what I did? Asked Wilfrey.

Absolutely not! What were you thinking, Wilfrey?

I never intended the spell to...

But it did! They're all dead, Wilfrey! You killed them, damn it! You murdered them – their men, their women, their children...

Damn you to hell, Barlow!

Stop it! Stop fighting! Cried the one in yellow.

Guys, come on. This has gone far enough. Stated Danagan.

So, this is how it ends. Said the one in blue.

No! We're not ending anything! Snapped the one in yellow.

Yes. He has a point, Danagan. This is the end. Replied Barlow.

Rudgaf observed as Barlow stood up and spread his arms out to make a proclamation.

Because of his heinous crimes against King Narvis and the northern dwarven kingdom, I make a motion to ban Wilfrey from the tower and disassociate him from our brotherhood.

No… whimpered the one in yellow.

Are you nuts? Asked Danagan.

Is that really how you feel, Barlow? Asked Wilfrey.

It's what is just.

To hell with justice for one, damned minute! This is Wilfrey we're talking about. Responded Danagan.

Don't be absurd, Danagan! Justice visits the iniquities of the stranger and the neighbor, alike. The dwarf and the elf are both subject to it as much as the goblin and the orc. The friend must fear it, as well as the father, the mother, and even the brother. When they give into the evil imagination of the heart, then…

What is justice without mercy? Sobbed the one in yellow.

He is our equal. Do we really have the right to throw him out, Barlow? Asked the one in blue.

He lost his rights as an equal the moment that he casted that spell.

Well, I don't agree with this. Any of it. It's bullshit. Said Danagan.

Something must be done, though. We can't continue with this kind of distrust. Said the one in blue.

The way I see it, Barlow is the only one with the problem. So, why doesn't he leave? Asked Danagan.

No! No one is leaving! I'll reduce this tower to ash before I ever see anyone forced to leave! Screamed the one in yellow.

Well, something has to be done. Said Barlow.

Rudgaf finally spoke.

I'll go.

Wilfrey quickly rose from his seat and spoke.

Rudgaf, no…

It's okay, Wilfrey. After all, this is all my fault. I'm the one who forgot to tell you about the stone.

But, Rudgaf…

Don't put all of the blame on yourself, Rudgaf. Said Danagan.

It's fine. I accept all of the blame. Let their blood be on my hands.

But, Wilfrey was the one… Said Barlow.

Wilfrey did nothing wrong. The blame is mine and that is that.

Silence, except for the sobbing of the one in yellow, filled the room as the wizards, baffled by the conversation, stared at each other.

I'm going to go pack my belongings.

Where are you going to go, Rudgaf? Asked the one in blue.

North, I guess. I have a lot of sins to atone for.

That's suicide! Exclaimed Danagan.

It is what it is.

There was a long pause before Barlow spoke.

Since it was my judgment that ultimately led you to make this decision, I shall accompany you on your quest. Although, I'd feel a lot safer if three of us went.

I'll go with you. I don't have anything more interesting to occupy me at the moment. *Said the one in blue.*

Then it's settled. It'll be me, Rudgaf, and Thome that leave.

This isn't happening…this isn't what's right. *Said the one in yellow.*

I have to agree with the little man here. You don't have to do this, Rudgaf. *Said Danagan.*

Rudgaf smiled. He then walked to his room to pack his belongings. The three wizards left that afternoon.

As they walked through the garden that Wilfrey and Barlow built, Rudgaf looked back to see his once, beloved home – filled with his friends and brothers, fade into the distance.

I didn't mean it. I didn't…

Rudgaf awoke with the Sun, as was his custom. He sat up and slowly shook his head as the sunlight peered in through the window in his room.

"Good morning!"

Rudgaf jumped with a start and noticed that Ramona was sitting on top of the dresser across from his bed with a handful of steamed towels and a pitcher of hot water.

"Oh, it's you. How long have you been sitting there?"

"Not long. The inn keeper was going to bring these to you, but I figured that I would do it." She said as she handed Rudgaf the towels and the pitcher of water.

"Did you sleep well?" She asked.

"Not really. How about you?"

"Sure."

"What's that supposed to mean?"

"You should get cleaned up. I'll meet you downstairs."

"Huh? Oh, alright."

Ramona sat up, opened the door, and exited the room. After she left, Rudgaf sat and thought for a bit, and then undressed and washed himself. Once he was finished, he replaced his clothes, his cloak, his boots and, finally, his hat, and exited the room to make his way downstairs.

Once he arrived, he noticed that Ramona was, once again, sitting in his "favorite" spot, so he, again, sat in the seat across from her. The inn keeper came around with a breakfast that consisted of quail eggs, freshly made biscuits, and sliced apples. Rudgaf eagerly broke his fast while Ramona picked at her food.

"Not a fan of eggs?" Asked Rudgaf.

"Huh?" Ramona asked with a start.

"No, it's not that. I'm just not in the mood."

The inn keeper, overhearing the conversation, piped in, "Well how's about ye tell me, next time, so I do'n go wastin' goo' foo' on ye?"

"You were serving it to me to eat, anyway. What's it matter what I end up doing with it?"

The inn keeper snorted as he snatched the plates away from Ramona and walked away in a huff, mumbling something about how disrespectful elves are.

"What's his problem?" Asked Ramona.

"You insulted his cooking."

"How? I didn't say anything was wrong with it."

"But you didn't eat it."

Ramona rolled her eyes, "Dwarves are so sensitive."

The inn keeper made another go at their table and said, "Well, I know that me wizard friend, 'ere, likes ma cookin' a whole bunch!"

"Indeed, I do." Responded Rudgaf.

"Oh, do'n I know it! Look at dat we li'ull tummy!" Said the inn keeper as he poked Rudgaf's midsection.

Rudgaf raised an eyebrow, "Don't do that, again."

"Uhh…yeah. Sorry." Said the inn keeper as he blushed and returned back to his duties.

"I'd say that you made a friend. Although he is a little too…happy." Said Ramona.

"Well, at least he can cook."

Ramona chuckled as Rudgaf finished up his meal and brushed the crumbs off of his beard. Getting up, they both thanked the inn keeper for the hospitality, picked up their weapons, and exited the establishment.

Upon exiting, Ramona strapped her bow to her back, along with a quiver of arrows. The quiver was a normal, everyday quiver made of lisk leather. However, the bow was quite ornate and featured spiral patterns made of gold and marble. It looked rather expensive. And heavy.

"That's a nice bow you have, there." Said Rudgaf as they walked through the door.

"Ah, yes. Thank you."

"How did you come about it?"

"It was a gift from a lover."

"I see." Said Rudgaf. He sensed a bit of hesitation from Ramona so he decided not to press the issue any further.

"Where are you headed?" Asked Ramona as they both trotted down the dirt path the led out of town.

"Back north," said Rudgaf, "I need to inform my friend at the tower of what transpired in Behnon."

"Do you mean Thome or Barlow?"

Rudgaf smiled, "Most people do not even know me by name and, yet, here you are – listing off the names of all of my companions as if it were common knowledge."

"Well?"

"Well? Oh, yes. It's Barlow. Thome went off on some sort of errand."

"An errand? What for?"

"He didn't really say but, of course, Thome will be Thome."

Rudgaf laughed as they both made their way to the remainder of the marketplace. Despite yesterday's events, it was good to see that everything was operating and things were, "business as usual". Indeed, nothing can keep a dwarf down.

Both Rudgaf and Ramona smiled and laughed as they talked about old stories while casually making their way through the marketplace. At around the tail end of it, and within eyesight of the gate, however, Rudgaf felt a tingling sensation on the back of his neck, followed by a queasy feeling in his stomach.

"Stop." Said Rudgaf as he held his hand out to stop Ramona from venturing forward.

"What? What's wrong?"

"Something is not right, but I can't place it."

Rudgaf focused for a moment while he attempted to find the source of the disturbance. Closing his eyes, he concentrated and focused on the moment in time insomuch that, in his mind, the events of the day were passing by at an increasingly slower rate.

That's when he felt it. There could be no mistake about it. He could see it in his mind.

The event was slow, in his mind, yet instantaneous to everyone around him, including Ramona. Rudgaf held out his hand just in time to catch the arrow between his thumb and forefinger before it pierced his left temple. Like a statue, he stood there, grasping the arrow before he incinerated it.

"Son-of-a-bitch!" Cried Ramona.

The crowd in the marketplace, startled and afraid, cried out in terror. Soon, the peaceful scene was replaced with the chaos of rampant dwarves attempting to find shelter in case more projectiles decide to make their way over to them. The sound of business, happiness, and merrymaking were soon replaced with a cacophony of fright.

Amongst the chaos, Rudgaf was able to observe that, on one of the houses that was over a hundred yards distance from where he stood, a faint, black figure was jumping off of the rooftop and into the crowd below.

"Did you see that?"

"Yeah." Said Ramona as she shook her head in disgust.

"But, why?"

"I don't know, but you're lucky to be alive."

"Yes." Agreed Rudgaf as he stared down at the ashen remains of the arrow that nearly ended his life.

"I don't know what's going on," continued Rudgaf, "but I bet the shooter knows something."

Ramona, understanding what the wizard was implying, nodded her head and followed him through the streets as he made haste towards the sniper's coop.

When they drew near to the house, Ramona knelt down to study the tracks on the ground.

"Any luck?" Asked Rudgaf.

After a few moments of silence, Ramona stood up.

"No. He didn't leave any discernable tracks. The Behun guard are trained to be as light footed as possible, you know."

Rudgaf tsk'ed for a bit and then started to ask the dwarves in the area if they had seen anyone run through the area. After questioning a few dwarves, the consensus was that they did, indeed, see someone run through the area and that this someone was, most assuredly, headed for the southern exit in town that led towards the marshlands.

With the information at hand, Rudgaf headed toward the exit. Just before he set foot into the last vestiges of forest before coming to the dreaded marshlands, he turned towards Ramona who he had just noticed had still been following him.

"You don't have to come with me. I'm sure that you have your own business to take care of." Said Rudgaf.

"This is my business, now. An elf, more importantly, a member of the Behun guard, just tried to assassinate someone. That is strictly against our code. It's not the elven way."

Rudgaf shook his head. Without further pause, they made a heading through the exit and into the forest towards the marsh. After a few moments of walking, Ramona spoke, once more.

"Let Justice come unto him. Her tax is heavy and her coin is crimson."

~CHAPTER THREE – EXODUS~

Three weeks we spent journeying without retire, forced to take the long route through the swamp,
cutting up through the jungle and into the marshlands. Much to our delight, the marshlands were
quite vast – far larger than the dank swamp that we had just endured.
The acid rain burned holes in our cloaks.

A somewhat elderly man sat at a desk made of pine, studying a dusty tome. His eyes peered through the text as if they were surveying the scene for scoundrels. He adjusted himself in his chair, shifting the grey cloak that he wore over his baggy, green robe. Impatiently, he tapped his foot as he read while squinting his eyes due to the lack of candle and sunlight, ruffling his thick brows that sat comfortably underneath the wide brim of his pointy, green hat.

His slightly, gnarled fingers combed through the pages with great speed. Then, suddenly, they slammed the tome shut, kicking up dust, everywhere, as the man shook his head in frustration. Leaning back in his chair, he rubbed his beard and contemplated.

"Where could Rudgaf be?" He said, out loud.

Rudgaf should have been back, by now. A journey that was set to take him no more than five days has now seen him absent for well over a week. The man in green sighed in worry.

The old fool probably got distracted, somehow.

It had been lonely in the tower without the Lord of Red. The green wizard had great difficulty passing the time in his absence, choosing to read random tomes out of their vast library in order to keep himself occupied.

After reading through them all numerous times (this particular volume he had already read thrice, being the excellent reader that he was), he had finally lost his patience.

Maybe I should go look for him?

Barlow stood up from his chair, surveyed the room, took a deep breath, and pondered his own question. He stood in the same spot for the space of a few minutes when he heard a familiar sound, the sound of someone tapping on a thick, piece of wood. There were three taps in succession, to be exact, followed by a brief pause and then another three taps in succession.

Who could that be at this hour?

Although it was around noon and a perfectly acceptable time to knock on someone's door, Barlow had not been expecting any company and he found the occurrence to be rather unsettling.

The Lord of Green girded himself up, walked down the spiral staircase made of stone, passed the dining floor, and walked up to the pine door on the bottom floor of the tower. Without any further delay, he opened it. Before him stood three dwarves in triangular fashion, each wearing horned helmets with the northern, dwarf insignia bore into the front of them (an image of a pine tree being struck with a bolt of lightning, encompassed by a circle). They bore no sign of rank which, Barlow knew all too well since he had spent numerous years around the northern, dwarf army, meant that they belonged to the, "intelligence" department. The dwarf at the head of the formation spoke, first.

"Afternoon, Lord of Green. Might we com'in fur a spell?"

"Certainly." Said Barlow as he stepped to the side of the door and motioned them in with a sweeping arc of his hand.

Barlow stood next to the door as he waited for the three dwarves to step in. When they had all entered, he shut the door behind them, turned to face them, and spoke.

"You may hang up your hats and cloaks on the rack next to me." Barlow said as he pointed towards the coat rack.

"No need," said the lead dwarf, "this won't take long."

"Very well. To what do I owe the pleasure?"

The lead dwarf cleared his throat and spoke.

"The siege of Behnon."

"I beg your pardon?"

"What do ya know about it?"

"Nothing more than what his majesty allowed my companion to be aware of. Why do you ask?"

Another dwarf spoke up.

"We have reason te believe that yer companion and another wizard may be involved, somehow."

Shocked, Barlow asked, "How have you come to this conclusion? Did not his majesty send the Lord of Red to investigate? How could he have had something to do with the siege if he wasn't even present in the city at the time that the event took place?"

The lead dwarf took the charge, again.

"Ya see, we've enlisted the help of the dread eagles."

"You cannot be serious!" Said Barlow with a gasp.

"They've proven quite useful."

"Regardless, what does that have to do with Rudgaf?"

"They saw 'im doin' 'is "investigatin'". It looked mighty suspicious."

"How so?"

"Well, fur starters, he tried to hide from 'em."

"Of course he did."

"Oh, but I'm not finished!"

"Go on."

"Right after he left, the whole, damn city was burned down!"

"What?" Said Barlow, in shock.

"On toppa that, there was another wizard there, dressed in grey. We believe 'im ta be the filth from the east tower."

"I see." Said Barlow as he rubbed his beard and stared at the floor.

The third dwarf spoke up.

"Did ya know that he was gonna be there?"

"I had no idea, I can assure you. I haven't spoken to him since before you were born."

The lead dwarf took the reins, again.

"Well, anyways, that scum'o'the'earth invaded a dwarven, mining town a few days back, now. He destroyed part of their marketplace and killed a civilian."

"That can't be true, good dwarf." Retorted the green wizard as he snapped his head back up.

The second dwarf spoke.

"Oh, but it is! He even shot one of our birds, dead!"

"My sympathies."

"He probably ate it," said the third, "the brute!"

"Dread eagle is a fine meal." Said Barlow, chuckling.

The dwarves simultaneously shuddered in disgust before the lead dwarf responded.

"Now it's you who cannot be serious." He said with disdain.

"As serious as the possibility of a wizard, and yes, even Danagan, murdering innocent civilians, regardless of his relation with the northern dwarves."

"It's been done before!" Piped up the second while slamming his fist down on a nearby table.

Barlow paused for a moment and then responded.

"That was a long, time ago and a completely, separate issue." Replied Barlow with his teeth gritted.

There was a long pause before the dwarf in front spoke, again.

"You'll hav'ta forgive me friend. Travelin' 'ere from the capital would leave anyone in a foul mood, not te mention that it's colder than a hag's teet, out there."

"Very well." Said Barlow, annoyed.

After a moment, Barlow spoke again.

"I'm sorry, but I cannot help you any further. Everything I know about what happened to the elven city was in the letter that his majesty sent the Lord of Red."

"What about the Lord of Blue?" Asked the second.

"He left on a journey to the west some time ago."

"I see."

"Well, we won't be any more of a bother to ye." Said the one in front.

"Again, I apologize that I couldn't be of more assistance. If there is anything that I can do for you, you be sure to let me know, alright?"

"Aye, we will. We consider ye te be a brother. We'll never forget what ye and yer friends have done te help us." Said the one in the front.

"It was the least that we could do."

"Well, you'll always be a friend ta us, despite all of this chaos goin' on 'round us." Said the second.

"Believe me, we did'unt even want te question ye. We're jus' tryin' te make some sense outta this." Stated the first.

Barlow smiled and spoke.

"I understand."

The first bowed to Barlow, followed by the second and the third as Barlow opened the door and the dwarves scuffled out. As they were leaving and before they came to a ridge in the distance, Barlow shouted to them.

"Give my best to his majesty!"

They all turned around to face the tower and shouted, "Aye!", before continuing on their journey towards home.

Barlow slowly pushed the door and, after a few creaks and a thick thud, it shut. He thought for a moment and, then, without further delay, he activated the deadbolt locking mechanism on the door, just in case. The deadbolt clicked in place, a sound that the green wizard thought to be very satisfying.

He pondered some more.

I wonder what is going on over there?

~

"Don't touch the frogs here." Said Rudgaf as he and Ramona trudged through the depths of the marshlands.

They were one day removed from the shooting incident at the dwarven, mining town. Ramona had been responsible for tirelessly following the tracks of the would-be assassin through the swamp. They weren't hard for her to follow, what with all of the soft ground and mud around, however, it was clear that they were dealing with a fellow who possessed great speed. Despite their fervent efforts and lack of rest, they had yet to spot him and were forced to continue exploring the vastness of the marsh. Still, despite the fact that the elf had quite a spring in his step, Rudgaf was surprised that the shooter hadn't spent a little more time attempting to cover his tracks, given the effort that he had put into hiding the ones that lead to the marshlands in the first place. Being the novice scouter that the Lord of Red was, the tracks in the ground were so obvious that even he could have followed them without much of an effort.

"Why?" Ramona asked as they continued to walk.

"They leech blood. It is quite a disturbing sight to see one do its work. You can, quite literally, see them getting fatter while they suck the life out of you."

"It's quite painful." Rudgaf added after a pause.

"I'll keep that in mind." Said Ramona without a hint of worry.

Rudgaf shrugged off her lack of care, deciding that it must have been due to a lack of sleep and surroundings that were, in general, rather dismal, at best.

After a while, Ramona paused, looked up at the sky, and sighed.

"What's the bother?" Asked Rudgaf.

"This guy is fast," Ramona remarked, "I don't know if we'll be able to catch him."

Ramona quickly snapped her neck from side to side, creating a, "popping" sound.

"And all of this looking down is bugging the hell out of my neck."

Rudgaf scratched his head.

"Want me to scout for a while?" He asked.

"Pah," Ramona snorted, "you couldn't tell an elf from a hydelisk!"

"Hrmph," Rudgaf scoffed, "hundreds of years of study and observation and, here I am, stuck with shoes filled with mud and a smarmy-mouthed elf."

"Whatever." Said Ramona as she continued to lead the way.

Several hours went by as they continued to drudge through the marsh and hopping over moss covered logs, only stopping once when Rudgaf lost his boot, causing him to pillage the mud with his foot, which, as you could well imagine, displeased him, greatly.

The sky was starting to show signs of aging as the Sun set over the horizon and the blazing blue gave way to the orange glow that sunsets are known for. It was then that both Rudgaf and Ramona stopped, suddenly. Ramona tilted her head to the side, slightly.

"How did he…?"

They both stared into the distance as they grasped the severity of the situation. Rudgaf stared down for a moment and pondered. If only the body of water that laid before him were clear, he could see his own reflection. However, all that he could observe was the brackish, algae infested lake that might as well have been a mountain or, perhaps, an impregnable fortress that, somehow, the shooter was able to conquer.

"Barrier Lake." Said Rudgaf.

"It seems that we have reached an impasse." He added after a pause.

"Well, it wasn't an impasse for him, now was it?"

"That would be most surprising, indeed! The southern elves have used this lake to their advantage for generations. I'm surprised that you are unaware."

"Why is that?"

"Thome built it to prevent the eastern elves from invading the, "junglies", as you call them."

Ramona glared at the lake, as if trying to evaporate it.

"This would have forced the eastern elves to take the mountain pass into the jungle, which the goblins certainly would have objected to."

Rudgaf cleared his throat.

"It was quite a fiasco," said Rudgaf, "Thome and King Nolan nearly came to blows! Luckily, King Ralis stepped in to settle the whole thing."

"Rudgaf!" Snapped Ramona.

Surprised, Rudgaf responded, "Yes?"

"How are we going to get across this thing?"

"Ah, there is that." Said Rudgaf, still rubbing his beard.

Rudgaf pondered for a while as Ramona tended to smacking the mosquitos that decided to make a feast out of her bare calf muscles. He allowed his mind to meander to a previous conversation that he had with Thome hundreds of years ago about this very lake.

As Thome was building, "Barrier Lake", Rudgaf remembered him mentioning something about getting across it. With Thome being present, they could've just walked across the lake. Since Thome was not present, Rudgaf thought, they would have to find another way.

Swimming is no good.

Indeed, swimming was not a viable option. The water, being thick and concentrated with high amounts of mud and algae, would cause them to sink before they could even put their minds to swimming. Since drowning was not an option, Rudgaf pondered further.

I thought that Thome had mentioned a way to get across the lake, should he not be present with us when one of us needed to get across.

Rudgaf thought harder.

Joem would certainly need to know of this. I haven't seen him in a long time, though, so maybe he forgot, as well.

"I know!" Blurted Ramona, suddenly.

"Huh?"

"You're the wizard of fire, right? Why don't you just turn the water into steam so that we can walk across the bottom?"

"That will not be possible." Rudgaf responded, disappointed.

"Why the hell not?"

"You see the fog coming off of the top of the water?" Rudgaf asked Ramona as he pointed toward the thick puffs of fog that floated above the water's surface.

"Yeah?"

"It's highly flammable. I could evaporate the water, if you insist, but the aftermath would do a little more than singe our eyebrows."

"Damn it!" Screamed Ramona as she stomped the ground in frustration.

There was a long wave of silence before Ramona spoke, again.

"We've just got to find a way."

"Are you sure he even made it across?" Asked Rudgaf.

Ramona turned toward Rudgaf and said, "Of course, I'm sure."

"Really?" Inquired Rudgaf. "He could have just attempted to make it across, but drowned in the process."

"Don't be absurd. I can see elf tracks leading out from the other side, going further on through the marsh from here."

Shocked, Rudgaf responded, "You can make out tracks from this distance?"

"What kind of an elf would I be if I couldn't?"

Rudgaf shrugged his shoulders and continued to think. If only he could remember, he thought, what Thome described as the way to get across the lake without him.

If you ever need to get across without me, just remember that you have to be nimble.

Be nimble?

Rudgaf got it.

"How agile are you?" Rudgaf asked.

"You're joking, right?" Ramona scoffed.

"Fine, then. You see those lily pads out on the water?"

"Yeah." Said Ramona as she peered out onto the lake to stare at the wide, green lily pads that sat peacefully upon the dark surface of their mother lake.

"They're not normal lily pads. You can jump on them."

"No way!" Gasped Ramona.

"But, there is a catch," added Rudgaf, "they are magical, after all."

"Ok, then. What's the catch?"

"Each lily pad is a part of a combination. Simply put, you have to jump on them in a certain order to be able to make it across the lake."

Ramona sighed, "Really? Is that what you wizard's do in your spare time? What a stupid idea."

"You must admit though," said Rudgaf as he tilted his head, "it serves its purpose."

"Being?"

"Thome didn't want just anyone getting across. He only taught the combination to certain people."

"And now it's all up to your memory to get us across this lake?" Ramona asked, turning pale.

"Well, yeah." Replied the red wizard, sheepishly.

"And I don't suppose that we'll survive if we step on the wrong lily pad, right?"

"Well, if we step on the wrong one, it will collapse and cause us to sink into the lake. So, no, chances are not likely that we would survive such a mistake."

"Great." Said Ramona, rolling her eyes.

Rudgaf shrugged.

"Would you like to go back, then?" He asked.

Ramona raised an eyebrow.

"Don't pretend like you don't want to find this guy as bad as I do." She retorted.

Rudgaf smiled.

"The lily pads it is, then."

Rudgaf girded himself up and began to wade out into the lake where the lake remained shallow. He turned back at Ramona whom, he had noticed, was not following him, quite yet.

"You coming?" He asked.

"Disgusting." She said as she reluctantly stepped into the water and began to wade out.

"It wreaks, too!" She added.

"Yeah," said Rudgaf, "that's the gas that I was talking about, earlier. It's methane."

"Lovely."

"Thome added a rather repugnant smell to it so that I wouldn't forget about it."

"Nice of him."

"I thought so."

Ramona sighed as Rudgaf led the way to the first lily pad. Laying his forearms flat on its surface, he hoisted himself up.

"This is the first lily pad," Rudgaf remarked, "and it's also the last part of the lake that won't be over our heads until we get to the other side."

"I hope that we can reach the other side of the lake before nightfall." Grunted Ramona as she hoisted herself up to stand alongside of Rudgaf.

"I know. Unfortunately, I won't be able to light our way and it's going to be exceedingly dangerous to attempt to do this in the dark."

The Lord of Red surveyed the area and observed that, from his lily pad, he could see two more within jumping distance that sat, quietly, next to each other.

"Memory, don't fail me now!" Rudgaf said out loud as he jumped towards the left most lily pad.

Rudgaf nimbly landed on the aforementioned lily pad and, to his joy, it supported his weight without effort. Ramona shook her head in approval and followed suit.

Two more jumps did Rudgaf make in similar fashion on lily pads that were aligned the same as the first pair. The correct choice was the left lily pad on the first jump, and then one that was directly in front of him. Ramona tagged along behind the wizard, surprised that he was able to memorize the sequence and that he hadn't drowned to death, already, leaving her stranded in the middle of the lake.

Rudgaf made two more jumps on lily pads which, if he were facing forward, would have been directly to his right. His next destination laid directly in front of him, but was quite some distance away from the lily pad that he was currently calling, "home". In preparation, the wizard swung his arms and then, swallowing hard before he did so, he leapt toward his goal. He felt his feet nimbly land on the lily pad, but as suddenly as they landed they also swept out from under him, and he felt himself falling into the arms of death.

Quickly, without even thinking about it, he was able to grab a hold of the edge of the lily pad before the rest of his body, most of which was already underwater, sank into the depths of the murky lake.

"Are you ok?" Ramona shouted.

"I think so. That certainly was a close one, though!"

Rudgaf hoisted himself up onto the lily pad with great difficulty, his body feeling quite heavy in the water that wanted nothing more than to envelope him completely. When he felt that he was secure on the platform, he stood up and rung out his robe, which was irreversibly filthy at this point, in order to attempt to reduce his weight.

Shaking off his fear over what just transpired, he made two more jumps – the first one to the left and the second one forward. He then made one to the left, then forward, then to the right, and forward, and repeated the pattern a few times, being extra careful not to slip as he did, before. Thome always liked patterns, Rudgaf remembered, which seemed quite odd to him because the rest of his actions always appeared to be quite erratic.

The red wizard jumped to the right and then forward twice, which he repeated a few times. It was then that he came to another impasse.

Hmm…I don't remember what to do, next.

Ramona caught up with him and joined him in staring at the field of lily pads surrounding them. They might as well have been a field of mines, she thought.

"Well? What are you waiting for?" She asked.

"There is a particular pattern, here," said Rudgaf, "and I can't remember what it is."

"Do you have any idea, at all?"

"Well," said Rudgaf, "it is a rather simple pattern. You're either supposed to make four jumps to the right and four jumps forward, or four jumps to the left and four jumps forward. I, however, cannot remember which."

"Well, you have to make a decision, soon," Ramona said in a panicked tone, "it's almost nightfall and we won't be able to see where we're even jumping!"

"I know! Just let me think for a bit."

The Lord of Red pondered next to the impatient elf for a time. Meanwhile, the sky was getting darker and the lily pads were becoming dim in the growing night.

"Rudgaf…"

If only I could remember…

"Rudgaf…"

Which way was it?

"Rudgaf!"

Gah!

Rudgaf, tiring of the elf's impatience, took a leap directly to his right, closed his eyes in midair, and hoped for the best. He felt his feet land and then, moments later, he heard a clapping sound coming from behind him.

"You did it!" Cheered Ramona.

Rudgaf smiled.

"I knew that I would remember, eventually."

Rudgaf and Ramona, after having much success, continued the pattern – jumping to the right three more times and then forward four times, until they reached the end of the embankment and were safely on the ground.

Ramona sat down while Rudgaf leaned over, putting his hands on his knees and taking deep breaths. He was exhausted, yet extremely thankful to be done with the ordeal. One thing was for certain, he thought, he was going to hate trying to do what he just did, again, except in reverse order.

As Rudgaf was staring at the ground, he noticed that, indeed, Ramona had been right about the tracks leading away from the lake. But how could a member of the Behun guard know the correct jumping pattern in order to make his way across the lake? Only the wizards and some of the southern elves knew how to do it.

"I still don't understand how a member of the Behun guard could have known how to get across that lake." Said Rudgaf.

"I don't know," said Ramona, "a series of lucky guesses?"

Rudgaf raised an eyebrow.

"Now look who is being, 'absurd'."

Ramona shrugged.

"It is what it is."

Rudgaf scoffed as he caught his breath and they continued on, making as much use of the remaining daylight as they could before they had to attempt to make a home of their dank surroundings for the night.

The wizard shivered, slightly, as a sudden breeze caressed his backside and reminded him that his clothes were soaked from his earlier expedition into the lake. He continued to trudge through the mud for a few steps when a breeze hit him, again, except across his legs, this time.

Blasted draft!

Determined to not let the cold bother him, he pressed on, only to, somehow, lose his footing as he was tripped up by some object that made a home in his path without his being aware of it. Tumbling forward, Rudgaf held his hands out and was able to stop himself from landing face first in the mud, instead landing on his hands and knees.

"What a fine mess," he said as he shook the mud off of his hands, "watch your step, Ramona."

No response was given.

The wizard perked up and said, "Ramona?"

Still, there was no response.

Rudgaf hoisted himself up from the mud and turned around. The first thing that he noticed is that there was nothing on the ground, in front of him, to which he could have tripped on. The mysterious object was gone. That's when he noticed, as he stared at the ground and turned his head toward his left, that the object had moved, and was still moving.

A tail?

Indeed, it was a tail – scaly, blue, and had nearly as much girth as a tree trunk. Rudgaf followed the tail with his eyes, up and up, along the scaly back of its master who towered over him and everything else in the surrounding area. It was a large creature, one that Rudgaf, given his current position, couldn't see around, as if it were a giant wall. The wizard continued to look up and, upon the behemoth standing in front of him were three heads, attached to three, very long necks. Before Rudgaf had time to get lost in his observations, he heard a small voice from the other side of the mountainous monster, calling out to him, meekly.

"Um…Rudgaf?"

"I'm here." He replied.

Upon hearing this, the left most head of the creature (from Rudgaf's perspective), turned around to face him, its neck contorting to accommodate the function. The head, seeming to have a mind of its own, gave a loud, "hiss", at Rudgaf while the other two heads focused their attention on Ramona. The wizard winced, slightly, as the billowing lungs of the giant serpent went on a rampage of, "hissing" and ringing his ear drums.

"Rudgaf…what the hell is it?"

Rudgaf didn't like what he was about to say.

"It's a hydra."

"A what?!" Screamed Ramona as she carefully took a few steps backwards.

The hydra hissed at her.

The third head, which was facing Rudgaf, however, had a different plan in mind. Noticing that the wizard had not fallen back, it outstretched its neck and snapped at him. The wizard smelled its rank breath invade his nostrils as he barely was able to dodge the advance by leaping backwards.

Ramona, seeing that at least one of the heads was distracted, took the opportunity to take out her bow and sink an arrow into the back of the skull of the head that got out of line.

"Direct hit!" She yelled, expecting the head to topple over.

"Oh, no." Said Rudgaf.

The arrow that she was certain would have caused the death blow served only to enrage the beast, as it turned its third head back towards Ramona and snapped at her, the other two heads following in succession.

Ramona dodged the third head by jumping backwards as it lunged forwards, much like Rudgaf did, landing in a sitting position on the ground. The second head came in from her left and she quickly rolled out of the way, launching herself off of the ground with her hands. Before she had time to recompose herself for the next attack, the first head came in for the kill, plunging itself forward. Before it could fully reach Ramona and deal, what surely would be, a death blow, it was forced to stop short and be delayed from its prize. All three heads squealed and hissed simultaneously as, being distracted as it was, it had forgotten all about the wizard behind it who was now wielding a flaming sword and who had just left a sizeable gash across its back.

The hydra, incensed, turned its fiery ardor to Rudgaf, who jumped out of the way of the attacks of two of the heads, but was caught by the third head in mid-air as it smacked him and sent him sailing into the mud. Rudgaf, his face to the ground, rolled over as quickly as he could to see the very same head, staring directly at him, not more than a few feet away. Without even a thought, Rudgaf outstretched his hand and expelled a ball of fire into the visage of the third head, catching it by surprise. Distracted by its new wound, Ramona took the opportunity to shoot again. Rudgaf heard the elven arrow as it "zinged" by with alarming speed. The wizard quickly focused his sight on Ramona's target, and noticed that her arrow had sunken deeply into the left eye of the third head of the beast. It hissed and screeched an ear piercing screech that hurt Rudgaf's teeth as it writhed in pain and sent the other two heads in to do its bidding.

The second head sailed in with its teeth barred at Rudgaf. The wizard leapt backwards as quickly as he could, but the foul monster ended up with a piece of his cloak. The first head flailed itself around in a circular motion in the air, distracting Ramona before it came sweeping down across the ground, tripping her up and sending her flying head over heels. As she was up in the air, the second head came by and smacked her, spiking her head first into the ground.

"Ramona!"

With the elf out of the way, the two heads turned their attention completely to Rudgaf. They hissed at him, once more, almost as if they were laughing at him. The second head lunged forward, but Rudgaf was able to side-step it just in time. Carefully and quickly, he planted his feet on the side of the head of the serpent and leapt into the air. He then stretched out his hands and launched two, large fireballs towards both heads, which exploded upon contact in a fury and toppled the hydra over.

The behemoth roared as it failed to weather the power of the blasts. The ground rumbled and quaked in the aftermath of the great beast tumbling over and hitting the dirt.

Rudgaf landed on his side, hard, and felt his left arm go numb. He stared at the hydra, intensely, as if trying to burn through lead, for he knew that the fight was far from over. The wizard sat up, but before he had time to stand, the hydra's tail cracked him across the face, the force of which sent him soaring through the air and toward the edge of the lake.

With great effort, the hydra managed to find a way to stand upright once more. With the faces of two of its heads burned black, and its third head still unable to do anything useful, it slowly slithered its way towards the lake in an effort to be rid of the wizard once and for all.

It failed to notice that, miraculously, Ramona had already recovered from its previous attack and was taking aim. This time, she sent an arrow sailing into the throat of the second head, which did little more than garner the attention of the angry giant.

The third head, deciding to deal with its pain, for it had quite enough of the elf for one day, cocked back and delivered a large stream of black goo towards Ramona that quickly burned everything within its wake. It was a highly potent acid of which Ramona quickly discovered when she was unable to dodge the attack completely. Before she knew what was happening, she noticed that she was experiencing a sharp, burning sensation on her right hand. She looked down and observed that the acid had burned straight through her glove and was just starting to eat her flesh. The elf swiftly removed the glove and threw it on the ground before the acid was able to do any more damage.

"Alright, you bastard. You've lived long enough."

In a blinding rage, she pulled out the two daggers that she kept sheathed near her hips and leapt in the air towards the hydra with reckless abandon. The attack took the monster by surprise for, before it even could see what was transpiring, Ramona had already run up its back and planted one of the daggers in the left eye of the second head. In anger and frustration, the first head curled around and snapped at her, but missed. Ramona then jumped on the first head of the hydra, but before she could plant a dagger in one of its eyes, the beast started to swing its head in an attempt to shake off its attacker.

Ramona swung in the wind, barely able to hold on to the thrashing creature. Her legs flailed every which way, but she refused to let go. The second head was completely incapacitated and could do nothing to draw her off. The third head wanted nothing more than to chomp her into bits, but was afraid of injuring the now flailing first head.

Out of desperation, the hydra slammed its head on the ground, causing the ground to quake violently. Ramona shook, but still would not relinquish her grip on the beast. It slammed its head again, and again, and once more but, despite its best efforts, Ramona would not give up. Thinking quickly, the hydra slithered its way toward the lake where the wizard laid. Taking advantage of the break in the action, Ramona climbed up toward the head and attempted to plant her second dagger into its left eye. However, before she had a chance to do so, the hydra had already arrived at the lake and, without any delay, it sunk its head into the water in an attempt to drown the elf.

Ramona held her breath and clenched tightly. She couldn't see anything, but she knew what she had to do. Quickly, she started climbing down the neck of the creature in an effort to use the hydra to escape the lake. Sensing movement, the beast outstretched its neck even more, sending Ramona even further into the depths of the lake. The elf scrambled quickly, but every time she felt herself make progress, the hydra was somehow able to stretch its neck further down into the water.

The elf started to lose consciousness and her efforts waned. She had run out of ideas, out of luck, out of time, and was about to run out of air and become another victim of, "Barrier Lake". She wondered how Rudgaf was doing, and sincerely hoped that he would be able to survive the onslaught of the creature without her help. She started to fade.

Above the water's surface, the hydra heard a shout.

"Hey! Over here!" Screamed Rudgaf from a lily pad located deep into the lake.

Infuriated that the wizard was still alive and standing, the hydra forgot all about Ramona and flung its first head up into the air, dumping Ramona onto the ground, behind it. It roared with rage and shot acid breath from all three of its heads, but to no avail. The Lord of Red was too far out. It had no choice but to heed his call and join him in a dance to the death.

"Ramona!" Cried the wizard.

Ramona attempted to shake the cobwebs out of her head. She was cold and dripping wet, but hadn't the energy to care. She opened her eyes and noticed that her vision was blurry and that the world swayed around her.

"Ramona!" Yelled Rudgaf, again.

The hydra, undistracted by the wizard's calls for his companion, advanced toward the lily pad that Rudgaf was standing upon with great speed. It was almost within an adequate range to stage an attack.

"Ramona!" Cried Rudgaf a third time.

"Ye…yeah?" She responded.

"Run! Get away from the lake!"

Ramona's eyes widened.

"Shit." She said as she stood up and ran as best and as fast as she could.

The elf was able to gain some ground before the hydra was able to get within striking distance of the wizard. It looked to take him out with one, fell swoop. Arching its first head back, it prepared to dive in for the kill.

Rudgaf had noticed that he couldn't raise his left arm any longer when he was making his way across the lily pads. He was forced to just let it hang, lifelessly, to his side. He found that he had reinjured his ribs, and winced with every movement. As the hydra lurked ever closer to where he stood, he mustered up the last remnants of his strength and began to speak.

"The flame of the ancients, the embers of Mount Shuun where dragon's fire doth roam, burn thy victim whole. Hear its wretched moan upon the fires of the dwarven hearthstone." Rudgaf spoke, softly.

The hydra barred its teeth.

Louder than he spoke before, the wizard said, "The heat that shapes the iron in the hands of the dwarven throne, may it melt your flesh and char your bone."

The hydra began to advance.

"Do you know where you go? Where demons rest on burning coals. Where you will look out beyond the ashen shores and, lo, an ocean of flames shall welcome you home."

The hydra began to swoop in.

Screaming with all of his might and energy, the wizard declared, "Do you go where I go? No! Where ne'r will you be quite the same, where the Sun shall beat down on you all the day, where ne'r shall water pass between your lips, where ne'r your face a cool breeze shall kiss, where ne'r shall you find shade by the moonlight, where magma rains from the skies at night, ne'r shall joy and happiness reach you anymore: To hell! To heat! Death greets you at the door!"

Rudgaf felt the breath of the monster as it swooped down to do him in. Just before the hydra was able to reach him however, Rudgaf covered himself, completely, with his cloak and let loose a fireball into the air.

What transpired afterwards was a terror storm. Rudgaf felt himself being hurled into the air. He heard a loud explosion and a terrible shriek. He felt the heat of the destruction of which he wrought. He then knew no more.

~

"Ale."

The barkeep raised an eyebrow at Danagan, unaware of whom he was serving, as he grabbed a tall mug from behind the counter, flipped open the tap, and allowed the light peering in through the clear glass to dim with the amber elixir. Handing it to him, the barkeep spoke.

"We don't get many of your kind around these parts."

Danagan smiled at him from underneath his black hood, flipped him a coin, and walked away. Carrying his mug of dwarven ale, he proceeded to walk to the table located in the far, back corner of the room and sat down so that he was facing the door.

He sipped, casually, as he allowed the brew to slowly caress his throat and warm his belly. The dwarves certainly know how to make an ale. It had been several years since Danagan had indulged himself in some. While he was enjoying it, he thought for a moment.

I hope this guy shows up.

The, "guy", that he was referring to was an informant that he had been lead to through his research into the events at Behnon ever since he had conversed with the Lord of Red. That was around three weeks ago, now. He had attempted to gain an audience with King Duhan, the king of the southern, or, "jungle" elves (junglies), but the king's servants kept giving him the run around. Since he couldn't get an answer about King Nolan's strange behavior and the trade embargo that King Duhan placed against the eastern elves straight from the horse's mouth, Danagan had to resort to other methods.

A few bribes, threats, and a little bit of blackmail led him here, to the, "Preying Panther", a cozy, little pub near to the capital of the southern elven empire known as, "Leshish", which, in the common tongue, means, "Less is More".

And, indeed, that is a principle that the southern elves live by. To them, the pomp and grandeur of other kingdoms – often displayed by their outward appearance through their vast cities and exhibition of tremendous wealth, only served as a display of their inner ignorance. It is their belief that it is the land that provides people with wealth, therefore they have nothing to brag about. "Let the land show its grandeur", they say, as they always do their best to respect it, tend to it, live for it and, yes, die for it, as well.

Because of their strong connection with nature, they have a very unique affinity with everything that involves it. Southern elves, for instance, are excellent healers and are able to use various roots and herbs to cure almost any ailment imaginable. They are always well fed. In fact, they eat better than any other kingdom or race. Their ability to farm is impeccable. The southern elves can out farm any other civilization in existence, often doubling or even tripling the output of food grown of any other nation. Their country also houses the greatest hunters as their ability to track, trap, and shoot down game is rivaled only by the eastern elves – a skillset handed down by their ancestors that also inhabited the jungle before they moved to their current place on the continent.

The warriors of the southern elves are also very capable, but never see battle. It is a well-known fact that the southern elven kingdom is, by far, the most secluded kingdom on the continent – protected by the dense swamp and marshlands to the north, and surrounded by mountains on both their eastern and western ends. This seclusion has allowed them to build up a vast amount of natural resources, although, you would never be able to tell just by taking a gander.

Homes and buildings were simply constructed out of thick bamboo that is native to the area. Even the, "palace" is constructed the same, although is a bit bigger than the homes of the commoners. The only other buildings that are larger than the palace are the halls. Each profession has its own hall, for example, the warriors have their own hall, so do the farmers, the construction workers, the hunters, etc. Only smaller meals are eaten, privately, within one's own home. The main meals of the day, of which there are three, were always eaten within one's respective hall in a family-style setting. So, the farmers would all get together and eat in their hall, the construction workers in their hall, the hunters in their hall, and so on and so forth. Even the royal family operated this way, alternating halls on a daily basis.

A first time visitor to the land, by the way, would have an extremely difficult time telling the royal family apart from the rest of the commoners. They all dress in similar clothes, talk similarly, and act similarly to everyone else. They very nearly *are* everyone else.

King Duhan has two children which he has raised as a single father since they were born, their mother having passed away while in labor. They are not privately schooled. Every morning, King Duhan packs a meal for them, refusing to let his servants do this as he considers it to be a part of his fatherly duties, and sends them off to attend school with the other children. During the day, King Duhan will leave the palace and help the farmers, construction workers, hunters, or whomever else he feels like helping on that particular day. He always insists on participating in manual labor because, according to him, sitting on a throne all day causes you to become gluttonous, feeble minded, abusive, and disconnected from the concerns of your people.

The system of government is rather unique, especially for a monarchy. When King Duhan ascended to the throne, he decreed that there should be a Senate containing ten representatives of whom his own people elected. Every two years, the people of the kingdom would simply cast a, "yes" or, "no" vote as to whether or not they wanted to keep a particular senator in power. It wouldn't be until a senator was voted out of this position that anyone else was allowed to make a run for the empty seat.

The Senate's duty to the country was simply to listen to the people. Every day, they would welcome people in to the, "Senate Office", located at the very heart of the capital, and listen to any concerns that any person may have. After one month of doing this, the Senate would rendezvous with King Duhan, discuss the matters, offer advice, and allow the king to come to a decision. Once this was finished, the process would start all over again.

The southern elven kingdom is the leader in the field of political rights and activism, and King Duhan is often seen as a visionary in this field.

Danagan continued to sip his ale and stare intently at the door. Before another moment went by, the door flung open, crashing into a bell that roosted over the top of the doorway. It made a rather, pleasant jingle when struck.

The new visitor was abundantly lengthy and was forced to duck under the doorway as he entered, quite a rare sight to see as all elves are also rather tall and their buildings are constructed specifically to accommodate that fact. The visitor closed the door behind him.

As he stood there, surveying the area, the barkeep raised an eyebrow in his direction, only able to see the long, scaly snout that protruded from his black hood.

"Another one." Stated the barkeep, calmly.

"Where?"

"Over there." The barkeep responded as he pointed toward the back corner of the building.

The visitor, with his massive tail dragging across the floor, proceeded towards his destination.

"I don't suppose that you're going to be buying anything." Stated the barkeep, matter-of-factly.

The visitor stopped and snorted before he pressed on.

"Didn't think so." Muttered the barkeep to himself as he continued his previous exercise of shining his glass mugs.

Our newest guest decidedly stepped his way toward the back of the establishment where he was greeted by another fellow that wore a black hood with red trim, sitting and casually sipping on ale. The visitor sat in the seat directly across from him.

"It's about time," said Danagan, "I've nearly finished my ale."

The visitor, in a flash, licked his nose with a forked tongue before he spoke.

"Drinking on the job?"

"I had to do something while I waited for your lethargic ass. You're nearly an hour late."

"I was...tied up in other matters."

"What other matters?"

"None of your business, human." The lizard hissed.

"So much for friendly conversation." Said Danagan as he threw back his hood. The lizard did much the same.

"Danagan?!" The lizard stated in surprise as the Lord of Grey's countenance came into the light.

"Yeah, it's me."

"I had thought that I heard your voice, but I dismissed it for a lack of sleep."

"Your senses aren't as dull as I thought."

The lizard jeered.

"I've been doing a fine job leading the men since you left."

"Oh?" Asked Danagan.

"That's right. I've lead the guild into a state of prosperity that you couldn't have ever even dreamed of."

Danagan took another sip of ale.

"You were always soft, Danagan," stated the lizard, sneering, "I can see that you still are."

"At least I don't have to lick my eyeballs."

The lizard hissed, again, as he followed the suggestion.

"What the hell do you want?" The lizard asked.

"Information, Tecza. That is all."

"Information? Is that all?" Asked Tecza as he scratched his chin.

"As I've said."

"Do you have the coin?"

"That depends on how useful you are."

"What do you want to know?"

"First thing, I want to know about this trade embargo."

Tecza shrugged, "What's there to tell?"

"Don't bullshit me, Tecza."

The lizard grinned, exposing a full set of cuspidated teeth, as he motioned his scaly hand in a come hither fashion.

Danagan tossed him a bag of coin.

"Do you know that King Nolan put a price on the goblin king's head?" Asked Tecza as he loosed the string of his prize and began to count.

"I'm aware of that."

"There's your answer."

"That's really what all of this is about?"

"Well, look at him, Danagan. Prancing around here as if he's just some common rabble. It's a joke, a front to support his moral complex."

"Your point being?"

"My point being that he doesn't take kindly to assassins or anyone who supports them. He considered King Nolan to be a brother, but looks at this latest move to be a severe dishonor to all of elven kind."

"So, this is just a punishment, then?"

"Precisely. Duhan knows that Nolan needs the trade line open a lot more than he does. Nolan will either admit to his wrong doing or see his people starve to death and his finances crumble into dust."

"Hmph," snorted Danagan, "strange sense of justice."

Tecza ignored the comment. Danagan rubbed his chin for a bit before pressing the lizard further.

"There's something you're not telling me."

"Whatever do you mean?" Tecza asked in an innocent tone as he rattled his weathered fingers on the table top.

"The goal of this endeavor is to hurt Nolan, economically," said Danagan, "yet, he was still able to keep a record breaking price on the goblin king's head. In fact, after the trade embargo was enforced, he *raised* the bounty. Explain that."

"I'm afraid that I don't understand your question." Responded the lizard, snidely.

Danagan rolled his eyes as he tossed another bag of coins into the air to be greeted by eager hands.

"Do we have an understanding now?" Asked Danagan, frustrated.

"Oh, yes. Now you're speaking my language."

"Well?"

"Oh, right," said Tecza, distracted by his newly acquired wealth, "he has an influential power providing him with the funds he requires."

"Ok, then," said Danagan, smiling, "who?"

"Hmm?"

"Who's backing Nolan?"

Tecza began to sweat as he suddenly came out of the trance that the gold had seemed to put him in and realized that he'd already let greed allow him to divulge too much information.

"I don't know." He mumbled.

"You know," said Danagan, "for someone who has lead his guild into a golden age of prosperity, you seemed awfully eager to take my coin."

Tecza licked his left eyeball.

"What's the matter," added Danagan, "the gold has caused you to slip this far, why not go all the way?"

The lizard patted his brow.

"Who is backing Nolan?" Danagan pressed.

"I can't tell you that." Stated Tecza with changed pitch.

"Why not?"

Tecza refrained from answering.

"Come, now, don't be shy." Said the grey wizard with a toothy smile.

"He'd kill me if I told you." Said the lizard, swallowing hard as he did so.

"Who'd kill you?"

"My boss."

"Who's your boss?"

"I can't tell you that, either!" Cried Tecza, his voice having changed pitch into a screech.

"You're pissing me off, Tecza. Don't piss me off."

"We…well, what do you want me to do?" Tecza whimpered.

Danagan grinned.

"I want you to tell me what I want to know."

"But he'll kill me!"

"If you don't tell me, I'll kill you, myself, and your little, "barkeep" friend, over there, won't be able to do a damn thing about it."

Tecza's eyes widened.

"How...?" Asked Tecza, so shocked that he couldn't even complete the question.

"I'm not an idiot."

Tecza gritted his teeth and slammed his fist upon the table.

"Taarok." Tecza answered, spitting his reply out from his grinding teeth.

"Who?"

"My boss. His name is Taarok."

"Taarok," said Danagan, "that sounds familiar."

The lizard licked his nose.

"Why does that name sound familiar, Tecza?"

"I don't know." The lizard replied, sheepishly.

Raising his voice, Danagan repeated, "Why does that name sound familiar, Tecza?!"

Tecza shook his head furiously and screamed, "I don't know!"

Danagan sat halfway up out of his seat, grabbed the lizard by the throat and squeezed.

"Where the hell have I heard that name, Tecza?!" Danagan shouted.

Tecza choked and sputtered, attempting to formulate some sort of response. Danagan squeezed harder as the lizard began to gargle and struggle to get free.

"The orc..." Tecza muttered.

"What? I can't hear you!"

"The orc and goblin war!"

Danagan loosed his grip a bit.

"You mean the, "War of the Mountain"?"

"Yes!" Tecza screeched.

Danagan released his grip on the lizard's throat and sat back down.

"That was over five hundred years ago, you crazy lizard."

Tecza rubbed his throat.

"I know." He responded in a rasp.

Danagan rubbed his chin and mused on historical events for a moment before he continued.

"That still doesn't answer my question."

"Don't you know anything about history?" Snapped the lizard.

"What do you mean?"

"Don't you remember reading about the orc who went insane?"

"Go on." Insisted Danagan, amused.

"When the war was nearing its end, the orc king was set to surrender to the goblins and sign a peace treaty, relinquishing half of their mountain territory to the goblin king."

"Yeah, I remember that, but someone stopped it."

"That's right. A crazed orc staged a coup on his own kingdom, killing the king and launching an ill-fated assault on the heart of the goblin capital."

Tecza cleared his throat.

"The bastard almost won, too. He slaughtered the goblin king but was stopped short of sacking the entire city by the goblin king's son, who got him in the back of the neck with an arrow."

"I remember reading about all of that. What's your point?"

"That orc, his name was Taarok. My boss is that orc."

Danagan laughed.

"Your boss is Taarok, "The Mad"?" Danagan asked with a chuckle, "That's the dumbest thing that I've heard in quite a while, Tecza."

"It's true!" Tecza screamed.

"Don't be absurd! Firstly, he was killed in battle and secondly, he would be close to six hundred years old by now. He'd be twice dead."

"That's what I thought, too."

Danagan's eyes widened.

"You're being serious."

"As always!" Said the lizard, still tending to his throat.

"But, that's impossible. How is he still alive?"

"That is something that, quite honestly, I don't know. But, I tell you, he lives."

"So, you're working for him and he's working for Nolan."

The lizard gulped.

Danagan leaned forward in his seat, "So, who's Nolan working for?"

"Like I said, I can't tell you."

Danagan extended his arm and the lizard felt cold steel against his throat.

"I told you not to piss me off."

~

The Lord of Green blew out the last, lit candle that rested on the floors beneath the floor of his bed chamber. Indeed, another day had given way into night, and yet...

Rudgaf had still not returned.

Barlow had become worried about his old friend weeks ago, but had dismissed his suspicions. After all, Rudgaf was never of the punctual sort and, certainly, if he had returned within a timely manner, it would have seemed more suspicious to the green wizard than if he had operated by normal procedure.

But *weeks* late? That was unprecedented, even for Rudgaf.

Barlow was unsure of what to do or how to react. He pondered, for a moment.

As if the lack of intelligent conversation wasn't enough to drive one mad, the dwarves have been a bother to me every day since the first that they visited.

Barlow stretched and yawned.

Every day, they come here asking for him and every day I have to tell them that I have no idea where he is. I think that they're beginning to grow suspicious of me, as if they weren't paranoid enough already.

The green wizard climbed the final staircase that lead up to the top floor of the tower and took a left to arrive at his bed chamber. His bed was rather a mess as he hadn't bothered to make it since the night before Rudgaf left. His sheets had fallen off some time ago, and he never bothered to replace them, instead just choosing to discard them into the corner of the room. His only blanket was in a heap upon the bed. One of his pillows was on the floor – a product of a horrible nightmare that he had dreamed the previous night.

He picked the pillow up from off of the floor and tossed it in the general direction in which he wanted it to lay. He then plopped down on the bed, bouncing slightly, without bothering to undress.

Maybe I should look for him after all.

The Lord of Green sighed.

These dwarves have been taking this matter rather seriously. I'm shocked that, given when it happened, no one seems to have an answer yet. I wonder if Rudgaf found anything? What if what he found put him in some sort of danger?

Barlow nodded his head.

I'll have to go look for him in the morrow.

Deciding upon leaving in order to find his lost friend in the morning, Barlow closed his eyes in an attempt to sleep.

The attempt would be in vain, however.

Before Barlow could even get a whiff of rest, he heard a loud, banging sound on the door to the tower, accompanied by loud voices.

"Open up, wizard!" Wailed a voice from outside.

What the hell?

The Lord of Green scurried up and ran to a nearby window that overlooked the courtyard to see what the cause of the commotion was. As he stared down upon the world, he was able to gaze upon a large troupe of dwarves, clad in iron armor and armed to the teeth.

There must be over a hundred of them out there!

He observed as one of the dwarves, carrying a bow, dipped an arrow in oil, lit it on fire, and shot in his general direction. Barlow swiftly stepped to the right side of his window, just in time to not take an arrow to the face, as the projectile sailed through the aperture and landed on his bed, setting it ablaze. Barlow quickly grabbed his wash bucket in a panic, which he had conveniently filled for his morning preparations, and soaked the bed and the fire until nothing was left but a small, puff of smoke.

"We know you're up there, wizard!" Cried one of the dwarves.

"Surrender now or die!" Screamed another.

"Not likely." Retorted Barlow as he grabbed his gnarled, wooden staff and scurried down the stairwell.

Before he had time to make it to the bottom floor, his ears were greeted with more, loud, banging noises on his front door. Thrice he heard it, and the fourth time the door came crashing down to allow his eyes to be greeted with irate dwarves that came swarming through the open doorway in order to do the wizard in.

One dwarf with a glowing, red beard bounded up the staircase to meet Barlow in combat. He hefted his axe and swung it in a downward arch, attempting to cleave the wizard in two. Barlow was able to block his advance by holding his staff in a horizontal direction in the air, which he followed with a stiff kick to the dwarf's face that sent him fumbling down the stairs and crashing into two of his companions, all three now laying in a heap on the floor.

Another dwarf, this one with a braided, black beard, growled at the sight of his moronic compatriots, ran up the stairs and tackled Barlow to the ground before the wizard was ready. In a fury, the dwarf began an attempt to pound his fists into Barlow's head, but the wizard was able to block most of these attempts before dealing a head butt to the bridge of the dwarf's nose. Knocked out and of no further trouble, the Lord of Green brushed him off and stood, once more. He then ran to the bottom floor before more dwarves had the time to enter.

Barlow was immediately greeted by a sword wielding assailant that lunged at the wizard's belly. The green wizard side-stepped his attack and when the dwarf turned back around to face him, he was greeted with the wizard's staff which clonked him upside the head.

Two more attempted to enter the doorway, but Barlow had a plan. He quickly pointed at one of his carnivorous plants that graced the main hall with its beauty and commanded it to grow to herculean proportions. The newly, arisen predator then hurled itself at the doorway with its mouth agape. The dwarves, understandably, screamed in terror as the hungry flower, armed with teeth as sharp as knives, engulfed them in its mouth and chomped down. All that could be seen were the stubby legs of the dwarves, kicking in desperation, right before the plant swallowed and fully absorbed its meal.

Not at all pleased with what just transpired, several dwarves rushed at the predator and began hacking away at it. The flower was able to rip a few more chunks out of its opponents – an arm and a leg, or two, before meeting its end at the hand of the dwarven axe.

Meanwhile, with the flower being an affective barricade, preventing dwarven access to the front door of the tower, a few dwarves took it upon themselves to hoist up a battering ram and smash a sizeable hole into the side of Barlow's home.

Barlow, seeing this as an opportunity to escape a battle of which he surely was doomed to lose, ran toward the newly formed orifice before any of the dwarves had a chance to pile in. The Lord of Green, getting a running start, quickly planted a foot at the base of the opening and then, with the agility of the young farm boy that he once was, hopping over his fence when called in for supper, he leapt a great leap over the heads of his attackers and rolled into the dirt on the outside.

Unfortunately, however, as he stood and gazed onwards, he could not help but notice that the twenty dwarves he had just left behind him only yielded fifty more in front of him.

"This could get ugly." Said Barlow to himself.

"Please don't." Whimpered the lizard.

"Who did you call, 'weak'?" Danagan said with a sneer.

"I'm…sorry."

"Now who's the weak one, you silly son-of-a-bitch?" Mocked Danagan as he pressed his knife against the lizard's throat even harder.

"Please, no!"

"Then tell me, damn you!"

"Ok! Please, just don't hurt me." Tecza sobbed.

Danagan relinquished the knife.

"Please, don't tell anyone that I told you this."

"Just go on." Said Danagan.

Tecza rubbed his throat, gently.

"It's…" He said with hesitation.

"Spit it out."

"Damn it, Danagan!" He screamed as he hissed at the wizard, who calmly smiled back at him.

"I…don't know! I don't think that Nolan's working *for* anybody, but two names came up! Some guy named Mazuumanesh and another guy named Wilfrey."

Danagan frowned.

"You're lying to me. Now you die." Said Danagan as he landed a swift, left hook to the jaw of the lizard's face, sending him promptly out of his seat and onto the floor.

Danagan quickly jumped on top of his chest and pinned him down before he had a chance to move. He then unsheathed his dagger and stared at it.

"You see this?" He asked the lizard.

Tecza shook his head, quickly, as his eyes were widened and fixated on the blade.

"This time, it's going for your throat and not stopping."

The Lord of Grey sent the dagger soaring toward Tecza's throat until the lizard let out a haunting wail that made him sound like a dying animal of some form. Ironically, that's exactly what Danagan had in mind.

"Wait!" He screamed. Danagan stopped the advancement of his blade.

"Why the hell should I?" Said Danagan as he swatted the lizard across the face.

"Tell me why I should wait!" He screamed again, striking Tecza, once more.

Tecza, now bleeding from his mouth, spewed some of it forth as he attempted to speak.

"I'm not lying, Danagan! Please, have mercy!"

Danagan swatted the lizard, again. A tear streamed down Tecza's face.

"Look at me, Lord of Grey. Death awaits me. I'd do anything to save my own life at this point."

"Including feeding me a line of bullshit?"

"I'm telling you the truth!" Tecza screamed as Danagan punched him in the jaw, causing the lizard to wail in distress, again.

"Time to die." Said Danagan as he pressed the blade on the lizard's throat.

"Please! Why would I tell you something that I knew you wouldn't believe if the goal was just to save my own hide?"

Danagan stopped and thought for a moment. He then put the dagger away.

"You're...not lying." He said.

"No! Now please, don't kill me!" The lizard bleated.

The wizard sat up, grabbed Tecza by the collar, hoisted him up and slammed him against the nearby wall.

"I have the name. Now I want to know the why."

"Nowhere ta run now, ya bastard." Stated one member of the drove of dwarves that stood before the Lord of Green.

Barlow readied himself.

"Get him!" They screamed as they rushed him.

The green wizard quickly pointed at the surrounding trees and waved his hand forward. In a rush, the ground quaked, the dirt shifted, and one dwarf stumbled, followed by another, and then a few more, until half of them were either in the dirt or tangled up in the tree roots that had heaved themselves above the ground.

The dwarves were in shock and dismay. Some of them began to retreat for fear of the wizard's might. Others, however, pressed forward, determined to see the wizard in pieces. Still others, seeing the plight of their comrades, began an attempt to free them by chopping at the entangling roots.

Another group came lunging at Barlow, but he quickly thwarted the attackers by commanding the very vines of his vineyard to wrap the dwarves up in their shrill embrace and pin them against the wall, disabling them. The dwarves screamed, but all that could be heard was muffled as the vines squeezed tightly against their mouths.

One dwarf, whom Barlow quickly noticed was the commander of this fine operation, shouted to his men.

"Can anyone kill that son-of-a-bitch?!"

A throng of dwarves armed with bows, after hearing their captain, took aim and began firing at the wizard. Barlow, having much the same ability to detect projectiles as Rudgaf, began to dodge them. He ducked under one, and swayed to the right as one, "zinged" by, barely gracing his ear. Barlow felt his ear and returned with a bloody hand.

The wizard sneered in anger and pointed at the trees behind the archers. A crackling sound filled the air, followed by several creaks as if a throng of oaken doors were being opened all at once. This was followed by a shriek of fright as the mighty limbs of the trees came crashing down on the dwarves, crushing them as the weeping warriors smacked the ground in rage.

The remaining forces, of which there were still many, shouted a blood cry and charged the wizard all at once, hoping to overwhelm him. He met one with his staff and smacked him in the face. The wizard then took a hit with the hilt of a sword, sending him crashing to the ground. Another dwarf swung an axe at the ground, hoping to cleave the wizard, but he was able to roll away from the blow.

Closing his eyes for just a split second, the wizard muttered something under his breath and then, without delay, the invaders were sprayed with thorns which pierced their skin, kissed their throats and stormed their eyes. Some of the dwarves screamed in sheer pain as the thorns hit more sensitive areas. Other dwarves continued their attack.

Barlow knew that he couldn't keep this up. He was on the ground, severely outnumbered, and growing very tired. He thought for a moment, searching for a viable alternative, but, ultimately, he knew what had to be done.

Swiftly, the wizard pointed at a nearby tree, which let down its mighty branches and hoisted him up into the air. The dwarves quickly shot at him from every angle, but he was able to dodge as he quickly brought life to more trees and skipped along their branches into the moonlight. Onward and onward they carried him, until the fight was just a bad memory and the sounds, thereof, faded into silence.

Bounding across tree tops for some time, he eventually took a break in order to catch his breath. The wizard turned around to face the nexus of his exodus, where he could see his former home, glowing in the distant backdrop.

Indeed, he knew what he had to do. The tower, his home, was no more.

The wizard felt a tear stream down his cheek.

~

"You'd best start talking." Asserted Danagan with his face pressed up against the opposing face of the lizardman.

"I don't know! I don't know, I tell you!" Screeched Tecza.

"You *do* know."

"Only rumor and speculation, I can assure you."

"Enlighten me."

"It's just mindless drivel."

Danagan gave the lizard a swift knee to the gut as Tecza exhaled, sharply.

"Enlighten me." Danagan repeated.

"I don't know," said Tecza, catching his breath, "something about ridding the world of the lesser races and creating a new empire."

"Anything else?"

"That's all! I swear!"

"And what of the other two names you mentioned? Wilfrey and…who was it?"

"Mazuumanesh." Said Tecza as he rubbed his midsection.

"Right. Mazuumanesh. I know the Wilfrey part is a load of bullshit, so we can skip over that. However, who is Mazuumanesh?"

"Honestly, Danagan, I've never met him. I haven't even had much of an occasion to see my boss face to face."

The lizard adjusted his jaw while he continued, "There's only so high a lowly servant like me can go."

"Fine, then." Said Danagan as he hurled the lizard back into his seat.

The Lord of Grey smiled at Tecza as he replaced his hood.

"You were always soft, Tecza. I can see that you still are."

Tecza raised his hand and wiped his snout.

Danagan, giving a chuckle, picked up his mug and finished off the remaining ale. He then gave Tecza a sneer.

"Be seeing you." He said.

The wizard then began to hum a dwarven tune before walking out of the bar.

The barkeep calmly watched the Lord of Grey make his exit, and then ran over to Tecza in a hurry.

"Are you ok?" He asked the lizard.

"Yeah."

"You took a hell of a beating." Stated the barkeep with furrowed brows.

"Yeah. Pretty good act, eh?" Said the lizard, wiping his snout, again.

The lizard chuckled before continuing, "Had tears and everything."

"You had me fooled." Said the barkeep.

"I want you to send a message to Taarok."

"Alright, no problem. What should I tell him?"

"Tell him the plan worked. The wizard should be heading his way."

"How do you know he'll be heading up north?"

"I know Danagan. He's stupid. He'll try to go right to the king and attempt to rough him up like he did to me. He won't get his chance." Said the lizard, chortling.

"I'll get on that right away." Said the barkeep as he scuttled off.

"Oh, Danagan," said Tecza to himself, "if only you knew the pain that we're going to inflict on you. If only you knew."

The lizard licked an eyeball.

~INTERLUDE ONE~

"Achoo!" Exclaimed the man in blue as he let loose a terrible sneeze.

"Oh, dear! Many blessings!" He said to himself.

"Don't you mean, 'Gesundheit'?"

"You bless your way, and I'll bless mine!" He shouted, angrily.

He paused for a moment, taking off his pointy, blue hat, holding it against his chest, and looking up toward the ceiling of the tomb that he had found himself ensconced in.

"Oh, dear me! There I go again!"

The Lord of Blue laughed excitedly.

"It's just been so many years since I've…" He said to himself, trailing off.

He coughed and gave a slight sniffle.

"…So many years."

Giggling to himself evermore, he marched forward with a lit torch in hand into the depths of the dusty tomb.

"I wonder if it is really here." He stated to himself again, as he, hunched over with his right hand upon the wall, gently felt the cracked, stone surface while he hobbled onward with exceptional rapidity.

"Yes, yes! It may be!" He exclaimed, smiling from ear-to-ear.

He held a torch in his left hand, which was now becoming of use as he moved further and further away from the warm, inviting sunlight that peered in through the entranceway.

The Lord of Blue scuttled his feet while he walked, as he often enjoyed doing, kicking up dust and sand that had collected on the floor through the passing of years. Coincidentally, this exacerbated the problem that he had, before, causing him to excuse himself in both frustration and delight as he had done before.

The blue wizard, still hurrying along, kept turning his head from side to side in an attempt to catch every detail. He giggled to himself as his hand ran through a spider's web, the owner of which he picked up to observe.

"No food in here, little friend!" He shouted as the spider made a quick attempt to crawl up his arm.

Thome grabbed hold of the spider with his teeth before it had an opportunity to crawl up the sleeve of his cloak. He bit down, hard, and crunched into it, feeling a flurry of viscera flood his mouth and invade his senses.

"No food, indeed!"

Thome laughed, loudly, disturbing the dust on the walls.

"Indeed." He said as he rubbed his teeth with his tongue.

After he was through with his snack, the Lord of Blue pressed onward, further penetrating the tomb.

A short while later, his eyes were presented with a peculiar sight. A small boy, who couldn't have been much older than ten, was huddled against the left wall of the tomb.

Thome observed, but couldn't make out the face of the boy as he sat there with his knees in his face. Some of the ground around him was wet. The boy sobbed and gave a clue as to why this was so.

"Little boy?" Said Thome with a look of inquiry.

The boy sobbed again.

"Little boy, why are we upset?"

The boy sobbed again, but slowly began to answer.

"I'm lost." He finally responded.

"You? Who is asking you? Why are we upset?"

The boy lifted his head and stared at the wizard.

"I don't know," he stated, raising an eyebrow, "why are you upset?"

The wizard scoffed before he responded.

"It is rude to answer a question with a question."

"Who are you?" Asked the boy with confusion.

"Nuh-uh! Not until you provide an answer! Normally, we would ask a question and you would respond, allowing you, then, to make an inquiry of us. Is that not the social norm in this region?"

The boy shook his head, too confused to continue weeping.

"Well, of course it is, sir!"

"Well?" Asked Thome as he placed his hands upon his hips, nearly lighting himself on fire with his own torch.

"Well, what?"

Thome sighed.

"The question was, 'Why are we upset?', to which you never gave a proper response."

The boy coughed as he inhaled the staleness of the tomb.

"Because you're stuck in a tomb." He responded.

Thome gave a belly laugh.

"Surely you jest! I'm here of my own accord."

"You came in from out there?"

"Out where?"

"From the outside?"

"What is, 'outside', but an inside without a roof?"

The boy laughed, wiping the tears away from his eyes.

"You sure are strange, mister!" Exclaimed the boy.

Thome tilted his head to the side and asked, "Who are you talking to?"

"You, sir!" Responded the boy as he stood up and brushed the dust from off his clothes.

"Why are you here, little boy?" Inquired the wizard.

"I don't know."

"How did you get in here? The entrance was sealed off before I entered."

The boy stared at the floor.

"I don't know that, either, mister."

The boy sobbed again.

"Can you help me get out of here?"

"Can I?" Asked Thome as he began laughing again, startling the young boy.

"Of course we can! We can do anything!"

"We?" Inquired the boy.

"Yes, 'we'. You and me. You and I. I and you." Stated Thome as he began laughing again.

The boy scratched his head and Thome continued with his outrageous chortling, hopping up and down while pointing his fingers into the air.

"Us and you! You and us! We can, we can, we must! But..."

Thome stopped bouncing and cleared his throat.

"You have to help me with something, first."

The boy hesitated for a moment, muddled by the wizard's display.

"What do you need help with?" He finally asked.

"Just *who* are you talking to, boy? Are you daft? Do you have a fever?" Asked the wizard as he swiftly placed his free hand on the boy's forehead.

He was very cold.

Thome chuckled some more before he said, "How very odd!"

"You're one to talk, mister." Responded the boy as he swatted the wizard's hand away.

The boy wiped his cheeks again before he continued further.

"What do I need to do?"

The wizard smiled, "A proper question. All you have to do is follow me until I find what I came here to find."

"What are you looking for?"

Thome gave a wink.

"You'll see when we get there."

The Lord of Blue scurried off ahead, while the boy reluctantly followed. He had to jog to keep up with Thome's pace, coughing and wheezing while he did so.

"Come along, come along! Don't dawdle!" Cried the wizard.

The boy followed Thome further into the depths of the tomb, down the hallways and around the bends until they found a set of stairs of which they descended. Shortly thereafter, they were met with a sealed door, barring them from venturing further.

Thome quickly observed the wall that surrounded the doorway, tossing the torch from hand to hand as he made use of its light. He observed that there, etched into the wall, was ancient, dwarven writing.

"Dark dwarf writing, sir?" Inquired the boy.

"Indeed, indeed!" Shouted Thome with glee.

Upon further inspection, he noticed a short line of text that peeked his interest far more than the others. He held his hand up to it, feeling the cool of the stone upon his skin, allowing himself to become entranced by the feeling for some time.

"What are you doing, sir?" Inquired the boy, coughing.

"Shh!" Responded Thome.

The boy, worried about his newfound companion, observed the wizard's face, which was now pale. His eyes, once vibrant and filled with life, were now rolling into the back of his head.

A rumbling came over the ground, quaking their feet. Thome sighed as the boy observed a faint, blue light slowly surround the wizard. The quaking continued further, becoming so fierce that the boy could no longer stand. As he attempted to touch the wizard in an effort to free him from his trance, the quaking knocked the boy onto his rear. In terror, he tucked his face into his knees again and started to cry.

However, before he could really get any tears going, the quaking stopped. Curious, the boy slowly lifted his head up from his knees and stared at the face of his companion, which was now back to normal and smiling at him.

"You may want to hold your breath." Said the wizard as he pointed toward the wall.

The boy stared at the object of Thome's attention. The text that the blue wizard had once covered with his hand was now giving off a faint, blue glow. The boy turned his head toward the wizard again, who was still smiling at him in the same manner that he had been before the boy had turned his attention toward the ancient text.

That is when the boy heard it, his ears peeking up with the noise. He couldn't identify what it was, though.

"What is that noise?" He asked.

"The voice of many waters." Responded the wizard.

"I don't understand." Said the boy, shivering with fright.

"Fear not." Said Thome as he stared at the ceiling.

"You never told me your name." The wizard stated after a brief pause.

"My name?"

"Yes. What is your name?" Inquired Thome.

"Mendax. My name is Mendax."

"Good, good," said the wizard, "my name is Thome. Hold your breath."

The boy took a deep breath and pinched his lungs tight. The noise that he heard was very loud, now. He continued to shiver with fright, but the wizard, who was now staring at the wall, began to hum a gentle tune which served to calm the boy's nerves a bit.

The noise cascaded off of the walls as the wizard continued to hum. The boy observed as Thome waved his hand across his torch, which was now surrounded by a blue light. Thome continued to hum and smile, as if nothing seemed out of the ordinary.

The sound was so deafening and so near now, that the boy could barely make out the tune that the wizard was humming. He continued to watch the wizard, who now held his arms out into the air and stared at the ceiling as if ready for the noise to swallow him. The boy, terrified and unaware of what was happening, closed his eyes as if ready to accept his fate.

Not more than a moment later, the rushing water collided with them, flooding the room and enveloping its inhabitants. The text on the wall began to glow very brightly as the water splashed against it.

The boy could feel himself moving forward and, for an instant, he was filled with the fear of hurdling into the stone. However, before he could give it much thought, he heard a loud crash and, not long after that, he was down on his hands and knees, dripping wet and coughing. He turned his body around to lay on his side when he noticed, much to his amazement, that the wall had been completely destroyed and they were now on the other side of it.

Thome walked by and stared down at the boy, lit torch in hand.

The boy coughed again.

"How is it that we are soaked from head to toe, but your torch still burns, sir?"

Thome stared at his torch.

"We protected it." He said, waving his hand across it and extinguishing the blue light that once surrounded it.

"Why didn't you do that for us, sir?"

"Where would be the fun in that?" Asked the Lord of Blue, laughing.

Thome held out his hand for the boy, of which the boy grasped, tightly, as the wizard hoisted him up.

"Come, come! We've almost arrived."

The wizard scuttled off once more, and the boy curtailed him. They traveled down a few more hallways and crossways, of which Thome always turned left, and descended, yet, more stairs. As the young boy suspected, they were greeted with another, blocked doorway which barred their path.

Thome held the torch up to the door and studied it. A small handprint was embedded into the door.

"Most interesting!" Exclaimed the wizard.

"What do we do now?" Inquired the boy.

Thome pondered for a moment and rubbed his beard with his free hand. After a few moments, he snapped his fingers.

"Boy, give me your right hand." Said the wizard as he snatched the boy's hand, declining to give him any say in the matter, and pushed it into the shape that was lodged in the door.

The boy gasped as he felt the walls rumble just a moment after touching the door. He then felt the door start to move as he quickly returned his hand to his side. The imprint, which was quite innate before the boy had touched it, was now glowing a faint brown. The door, which was nothing more than a stone wheel, slowly rolled out of the way, allowing the wizard and his companion to enter.

The boy glared at the wizard in astonishment.

"Why did my hand do that?" He asked.

Thome shrugged his shoulders and pressed onward. The boy, having no other choice, did much the same.

They passed through a small hallway and down a few steps until they encountered an oblong stone structure with another, large slab of stone fallen to its side, haphazardly.

Thome rubbed his beard and peered inside of the structure, studying it with torchlight.

The stone coffin had been vacated.

"Oh, dear." Said Thome.

"What's wrong?" Asked the boy as he drew closer to the coffin.

"Gone, gone!" Shouted the blue wizard.

"What's gone?"

"The stone, the stone!"

"What stone?"

"*The* stone, boy!" The wizard shouted.

The Lord of Blue stared into the coffin for a moment.

"The body...the body! Stolen?"

Thome began to laugh out loud.

"Removed? Taken?"

The boy backed up a step as the wizard began to prance around the coffin.

"Thief! Thief!" He shouted as he pranced on and on.

"Stolen?" He asked once more as he stopped in his tracks and stared into the coffin.

"Impossible." He stated.

"Who?" Inquired the boy.

The wizard began to laugh, once more.

"But who? Who could possibly have it?"

"Have what?"

"The stone! *The* stone, boy!"

Thome walked toward the boy and placed his hand on the boy's shoulder.

"Do you remember anyone coming out of the tomb?"

The boy stared down at the floor.

"Someone is missing." Said Mendax, sadly.

"Indeed!"

The boy looked up at the wizard with worried eyes and said, "Someone close to...me?"

"Good, good! Come, let's get you out of this tomb." Said the wizard as he snatched the boy's hand and began to drag him along.

The boy kept up as best as he could, but as they wound down the hallways and up the stairs, traveling for what seemed like an eternity in the darkness, he began to feel weak when they were near to the entranceway and the light from the outside beckoned them further. Soon, the boy had no choice but to drag his feet.

Thome halted his advance and let go of the boy's hand, allowing him to drop to the floor.

"What is wrong with us?" Inquired the wizard.

"I'm too weak." The boy responded, slowly.

"What about us? What is wrong with us?"

The boy began to laugh.

"I'm unstable." He stated, beginning to roll around on the ground while continuing to laugh.

"Oh, dear me!" Exclaimed Thome with widened eyes.

The boy began to cry.

"I can't hold on! I can't hold on!" He shouted as he clinched onto Thome's robe.

"Save me! Save me!" He shouted.

The boy began to laugh again as he slowly started to foam at the mouth.

"Can't you save me?" He cried.

Despite the boy's pleas, all that the wizard could do was shake his head, "tsk", and take a step backwards.

The boy reached out for him, but couldn't move. He gurgled and spat, the foam from his mouth now exceedingly great and dripping onto the dusty floor. Unable to breathe and filled with instability, the force overtook him and he exploded into a dark cloud of energy, the wisps of which collided with the walls of the tomb until nothing remained.

Thome, alone once again, walked toward the site of the explosion after the energy cleared and knelt down. Upon the floor where the boy had once laid appeared to be a stone of some form. The wizard picked it up and held it against the light, which refracted as it journeyed through the object, its crystalline structure twinkling in Thome's eyes.

"Interesting."

Thome paused for a moment and took a deep breath before he returned his attention to his newly found treasure. He peered through it as he rotated it in his hand.

"Indeed, indeed."

Not knowing why, but just because he had a strong feeling that he should despite his better judgment, he hurled the crystalline fragment at a nearby wall as hard as he could and watched it shatter into pieces.

The Lord of Blue was immediately overwhelmed with a feeling quite indescribable to him. His vision, which had once been cloudy was now clear and pure like the waters that had rushed forth to carry him away, earlier. He closed his eyes and then reopened them. Astonished, he peered around the tomb as if he had just arrived there at that very moment.

"Thank you, Wilfrey." He said to himself, smiling.

A small tear of joy ran down his cheek as he exited the tomb and reunited with the light.

~CHAPTER FOUR – ALLIANCE~

The three weeks' journey through the jungle, swamp, and marshlands reached its conclusion, and not a moment too soon. We had trudged through an endless mud and a torrent of rain that softened the ground and cracked the mind. We pressed on, although it seemed as if our visitation would never end – driven by our one desire, our one goal that snapped at our heels and bit our backs like a taskmaster's whip.

We finally reached the forest, just before the summit of the orc mountains, where we were refreshed by a friendly troupe of elven players…

There he sat, a vigil for the unconscious. The trees had managed to take him this far, but he lacked the strength to command them to carry him any further.

His flight from the tower had not been a steady one. He'd already expended a vast amount of energy in escaping from his dwarven assailants and it, not surprisingly, took quite a bit of strength and concentration to command the trees, most of which have stood petrified in space, save for a bit of sway from a whipping wind, for hundreds of years, to gently lift forth their ancient branches and physically carry the wizard through the sky unto safety.

The Lord of Green knew his destination, too, of that he was sure. Given the sudden urgency of his adventure, he hadn't had time to actually plot out the course that he was required to travel from the tower to the eastern, elven capital of Behun, but he knew the general direction. Barlow, in a state of deep thought and tired as he was, hadn't been able to let loose enough of his mental capacity to pay attention to how long he had been traveling, lest he lose control of his spell and tumble to an early grave, but he swore that he must have seen at least three sunsets before he finally had to give in to exhaustion and command that one of the trees gently place him on the ground. It was here, his back supported by the trunk of the very tree that gently caressed him and returned him to the safety of the ground, that he collapsed in on himself and feinted. It is here that we now find him.

So, too, did a man who happened to be, as it would appear, aimlessly wandering through the forest. He was a strange sight, to be sure. His demeanor refused to match his apparent situation. At a glance, it would seem that he was quite lost, but he wandered along, haphazardly at best, with a dazzling smile plastered upon his face. He had curly, brown hair and a short, yet thick, brown beard that he took sincere care of. His eyes were blue – a piercing blue that was as intense as a roaring fire. He wore a plain, brown robe made of leather, which tied at his waist and would have buttoned all the way from his knees to his throat, had he bothered to button the final three buttons. His chest was exposed as a result, revealing thick, black hair.

The strange man, after hopping over the roots of various trees like a school girl, caught a glimpse of the unconscious wizard, the sight of which left him grinning from ear to ear.

"Oh?" He uttered, but not in surprise, as if he had been expecting to find him all along in the same length of time, manner, and area that he had, indeed, found him in.

If you recall, earlier you learned that Barlow created a large forest that extended from the northern, dwarven kingdom all the way into the eastern, elven kingdom. To put it quite plainly, Barlow was quite the expert in all things involving nature. Because of this, he knew every tree in his forest, every shrub, every creature that came into and out of the forest, every flower, every rock, every blade of grass, and just about everything of anything else that you may find in any, given forest.

The trees, however, were special. Some were even more special than others and, through much concentration, Barlow could actually hold conversations with some of them. Others, however, could only take orders, which is still quite an impressive feat for any tree. Among the other tasks that these trees performed was keeping a watchful eye on everything that came into the forest and warn Barlow of any impending danger – especially when it came to strange men attempting to sneak up on the wizard when he is vulnerable.

The wizard's eyes shot open and glared upon the sneaky one who had, at one time, thought himself to be far too stealthy to be caught by an ever watchful eye. The man, surprised, but not in the least bit frightened of the Lord of Green, stopped in mid step and cocked his head in inquiry. Frozen within the space that he occupied, he listened to the wizard speak.

"Who are you?" Asked Barlow.

"Don't you already know?" Replied the man, sardonically.

The Lord of Green carefully hoisted himself up into a standing position, almost surprised that he was able to do it with such ease, before he continued.

"You've never placed a foot in my forest, before," remarked Barlow, "if you had, I would have known you – every inch of you, from your feet to the very hairs on your head."

"Oh, I've been here, before," remarked the man as the wizard scoffed, "you've just never paid me any mind."

"Impossible."

"Not quite," replied the man as he finally finished his forward progress, "you see, I have been here, before. I've tread through this ancient forest before it was even known as a forest and before you even came to know the first light outside of your mother's womb."

Barlow rubbed his beard and said, "Go on."

"My feet have touched the soil of many a place," continued the man, "I have walked to and fro, up and down."

"Why is it that I find you here, now?"

"That's a good question. I have an even better one – what do you want?"

Barlow shook his head, "It is you whom I caught slithering about. It is you who should answer your own question."

"Humor me, if you would be so kind."

"Humor me, first."

The man gave Barlow a large grin and said, "I cannot rightly answer you until you first answer me."

The Lord of Green waved the man away and said, "Be gone. I've no time for your tomfoolery."

The man 'tsk'd' and responded, "I must be mistaken, then. Do pardon me."

Barlow raised an eyebrow and said, "Mistaken about what?"

"Well," said the man as he cleared his throat, "I had thought it was said that the ones who wear the colored robes are impervious to the effects of time."

"And just who told you that?"

The man smiled and responded, "A friend."

"No friend of mine, I can assure you."

"And how could you be so positive of that to make such a bold claim?"

The wizard crossed his arms and snarled, "The way that you talk and snoop about, I wouldn't at all be surprised if you made home to a den of lizards and conversed, daily, with serpents."

The man laughed and said, "You dare call King Nolan a lizard or a serpent?"

This shocked the wizard, an effect that he felt he let show on his face. He damned himself for it before continuing, "The honorable king of the eastern elven empire calls you friend?"

"Indeed, good sir!"

"Do you carry any proof of this?"

"Certainly!" Exclaimed the man as he tossed the wizard a small badge.

Barlow carefully studied the badge as he held it up to the sunlight. It was made of pure gold and had the kingdom insignia imprinted into it – one circle encompassing nine. Indeed, it was the badge that was given to any ambassador to the kingdom that allowed them safe passage to and from its borders, as well as allowed the carrier to seek an audience with the king at any given time. Barlow knew it all too well, for he carried one just like it.

The Lord of Green shook his head and said, "My apologies."

The man, continuing to grin, simply shrugged and asked, "So, what is your answer?"

"To what?"

Barlow's poking only served to make the man smile even wider before he said, "What do you want?"

"I want to see King Nolan."

"No, you fool!" Said the man in disgust.

"I beg your pardon?"

"What do you want?"

"I've already told – "

"Barlow, Barlow, Barlow." Said the man, shaking his head and coming closer to the wizard.

"What do you *really* want?" The man continued.

"I..." Said Barlow, stunned at the man's sudden approach as he put his arm on the wizard's shoulder.

"What happened to your tower, Barlow?"

"It...it burned." Answered Barlow, as if it were a rote response that he hadn't even put thought into.

"And whose fault was that, Barlow?"

The green wizard hesitated, but eventually said, "The northern dwarves."

"The northern dwarves?" Asked the man.

"Yes. They attacked me in the middle of the night and scorched my home." He stated, wondering why he even felt the urge to talk about the situation with a stranger in the first place.

"Just your home?"

"No," said Barlow, "I mean, it was Rudgaf's and Thome's home, too."

"And where are they now?" Said the man, almost whispering.

Barlow strained not to say anything else, but he felt his natural barriers to the world crumble before his feet.

"Thome went off to the desert, but Rudgaf..."

"Where was Rudgaf?"

Barlow stared at the ground and spoke, "He was away on an errand, but he..."

"Should have been back in time." The man continued, slowly nodding his head.

"In time." Barlow repeated.

"In time for what, Barlow?"

"In time to..."

"To save you, Barlow? To save your home?"

"Ye..." Said Barlow, unable to finish his sentence.

The man, now frowning, attempted to lock eyes with the wizard, but Barlow was still staring intently at the ground.

"But you've been there for him a plenty, haven't you, Barlow?"

"Yes." Replied Barlow, reluctantly.

"And you have saved his life on numerous occasions, haven't you, Barlow?" Asked the man in a gentle voice that was as smooth as silk.

"Of course. He's my friend."

"Wouldn't it be nice, Barlow, if this same kind of love was extended to you as well?"

Barlow didn't know how to respond, so he remained silent while the man continued.

"Rudgaf, Rudgaf. Always getting into trouble is that Rudgaf. Always forgetting things. Always blundering things. Yet, he's the one that everyone seems to cherish."

Barlow, although he attempted to keep his feelings at a simmer, felt a sudden rage build up inside of him.

"Why isn't it you, Barlow? You always do the right thing, Barlow. You're always the one making sacrifices, Barlow. You stand for justice and righteousness. Why is he considered to be the best of all of you, Barlow?"

"What...what are you doing to me?" Asked the wizard.

The man breathed in, deeply, and said, "I know what haunts you, my friend. I can feel the quivering in your heart. It boils over with rage, daily, hourly, minute by minute, second by agonizing second. You want to let it out, don't you?"

"No...no. What are you?" Asked Barlow, shaking his head as if trying to clear his thoughts.

The man gently placed his forefinger on Barlow's chin and raised his face up until their eyes locked before he spoke again.

"I'll always be here for you, my friend. I'll support you whenever he crumbles."

Barlow shook his head and snapped at the man, "You speak of that which you know not! Be gone, snake!"

"The truth can be painful, sometimes, Barlow." Assured the man as he stretched out his hand to reach for the Lord of Green.

Barlow immediately smacked it away and said, "You know nothing of truth. Be gone, foul spirit!"

The spirit laughed and replied, "So, you know?"

"It's written all over you. Your words intoxicate like wine and hemlock."

The spirit shrugged, "All I do is reveal what it is that you truly want. Nothing more, nothing less."

"You know nothing," replied the wizard, "a pure heart is something that you cannot comprehend."

"My, my," replied the spirit, chortling, "whoever said that your heart is pure?"

Enraged, the Lord of Green took his staff and pointed it at the spirit, the aftermath of which sent him flying into a nearby tree, where he remained pinned by a magical force.

Barlow stepped forward, his staff still pointed at the spirit.

"Foul, contemptuous creature!"

The spirit laughed and responded, "What are you going to do, kill me? You can't kill what you can't understand."

Barlow stopped short at this. The fact crossed his mind that he wasn't dealing with mere flesh and bone. He was dealing with a spirit, the very essence of someone's deep, evil emotion. No, he thought, he couldn't be killed, but there were other methods, and Barlow knew just what to do.

"Your move, wizard." Grunted the spirit.

"Very well." Said Barlow, snarling.

Barlow closed his eyes and focused deeply. Inside his mind's eye, he could see his surroundings, but not in the same manner that they would normally be seen in. He focused harder and looked upon the life force of the forest, *his* forest, the one that he created by the power of his hands, with care and love, something that he knew and the spirit knew not.

"And now this spirit dares to defile my sanctuary?" Thought the wizard.

Barlow felt a rage boil over inside of him as he directed his will toward the tree in front of him, the same one that he held the spirit trapped against. He extended his will forward and felt the life energy of the tree, which he turned inward on itself and, consequently, through the spirit.

He heard a scream come from, at least what sounded like, the correct direction.

The Lord of Green shook a bit, which nearly broke his concentration, when he felt a cold sense of delight flow through his veins at the sound of the spirit's shriek. He regained his composure and dismissed the feeling, however, continuing to turn the energy of the tree in on itself.

When he felt that no more could be done, he opened his eyes and gazed upon the tree, the spirit having vanished out of his sight.

The Lord of Green shook his head and hoisted up his staff. With one swoop he knocked it against the tree and left a gash in it, so that all would know of the evil that lied therein.

Satisfied, he turned away from the tree and headed toward his destination – the city of Behun.

Barlow had never seen a spirit before, let alone fought one. Granted, he knew of their existence by the way of ancient texts that he and his companions had poured through in the central tower so long ago, but they were thought to be long extinct.

Their return was quite troubling, Barlow thought.

Even more troubling was the fact that he was carrying a badge that signified that he was the ambassador to the king of the eastern elves.

"What was he doing with such a thing?" Said Barlow out loud.

He rubbed his beard in thought as he walked through the forest toward the capital city of Behun.

"Where could he have gotten it from? Did King Nolan really gift it to him?"

He wanted to dismiss it outright but, for some reason unknown to him, his mind just couldn't let it go. If it were the case that the king was consorting with evil spirits, thought the wizard, then he could be headed into some sort of trap. A million thoughts started buzzing through the wizard's head all at once. What if King Nolan was conspiring with King Moldof?

Perhaps sending Rudgaf to investigate the city of Behnon was all a part of the setup in order to weaken the tower's defenses and make sure that the green wizard was as vulnerable as he could possibly be? If that were the case, Nolan would be in for quite a surprise, Barlow thought, when he showed up at his doorstep.

The wizard shuddered at these thoughts.

"It was bad enough having one entire kingdom conspire against us, but now two? And if so, why?"

Why, indeed. Well, for starters, thought Barlow, there was business involving the northern dwarves and one of Barlow's former companions, Wilfrey, several years ago.

"But I've more than made up for that." He said, waving off the thought before it came biting back again.

Had he? Surely, he must have. Look at all that he did for the dwarves. They would be kingdomless without him – just a small group of wandering vagabonds forced to seek shelter amongst foreigners on the continent – always mistrusted, always downcast. Barlow saved them from all of that. The very forest that he was walking through at that moment was a testament to that fact. It provided them with an infinite supply of food, shelter, and wealth, given time enough for it to grow – more than enough to make up for their loss.

Or was it?

"Was justice really served?" Contemplated Barlow.

The Lord of Green spat upon the ground and thought of Rudgaf. At times, thought Barlow, the Lord of Red could be unbelievably selfless. Had the Lord of Green had things his way, he would have thrown Wilfrey out of the tower and into the hands of those that he wronged. But Rudgaf, the soft hearted fool that he was, couldn't believe that the Lord of Brown would commit such a foul act on purpose. Rudgaf had insisted that it was an accident, but Barlow knew better. What choice did he have, though? When Rudgaf offered to risk his life by leaving the tower and allowing Wilfrey to stay, how could Barlow not follow suit? It would have been wrong to allow his companion to endure the kind of hostility that he was sure to face when he arrived at what was left of the northern, dwarven capital of Narvas in order to attempt to pay off a debt that, had justice prevailed, Wilfrey would have paid off through either toil or blood.

Perhaps justice didn't prevail at all, Barlow thought. Perhaps justice was not served. Perhaps justice sought its revenge upon his soul, seeking vengeance against him for turning his back on her and showing mercy where mercy should not have been shown.

That must have been the answer. Rudgaf, he was convinced, could not understand this. It wasn't Rudgaf's place amongst the wizards to exact justice and to be the beacon of righteousness that Barlow was, nay, is. Now, as fate would have it, the world has turned on his kind – the ones who held the power.

"The power to do what?" Thought Barlow.

His own mind answered him.

"The power to save the world from itself."

Barlow trotted through his forest with purpose. He knew his destiny. He knew that he was surely meant to be the one to direct the power that only he and his companions possessed. He was the guide through the labyrinth. He was the torch in the darkness.

Indeed, he knew now that he was in the wrong. He shouldn't have left the central tower along with Rudgaf on that fateful day. Wilfrey should have been forced to pay his debts – Rudgaf had no right to bear that debt upon his shoulders. Perhaps it wasn't even selflessness that drove the Lord of Red to do what he did – perhaps it was greed. Perhaps it was his inability to do what is right when justice comes to settle a debt with a loved one. It can be easy to serve justice until she strikes your own home. But, thought Barlow, that is what he was there for – to provide the strength to his companions so that they may serve justice no matter the cost. It was clear to Barlow, now, that Rudgaf's act had been nothing but a hindrance to his service.

"I've failed you once, my lady, and I'll not fail you again."

Barlow smiled as he continued on, the city gates now within his sight. It might have been due to exhaustion, but the Lord of Green swore that the city had a faint glow that made it appear illuminated. Whatever the cause, it was a sight that calmed his heart and helped to remove the remainder of doubt that he had still held within his mind.

~

Danagan raised up a glass and quickly took down a clear liquid that was unidentified to him, but tickled the back of his throat a bit on the way down.

As the Lord of Grey finished his drink, he carefully set his glass down upon the bar table in front of him and nodded toward the bartender, whose rotund belly rippled from laughter at the mere thought that Danagan actually wanted more.

He smirked and said, "You actually want more?"

Danagan rubbed his chin and replied, "Problem?"

"Don't you think you've had it, huh?"

Danagan held out a hand to his doubter and kept it steady.

"Satisfied?"

The bartender looked impressed, poured Danagan another drink and slid it across the bar into Danagan's hand like an old pro which, in fact, he was.

The wizard smiled a bit and raised the glass up to his lips, but caught the bartender's gaze before indulging in his beverage and decided to make a pause. He set the glass down upon the bar top slowly and carefully before he spoke.

"Do you take as much of an interest in the rest of your customers?"

The bartender seemed caught off guard and only managed to reply, "Huh?"

Danagan slowly turned his glass and replied, "You're staring at me."

The bartender seemed slightly sheepish and responded with some effort, "You're strange."

Danagan chuckled, "You're the one staring."

The bartender fell silent and started to shine a glass to busy himself. Danagan, out of interest or maybe even pity, decided to continue the conversation.

"What's your name?" He asked.

The bartender grunted, "Fader."

Danagan almost scoffed, but caught himself and said, "I'm Janon."

"That's a good name, although a bit more common than I would have expected from a guy like you."

Danagan shrugged while Fader continued, "You from around here?"

"You could say that, I guess."

Fader grew silent again, so Danagan took the opportunity to slug down his drink, setting down his glass and wiping his mouth with a sleeve before continuing the conversation.

"How about you?"

Fader, seemingly unaware of the context, simply replied, "Eh?"

Danagan sighed and said, "You from around here?"

"Oh," said Fader, "yeah. Born and raised."

"Have you been tending bar for very long?"

Fader nodded, "Close to thirty years now."

Danagan frowned and rubbed his chin, pretending as if he thought that was a long time.

Fader busied himself by cleaning Danagan's newly used glass, grunting as he did so.

"What?" Asked Danagan.

Fader gave a nod of his head in order to indicate something behind Danagan and said, "Her."

Without looking, Danagan responded, "Who?"

Fader smirked, "That elf at the table back there."

"What of *it*?"

"She's been glaring at you this entire time."

Danagan shrugged, forcing the bartender to scoff and say, "This generation...you never have any fun."

The wizard laughed at that and said, "It's because I already knew."

Fader raised an eyebrow and asked, "How? Got eyes in the back of your head?"

"Let's just say that, in this case, I have eyes for what lies before me and behind me." The Lord of Grey replied, smugly.

"In, 'this case'?" Asked Fader.

Danagan smirked and then leaned over the bar, grabbing the bottle containing the mysterious liquid that he was ingesting. Popping off the top, he drank.

At first, Fader seemed surprised, but after he remembered how much Danagan had taken in already, he sloughed it off and turned his attention back to the elf.

"She's heading this way, you know." He said.

"I know."

"But…" Fader protested.

"The eyes." Said Danagan, smiling.

Fader gave a look of disapproval, as if contemplating an attempt to force this stranger out of his establishment, but he thought better of it and, instead, decided to tend to some other customers that were a bit more, "normal".

The elf in question took a vacant seat next to the Lord of Grey while he took another sip of his bottle. He was the first one to break the silence.

"What are you doing here?" He asked.

"You knew I'd come." She replied, smugly.

Without looking at her, Danagan replied, "But, why?"

The elf drew closer to Danagan until her lips were barely pressing upon his left ear. She spoke, then, her voice like silk running up and down the wizard's spine, around him and through him, she said, "Don't I always?"

Danagan shivered uncontrollably, damning himself for it. He thought homicidal thoughts that were quickly beaten back by a strange taste for the depravity of it all. Snapping out of it, as if he were in a trance, he quickly felt his rage build again just to be bitten back like before. As much as he tried to draw away, his efforts just brought him closer to the elf.

Despite seeing that she was going to be there, the Lord of Grey had failed to see his insufficient preparation.

Danagan turned toward her, refusing to lock eyes, "What do you want with me?"

The elf gently placed her hand, which emitted a slightly cold aura in contrast with the smell of wildflowers that Danagan was picking up from her hair, upon his chin and, despite his best efforts which culminated to something quite feeble, she lifted up his head and forced him to gaze into her soul destroying, green irides.

"It's not what I want," she said, gently, "it's what you want."

Before Danagan could even think to protest, he realized that his surroundings had changed as if his world was completely swept out from under him without his knowledge like a professional busser would, pulling away the tablecloth without even causing the remotest sense of a clattering of dining ware.

Gazing about, Danagan soon realized that he was standing in the middle of the square of the elven city of Behnon. Before him, the same pile of bodies, massacred by what he could only assume to be orcs, laid in the same heap that he had seen them in weeks before.

The Lord of Grey, staring at them hard, said, "Why have you brought me here?"

The elf, her golden hair reflecting in the warm sunlight, swept her hand through the air as if presenting the carnage to the wizard and said, "Look at them."

"What about them?"

The elf sighed, "Why do you care about them?"

Danagan looked away, "I don't."

The elf tilted her head, "Oh? Why are you out helping Rudgaf, then?"

The wizard spat on the ground and turned his back to the elf, "I care about the injustice of it, that's all. As far as these people…I never knew them."

At that moment, Danagan heard a rustling coming from his left. He turned his attention to it and, to his amazement, it was coming from the heap of bodies as several of them had begun to reanimate before his widened eyes.

"Tatiana," uttered Danagan, "what kind of sorcery is this?"

Tatiana, with the grace of a ballroom dancer, slid closer to Danagan and began to gently brush her hand through his jet black hair.

The bodies, with their mortal wounds healed, slowly approached the wizard. Their movements were completely in sync, as if they were of one mind and one body. They marched forward in perfect time like a well-made clock, like a unit, like an army. However, as suddenly as they began, they stopped. Slowly, yet precisely, they raised their hands and pointed directly at Danagan.

"What are they doing?" Asked the Lord of Grey.

Tatiana did not deign to answer him.

"Look at him!" They cried out in a booming voice.

Shockingly, they then began to act as individuals. One of them spoke, then, shouting, "The wizard filth!"

Another said, "What is his kind doing here?"

Yet another muttered, "I'll never understand why we must tolerate his presence."

Still another screamed, "He's not normal!"

Danagan scoffed as if the entire thing didn't bother him.

Tatiana, who was watching the scene unfold, returned her attention to the wizard and said, "Why do you act thus?"

The Lord of Grey crossed his arms, "Because it really doesn't matter."

The elf 'tsk'd' and said, "Yes, it does. After all you've done for them? The hundreds of years of service?"

"I only did what I was supposed to."

"And who is the judge of that?" Asked Tatiana, raising her voice.

The wizard gazed upon her, wanting to say something profound but could only manage to say, "Tatiana…"

Still glaring at Danagan, she pointed at the gang of elves and said, "They hate you! They revile you! After all of the things that you've done for them! All of the things you sacrificed…your life…"

Danagan held out his hand and touched her shoulder.

She then muttered, "Me…"

The wizard whispered, "What will you have me do?"

The elf locked gazes with him, then, her eyes shimmering like crystal, "Let it go. Forget about your quest, forget about the elves, forget about Rudgaf, forget about all of it and come and be with me."

Danagan looked away, "You know that I can't do that."

"Why?" Asked the elf.

Danagan refused to answer until the elf, working her magic again, was able to gently place her slender hand upon Danagan's chin and force him to look at her once more.

"Why?" She repeated.

"Because…" Whispered Danagan.

"Because?" She repeated.

"You're…dead."

Danagan sighed and stared up at the sky, "All of this…it's not real."

The elf remained silent.

The wizard continued, "The power within my hands…it's causing this. It's causing me to go mad."

The elf spoke at that and said, "What are you talking about?"

"When we saw the might of the black lesser stone, what it did to those who held it…well, we knew that the same thing could happen to us – the ones who inherited the power derived from the Lord of Black, the first one who wielded the power of the stone."

The wizard turned his back to the elf and continued, "The black lesser stone was so powerful that those who wielded it, yet had a flawed mind, would almost instantly start to succumb to the madness."

"And what of you?" Asked Tatiana.

"All of us…we had gone so long without any symptoms, we had just foolishly hoped that our minds were free of error. Yet…I knew the truth. I'm certain that they did, too."

Danagan turned back toward the elf and said, "You see? That's how I knew you were coming. You're a product of my mind. The entire world, from the bar to here, has been nothing but a creation of my own, assaulted imagination."

Tatiana began to chortle. Before Danagan could address it, however, the crowd behind him grew restless and started calling for his head.

The Lord of Grey started to turn his attention to the crowd, but the elf stopped him and asked, "Do you love me, Danagan?"

Startled and confused, the Lord of Grey nodded his head.

Tatiana continued, "Illusions aren't so simple, my love. Though you think that this is nothing but a product of your imagination…"

Suddenly, Danagan felt a sharp pain in the back of his head. He quickly placed his hand on the affected area and, pulling his hand away and placing it in front of his face, he gazed upon his own blood. Shocked, he quickly whirred around and glared at the angry mob, then at the ground where it was that he noticed a rock.

"…What happens in this world has real repercussions."

Danagan quickly turned his attention back to the elf and said, "That's not possible! I should've felt that coming!"

"Danagan…" said Tatiana, gently, "my master has room for you in his house."

The wizard tilted his head, "Your 'master'?"

The elf smiled, "When you left me, that day, I never could recover. I lived every day in sadness…jealousy…fear…"

"Tatiana, I'm sorry."

The elf nodded, "I know, just listen."

Danagan then started to hear a faint rumbling in the distance. He held his hand up in the air to stop Tatiana in midsentence and said, "What was that? Did you hear that?"

The elf looked around, then said, "Just listen. Do you know how I died?"

Danagan glared at the ground, "Yes…you died in childbirth."

"Oh, Danagan," protested the elf, "don't be so foolish."

The Lord of Grey's eyes widened, "What do you mean?"

"It was *him*." She said.

This caught Danagan's attention, forcing him to snap his head up and stare into the elf's eyes.

"*Who*?" He asked.

The rumbling started to grow louder, but the wizard ignored it.

"You know who!" Tatiana shouted.

"Taarok." Danagan uttered as the rumbling seemed to grow even louder at the mere mention of his name.

"He came to our village," said Tatiana, "we were there supporting the goblins. He captured all of the women and had his choice of which ones to…"

Danagan swallowed hard, "And then?"

"And then?" Asked Tatiana. "And then I killed myself and our child! I'd rather that than serve him for the rest of my life!"

The elf continued to speak, now not having a choice but to shout, "It was then that the master came unto me and he said…"

"Tatiana?"

The elf repeated, "He said…"

The rumbling was so loud now that Danagan could barely hear the elf, although she was shouting at the top of her lungs.

"What did he say?!" Screamed the wizard.

The elf looked around frantically as if in a true panic and then shouted, "He's coming!"

Danagan swiped a hand through the air, "I don't care! What did he say?!"

"Run, Danagan! Run!"

"No! What did he say, damn it?!"

It was then that the Lord of Grey lost all vision and was left in a state of complete darkness and silence. To him, at first, it seemed to be lonely, but, then, he could feel the presence of his long, lost love, allowing him to bask in the peacefulness of his apparent solitude.

He heard a voice after but a moment, then. He could barely hear it at first, but it gradually became louder and louder still. When it was but a whisper, just enough for Danagan to make it out, he recognized it as the voice of the elf.

Into his mind she uttered the words, "Though you are dead, yet shall you live."

"Lord of Green! What a pleasant surprise." Said King Nolan, his eyebrows arched in suspicion.

Barlow stiffened his back at the remark and, slamming the bottom of his staff upon the ground with a resounding, "thud", simply replied, "Is that so?"

King Nolan guffawed at the retort and inquired, "Whatever do you mean?"

Barlow had, unfortunately, failed in his attempt to cast out his anger despite a valiant effort to do so between his encounter with the spirit and his arriving at the city gates. The elves in the area, being overtly suspicious of all of the wizards, not just Barlow, primarily gave him a welcome as cold as the steel garbs of the guard in the royal throne room, which was where the Lord of Green was currently. He admitted to himself at that time that their attitude didn't help much to improve his mood and if the pleasantries presented to him by King Nolan were, indeed, fake, then he wished to cut through them with a steely eye for detail that not even a dread eagle could hope to match; The Lord of Green would know, then, that he was wasting his time. In fact, at this point, he began to think, perhaps it didn't even matter if the, "damned elf", was being sincere or not for the sooner that he could leave the never yielding glare of the inhabitants of that awful place, the better.

Upon his ivory throne, the King of the Eastern Elves, as was his official title, rubbed his chin and grinned at the wizard. He then motioned to his left in a come hither motion in order to garner the attention of the royal secretary who was, interestingly, as Barlow noted, completely dressed in black. King Nolan then proceeded to whisper something into the secretary's ear while Barlow crossed his arms in impatience.

After a few moments, Barlow was about to interject as he was growing a mite bit tired of not being addressed, but before he could utter a word, King Nolan's secretary shot him a kindly eyed stare, smiled, and said, "Lord of Green – please follow me."

Barlow scoffed audibly as he followed the female elf through the corridor to the left of the throne, not caring to give the king a glance as he passed him, and down a stone hallway that was barely lit by the sparse array of torches that were placed seemingly randomly on both sides of the cold grey.

"Hmph." Said Barlow.

To his surprise, the secretary responded, "Yes, Lord of Green?"

Barlow cleared his throat, "This section of the palace was built in a hurry."

The secretary nodded as she continued to lead the way and said, "Indeed, good sir."

"Where are you taking me, secretary?"

"To the war shelter."

Barlow rubbed his beard and raised his eyebrows, "Whatever for? Are we expecting a fi_"

"Please," interjected the secretary, "do not tarry, my Lord. All will be made clear shortly."

Barlow protested, "For a people that treat me with such suspicion, you are certainly asking me to place a lot of trust in you."

"I'm sorry that you feel that way, my Lord. I assure you that King Nolan did his best to treat you with honor and respect in his court."

Barlow laughed, "You must not have many happy returns."

The royal secretary stopped, then, but didn't look at Barlow while she stated, "It is one of my duties, good Lord, to treat all of my King's guests with dignity and respect. However, I am new to the position and being that I am inexperienced, you, sir, if I may be so bold as to say, you are making it incredibly difficult to hold my tongue – complaining about a lack of smiles and warmth in such a time of grieving."

She resumed her stride, then, at a newly formed, rapid pace that forced the Lord of Green to nearly require a jog to catch up with her as she continued to speak, "We lost many on that day, sir wizard. I, myself, lost my brother. Our parents had passed away when we were children. He was the only thing I had – my own flesh and blood."

"I'm sorry." Barlow said sympathetically.

"The worst part of it all was that no bodies could be recovered after the city was reduced to ashes, save for that of one orc."

Barlow stroked his beard and asked, "That doesn't strike you as odd?"

"I don't care about the oddity of it all, wizard."

"Aren't you in the least bit curious? I mean, it just seems a bit convenient that…"

"That what, good wizard?" She spat.

Barlow didn't respond, so she continued, "That coward, King Colibrim, sitting up in his damned mountains…he always uses the orc tribes to do his bidding. So they left one behind on accident. Who cares? We would've known he was behind it, anyway."

"It's funny…" Said Barlow.

"What's funny?"

"Well," explained Barlow, "the northern dwarves were blaming Rudgaf and Danagan for the whole thing."

"Hrmph," she snorted, "I know not of this, "Danagan", you speak of, but I do know enough about the Lord of Red to know that he had nothing to do with it."

The Lord of Green crossed his arms, "This all strikes me as odd. Orcs found at the city…the goblin king's involvement…the dwarves blaming Rudgaf for the whole thing when it was King Moldof, himself, that sent Rudgaf to investigate in the first place."

The royal secretary stopped at that and asked, "He did?"

"Indeed." Replied Barlow.

"How?"

Barlow tilted his head, "What do you mean, 'how'?"

"When did the Lord of Red receive word about the attack?"

The Lord of Green stared up at the ceiling in thought then replied, "Several weeks ago, now. Why?"

"You're right," replied the secretary, "this is all very odd."

"What do you mean by that, my lady?" Asked Barlow.

"It's urgent that you speak with my king, immediately."

"Why? What is going on here?"

"Look," she said, finally turning around to address the wizard, "it's four days travel from here to Behnon, correct?"

Barlow nodded.

"So one of our scouts would've had to have traveled four days from the capital to Behnon, see the city in ruins, travel four days back to the capital and report the incident."

"Of course, of course." Said Barlow.

"Then a messenger…"

"Right," interjected Barlow, "a messenger would have to go from the capital to report the incident to King Moldof…"

This time the elf interjected, "Of his own volition, mind you, because we wouldn't have sent him ourselves."

Barlow was caught in surprise by that remark, as he had never even thought of that and just how odd the letter from King Moldof was. He slammed his staff down on the floor in frustration, wishing that Rudgaf would for once learn to stop being so hasty.

After a few moments thought, Barlow continued, "And he wouldn't be allowed to use the mountain pass, forcing him to travel over the mountains and adding another two weeks onto a one and a half week journey. Then it would take another three days for the letter to get from the dwarven capital to our tower."

The elf nodded, "Correct, so Lord Rudgaf would've received the notice over a month ago."

The Lord of Green tapped his foot, "Indeed, I told you that he received word of it several weeks ago."

"Well, that's just it, my Lord."

"What is?" Asked the wizard as he began to wonder if they would be beating around the bush for an eternity at this point.

"The Lord of Red left Behnon just after our scouts arrived and…"

"And?"

"You see," she continued, a bit panic stricken, "that was the first that we'd heard about the attack and…"

The wizard widened his eyes as she continued.

She hesitated at first as if trying to put the pieces together in her head. When she couldn't, she simply responded, "I know this doesn't make any sense, but it's true. We only heard about the attack a little over a week ago!"

The Lord of Grey slowly came to as the world folded around itself to form something new, yet familiar to him. He found that his eyes had once again started to see reality and his mind was free of the fog that often accompanies his hallucinations. When he had fully come to, he noticed that he was still sitting in the pub that his mind had vacated earlier. He quickly shot his head up and locked eyes with the barkeep.

"Are you ok?" Asked Fader.

Danagan shook his head and screamed, "You've got to get out of here, now!"

Fader raised an eyebrow and said, "What are you talking about?"

The barkeep was about to rip into the wizard, then, accusing him of playing a foolish prank and scaring his customers when an audible rumbling interrupted his thought process.

Danagan quickly shot a look at the door behind him, then glared at Fader and screamed, "Get the hell out of here, now!"

Fader, again, was about to protest but was interrupted by the sound of a large trumpet blast that rattled his skull and shook his faith. At this point, the rest of the guests began to shout for fear and scatter toward the door, doing a better job of disabling each other from leaving by blocking the doorway than they did of actually exiting the establishment.

Fader looked at Danagan and said, "What was that sound?"

"That was the sound of death." Replied Danagan, coldly.

The trumpet blasted again, even louder than before, causing Fader and several of the guests that remained to cover their ears.

"No." Stated Fader after the trumpet sound faded.

"What?" Inquired Danagan.

Fader's only response, then, was to shake his head, duck underneath the bar and then return with sword in hand – a falchion with a leather bound grip. He unsheathed it quickly and smiled at Danagan.

The Lord of Grey widened his eyes and said, "Are you nuts?"

Fader responded only by tilting his head.

Danagan continued, "Those are orcs out there!"

The barkeep shrugged.

The wizard pressed further, "You'll be killed you old fool!"

This time, Fader responded, "I stay here, I die. I run, I die. I fight, I die."

Danagan was stunned by this at first, but then smiled and said, "You've got gusto, I'll give you that."

The Lord of Grey turned his attention back to the door and, at that moment, heard a loud crash that quaked the very foundations of the pub and knocked him over the bar and into Fader's arms as they both tumbled to the ground. The wizard recovered quickly and stood back up to survey the damage. Firstly, he took note of a large boulder near to the bar that wasn't there just a moment ago. He then noticed that the roof now had a sizeable hole in it and that most of the front of the building was gone, allowing him to see outside.

"They have a trebuchet." He said to himself.

Everyone, with Danagan and Fader being the only exceptions, that survived the initial attack were now fleeing for their lives, the cries of horror and anguish that were all too familiar to Danagan now filling his ears as they were all shot down by orcish archers while they attempted to leave through the front of the pub.

Fader shook his head as he slowly sat up and looked over the bar in both dismay and rage.

"I'm gonna kill 'em!" He shouted.

Danagan turned his attention, now, to the barkeep and noticed a slight change in his companion. His clothes seemed strangely different, closer to what Danagan was wearing and to make matters even stranger, he was no longer wielding a falchion, but was, instead, wielding a pair of daggers not unlike what the Lord of Grey wielded.

"Who are you?" Asked Danagan.

Fader laughed and said, "Never mind that, boy!"

Before Danagan could protest, Fader wrapped his arm around the wizard's shoulders, pointed out at the invading army and said, "We're going to charge those sons-a-bitches, you hear me?"

The Lord of Grey returned his attention to the army in an attempt to count what they were up against, but failed to estimate their number due to sheer volume alone.

Danagan glared back at Fader. Fader shook his head, pounded his chest proudly and said, "Believe in yourself, Danagan!"

The Lord of Grey, astonished at the statement for the fact alone that he could've sworn that he gave the barkeep a fake name, began to raise an inquiry, but, instead, nodded his head and, together with his companion, took daggers in hand and rushed forth to steal their souls from the iron grip of death itself.

To the eyes of the orcs, the Lord of Grey vanished as he stepped out of the pub. In reality, as they soon found out, their eyes deceived them when Danagan and, to Danagan's amazement, Fader was on top of them with blades of rage stabbing here and slashing there. The entire, front line was completely caught off guard as they attempted to pounce on their unseen enemies to no avail.

What was left of the front line regrouped and, together, they attempted to corner the Lord of Grey. However, whenever they thought they might've had him, Fader would appear as if created of an ocean mist, leaving three dead orcs in his wake before vanishing again. Then, by the time the remainder of the line would react to him, Danagan would appear as if created of smoke, leaving, again, three dead orcs in his wake before disappearing again and repeating the cycle.

It was only a matter of seconds before the two reappeared, side-by-side, boldly standing before the remainder of the orc army – the entire front line now dead at their feet.

An instant passed as the two forces stared each other down, but, even to Danagan, who sometimes defied even time itself, the moment seemed an eternity.

The silence was broken, time returned to normal, and reality reigned again when, out of nowhere, Fader shouted at his enemies, "You bastards!"

The Lord of Grey clenched his daggers, feeling a surge of strength run through his veins that he had never felt, before. All he knew, then, was his enemy. He knew no anger, no fear, no sadness, no regret, no doubt – even when the entirety of the army started rushing at him, even when he could see the archers readying their bows, preparing to fire hundreds of arrows that normally couldn't be dodged, not even by Danagan, although this fact had completely left him.

"Look at these bodies, Lord of Grey." Said Fader.

Danagan grunted as Fader continued, "Do you now believe in what you are?"

The enemy picked up their pace then, being a mere few feet away from engaging their enemies. The arrows had already been fired. Death made its move.

Fader continued to speak, "Put away your past – leave no room for regret. You are no longer what you once were."

The orcs were close enough now to warrant raising their axes, preparing, then, to break their enemies into a thousand pieces. Death yielded its turn.

"Do you know who you are?!" Shouted Fader.

Danagan screamed at death, daring it to strike, as Fader roared, "You are the Lord of Grey!"

The Lord of Grey swung at his attackers wildly, but missed. When he turned back around for another strike at his closest enemy, he noticed that his assailant was gone. The wizard looked around, frantically searching for his enemies. However, there was no one left in sight. Even Fader had managed to vanish without him taking notice.

Death had retreated.

In the wizard's mind, he heard a familiar whisper. His voice, once boisterous, but now faint, said in a soothing tone, "Your faith has saved you".

The Lord of Grey smiled and said to himself, "Wilfrey...it was you all along."

Danagan then sheathed his daggers and trudged up to the top of the hill where death once proudly stood.

He stared out at the horizon and thought on the orcs, he thought on Tatiana, and he thought on his past.

Tecza, even, crept into his mind, along with the harsh treatment that the wizard had shown him. To his surprise and dismay, he felt sorrowful for what he had done to the lizard for as despicable of a creature that he was, Danagan knew that he didn't deserve that kind of treatment.

The wizard muttered to himself, "Have I really changed, Wilfrey?"

The Lord of Grey looked at his hands for a moment, then said, "Are these hands truly capable of good?"

The wizard breathed in deeply. It was a cold night, the coldest that he had felt in quite some time. He watched as his breath left his lungs and dissipated into the night sky, cloudy as it was, yet, clearing.

"What if I lose faith, again, Wilfrey? What if I don't believe?"

The Lord of Grey shook his head as if attempting to vacate his mind of his thoughts. With a clearer head, he started down the other side of the hill, advancing ever forward even though he knew that Taarok would be waiting for him.

"What are you thinking, my Lord?" Asked the royal secretary.

Barlow sat in an uncomfortable, wooden chair in the midst of the cold, grey walls of the elven, war shelter, attempting to clear his head.

The Lord of Green sighed, "I'm not sure what to think…what was your name, again?"

The secretary raised an eyebrow and asked, "Hmm?"

"Your name," said Barlow, "I never caught it."

"Oh," she said, nearly laughing, "I nearly forgot, didn't I?"

Barlow shook his head.

The secretary continued, "It's Tatiana."

"Ah," responded the Lord of Green, rubbing his beard, "that's a beautiful name."

Tatiana gave a quick bow and said, "Thank you, Lord Wizard."

"Please, just call me Barlow."

Tatiana smiled at that, her face glowing. It wasn't until then that Barlow had noticed just how beautiful she was. He noticed her hair, first, and how it looked as if it were made of pure gold. Even in the dimness of the insufficient torchlight, it seemed to glow as bright as a morning Sunrise. His attention shifted to her eyes next. They were green, greener than even the Lord of Green had ever beheld in anything before, as if the very definition of the color had been lost upon him until that moment. They shimmered like crystal, enough to convince even the most astute fortune hunter that they weren't eyes at all, but precious gems. Despite his fortitude and to his surprise, he was unable to lock eyes with her for long, for they caused a quaking within the depths of his very soul. At this, the Lord of Green scoffed and dismissed the feeling as mere infatuation with beauty, despite not having felt that way about anyone in hundreds of years.

Barlow cleared his throat and asked, "And you said that you were new to this job?"

The elf nodded and said, "Yes, I was merely a guard beforehand."

"That's quite a change in profession."

"Yes, I suppose it is."

The Lord of Green scratched his head and asked, "How does a guard become the royal secretary?"

She smiled at him, perfectly and said, "The king was swayed by my diplomatic tongue."

The wizard laughed and said, "Oh, no doubt."

There was a silence for a time, then, before Tatiana said, "So…getting back to the matter at hand…"

"Yes," said Barlow, "when is the King coming?"

The elf looked down the dark tunnel, then back at the wizard and said, "He should be here any minute."

It was at that moment that the Elf King appeared before Barlow's eyes as if being formed from the darkness of the hallway itself.

Upon entering, he gave a quick bow to both the wizard and his royal secretary. At that, the secretary bowed to both the king and the wizard and said unto Barlow, "It's been a pleasure."

Barlow bowed and replied, "The pleasure was all mine."

She shot him another glowing smile in approval of his remark and then rejoined the darkness of the hallway.

The Lord of Green returned his attention to King Nolan at that moment and asked, "Why am I here?"

The King smiled and said, "I am happy to have you here."

"Oh," asked Barlow, amused, "why is that?"

"I had feared that this world had lost you."

Barlow crossed his arms at that while the King continued, "Our scouts from Behnen reported that they could see the smoke from your tower even from their positions."

"So you know." Replied the wizard.

Nolan nodded and said, "Yes, and I know that the destruction was at the hand of the Northern Dwarves."

Barlow's eyes widened. After getting over his shock he asked, "How could you possibly know that?"

The King waved off his question and said, "I know about the letter as well."

Barlow took a step back at that and said, "That's not possible."

The King smiled and said, "Much is possible, old friend."

Nolan began pacing back and forth as he continued to speak, "Love, lust, avarice, betrayal, a frantic grab for power, the resurrection of powers long forgotten. Even now, in my great kingdom, my people are starving to death."

Barlow had nothing to say to that, so he let the king continue, "I've been betrayed, Barlow. Our elven cousins want little more to do with us. For no, just cause they block trade with us, forcing my people to migrate in droves to our northern boundaries in order to take advantage of the beautiful forest built by your hands that, miraculously, crept into our lands."

Nolan sighed, then continued, "And now King Moldof turns against us, taking advantage of our overly exposed, northern borders."

"I must object to that claim, your majesty." Protested Barlow.

"Hmm," replied the King with candor, "I figured that you would. I know of your friendship with the dwarves."

"Hmph," replied Barlow, "whatever friendship I had with them clearly wasn't there to help my cause while they burned down my home and attempted to murder me."

"It's Moldof's doing, you know."

"But why?" Asked Barlow.

"For what else? Land, power, dominion, and any other thing that a king would desire to obtain."

Barlow, unconvinced, asked, "But why would King Moldof be so bold as to think that, in his kingdom's continuing weakened condition, he could possibly defeat the Eastern Elven kingdom and what does that have to do with me and Rudgaf?"

The King rubbed his chin and said, "To your first question – the entire continent is fairly aware of our current condition. No trade means not only no food, but reduced capital. I would be lying to you if I said that my people's faith in me hasn't dwindled significantly recently and, for my soldiers, faith alone isn't enough to sustain their effort."

"You mean that they're abandoning your cause?"

Nolan sighed, took a seat across from the wizard and said, "Unfortunately. I mean, many are still loyal, but we are weakening every day."

The King then spread his arms out and said, "And the massive immigration is putting strain on our northern cities, as well as causing us to have to spread our remaining forces too thin."

The Lord of Green slowly nodded his head while Nolan continued, "It's, frankly, the perfect time to strike."

Barlow rubbed his beard and asked, "And for my second question?"

King Nolan crossed his arms and said, "Isn't it obvious? Moldof wanted you out of the way. He sent you a fake letter, knowing that by the time Rudgaf was able to see the fate of Behnon for himself, the orcs would've already have disposed of the city."

"Wait," protested Barlow, "you're jumping all over the place. First, you're accusing the dwarves of treachery and now the orcs. Even your own secretary had thought that King Colibrim was behind the attack."

"Two words, Lord Wizard – dread eagles."

Barlow nearly gasped and replied, "So it *is* true."

"Hmm," replied Nolan, "so you knew about that already."

The Lord of Green took off his hat and wiped his brow before responding, "Some members of the dwarven interrogation force had mentioned something about them. I had thought that they were lying in hopes to coax information out of me."

The elf's eyes widened at that.

"Honestly," continued Barlow, "I'm shocked that they were so bold as to openly admit to the act. It's in direct violation of the, "War Powers Treaty", you know."

"Yes," said King Nolan, nodding his head, "it is."

"It's obvious that King Colibrim sent orcs to attack the city," said Barlow, scratching his head, "and I can only assume that you made the assumption that the dwarves were involved because of the hatred between the goblins and the dread eagles."

"Right. The goblins, no matter how desperate, would never contract dread eagles for use in any situation, but especially not to…"

Barlow was confused by the king's sudden pause and asked, "Especially not to what?"

Nolan put a hand over his mouth and glared at the ground while he spoke, "Have you heard from Rudgaf at all? I mean, ever since he left?"

Barlow shook his head and said, "No, I haven't. Why?"

"Because the dread eagles certainly spotted him in the city and no one has seen or heard of him since he left my scouts in Behnon over a week ago."

Barlow's eyes filled with fear, "No...you don't think..."

Nolan removed his hand from his mouth, looked up at the wizard and said, "I don't know. I think that King Moldof sent Rudgaf there to get killed, making it easier to take you out because you were alone at that point. He obviously failed in his attempt to assassinate you, but whether or not he succeeded with the Lord of Red is up for debate."

Barlow shot up out of his seat and screamed, "By my foot, if they've harmed Rudgaf..."

Now it was the Lord of Green's turn to pace about the room while he continued to speak, "They set us up, after all we did for them. They set us up to die. They destroyed my home. They murdered hundreds of innocent civilians."

King Nolan interjected, "What are you thinking, Lord of Green?"

Barlow stopped pacing in order to look at Nolan's eyes. He then slammed his staff upon the ground and said, "I am the Lord of Green, the law bringer, the exacter of Justice. How can I let these sins go unpunished?"

The wizard then glared at the elf as if trying to burn a hole in him and said, "And you...oh, how far have you fallen!"

The King was taken aback by this statement and replied, "What do you mean by that?"

"This!" Shouted Barlow as he rummaged through his cloak. However, for some reason, he couldn't find what he was searching for.

"What?" Inquired the King.

"Bide a moment." Said Barlow as he continued to search about his person. He pressed on with this activity frantically for a few minutes until he lost his patience and threw his arms down in disgust.

"I cannot find the blasted thing!" The wizard shouted.

"What were you looking for?" Asked Nolan, his mouth watering with curiosity.

"A badge – the very same that you give to all of those whom you favor."

Barlow scoffed in frustration before continuing, "The very same that you gave to me."

King Nolan smiled and asked, "Do you still have yours?"

Barlow searched his outer pockets and began to answer in the negative until his hand touched the object in question. Pulling it out slowly, he held it up to his face, astonished and said, "Funny...I don't remember taking it with me."

Nolan tilted his head and said, "Barlow?"

Barlow didn't respond, so the King tried to grab his attention once more and said, "Lord of Green?"

The wizard, however, couldn't help but continue to stare at the badge, as if in a trance from the fact that he was surely convinced that the very object he grasped within his palm shouldn't even be in existence. To him, for reasons that he couldn't wrap his mind around, his confusion wasn't simply due to a matter of forgetting that he brought it with him.

"Are you ok?" Asked the king.

Barlow snapped his head up as if being awoken by a dream and responded, "Of course I am! I was just thinking."

The king rubbed his chin and asked, "Are you sure?"

Barlow scoffed at that and said, "Never mind that. What I was trying to tell you is that I have, or had, another badge just like this one."

"I see," said Nolan, nodding his head, "where did you get it from?"

Barlow, still slightly mystified, put the badge back in the outer pocket of his cloak and said, "A man. An evil man that dared to defile my forest."

Barlow stared at the ceiling in thought before continuing, "No, he wasn't a man. He was an evil spirit – the stuff of legend. He gave me his badge as proof of his friendship to you."

Barlow looked for a reaction from the king at this revelation, but found nothing.

"Did you hear what I just said?" He asked.

The king slowly shook his head and said, "It's time that I told you the truth, Barlow."

Before Barlow could inquire as to what the king meant by that statement, Nolan had already vacated his seat and, in a brilliant flash, disappeared in a blinding light. The Lord of Green shielded his eyes as best as he could, but had to let a few moments pass in order for his eyes to readjust.

When the residual effect cleared, Barlow beheld before him a pale man, completely dressed in brown from head to toe. His face, Barlow noticed, was rather young – no more than forty years of age – and full of life. All of his elven features were now gone, leaving behind a facial structure more akin to that of a human. In fact, Barlow reckoned, what he was looking at was incredibly human and, also, incredibly familiar to him.

At first, the Lord of Green had difficulty forming the words that he knew must be spoken, but after a moment he was, at least, somewhat able to overcome his shock and utter the word, "Wilfrey."

The Lord of Brown smiled and said, "It's been a long time, old friend."

Barlow remained silent.

Wilfrey frowned, "You haven't forgiven me for what happened back then, have you?"

The Lord of Green shook his head, "You never paid for your crimes."

"Please," protested Wilfrey, "there are things that you do not understand."

Barlow raised an eyebrow and remarked, "Oh? Just what do I not understand, Wilfrey?"

The Lord of Brown sighed, then replied, "I was not strong enough to defeat that evil spirit."

"Ah," said Barlow, "so it *did* come to you."

Wilfrey nodded his head and replied, "Yes, it has been tormenting me for a long time. Even back then."

The Lord of Green crossed his arms and said, "What are you getting at?"

"The madness, Barlow."

The green wizard felt a quivering within his heart and said, "You've been afflicted?"

"Yes, my friend. We both have."

Barlow shook his head and said, "No. Surely not I."

"I'm sorry," responded Wilfrey with sadness, "only the afflicted can see that spirit."

"Who…or what is it? Do you know?"

The Lord of Brown shook his head and said, "It is the Spirit of Want."

"The Spirit of Want?" Asked Barlow.

Wilfrey brushed a hand through his hair and said, "It is an evil spirit that preys on the flawed mind, convincing the afflicted to perform horrible deeds in the name of avarice."

The Lord of Brown slowly shook his head as he continued, "I didn't mean to do what I did back then. I didn't even know what I was doing, really. He convinced me that it was the best course of action. All I wanted to do was protect my friends."

Barlow sat down and put his head in his hands. After a minute or two, he grunted his frustration and said, "I…misjudged you. I've seen the power of this spirit first hand."

Wilfrey looked at Barlow, but didn't respond, so Barlow continued, "I was barely able to escape the snare of his honeyed words, but I did. I trapped him within a tree in my forest. He'll never bother us again."

The Lord of Brown nearly jumped for joy at that and replied, "I knew you would!"

Barlow looked up, surprised at that statement and said, "You knew that he would come to me?"

Wilfrey nodded, "Yes. I knew that he had to, being that he was the one responsible for what happened to the Northern Dwarves back then. I knew that he would have to answer to you – the law bringer, the warrior of Justice."

Barlow smiled and said, "And let your sins be placed upon his head. His punishment has been carried out. Justice has been served."

Wilfrey smiled at that, but then turned away.

"What ails you, Wilfrey?" Asked Barlow.

The Lord of Brown stared at the ceiling and said, "He's back, you know."

Barlow scoffed and asked, "Who? The spirit?"

Wilfrey shook his head, "No, I'm certain that you've disposed of him."

"Then who?"

The brown wizard delayed for a moment, as if trying to find a way to break the news.

Barlow, growing impatient asked, "Who, Wilfrey? Who is back?"

"The Lord, Barlow. The Lord of Black!"

The Lord of Green shook his head and said, "That's impossible. The heir to the black, lesser stone was taken care of. The stone, itself, is lost forever."

Wilfrey turned back to face Barlow and said, "It's true, Barlow! I can feel him."

"How can that be possible?"

"He is in spirit form, only. He seeks his full power again. He seeks the black, lesser stone."

Barlow crossed his arms and replied, "Well, that shouldn't be a problem. The only one that can get it back is you."

The Lord of Brown nodded, "Precisely. That's why Moldof wants my head."

The Lord of Green raised an eyebrow and said, "I don't understand."

"Like I said," explained Wilfrey, "he is in spirit form, only. In order to enact his will on the physical plane, he created for himself an evil conduit to whom he was able to give but a portion of his dark power."

"That conduit," continued Wilfrey, "I'm fairly certain is Moldof."

"Even if that were true," protested Barlow, "how would killing you help? Your soul is forever linked to the stone. If you die, no one else can inherit the stone's power. The power can only be given by the bearer. It cannot be taken by force."

Wilfrey shook his head, "You're wrong, Barlow."

"What?!"

"The conduit is a necromancer!"

"No," cried Barlow, "that cannot be true!"

"It's true. All he needs to do is kill me, then he can strip my soul from the stone, leaving it as a blank canvas to whomever is bold enough to receive its power."

Barlow swallowed hard, "I forgot that necromancy was a possibility. That's the reason why we placed the protections on your tomb in the first place."

The Lord of Green felt a shiver up and down his spine, then continued, "He could reverse your spell and obtain the black, lesser stone."

"And with that power..." Said Wilfrey.

"He could merge himself..." Continued Barlow.

"Right," said Wilfrey, "he would be the dark lord, the Lord of Black."

"Mazuun." Said Barlow, nearly afraid to even state the name.

The Lord of Green shook his head in anger and said, "Moldof must be stopped."

"What do you suggest?" Asked Wilfrey.

The Lord of Green thought on that question for a moment, even though he knew that his mind was already made up. He nodded his head in approval of himself and said, "Give me your finest men, Wilfrey. It's time for war."

Wilfrey looked away and said, "If that's what is required. I mean, you know what's best."

The Lord of Green raised his staff and said, "Fear not, Wilfrey. What you do to them, now, is what is just and pure. They must pay for their crimes against the world."

Wilfrey sighed and said, "You can understand my hesitation."

Barlow nodded and replied, "Of course."

The Lord of Brown bit his lower lip and said, "Are we really going to do this?"

The Lord of Green locked eyes with Wilfrey and said, "Let Justice come unto them. Her tax is heavy and her coin is crimson."

~CHAPTER FIVE – SOUL BOUND~

The western orc mountains were all that remained between us and the desert – where lied our ultimate destination. That fact did nothing to lift our moods. Two weeks we spent traversing the mountain range, greeted only by the solemn faces of orcs, led to the north in disbanded tribes by their new, goblin taskmasters. War is always filled with atrocities such as these – each side packed to the brim with egos and glory seekers all convinced that the end justifies the means.

…But it's never until the end that they realize that there is no majesty in tears and no glory in death.

Rudgaf awoke, startled and disturbed. He had just suffered from a horrible nightmare of a patch of earth giving way and swallowing him whole. As much as he struggled and dug at the ground in an attempt to free himself, he was eventually enveloped by soil and suffocated.

He inhaled deeply, filling his lungs as if it were that, just a moment ago, he could no longer enjoy such a simple pleasure.

Rudgaf noticed that he failed to feel any pain when he breathed in. He glanced toward his side and raised his once, broken arm into the air. It was fully functional once more.

The Lord of Red peered at his surroundings. It was relatively dark in the room, save for the few rays of sunlight that seeped in through the bamboo door in front of him. He noticed that his bed was a tad bit prickly, but warm, likely made out of feathers or possibly hay, which was now poking at him through his sheets.

His clothing was gone, save for a pair of undergarments of which he had never seen before. Next to him, he noticed, was a wash bucket, bowl and some cloth of which to clean himself with. He slowly sat up, turned his feet around, and did just so.

After he was through washing, the red wizard noticed that some fresh clothing was set on a table next to his bed. He picked up a shirt and glared at it – green and brown - rather simple. Rudgaf immediately slipped it on, followed by pants and pointy, brown shoes. He had assumed that his clothes, including his favorite hat, were all destroyed or lost in the explosion. A true pity, he thought.

He mused over his new attire for a moment.

Quite baggy. Then again, jungle elf clothing always is.

The Lord of Red sat up and stretched. His muscles were tense as if he had been lying down for several days. He noticed that his knees quaked a bit as he attempted to walk, but quake as they did, the red wizard still managed to make his way to the front door. It was there, next to said door, that he spotted his sword – sheathed and ready to depart. Rudgaf exhaled in relief. He was afraid that he may have dropped it in the skirmish and a loss of such magnitude was not something that he was prepared to tolerate. After all, the hat was bad enough.

He quickly slung the scabbard over his shoulder, tied it off, and opened the door.

The Lord of Red's eyes were immediately assaulted by the sunlight. He attempted to shield away some of the pain, but to no avail. He pressed forward as well as he could, hoping to get used to the bright light of which he now knew that he had not beheld for at least a few days.

He made an exceedingly great effort to stare off into the distance and eventually was able to do so, allowing him to see a group of elven children playing with a darkly clad, pale elf in front of a few, stick huts. The figure in dark clothing, he observed, was kneeling down in order to attempt to make itself of equal height to one of the children and, handing the child a ball, watched as all of the children scurried off into the distance. As Rudgaf slowly approached closer, the figure turned its attention to the wizard, stood up and smiled.

"A little bright out here for you?" The figure called in a voice that Rudgaf immediately recognized as Ramona's.

The Lord of Red didn't feel like shouting, so he stumbled closer to Ramona before speaking, the elf being incredibly patient while he did so.

When the wizard was finally within a few feet, which took longer and far more effort than he would've preferred, he finally spoke, "It's as if the Sun were a foreign thing to me. Surely, I haven't seen it in days."

"Try weeks." Replied Ramona.

Rudgaf's face turned red at the remark, being embarrassed that he was down for that long. Perhaps, he thought, his actions at the swamp were quite foolhardy, but he didn't know what else to do against such a monstrous beast such as was the hydra.

The hydra!

"What of the hydra?" Asked Rudgaf.

There was a long pause between both Rudgaf and Ramona then. The red wizard had noticed a strange look in the elf's eye that he hadn't noticed before as if she were beholding him for the first time. It was then, to Rudgaf's shock, the elf drew in closer, wrapped her arms around the wizard and squeezed. Rudgaf, being stunned, first felt an inclination to withdraw, but eventually succumbed to Ramona's embrace, returning it as best as he could. Hopefully, he thought, she could tell that he cared.

"I had thought that a great evil had taken you." The elf said, letting go of her embrace and pulling away while she did so, but not unlocking with Rudgaf's eyes.

Rudgaf was slightly confused by the statement, but just repeated his earlier question, "What of the hydra?"

Ramona smiled a bright, deeply sincere smile at the wizard. He gazed upon her, then, the same way that she gazed upon him – as if seeing her for the first time. Her jet, black hair swayed in the wind with grace as if each strand were a ballroom dancer. He stared deeply into her steely, grey eyes which, as he had observed before, seemed beyond ancient to him and as if they, themselves, were the long and winding road of an incredibly prolonged life that stretched out for immeasurable miles, yet seemed undaunting, bidding the wizard walk it. Rudgaf thought for a moment, remembering a time where he would've found the elf to be very attractive, but, to his confusion, his feeling was deeper than that and he couldn't put a finger on what the feeling was or why he felt it.

After the two failed to exchange words for a few, precious moments, Rudgaf finally broke the silence and said, "Are you alright, Ramona?"

She, herself, seemed to snap out of a trance, then, and said, "Oh, yes. Thanks to you, that is."

There was another slight pause before she continued, "You saved my life."

The Lord of Red shrugged, "You had as much to do with that as I did. Where did you learn to fight like that?"

Ramona brushed a hand through her hair and said, "You could say that I'm self-taught."

The Lord of Red chuckled at that, leaving the elf to respond to him by saying, "What's so funny?"

Rudgaf smiled at her and replied, "Ever the enigma."

The red wizard then stared off into the distance, beholding jungle and a few huts. He recognized where he was – on the outskirts of the southern, elven kingdom. After his discussion with Danagan, it didn't surprise him at all that they weren't in the capital itself.

Breaking Rudgaf's observation, the elf said, "I owe you big time."

The Lord of Red cleared his throat and said, "It is nothing."

Ramona laughed under her breath and said, "It's more than anyone has ever done for me before."

The red wizard turned his attention to her then and asked, "Do you have any family?"

The elf shook her head.

"Any friends?"

"Well," she said, now staring off into the distance, herself, "there's you."

"Really? You consider me to be a friend?" Asked Rudgaf.

She nodded and replied, "After what you did for me, back there? I owe you my life, Rudgaf."

"Like I said," remarked the wizard, "it is nothing."

"You know," protested Ramona, "some may take for granted the good that you do, but I don't."

The elf stared down at the ground before continuing, "I've only known evil for most of my life. People sticking their necks out for me, well, I'm not used to that."

"Well," said Rudgaf with a grin, "get used to it, because I have a feeling that if you and I stick together, given our track record and all, I'll be doing it quite a lot."

The elf chortled at that and said, "We have had quite an adventure thus far, haven't we?"

Rudgaf nodded, "We certainly have."

They both continued to stare out into the jungle, then. After a moment, Rudgaf rubbed his beard and said, "May it never end."

Ramona sighed after a few minutes and said, "That reminds me."

The Lord of Red turned his attention to the elf and said, "Yes?"

"Well, firstly, no one has seen our sniper."

Rudgaf crossed his arms and replied, "Why doesn't that surprise me?"

"Secondly," continued Ramona, "you should see the village elder. He told me that when you woke up, he had urgent matters to discuss with you."

"I see." Said the wizard.

"He also saved your life with his medicine." She added.

"Speaking of which," said Rudgaf, "what happened, exactly?"

Ramona sat down on the ground and, staring at the sky, proceeded to answer Rudgaf's question, "I knew what you were planning to do when you told me to run. I didn't know where to go, so I ended up just running back to the lake and hanging onto the bottom of one of those magic lily pads until it was over."

"Then what?"

"Well," she continued, "I heard a loud explosion and the whole lake turned red. Even though I was underwater, I could still feel the heat of the flames."

"They didn't burn you, did they?" Asked Rudgaf with concern.

"No," replied the elf, "the water kept me safe."

The Lord of Red smiled and said, "Good."

"After it was over," said Ramona, proceeding with the story, "I climbed up to the top of the lily pad and…wow, Rudgaf. I wish you could've seen it."

"What happened?" Asked Rudgaf, his eyes glimmering with curiosity.

"The hydra was still there, except the entire upper half of his body, the entirety of it that was out of the water, was turned to ash."

Rudgaf nodded, as if expecting that result.

"Then a squall came through and carried all of the ash away, leaving half of a hydra sitting in the lake."

Ramona laughed before continuing, "I wonder what people will think when they go through there from now on? Imagine the stories, the rumors."

Rudgaf sat down next to Ramona and asked, "What happened to me?"

The elf shook her head and said, "I had trouble finding you at first. I was afraid that you had sunk to the bottom of the lake."

The elf had to take a pause, then, before continuing with her story, "I didn't know what to do, so I started to make a heading toward here in hopes that someone could help me. That's when I found you."

"Where was I?"

The elf shrugged, "I guess that the blast was so intense that it flung your body out in the distance. I was nearly a mile away from the lake when I found you."

The Lord of Red shook his head and replied, "Sorry to worry you like that."

"Your body," the elf continued, "was miraculously not burnt up. Most of your clothes were done for, though. Luckily, your sword was still on you."

The red wizard slapped his scabbard and said, "And I'm definitely thankful for that."

"Ah, but the hat, though." Said Ramona with regret.

"I know, I know. Don't remind me." Replied the wizard with grief.

Ramona snickered at that before continuing, "Well, I guess the rest is obvious. I flung you over my shoulders and carried you here where the village elder healed your wounds with jungle elf medicine."

"Ah, I see. It looks as if you and I are even, then."

Ramona scoffed, "Don't be ridiculous. All I did was carry you here."

"I still appreciate it." Insisted Rudgaf.

"Think nothing of it."

The Lord of Red cleared his throat and asked, "How bad was I?"

"Well," explained Ramona, "that was the strange part. You had a few, broken ribs and a broken arm, all of which the elder, the enigmatic, creeping…thing that he is, was able to somehow repair with ease, but…"

"But?"

"That's what scared me, Rudgaf. You were bedridden for weeks and we couldn't wake you up."

Rudgaf tilted his head and asked, "Why not?"

"We didn't know," replied the elf, "I still don't know why, exactly. He, as in the elder, was looking into it while you were down."

"Is that what he wanted to see me about?"

The elf shrugged, "Probably. Your breathing was shallow for a couple of weeks, even, and every night you would scream out in terror."

This surprised Rudgaf, who took a moment to speak, "I screamed?"

Ramona nodded and said, "Yeah. You'd scream and reach out as if being swallowed up by quick sand or something."

"I…remember that." Said Rudgaf, collecting his thoughts.

"Do you think that it means something?" Asked Ramona.

"I'm not sure," replied Rudgaf, "but, for some reason, it made me think of Wilfrey."

The elf raised an eyebrow and said, "The Lord of Brown?"

The wizard nodded and said, "I've been dreaming about him quite a lot as of late."

"Do you have any idea why?"

The Lord of Red sighed and said, "No…I wish I did."

"Don't worry," assured Ramona, "I'm sure that the answers will come to you."

Rudgaf nodded, "Yeah."

"In the meantime," continued the elf, "The elder may have some answers for you. You should go see him before it gets dark."

"You're right." Said Rudgaf, standing up and brushing some residual dirt and greenery off of his clothes.

"I cannot go with you," said Ramona with a half snarl, "he specifically asked to see you alone."

The Lord of Red scratched his head at the remark and said, "I wonder why?"

Ramona shook her head, "Not sure, but I'd be careful, Rudgaf. Despite him saving you, I suspect that he had ulterior motives."

"Ulterior motives?"

The elf nodded, "There's something not right about him. He's not an elf, for one."

"But he's the elder!" Rudgaf protested.

"Of only this I'm certain, that and his abilities. It's not like I could get a good look at him."

"Why not?"

"Well," explained Ramona, "he never once showed his face."

"Then how do you know he's not an elf?" Asked Rudgaf skeptically.

"Because he's half my height."

"Oh," said Rudgaf with a half-smile, "that would be a bit of a problem, wouldn't it?"

Ramona shrugged, "He could be a half dwarf. Such a thing is uncommon, but not unheard of."

"I'd be surprised at that, actually. I had been under the impression that a half elf could never attain the rank of village elder."

"I think," said Ramona, lightly tapping her chin with her forefinger, "that the junglies are a bit more lax about that sort of thing."

"Well, in any case," continued Rudgaf, "what else was odd about him?"

Ramona sighed, "A lot of things. Too many to name, really. Even the way that he spoke was strange, as if he were trying to sound...older? I'm not sure if that's the correct way to describe it, but that's certainly what it seemed like."

"How...peculiar."

Ramona laughed at the remark.

"What is it?" Asked Rudgaf.

"Here I am warning you about how odd and suspicious this person is and all it's doing is igniting your thirst for adventure."

Rudgaf was about to protest at the remark, but then he happened to look down at his hands. They were trembling with excitement.

"I'm sorry," he said, "but I'm afraid that I'm not behaving quite rationally."

Ramona shrugged off the comment, "It's only natural, Rudgaf. You might be a wizard, but you're still a human."

"Hardly."

"That's enough, though."

Rudgaf sighed and surrendered to the point.

"Ok," said the wizard, "I'll make sure to fill you in on all of the details once I'm finished."

Ramona nodded, "Do you know where the elder's hut is?"

"Yes, I do. I'm quite familiar with the layout of this place."

Ramona stood up then and, putting a hand on Rudgaf's shoulder, said, "Be careful. I sense a great, unseen evil at work."

Rudgaf nodded, "As do I...and I will be."

With that, they parted ways – Rudgaf heading south toward the elder's hut and Ramona heading east toward her own.

Rudgaf pondered a bit as he made a heading for his destination and observed the village. All seemed quiet and peaceful, he noted, which was in stark contrast with every other place that he'd been to as of late. To his left and somewhat in the distance, he looked upon a farmer, cultivating what appeared to be wheat. The farmer, noticing Rudgaf staring, smiled at him and waved. The Lord of Red firstly went to tip his hat, but, remembering that he lacked one at that particular moment, returned a wave instead and pressed onward.

He passed between some huts and through some tall grass, wiping his brow of both internally and externally created humidity every now and then. It wasn't long before he could physically see his final destination waiting for him about a hundred yards or so away. Before he could continue further, however, he was waylaid by a young boy who tugged at his shirt.

Rudgaf, turning his attention to the boy, said, "What can I do for you, young man?"

The boy's eyes twinkled as he asked with hope, "Are you a wizard?!"

The red wizard nodded, "Yes, I am. But how did you know that?"

The boy looked around suspiciously, then beckoned Rudgaf to bring his ear closer, which the Lord of Red did without hesitation. Quietly, the boy replied, "You look smarter than everyone else here."

Rudgaf laughed at the comment and asked, "What is your name, boy?"

The boy smiled and said, "Mendax."

"Mendax?" Asked Rudgaf.

Mendax nodded.

"Hmm," said Rudgaf, rubbing his beard, "That's a human name."

"I know," replied the boy, "my father is a human, but my mother is...was an elf."

The wizard, "tsk'd", and asked, "What happened to her?"

Mendax, crestfallen, replied, "She died giving birth to me."

"Oh," said Rudgaf, shaking his head, "I'm sorry to hear that."

The boy sighed, then returned to smiling and asked, "Are you going to see the elder?"

"My," said the wizard, "aren't you the astute one?"

Mendax nodded and said, "My father says that I'm really smart! I'm at the head of my class."

"I don't doubt that for a second." Said Rudgaf. Then, reaching out his hand, he rubbed the child's head and said, "You run along now."

"Ok…but wait!" Exclaimed the boy.

"What is it?"

The boy laughed and said, "You never told me your name."

The wizard guffawed and said, "I didn't?"

"Nope!"

"Well," remarked Rudgaf, "that was awfully rude of me, wasn't it?"

The boy shrugged, "I guess so."

"My name is Rudgaf." Said the wizard.

"Oh, ok," said the boy, then, "you're very forgetful, aren't you?"

The wizard was beginning to become disturbed by the boy's observations, but just smiled and said, "You run along now."

"Ok," said Mendax, "I'll see you later."

The Lord of Red nodded and continued on his way to the hut, with greater speed this time than before, as if the task were ever the more urgent. It wasn't long before he came to a short ladder that lead up to the front door of the elder's dwelling. Still with urgency, the wizard swiftly climbed up the ladder without a hitch and entered through the door.

Before him, in the dimly, lit room, illuminated only by the outdoor light that peered in through the doorway, sat a small figure, the top of who's head, Rudgaf figured, would barely reach his chest if the figure had been standing – and Rudgaf was only of average height for a human. The figure was clad in a bright, yellow cloak with a hood thrown over the top, making it just dark enough for Rudgaf to be unable to see inside. The figure suddenly dove at him as the wizard approached, causing Rudgaf to quickly recoil.

"What are you doing?" Asked the wizard.

The figure laughed and Rudgaf immediately recognized the voice as that of a child.

"You're not the elder." Said Rudgaf as he slowly took two steps backward and laid a hand on the hilt of his sword.

"I am," said the voice, "only what the people that I help make of me."

Rudgaf immediately took his hand off of the hilt and relaxed.

"Don't you recognize an old friend when you see one, Lord of Red?"

Rudgaf's face immediately lit up into a bright, wide mouthed grin, "By the hairs on a dwarf's chin…Joem!"

Joem threw back the hood of his cloak, exposing his face, as dark as the underside of a patch of fertile sod, and a pair of piercing, yet gentle eyes – one blue and the other green. On his slightly large earlobes were two, small golden loops - common earrings for children from his tribe to wear. His smile was the purest and brightest that Rudgaf had ever beheld.

The Lord of Yellow knocked on his shiny head and said, "What were you thinking, Rudgaf? You nearly drew on me!"

Rudgaf scoffed, "Well, if you weren't acting so unsavory…"

"Unsavory!" Joem protested, "It's been over two hundred years since we last saw each other and this is the greeting that I get?"

Rudgaf smiled sheepishly, "You're right, Joem, but you certainly didn't help matters any – what with all that's been going on, lately."

Joem shrugged, "So, I have a flair for the dramatic. Is that any reason to lob my head off?"

"I hate plays."

"Since when?"

"Since forever."

"Even Escofchylus?"

Rudgaf crossed his arms, "Who?"

"Bah!" Exclaimed the yellow wizard, swiping his hand through the air, "How can you say that you hate plays when you've never even heard of Escofchylus?"

"Who?" Rudgaf repeated, smirking.

"Ugh, Rudgaf, come on. He's only the father of the modern day tragedy…and a really good cook to boot."

"Ah, that reminds me," interjected Rudgaf, "there's this great inn that I stopped in along the way that…"

"Umm, Rudgaf?" Interrupted Joem.

Rudgaf caught himself and said, "Yes, Joem?"

The Lord of Yellow pointed in a direction that indicated that something was behind Rudgaf. Quickly turning around, ready to pounce, the Lord of Red felt his muscles relax when he realized that it was none other than Ramona that Joem was pointing to.

"Mind if I drop in?" Asked Ramona, sitting down across from the yellow wizard before anyone could protest.

"Good." Said Ramona, nodding her head, as if all present had agreed to her request.

The Lord of Yellow placed his hands upon his hips and said to Ramona, "Ah, you're the elf from the other day."

"Ramona." She replied rigidly.

After an awkward pause, Ramona slapped her hands on her knees and asked, "So, where is he?"

"Where is who?" Asked Joem.

"You know," snorted the elf, "the elder."

Joem smiled shyly and scratched his head, but remained silent. After a moment, Rudgaf cleared his throat and replied, "That is the elder, Ramona."

Ramona raised an eyebrow at the Lord of Red, then looked back at the yellow wizard and asked, "How is this possible?"

Joem crossed his arms and asked, "What do you mean?"

Ramona studied the Lord of Yellow carefully and said, "You're half elf, which explains that, but...you're..."

"A child?" Finished Joem.

Ramona nodded and said, "Yes. How can a child be an elder of an elven village?"

Joem laughed and said, "I guess I'm just that great!"

"I beg your pardon?"

"That's enough, Joem." Said Rudgaf in protest. Then, after Joem was finished with his snooty chortling, Rudgaf continued, "Don't be fooled by appearances, Ramona. He's almost as old as I am."

Ramona's eyes widened at that and the Lord of Yellow gave her a cool smile.

"It's true," said Joem, "I'm five hundred and ten years old."

Ramona slowly nodded her head, then, and said, "It's good to finally meet you, Joem."

Now it was Joem's turn to be surprised, "You know who I am?"

The elf smirked and said, "Of course. I know a lot more than what is commonly known about you, you know. Your name, your specific abilities, your age, your alignment, your past life, the lesser stones...everything. I'm familiar with all of the wizards."

The yellow wizard shot Rudgaf a look of concern and asked, "How is this possible, Rudgaf? I mean, I know that word gets around, but that's some pretty specific information."

The red wizard shrugged, "Apparently she found the books."

"The ones at the central tower?"

Rudgaf nodded, "The very same."

The Lord of Yellow gasped, "There's no way. Those were destroyed."

"Or so you thought." Interrupted Ramona.

The elf laughed a bit afterwards and continued, "You ought to be more careful with your secrets. I even know about the black, lesser stone. Tell me, again...what became of it?"

Simultaneously, Rudgaf and Joem replied, but with different responses. Rudgaf said, "It was lost at sea." While Joem said, "It was eaten by a dragon!"

The Lord of Red stomped his boot on the ground and screamed, "Eaten by a dragon?! Joem!"

"Oops." Said Joem.

Ramona stood and turned to Rudgaf, "I knew you were making that up when I asked you about it earlier."

Rudgaf turned away, "It was for your own good. Damn it, Joem! You and your imagination!"

Joem shrugged, "It's ok, Rudgaf. I'm sure she would've found out eventually. She seems rather resourceful."

The yellow wizard locked eyes with the elf, then, and gave her a look that she couldn't quite discern while saying to Rudgaf, "Doesn't she?"

Ramona sloughed off the comment and said, "Where is the stone, then?"

"More importantly," interrupted Joem, "why do you want to know? Do you plan on becoming the new Lord of Black?"

"Is that even possible?" Asked Ramona.

The Lord of Red chimed in and said, "Not if you plan on keeping any shred of your sanity."

Ramona tilted her head and asked, "What do you mean?"

Rudgaf sighed and said, "The lesser stones grant the ones chosen to carry them great power, but it comes at a price."

The Lord of Yellow stared at the ground, "So...it's gotten worse, Rudgaf?"

Ramona snapped her head back to Rudgaf and asked, "What is he talking about, Rudgaf?"

The Lord of Red rubbed his beard somberly and said, "The hallucinations have started."

Ramona shot a look at Joem, who looked almost as if he were in tears. She then said, "You knew about this?"

"Yeah." Joem sobbed.

The elf walked over the Lord of Red, gently placed a hand on his shoulder and asked, "When? When did the hallucinations start?"

"I...I'm sorry, Ramona. I didn't believe it when I heard that the hallucinations could affect reality. I put you in grave danger. I didn't realize it until it was almost too late."

"What are you talking about, Rudgaf? When did you put me in danger?"

Rudgaf swallowed, "That hydra...you know how I tripped on its tail?"

Ramona nodded.

The Lord of Red continued, "Didn't you wonder how it came to be that we didn't even notice a tail as large as an evergreen just lying on the ground? I'll answer that for you – no, you didn't. You didn't at all wonder how it was that we could've missed seeing a three-headed lizard as large as a tavern until it was right on top of us."

"What are you saying, Rudgaf?"

"It wasn't there." Said Joem.

Ramona looked at Joem, then back at Rudgaf and said, "You know that's not true. I was there. I saw it. We fought it together."

Rudgaf nodded, "Indeed. We fought a hydra, there's no doubt about that."

The elf gave Rudgaf a puzzled look and asked, "Then why are you saying that it wasn't real?"

"Because hydras don't exist any longer."

Ramona crossed her arms and said, "Well, apparently they do."

Rudgaf shook his head, "You don't understand. It wasn't real until my hallucination made it real."

Joem tsk'd and said, "It looks like our hopes are dashed."

"What does he mean by that?" Asked Ramona.

The red wizard replied, "We were hoping that our minds weren't powerful enough to make the hallucinations become a semi-reality. It would appear that isn't the case."

Joem spoke up, then and asked, "But why did Ramona even see it, let alone nearly get killed by it?"

The Lord of Red looked up at Joem then and said, "I don't know, Joem. That's quite a mystery."

"Wait, wait, wait," protested Ramona, "the both of you aren't making any sense. I shouldn't have been able to see it? A semi-reality? What are you talking about?"

"I'll explain this one." Said Joem.

"Please, do." Replied Ramona, now turning her attention back to the Lord of Yellow.

The Lord of Yellow scratched his bald head for a moment, but then said, "It's sort of complicated, but to put it simply…well, if a normal person were to hallucinate, you could very well say that the hallucination is very real to that person, correct?"

"Yes, that makes sense." Said Ramona.

Joem continued, "But it's not real to anyone else, therefore it's not considered a reality because no one else in the world can actually confirm its existence. Since no one else can confirm that the hallucination actually exists, then it must simply be the product of the hallucinater's mind. Does that make sense?"

Ramona nodded.

"So," said Joem, "we've now clearly defined what imagination and reality are, but as happens quite often with things in nature, it's not quite as black and white as that. There's another state, called a 'semi-reality'. Rudgaf's mind is so powerful, you see, that whenever he hallucinates, the hallucination is actually real…sort of."

"What do you mean, 'sort of'?"

"Hmm," said Joem, rubbing his chin, "this might seem confusing, but bear with me. You're walking along with Rudgaf and Rudgaf tells you that he sees a hydra. You, however, don't see anything at all. Then a few more people come along and they don't see anything. So, by our definition, what Rudgaf is seeing isn't real, right?"

"Correct." Said Ramona.

"But then Rudgaf mysteriously gets flung in the air, horribly mangled, and then dies on the ground before you."

"Hey!" Protested Rudgaf.

Joem held up a hand, "It's just hypothetical, Rudgaf!"

Rudgaf snorted and the yellow wizard continued, "So, I ask you, Ramona. Was the hallucination real or not?"

Ramona shook her head, "By our original definition, it wasn't, but it obviously had a real effect."

"Exactly." Said Joem, smiling.

The elf protested, "What you're saying is insane."

Joem shrugged, "It's true, though. That's why this has become so dangerous."

Rudgaf interrupted, "What of you, Joem? Have the hallucinations started for you?"

Joem shook his head, "Not yet."

"Getting back to the original subject," said Ramona, "how did the both of you even find out about this?"

"Ah," said Joem, "a good question. Want to take this one, Rudgaf?"

The Lord of Red cleared his throat, "It came to me in a dream."

Ramona raised an eyebrow, "Are you serious?"

"Very."

"Mind explaining it to me?"

Rudgaf shrugged, "I had a dream quite some time ago that an old acquaintance of mine – an elf, ironically enough – came to me and warned me about my impending condition, explaining it all just the way that we told you."

Rudgaf chuckled a bit before continuing, "Of course, I originally wrote it off as nothing but an odd dream…that was until I started to forget things."

"So," said Ramona, "that's why you're forgetful? This…what do you call it?"

"We simply call it, 'the madness'." Answered Joem.

"At least," he continued, "that's what she called it."

"She?" Asked Ramona.

"The female elf in Rudgaf's dream. What was her name, Rudgaf? Ironically, I forgot it."

The red wizard raised an eyebrow, "Tatiana."

Ramona felt herself inhale quickly and damned herself for it.

"Hmm?" Asked the Lord of Yellow.

"Something wrong, Ramona?" Asked Rudgaf.

"It's…" stuttered Ramona, "well, it's probably nothing."

"Come on Ramona," insisted Joem, "you can tell us."

Ramona sighed, stared up at the ceiling for a few moments as if collecting her thoughts, then turned her attention to the Lord of Yellow and said, "I know an elf named Tatiana."

Rudgaf rubbed his beard, "I wouldn't make much of that. Tatiana is a fairly common name amongst eastern elves."

"Yeah." Agreed Ramona.

Joem tilted his head, "Still bothering you?"

Ramona nodded.

"Well," said the Lord of Red, "what does she look like, then? The Tatiana you know, I mean."

The elf rubbed her chin, "Well, she's exceedingly beautiful, even by elven standards. Her skin is the fairest I've ever seen on an elf. Her hair is as golden as the first rays of sunlight in the morning. Her eyes...her green eyes pierce through you, as if peering into your soul."

Ramona stared down at the floor, lost in thought, while the wizards looked at each other and nodded.

The elf grinned after a moment and said, "She even knew quite a lot about all of you...the wizards, I mean. That's how I found out about the central tower in the first place – she told me."

"I see." Said Rudgaf.

Ramona sighed, "I must admit that my curiosity got the best of me."

"Wait," interposed the yellow wizard, "why did she tell you anything about the central tower?"

"Why do you think? I asked her about it."

"Yeah, but why?"

Ramona shrugged, "Because she was the only one that I knew that would know anything about it."

"And how did you come to that conclusion?"

Rudgaf also joined in, "And why did you want to know?"

The elf quickly shot looks at both of them, threw her hands up in the air and said, "What is this? An interrogation?"

Joem quickly shook his head, "Nothing of the sort! We're just curious."

"Look," stated the elf, "why I wanted to know is my own business."

Joem looked slightly hurt, but simply said, "Fine, fine."

"Ramona..." said Rudgaf, gently.

The elf smiled, "It's ok, Rudgaf. There's just a lot of things about my past that I'm not ready to talk about yet."

Joem chewed his lip a bit, then said, "I don't mean to be pushy, but what about the other question?"

"That," said Ramona, "I honestly don't have an answer to. It was as if I was compelled in a way – like I knew that she would have the answers that I was seeking without actually knowing that she would."

"Elven intuition?" Asked the yellow wizard.

"There's no way," said Rudgaf, "there must have been some other force at work."

Ramona nodded, "Yes. It certainly felt that way."

The three of them sat in silence, contemplating various things for a few moments until Ramona broke the silence.

"Rudgaf?" She inquired.

The Lord of Red took a moment to respond to her inquiry, as if it took a moment for him to transition to reality from a deep thought.

Rudgaf said, "Yes?"

"Can you please explain to me why you thought it was better to lie to me about the black, lesser stone than to tell the truth?"

The Lord of Red sighed, "Some things should always remain a secret."

"So, the stone still exists? It wasn't lost?"

Rudgaf gave the elf a stern look and said, "The stone still exists. The key, however, is lost forever."

"The key?" Asked Ramona.

The room fell silent again, with the wizards both staring off in different directions, but ultimately towards the ground. After a while, Ramona asked, "What do you mean by that, Rudgaf?"

The elf looked at the Lord of Red, but he refused to answer or even make eye contact with her. She then turned toward the Lord of Yellow and he did much the same, save for a small stream of tears that ran from his eyes down to his chin, forcing him to wipe his face clean with the sleeve of his robe.

"Why are you crying, Joem?" Asked Ramona.

Rudgaf answered in his stead, "That stone was a curse to us from the beginning. It brought us nothing but pain, hatred and death."

"What happened?" Asked Ramona.

"Joem…" said Rudgaf, buying the Lord of Yellow's attention.

Joem sniffed, nodded and said, "It's ok. I trust her."

"Me too." Said Rudgaf with a smile.

The elf gave a quick look to both of the wizards and said, "Thank you. Both of you."

The Lord of Red rubbed his beard and said, "Now, Ramona, what I am about to tell you is incredibly sensitive information. Only the order of wizards knows this. I cannot even begin to stress the importance of keeping this information secret. Tell no one."

Ramona gave the red wizard a firm stare and said, "Ok."

The Lord of Red cleared his throat and said, "It started five hundred years ago. All of us – Joem, Danagan, Thome, Barlow, Wilfrey and myself – stumbled upon…no, that's the wrong word, really."

Joem interrupted, "We were chosen by."

The Lord of Red nodded, "Yes. At first it seemed as if we stumbled upon them, but they really chose us."

The elf scratched her head and asked, "Are you talking about the stones?"

"Exactly." Said Rudgaf.

"The stones were sentient?"

"Not really sentient," said the Lord of Yellow, "it was more like they were imbued with the will of their master. Him and, well…something else."

"Something else?"

Rudgaf explained, "We don't know the answer to that yet. Suffice it to say that the master willed the stones to find suitable bearers of their power, but the master had no say in the matter as to whom the stones would choose."

Ramona tilted her head, "But the stones didn't have a say in the matter, either, even though they made a choice?"

Rudgaf nodded, "Correct. They are, after all, only stones."

"I see." Said the elf.

The Lord of Red continued, "After we were chosen to inherit the power, we inexplicably dropped everything that we were doing at that moment and journeyed toward a location unknown to us at the time, but ended up being the central tower."

"You had no control over that?" Asked Ramona.

Rudgaf shook his head, "No. None of us even remember the journey. We just remember that Wilfrey was the first to display his power once we got there."

"How?"

"The tower," said Joem, "was buried underground. The Lord of Brown commanded the Earth to unveil it."

"Ah," said Ramona, "that explains why no one found the thing before all of you did."

"Correct," said the Lord of Red.

"I have a question." Said the elf.

"I imagine you'll have many, but go on." Said the Lord of Red.

"The 'madness', as you called it, has an effect on your memory, correct?"

"Just mine it would seem. It could do something different to everyone else, though. The hallucinations, however, are a shared trait."

"Ok," said Ramona, "but if it affects your memory, then how is it that you can remember all of this?"

"It only sometimes has an effect on my short-term memory. The only reason that I won't remember a certain thing in the long-term is because the 'madness' stopped me from remembering it in the short-term in the first place. It can be...frustrating."

"I imagine so."

"Did that answer your question?"

Ramona smiled, "Yes, thank you. Please continue."

"Very well. Nothing of great import to this particular story happened for the next one hundred years or so. We simply lived in peace, got to know each other, and helped each other explore our powers."

Rudgaf paused for a moment as the memories of a simpler time started to get him choked up. Ramona waited patiently for him to continue, which he eventually did, "Wilfrey and Barlow built a beautiful garden together around the perimeter of the tower. It was filled with the most beautiful flowers – lilies, lilacs, daisies, roses, sunflowers, tulips – just to name a few."

"It also grew all kinds of fruit and vegetables to feed us." Joem said.

Rudgaf continued, "I provided the tower with heat. With the help of Thome, I was able to create wonderful sculptures out of stone to decorate the garden."

The elf's mouth dropped a bit, "How did you do that?"

"Well, I used my power to superheat granite until it was molten. I would then shape the molten material the way I wanted while Thome would supercool it with his power."

Ramona frowned, "I wasn't aware that he was able to do that. I thought he only commanded water."

"Ah, but what is ice other than frozen water?"

"Point taken."

Joem chuckled, "How about that, Rudgaf? There was actually something she didn't know!"

The Lord of Red smiled, "I, too, am in awe."

The elf rolled her eyes, "Whatever."

"Anyway," commenced Rudgaf, "it was a paradise for us for one hundred years, but then the troubles started."

Ramona nodded, "Such with all tales bordering on morality plays."

The Lord of Yellow lit up at the elf's comment as he exclaimed, "A fan of theatre! Well met, Ramona!"

Ramona laughed, "Likewise, Joem."

The red wizard simply tsk'd until Joem said, "Sorry, Rudgaf. You were saying?"

"Right," said Rudgaf, "the troubles began when I was exploring around the tower. You see, the tower came equipped, if you will, with a room for all of us. However, for a reason unbeknownst to us, there was an extra room."

"Odd." Commented Ramona.

"Very," agreed Rudgaf, "but in any case, we used the room for storage. It was around this time that I started to forget things, so I was searching in the spare room for my alembic because I had somehow managed to misplace it."

"Your what?"

"My alembic."

Ramona raised an eyebrow, "What's an alembic?"

Rudgaf furrowed his brow, "It's a...distilling device."

"Ok," said Ramona, "why the hesitation?"

"Because," explained Joem, "Rudgaf invented it."

"So?"

Joem continued, "He uses it to make a liquor that no one else knows how to make."

"Really?" Asked Ramona, amazed. "What does it taste like?"

"Smoke." Said Rudgaf. "With a bit of an aftertaste not unlike a banana."

"Honestly, that sounds terrible."

"Hrmph!" Said the Lord of Red, angrily. "I haven't had time to perfect the recipe yet."

"Rudgaf?" Asked the yellow wizard.

"Yes?"

"Can we get back on topic?"

Rudgaf folded his arms, "I was just about to. Anyway, I went searching for my alembic when I noticed a bookcase in the back of the room that we had previously just ignored. I cannot discern the cause, but for some reason it caught my attention that day. I walked over to it, but as I did so I ended up stubbing my toe, shoving it out of place."

"And then what?" Asked Ramona.

"Well," said Rudgaf, "because the bookcase was no longer snug against the wall, when I went to set it back into its place, I noticed that it had been concealing a crawlspace. Naturally, I had to investigate."

"Naturally." Agreed Ramona.

"What I found there was rather odd."

"What did you find there?"

"Another room that we hadn't known about." Said Joem.

"Yes," continued the red wizard, "I found it to be most odd. It was fairly small, leaving only enough space for a small bed, a table and a bookcase. It looked as if the place hadn't been touched in hundreds of years because, well, it hadn't."

"Hundreds?" Asked Ramona, "Don't you mean one hundred?"

"No," said Rudgaf, "I meant hundreds."

The elf's eyes widened, "You mean someone lived there before you? A long time before you?"

"Oh, yes." Said the Lord of Yellow.

"Who?"

"I'll explain in a moment," said Rudgaf, "as I was saying, I found a desk in the room. On top of the desk laid a folded up piece of parchment of which I unfolded and read."

"What did it say?" Asked Ramona eagerly as if she were on a tipping point.

"Well, I'm paraphrasing, of course, but the note was actually addressed to us."

"Wait, what?" Asked Ramona.

Rudgaf shrugged in response.

"How is that even possible?"

Rudgaf stroked his beard, "Honestly, I don't know. It's obvious that either the author possessed enough power to have some semblance of clairvoyance or that he was simply hopeful that someone would find it."

"Do you think the latter is most likely?"

"Absolutely not." Said both of the wizards simultaneously.

The elf chewed her lip in thought while the red wizard continued, "I'm honestly surprised that you hadn't thought of this before, Ramona. We had to have a predecessor - the tower and the stones didn't just appear by their own will."

Ramona rubbed her chin, "Well, I knew that someone had to have created the stones, but until you mentioned how Wilfrey uncovered the tower, I honestly thought that all of you had built it."

"Not quite." Remarked Joem, smiling.

"Anyway," said the Lord of Red, "and again, I'm paraphrasing, the letter explained that there was, or should have been, another wizard living amongst us."

"Another? Who?" Asked the elf.

"The Lord of Black." Explained the yellow wizard.

Ramona slowly nodded her head as if the last piece of a puzzle had just been discovered.

"The Lord of Black should've been there with us," Rudgaf explained, "but he wasn't. The letter also went on as to why this would most likely be the case."

"So the author didn't know for certain that he wouldn't be with you?"

"He was fairly certain," said the red wizard, "but he probably wished to avoid an assumption."

"Sounds as if he lacked the knowledge to make an assertion." Said the elf.

Rudgaf scratched his head, "Maybe. I never made the claim that he was all knowing. Then again, neither did he."

"Ok," said Ramona, "so the Lord of Black wasn't with you. For some reason, he never made it to the tower. Why?"

"Because," explained Rudgaf, "as the letter stated, he probably wouldn't be there because..."

"Because?"

"Because the black, lesser stone drives people mad." Finished the Lord of Yellow.

"I don't understand." Said Ramona.

The Lord of Red slowly nodded, "That's alright. I'll do my best to explain everything."

"Well, I mean, I understand everything that you're telling me."

"What's the question, then?" Asked Joem.

Ramona brushed a hand through her long, black hair in order to remove it from her face and said, "This is what I'm not understanding - the author hypothesized that the Lord of Black wouldn't make it to the tower because the black, lesser stone drives people insane - but isn't that what's happening to both of you, all of you, as we speak?"

Rudgaf smirked, "You assume too much."

"Do I?" Asked Ramona. "What, praytell, am I assuming?"

"The assumption that you're making," explained Joem, "is that all of the lesser stones are equal in power."

A look of astonishment flashed over the elf's face, "They're...not?"

"So as to not mislead you," said the red wizard, "I will explain in further detail."

"Please." Said Ramona.

"All of the lesser stones, as in Red, Grey, Brown, Green, Blue and Yellow, are all equal, yet different, in power."

"I noticed," remarked Ramona, "that you forgot to mention Black."

"Black," said Rudgaf, "is special."

"Special how?"

"As you probably know by now," said Joem, "each color represents something in particular - a greater...what would you say, Rudgaf?"

The Lord of Red furrowed his brow, "Meaning? Purpose?"

"Purpose. Yes, that's probably the best word to describe it, however incomplete."

"Very well," said Ramona, "so what does Black represent? Evil?"

"Oh, no, no, no!" Exclaimed the yellow wizard.

"Then what, then?" Asked the elf in frustration.

The red wizard tsk'd and said, "It's important to not think in such a manner, Ramona."

"I apologize." Said Ramona, wincing.

Joem laughed, "There's no need to apologize, Ramona!"

Rudgaf nodded, "Joem is correct. You're new to this."

"Alright," said Ramona, "but could you explain to me why that line of thinking is incorrect?"

"Certainly," replied Rudgaf with a smile, "it's really quite simple. Each stone, each power, is capable of equal parts good and evil simultaneously."

"Huh?"

"It depends on the wielder." Explained the Lord of Yellow.

"That's right," continued Rudgaf, "a wielder of a pure heart is capable of good or evil. One who is purely good will only produce good and one who is purely evil will only produce evil."

Ramona nodded, "So, what are you, Rudgaf?"

The red wizard rubbed his chin, "Therein lies the problem."

"Of course," replied the elf, "nothing is ever that simple."

"Rudgaf," said Joem, "and myself are not pure of heart. We're not purely good, nor are we purely evil."

"So what happens, then? Do your powers always have a positive and negative effect?"

Joem grinned, "You're catching on, Ramona!"

The elf shrugged, "It just seemed like something you'd say. Anyway, how does this negative effect manifest itself?"

The Lord of Yellow gave a worried look and said, "The 'madness'."

"I think I understand now." Said Ramona, cracking her knuckles, "Mind if I take a whack at explaining this?"

"Go ahead." Said the Lord of Red.

"Thank you." Responded the elf with a smirk. "Every time each of you uses your powers, it drives you a little further into madness. However, because the black, lesser stone is more powerful than the rest of the stones, the one who inherits that power, if not pure of heart, whether this heart be good or evil, will succumb to the 'madness' at an accelerated rate."

"Almost." Said Joem.

"Almost?"

"It's not an accelerated rate."

"Oh," said Ramona, "then what is it."

Rudgaf spoke up, "It's instantaneous."

The elf laughed. Rudgaf simply glared back.

"Wait, you're serious?" Asked Ramona.

"Very." Said Rudgaf, sternly.

"But," protested the elf, "that shouldn't be possible! Should it?"

The room fell silent.

"Let me get this straight," continued the elf, "it has taken hundreds of years for you, Rudgaf, to succumb to the 'madness'..."

Rudgaf interrupted, "Well, I haven't succumbed to it yet. I've just only started to experience second stage phenomenon."

"The illusions."

"Correct. My first stage was forgetfulness."

"In any case," said Ramona, "it took you one hundred years to start experiencing the first stage, correct?"

The red wizard nodded.

"Now, before I continue - Joem?"

The Lord of Yellow snapped to attention, "Yes, Ramona?"

"What is your first stage phenomenon? That is, if you don't mind me asking."

Joem chewed his lip, "I...guess I don't."

"Then?"

"Hmm", said the yellow wizard with hesitation, "it's rather embarrasing, but..."

"Take your time." Said Ramona, gently.

Joem sighed, "It's an incomprehensible fear."

"Fear?"

The Lord of Yellow nodded, "Of anything. A shadow, a tree, a rock, a building...anything. It doesn't happen often and it never lasts that long, but it's completely paralytic."

"That's horrible." Replied Ramona with pity.

"It's alright, I've found ways to manage."

The elf tilted her head, "But you haven't experienced any second stage phenomenon?"

The Lord of Yellow shook his head, "Thankfully, no."

"Why do you think this is?"

Joem shrugged, leaving Rudgaf to answer, "Because his heart, while impure, is purer than mine."

Ramona nodded, "That makes sense."

The elf paused for a moment before continuing, "Back to the topic at hand - if it took Rudgaf one hundred years to start experiencing symptoms of the 'madness', but the inheritor of the powers of the black, lesser stone experiences the 'madness' instantaneously if not pure of heart, that means that not only is the black, lesser stone more powerful than the rest, but it is *far* more powerful than the rest."

The room fell silent again.

"Am I correct?" Asked the elf.

Rudgaf sighed, "You are."

The elf smiled and shook her head in disbelief, "That can't be possible."

"It is," said the red wizard, "each color is a representation - it has a greater purpose. Black represents..."

"Power." Joem continued.

"Pure might." Finished Rudgaf.

Ramona fell silent, so Rudgaf continued.

"The letter continued to say that if the Lord of Black hadn't come to the tower, then he assuredly succumbed to the 'madness'. If that were the case, then we had the unfortunate duty to seek the wizard out, kill him, secure the lesser stone and then dispose of it in any way that we could."

The elf looked stunned, "*Kill* him? One of your own?"

"Unfortunately."

"Horrible, right?" Added Joem, nearly weeping.

"But, why?" Asked Ramona.

"Because," explained Rudgaf, "the Lord of Black was incredibly dangerous - not just to himself, but to the world around him. That kind of power would be treacherous in anyone's hands, let alone the hands of someone that has fully succumbed to the 'madness'."

"He nearly destroyed us when we approached him." Said the Lord of Yellow.

"What happened?"

"He seemed to recognize us as soon as we came near to him." Said Rudgaf.

The elf raised an eyebrow, "How could he have known?"

"The black, lesser stone is a wonder of which we have yet to fully comprehend." Explained the Lord of Red.

"You mean that, to this day, the zenith of its power hasn't made itself known to you?"

Rudgaf shook his head, "Probably not even close."

"That's what got us into trouble to begin with." Said Joem.

"I'm sorry, Rudgaf," said Ramona, "you were saying that he recognized you?"

The red wizard nodded, "Yes. He fired upon us almost immediately."

"And you survived?"

"We were lucky," explained Joem, "he had become so mad at that point that he let control of his spell slip and it ended up backfiring."

"Backfiring?"

"Indeed," said the red wizard, "the result was an explosion that made the one at Barrier Lake look like a firecracker. It completely leveled the entirety of the city he was residing in."

"To be more precise," added Joem, "the blast radius was approximately a half of a mile."

Ramona swallowed hard, "How did you even survive an explosion of that magnitude?"

The Lord of Red explained, "Luckily, the Lord of Black had a tell. As in, we had some warning that his spell was going to backfire."

"But how could you have possibly escaped?"

"It was Danagan," said Joem, "he teleported us away."

Ramona scratched her head, "Did you know that he could do that?"

"Actually, no." Said Joem.

"Then again," continued Rudgaf, chuckling, "neither did he."

"What? Then how?" Asked Ramona.

"He just tried it and it worked, simple as that." Explained Rudgaf.

Joem smiled and said, "We're uncovering new depths to our abilities all of the time."

The elf shook her head, "What was the name of the city?"

Rudgaf stared at the ceiling for a moment, then said, "I don't remember."

"I do!" Exclaimed Joem.

"Ah," said Rudgaf, "please enlighten us, then."

"It was known as Taltains."

The elf shrugged, "I've never heard of it."

"Well, now you know why." Said the Lord of Yellow, grimly.

"After the ordeal," continued the Lord of Red, "we went back to the epicenter of the blast and there we found the black, lesser stone."

"You mean it was just lying there?"

Rudgaf nodded, "Indeed. When a chosen one absorbs the power of a lesser stone, the stone becomes a part of that wizard. When the wizard dies, the wizard's body vanishes, the stone returns to existence and the power returns to the stone."

"How...convenient." Said Ramona.

The red wizard shrugged, "I suppose so."

The elf stretched for a moment and then said, "So, then what happened?"

"Mistakes were made." Said Joem.

"Mistakes?"

Rudgaf continued to explain, "We didn't know how to dispose of the stone, exactly, so we decided to take it back to the tower until we could figure out what to do with it."

"Was that the mistake?" Asked Ramona.

"Not exactly," said Rudgaf, "the first mistake occurred when I attempted to light fire to a hearth in the same room that the stone was residing in."

"That doesn't seem like a big deal." Remarked Ramona.

"It really shouldn't have been, but there was something that we hadn't anticipated."

"What was that?"

"The stone," interjected the yellow wizard, "radiates power."

"So what does that mean?"

"It has the effect of greatly magnifying the power of spells that are cast near its general vicinity."

"So," said Ramona, "when Rudgaf tried lighting fire to the hearth..."

"I nearly burned down a section of the tower." Said Rudgaf.

"Apparently," added Joem, "Rudgaf had to call in Thome to stop the blaze, but of course Thome accidentally flooded the room with water for the same reason that Rudgaf nearly burned it down."

"Apparently?" Asked the elf.

The Lord of Yellow shrugged, "I wasn't there. I heard about it afterwards."

"You heard about it far too late." Rudgaf added.

Joem nodded while Ramona asked, "What do you mean by that?"

"After the room was flooded, I had to shatter a nearby window by kicking it in order to let the water drain out of the room."

"Thome couldn't dispose of the water?"

"Normally he could have, but neither of us wanted any more adverse effects to our spells because of the presence of the stone."

"Alright," said Ramona, "but what does that have to do with my question?"

The Lord of Red shifted uncomfortably, "After that little incident, I asked Thome to go tell everyone what had happened while I cleaned the place up."

"And?"

"Well, he did and he didn't."

Ramona gave a look of confusion, "He did and he didn't? How does one manage to do that?"

The Lord of Yellow gave a worried look, "He basically just came to us and said, 'I flooded the room', and then walked away without any explanation."

The elf raised an eyebrow, "But why?"

"The 'madness'." Said Joem, somberly.

"It was unfortunate," added the red wizard, "like I said, the first stage phenomenon of the 'madness' is different for every one of us. For myself, it presented me with short-term memory loss. For Thome, it presented him with an inability to accurately articulate his thoughts."

Rudgaf sighed before continuing, "This eventually evolved into incredibly erratic behavior."

"Thome's first stage phenomenon seemed to hit him harder than anyone else." Said Joem, nearly in a whisper, as if he were attempting to avoid speaking any ill of his comrade.

Ramona gave Rudgaf an inquisitive expression, "Was Thome experiencing his first stage phenomenon before this incident?"

The Lord of Red nodded, "Yes."

The elf shook her head, "Then why didn't you confirm that the details of the incident were successfully rendered to the others?"

The Lord of Yellow interceded, "He did! Well, I mean, he meant to..."

"He 'meant to'?"

Joem resumed his intercession, "He nearly immediately came to us with the stone and said that we quickly had to find a method of disposing of it because it was a great danger to all of us."

"But he didn't explain what happened?"

The yellow wizard shook his head, "We asked him why, but he forgot what had transpired already."

The Lord of Red pounded a fist into the floor, garnering the attention of both elf and wizard with which he did nothing except turn his head away in disgust at the entire situation.

Ramona turned her attention back to Joem, brushed a hand through her hair and asked, "What was your solution to the problem? That is to say, what did you decide to do about the black, lesser stone?"

Joem rubbed his head, "Do you know of King Narvis?"

The elf smiled, "Of course – the most famous king of the former northern dwarf empire. Who doesn't know about him?"

"Right," said Joem, "anyway, we were all good friends with him at the time. Word had gotten around about the massive explosion at Taltains and Narvis, being of the inquisitive sort, came to us to find out what had happened."

"Did you tell him?"

The Lord of Yellow nodded, "Yes and he was infuriated."

"With you?"

"Oh, no, no, no. He was merely upset with the situation. He immediately wanted to take action."

Ramona leaned forward, "Did he have a plan to dispose of the stone?"

Joem groaned, "Yeah...and it seemed like a great idea at the time."

The elf's forehead wrinkled with concern, "You make it sound as if the plan was foolhardy."

"Idiotic." Interrupted the Lord of Red, "It was completely idiotic."

Joem nodded in agreement, "We probably should have just plunged it into the bottom of the sea."

The Lord of Yellow paused and shrugged, "I don't know if even that would've stopped it, though."

"I guess there is no way to know for certain." Said Ramona.

Rudgaf fell silent and Joem placed his head in his hands.

The elf resumed, "You really shouldn't beat yourselves up over it. You can't predict the future…"

Ramona paused before finishing the sentence, then asked, "Or can you?"

Joem stared at her and replied, "If only."

The elf shrugged, "Whatever happened…I know there is no way that you could have predicted it. Like I said, you shouldn't beat yourselves up over it."

The Lord of Red sighed while the yellow wizard smiled and said, "Thank you, Ramona."

Ramona nodded, "Please continue your story."

"It's funny that you mention predictions in this case." Said Rudgaf.

"Oh?" Asked Ramona.

"Indeed, for Wilfrey warned us all, including King Narvis, that the plan would be a complete disaster."

Ramona tilted her head, "What was the plan, anyway?"

"Oh, right. I forgot to tell you, didn't I?"

The elf nodded.

Rudgaf continued, "In those days, the dwarves had engaged in a costly and harrowing expedition to reach the fires beneath the Earth."

The elf folded her arms, "I didn't know that an underground fire even existed."

"Neither did I." Said Rudgaf. "That was until I saw it."

"They reached it?"

"Yeah," said Joem, "they dug the most massive hole that I've ever seen in my life."

"You mentioned that it was costly, Rudgaf. Why didn't they get Wilfrey to help them?"

The Lord of Red tittered, "Then they couldn't claim the glory for themselves."

The elf scoffed, "Typical."

"In any case," the Lord of Red renewed, "with the project finished, the fire studied to the satisfaction of the dwarves, and the glory taken, King Narvis offered to hurl the black, lesser stone into the Earthly fires. In exchange, he merely asked Wilfrey to use his power to quickly cave in the Earth, filling in the seemingly endless pit and covering the stone along with it."

"Why did the dwarves want to fill in the pit after making such a strenuous effort to make it?"

"It was unsightly." Explained Rudgaf with a straight face.

"Oh, how awful." Replied Ramona, sardonically.

After a pause, Ramona added, "So Narvis disposes of the stone for you and, in exchange, Wilfrey saves them a ton of work."

The Lord of Yellow replied, "It seemed like a fair trade to us."

"Ok," said Ramona, "so the stone was officially disposed of. Job done, right?"

The Lord of Red winced as if his stomach was upset and said, "This is the part of the story that is the most difficult to relay."

The elf gave the red wizard a look of sympathy, "It's ok, Rudgaf. Take your time."

Joem whimpered, "This is the worst part of all."

Rudgaf soughed, "The Lord of Brown, Wilfrey, committed an egregious error."

Ramona lifted her brow, "Oh? What did he do?"

The Lord of Red slowly shook his head, "He failed to trust."

"Are you purposefully obfuscating?"

"No," said Rudgaf in a near sorrowful manner, "this is just a difficult topic to discuss."

The elf sighed, "You're right. I apologize."

"It's fine. I just…"

The Lord of Red paused a moment, swallowed, then commenced, "I don't want to make it seem as if Wilfrey is a murderer."

Ramona looked stunned and muttered, "A murderer?"

"Please don't say it like that!" Begged Joem.

"Joem, please calm down." Said Rudgaf, softly.

The elf raised a hand in the air and said, "I'm sorry. I didn't mean to offend you, Joem. I was merely taken aback by the statement."

The Lord of Yellow fell silent while Rudgaf continued, "Wilfrey…he didn't trust any of us."

"But why?" Asked the elf.

The red wizard stroked his beard, "I cannot discern why."

Joem piped up, "A lack of trust was Wilfrey's first stage phenomenon."

Rudgaf tsk'd, "I cannot concur with that."

The Lord of Yellow's face flushed with anger, "Oh, come on, Rudgaf! It's obvious!"

Rudgaf locked eyes with the yellow wizard, then looked away and said, "We have no proof."

"To hell with that!" Screamed Joem. "Wilfrey was our friend, our brother. He saved our lives numerous times and we saved his numerous times. Now you want to sit here and make the implication that, for no reason whatsoever, all of the sudden, out of nowhere, just when both you and Thome are experiencing first stage phenomenon, Wilfrey has an extreme lack of trust and commits an act of genocide?"

Rudgaf fell silent.

After a lull, the Lord of Yellow quietly said, "Bullshit."

The Lord of Red spoke up then and said, "I never implied anything. I just simply don't have any proof as to what inspired Wilfrey to do what he did."

Ramona interrupted, "That's enough. Stop it, the both of you. I know that this is a sensitive matter for the both of you, but it does no good for you to argue about it."

Both wizard's failed to respond to the chastisement, so after collecting her thoughts, the elf asked, "Joem, you mentioned genocide. What were you talking about?"

The yellow wizard stared blankly into the distance and said, "I cannot speak it."

The elf nodded and then turned to Rudgaf, "Can you, Rudgaf?"

The red wizard exhaled audibly and said, "Wilfrey didn't trust our judgment of King Narvis and the dwarves. He was of the mind that as soon as our backs were turned, King Narvis would attempt to dig up the black, lesser stone and claim its frightening power for himself."

"So? Seems like a logical thought to me."

"Nonsense." Protested Rudgaf. "King Narvis had no interest in losing his mind."

"I'm just saying," said Ramona, "kings are often power hungry."

"Power hungry? He was already the king of the most powerful empire in the world. If you ask me, he should've been more afraid of the stone being uncovered and upsetting the current order of things than he should've been tempted by it."

"Also a logical argument." Admitted the elf.

"In any case," said the Lord of Red, "Wilfrey should've trusted us. For whatever reason..."

"Rudgaf..." Interrupted a frustrated Joem.

Rudgaf smiled and said, "Very well. Because of his first stage phenomenon..."

"Thank you." Interrupted Joem again.

The Lord of Red continued, "Wilfrey didn't trust our judgment nor did he trust the dwarves. So, because of this, he placed a small spell on the Earth that covered the black, lesser stone that, in essence, kept the surrounding Earth active enough so that anyone attempting to uncover the stone would find that with every shovel full of dirt they displaced, the Earth would replenish the area with an equal amount of dirt."

Ramona folded her arms, "So it acted almost like quicksand?"

"In a way, yes. But only when dirt was displaced."

The elf shrugged, "Seems harm..."

Ramona stopped in midsentence as the magnitude of what Rudgaf was telling her had just dawned on her. She shook her head in fear, pity and amazement all at once.

"Oh, shit." She said.

"Yes." Said Joem, sadly.

"The stone." Added Rudgaf.

"That's what happened to the empire..." Whispered Ramona.

"The entirety of the city of Narvis, the northern dwarf capital, was swallowed up in a matter of three days. Millions of dwarves were buried alive. The empire fell shortly thereafter." Explained Rudgaf.

"So, does that mean that Wilfrey was right? Did someone attempt to dig up the black, lesser stone?"

The red wizard shrugged, "There is no way to say for certain, but with how much the stone magnified the power of spells, even the displacement of a grain of dirt would've started a chain reaction that would have yielded the same results, anyway."

Ramona nodded and fell silent.

Rudgaf continued, "After the capital fell, all of the wizards held a council in the central tower."

"And what happened there?"

The Lord of Yellow sobbed, "Rudgaf left us."

The elf gasped, "Did you really, Rudgaf?"

The Lord of Red nodded and said, "Wilfrey was incredibly angry with me for not telling him about the power of the black, lesser stone."

"But that wasn't your fault, Rudgaf." Said Joem. "You know that, right?"

"That's not how I felt at the time, Joem."

The Lord of Yellow sighed, "I know."

"Barlow...", said Rudgaf, "being the Lord of Green, the representative of justice, the law giver, passed judgment upon Wilfrey for his lack of trust resulting in an act of genocide and sought to banish him from the tower, which surely would've resulted in his death."

"Why is that?" Asked Ramona.

"Because," explained Rudgaf, "after the ordeal, we had many enemies. The dwarves were more lenient with the rest of us at the time, but they knew that Wilfrey controlled the Earth and were under the impression that he betrayed the dwarves on purpose. Because of that, they sought to kill him."

"But, wait," said the elf, "if Barlow sought to banish Wilfrey, why did you leave instead?"

Joem interrupted, "Rudgaf sacrificed himself to save Wilfrey. He allowed the blame for the crime to be placed upon his shoulders because he felt that his forgetfulness was the cause of the entire tragedy."

Ramona stared at the red wizard with mournful eyes, "That was very noble of you, Rudgaf."

"I would've done anything to save Wilfrey." Said Rudgaf. "At least I wasn't alone. Both Thome and Barlow ended up coming along with me."

The elf looked puzzled, "Why did Thome and Barlow leave the tower?"

"Barlow left because he was the one who motioned for Wilfrey to leave. He didn't feel right about not coming along with me after I decided to leave in Wilfrey's stead. As for Thome...his reasons are still unknown to me."

The Lord of Red exhaled and slumped back, "My hope was that if I left and offered the remainder of the dwarves my services in helping them rebuild their kingdom, they would leave Wilfrey alone."

"Did your plan work?"

Joem interjected, "Three weeks later an angry mob of dwarves armed with swords came to the tower demanding that we give up Wilfrey to them to be judged and executed."

Ramona tsk'd, "I see."

The yellow wizard resumed, "We couldn't give Wilfrey to them, but Wilfrey made it clear that he couldn't endanger both myself and Danagan by staying at the tower, so we concocted a plan to hold off the dwarves long enough for Wilfrey to make a break for it."

The Lord of Yellow cleared his throat and then said, "Danagan confused the dwarves with false images of himself and I scared them a bit by commanding lightning to strike near to where they stood. Wilfrey thanked us, escaped the tower, ran off to the desert and…well…that's the last that any of us would ever see of him again."

Ramona gave Joem a look of inquiry, "Why?"

Rudgaf continued for the Lord of Yellow, "Thirty-seven years later, Wilfrey was assassinated. The assailant is still at large."

The elf inhaled sharply. After she regained her composure, she simply said, "I'm so sorry."

The Lord of Yellow, crying, said, "He didn't deserve to die."

Rudgaf said, quietly, "The dark iron dwarves returned the brown, lesser stone to us out of honor for Wilfrey. Apparently, he had befriended them and helped them out quite a bit with irrigation systems."

Ramona nodded, "I can see how that can come in handy in the desert."

Joem said, "Now you see what Rudgaf meant by the key being lost forever. Wilfrey is the only one that can dispel his own spell."

The red wizard nodded in agreement and continued his story, "We then took the stone and constructed a special tomb in the desert. We interred the brown, lesser stone in the main chamber and sealed it off, using the brown, lesser stone with a spell that only Wilfrey could dispel. And it's there that it rests to this day."

Ramona processed this information. After a space of time, she asked, "Why are they called lesser stones?"

Rudgaf snapped out of a trance and asked, "What's that?"

Ramona repeated, "Why are they called lesser stones?"

"Oh," said the red wizard, "I don't know. That's just what the author of the letter that I found had called them."

"Oh. Who wrote the letter anyway?"

Rudgaf rubbed his beard, "His name was Zaan."

The elf didn't respond, so Rudgaf continued, "Zaan also explained that we had a master who went insane and created the lesser stones so that he could create a subservient army of wizards."

Ramona looked surprised, "And what was the name of your master?"

The Lord of Red shifted uncomfortably, as if it took a great effort for him to even utter the name, "Mazuun."

Ramona fell silent again. This time, Joem spoke up, "Is something wrong, Ramona?"

The elf shook her head, "There are a few things that don't make any sense right now. I have to sort them out in my head first."

Without warning, Ramona suddenly stood up and said, "Please excuse me.", before running out of the hut in a hurry.

After she left, Joem turned to Rudgaf and asked, "What was that about?"

The Lord of Red shrugged and said, "I don't know, but I think that we should follow her."

Joem nodded and said, "I agree."

Both wizards slowly stood up and stretched. As they were both approaching the door, they heard a shriek come from the outside. Quickly, they shot each other a look and then bolted out of the door and down the ladder.

At the base of the ladder, Rudgaf saw Ramona with a fearful look in her eyes, slowly backing away and staring at something on the ground.

"R…Rudgaf." Stuttered the panicked elf.

Before the Lord of Red could inquire as to what was wrong, Joem shouted, "Look, Rudgaf!"

The red wizard looked at the Lord of Yellow, who was pointing at something on the ground. Rudgaf looked down and immediately recognized a crystalline object as the very one that both he and Ramona had discovered in the copper mine in what seemed like ages ago. He noticed that the object was quivering as if it were willing itself to perform such an act. He also noticed that there was now a sizeable crack in its exterior.

"What happened, Ramona?" Asked the Lord of Red.

"I don't know!" Exclaimed Ramona. "I simply climbed down the ladder and the thing flew out of my cloak!"

"What is it?" Asked Joem.

"It's something that we found a while ago, just lying about in a copper mine." Explained Rudgaf.

"Right." Said Ramona. "After the explosion, I found it next to you and put it in my cloak for safekeeping."

"Tell me," said Rudgaf, "did it have that crack in it when you found it next to me?"

Ramona paused in thought, then said, "No."

"Are you certain?"

"Yes." Ramona insisted. "I would've remembered if it was damaged."

Rudgaf took a step toward the stone.

"Are you crazy, Rudgaf?!" Cried Ramona.

"A little." Replied the red wizard.

"Now is not the time for jokes!"

"Please be careful, Rudgaf." Said a worried yellow wizard.

What are you going to do, Rudgaf?

The Lord of Red paused in mid-step and said, "Did any of you just hear that?"

Joem shook his head, "No, Rudgaf. Hear what?"

"I did!" The elf exclaimed.

Joem quickly shot a look at Ramona and said, "Are you serious?"

"Interesting." Said Rudgaf. The red wizard then smirked and said, "Hello, Mendax."

The Lord of Yellow looked around frantically and said, "Who are you talking to, Rudgaf?"

"Are you talking to that child standing behind the crystal, Rudgaf?" Asked Ramona.

Joem glared behind the stone, squinting his eyes. After a few moments he threw his hands up in the air and said, "I don't see a child! What are you talking about, Ramona?"

"Joem," said Rudgaf, "she is again sharing my second stage phenomenon."

Joem's jaw dropped and said, "That's impossible!"

"It was possible the first time," said Rudgaf, "so why couldn't it happen again?"

Mendax gave Rudgaf a toothy grin, then turned his attention to Ramona and said, "Hello, mother."

Rudgaf went to speak, but was stymied by his surprise at the statement. Ramona took another step backwards and said, "Did he just call me mother, Rudgaf?"

Rudgaf nodded, "I believe he did. Any truth to it?"

The elf looked at Rudgaf, then back at Mendax and said, "I don't have any children."

The red wizard turned to Ramona and said, "Then why are you acting so scared?"

"Be…because he looks so familiar."

After a pause, she said, "I know him, Rudgaf!"

Mendax cackled and said, "You really don't get it, do you mother?"

"Shut up!" Screamed Ramona. "I'm not your damned mother!"

"I've had enough of this." Interjected Rudgaf. "What do you want, demon?"

Mendax grinned at Rudgaf and said, "What are you going to do, Rudgaf?"

The Lord of Red took a step forward and exclaimed, "Be gone!"

Rudgaf held up a hand and shot a ball of flame at Mendax, which went through the demon and exploded behind it.

The red wizard groaned and lowered his hand.

Mendax chortled and said, "Come, now, Lord of Flame. Surely you can do better!"

The Lord of Red spat on the ground before him. After a lull in conversation, Joem garnered Rudgaf's attention and said, "Rudgaf. The crystal."

Rudgaf stared at Joem, then back at the crystal, just as if the enigmatic message was clear. The Lord of Red stepped forward.

Mendax protested, "Don't you dare."

Rudgaf took another step forward.

Mendax again protested, "It won't do anything!"

The Lord of Red picked up the crystal.

Mendax screeched, "I'll be back!"

"Shut it." Stated Rudgaf as he threw the crystal to the ground, smashing it to pieces. Almost instantly he heard Mendax scream and saw him vanish into nothingness. Then, without warning, the Earth began to rumble and quake. Before Rudgaf could even think to do anything, the quaking stopped. Once he regained his footing, he noticed that a sizeable fissure had suddenly formed in the Earth before him.

"I see that, Rudgaf." Said Joem.

"So do I." Added Ramona.

Rudgaf stared at the fissure in the ground and quietly said, "Wilfrey..."

The Lord of Yellow nodded and said, "Wilfrey was in that crystal."

Ramona looked at both of them and said, "How is that possible?"

The Lord of Red ignored her and screamed, "Son-of-a-bitch!"

The elf turned to Joem, desperately and asked, "What's going on, Joem?"

Joem turned to Ramona and said, "A piece of Wilfrey's soul was in that crystal."

The Lord of Yellow began to cry.

"Wh...what does that mean?" Asked Ramona.

Rudgaf stared off into the distance and said, "Necromancy."

"That's impossible!" Screamed Joem.

"Why, Joem? Why is that impossible?" Asked Ramona.

"Because," explained Rudgaf, "only the Lord of Black has the power of necromancy."

"No..." said Ramona, collapsing on the ground.

"No...this can't be." She whispered.

The Lord of Red, almost insane with anger at the fate of his brother's soul, quickly turned toward Ramona and said in an irritated tone, "What are you talking about?"

The elf burst into tears, "I'm sorry. I'm so sorry."

Presently, Joem stopped crying, sniffled a bit, walked over to Ramona and placed a hand on her shoulder to comfort her.

"Explain yourself." Said Rudgaf, calming down a bit.

Ramona shook her head, wiped away her tears, sprang up and said, "Not yet. I'll explain on the way."

"Where are we going?" Asked Joem.

The elf locked eyes with the Lord of Yellow and said, "Danagan, Barlow and Thome are in grave danger. They may already be dead."

"What?!" Screamed Rudgaf.

"Don't say that, Ramona!" Exclaimed Joem.

"We have to go. Now. I'll explain on the way."

Joem, still staring at Ramona, searched her eyes. Satisfied, he simply nodded in agreement.

The Lord of Red, dissatisfied, but trusting of the elf, sighed and said, "Let's go."

~CHAPTER SIX – BETRAYAL AT MOUNT ER~

We finally crossed into the desert wastelands of the dark iron dwarves. Two more weeks of travel – slowed by the endless tide of dunes and sandstorms – and we finally made it to our destination. After spending a few nights in the various, scattered settlements that the dwarves had set up for themselves, it made sense to me how they were so hearty and why only a people such as they could possibly survive in such harsh conditions for so long. They shaped the land and the land, in turn, shaped them.
Mount Apollion laid before us…

The desolate peaks of Mount Er, where blizzards raged on so fiercely that the fresh accumulation of snowfall could bury an elf thrice over, where the wind whipped and cleaved the atmosphere with enough malice as to make one believe that they were just sliced by a pirate's cutlass, where the cold would eventually make the illusory effects of that thought a reality, where the northern dwarves preferred to call home, where sat the northern dwarven capital – Moldof, where the king of which the city was named sat amongst the slain bodies of his royal guard in fear before the might of two wizards.

It hadn't taken long for both wizards, working together, to seize control of the kingdom. As mighty as it was, its army was prepared to fight soldiers – certainly not the very trees in the forests that they were forced to march through or the very ground that they trod upon. One unit of foot soldiers were said to have been grabbed by branches of trees and hung from nooses made of vines. Another unit of bowmen were rumored to have simply been swallowed whole by the Earth, never to be seen again. Cities surrounding the capital suffered from earthquakes. Gardens turned against their keepers and shot venomous barbs which killed slowly and painfully. Sinkholes formed and buried homes, government buildings and public works. Mountains that had been dormant for centuries began to erupt, covering the land with ash that also smothered the Sun, leaving the kingdom in darkness. Then, as if matters couldn't get any worse, both wizards were supported from the rear by the eastern elven army, including the Behun Guard – the deadliest marksmen on the continent. Wilfrey, to the chagrin of Barlow, also contracted dread eagles and death hawks to hunt down any stragglers. As the Lord of Brown put it, "In these times, we must sometimes fight great evil with great evil."

And, in the eyes of both wizards, great evil laid before them.

"Stand down, traitorous scum!" Shouted Wilfrey to Moldof.

Moldof swallowed bile, took a moment to compose himself, pointed directly at the Lord of Green and said, "You, I know." He then pointed to the Lord of Brown and said, "You, I haven't met."

Wilfrey scoffed, "We haven't come to exchange pleasantries."

"What have you come for, then?" Asked Moldof. Standing up from his throne and slamming the handle of his axe down upon the floor, he continued, "You've murdered my people. You've ravaged my kingdom. You've most likely assured the destruction of my entire race. Why? Why have you done this?"

Barlow interceded, "We owe you no explanation, traitor."

Wilfrey turned toward Barlow and laughed, "He has the gall to speak of murder."

"I know." Replied the Lord of Green with disgust.

Moldof spat upon Barlow's feet, watched the wizard recoil with great satisfaction and then said, "And you dare speak of treachery. You came here centuries ago after your order committed an act of genocide. You befriended my people and swore that you were here to right the transgressions of the Lord of Brown. We trusted you again – even after such an atrocity, we trusted you. Now this."

Moldof shook his head, "Am I to presume that your friend, here, is Wilfrey, the destroyer of empires?"

The brown wizard looked away as if he were in shame and said, "It is I."

The Lord of Green placed a hand on Wilfrey's shoulder and said, "There is no need to be ashamed, Wilfrey."

The dwarven king stomped his foot in rage and shouted, "How could you say such a thing? How could it be that the *law* giver, the servant of *justice*, winks at an act of mass murder?"

The green wizard scoffed and said, "You speak of things of which you know nothing. In any case, the Lord of Brown isn't the one on trial here, you are."

The Lord of Green readied his staff before continuing, "And I am your judge, your jury and your executioner."

It was then that their conversation was rudely interrupted by a pounding at the double doors leading into the throne room.

"Wilfrey", said Barlow sternly, "you have to tell them to hold off."

"Why?" Asked Wilfrey with surprise.

"Because," explained the Lord of Green, "he's the Lord of Black."

Barlow glared at Moldof before shouting, "He'll kill them all!"

The Lord of Brown stared hard at Barlow, then at Moldof, then nodded and said, "Right." He then rushed toward the doors.

"So," said Moldof with a grin, "you know the truth."

The Lord of Green pointed his staff at the Lord of Black and said, "Did you really believe that you could conceal it from me?"

The black wizard chortled and said, "My creations are, indeed, strong."

Barlow scoffed, "I'm no creation of yours, I can assure you. You're nothing but a conduit, a puppet – you're not the real Lord of Black. I know you don't have the black, lesser stone in your possession."

The Lord of Green laughed loudly before finishing, "You're nothing but a hack!"

The Lord of Black frowned and said, "A hack am I?"

Barlow smirked, "You heard me."

At that moment, Wilfrey came running back into the room screaming, "They're not my men!"

The green wizard whirred around and said, "What are you talking about?"

The Lord of Brown shot Barlow a look of fear, pointed at the double doors and shouted, "They're coming!"

Moldof gave a hacking laugh, then flew into the air, much to the surprise of the two wizards, floated across the room to the double doors and hung in the air while the doors burst open.

The Lord of Green's jaw dropped. Overcome by shock, unable to act or even swallow, he was only able to mutter the words, "They're back."

"I'm home!" Shouted the wizard with joy as he shut the tower door behind him and hung up his hat on the nearby rack.

Thome peered around the first floor of the northern tower with his deep-set, almond eyes, as if he had never beheld the place before – even though he's called it home for hundreds of years.

The Lord of Blue rubbed his long, grey beard and said, "Where is everybody?"

Thome turned left from the doorway and started to climb up the stairs, but stopped as he observed that the walls were covered with scratches. He studied them curiously – most of them were faintly visible, but a few of them were deep-set, as if someone gouged the wall on purpose.

Thome felt his mouth turn dry as he said, "What happened, here?"

The blue wizard quickly continued up the stairs and into the second floor, where sat a small library and a desk. He took a step toward a bookcase, but tripped and nearly fell over a book that was laying on the ground. In fact, he noticed then, several books were scattered all over the place – a greatly unusual thing. Thome picked up the volume that he had tripped over and read the cover – "The North Country" was the title. Carefully stepping over the scattered remnants of his once organized library, he gently placed the book he held back into a bookcase.

The wizard turned around from the bookcase and observed the room in amazement – it was a complete disaster. Loose, red paper was flung around all over the place. Books were tossed around without a care to land where they may. Bookcases were tipped over. Quills were scattered and inkwells were spilled over, allowing their contents to drain. The cause of such disarray the wizard knew not, but he was determined to find out.

Girding himself up, Thome bit back his frustration with the state of things and continued to climb up the stairwell until he reached the third floor. The stairs ended, here, into a circular hallway surrounded by three doors, all of which were shut at the moment.

The blue wizard immediately made a heading for the door directly in front of him, which lead to his room. With purpose, he quickly turned the knob, flung open the door and gasped.

The wizard's room was completely destroyed as if by fire.

"Wh...what?" The wizard muttered to himself as he ran inside and toward the remnants of his bed, which weren't much to tell the truth – just a slightly melted and blackened steel frame. Thome scurried about the room, looking for more remains, but he ended up simply staring into the abyss represented by the blackened walls of his former quarters after having realized that he had already found all that remained.

Unblinking, the wizard turned himself around and stared out the aperture in his room that once held a window. A chilling breeze came in from the outside which smacked the wizard in the face, returning him to his senses.

Thome rubbed a hand through his hair and because there lacked a better thing to do he decided to exit his room, turn to the right, and open Rudgaf's room.

Where was found the same, exact thing.

"My...by all that's holy." The wizard uttered. Not even the bedframe remained in Rudgaf's room.

Thome spun back, exited the room of the Lord of Red, walked up to the stairwell and stared down.

"All of our personal effects..." He stated.

The wizard rubbed his beard and continued, "Centuries worth of notes on people, places, experiments...all gone."

The Lord of Blue, with extreme anger, pounded his fist on the railing, "And I wasn't here to stop it! All because of the 'madness'."

The wizard laughed to himself, "What a fool I must have sounded like. I wonder what my brothers made of me? I wonder if they even want me around anymore?"

The Lord of Blue felt a tear form in his eye, "I wonder if they still love me..."

"Heavens know," continued the wizard, "I would've gotten tired of me, too."

The blue wizard wiped the tears from his eyes with his sleeve, sniffed and said, "But I'm back now! I'll be there for all of you this time."

The wizard hoisted himself up from the section of railing that he was leaning upon, made to leave, then stalled and looked at Barlow's room.

"Why should I? It'll just be the same thing."

The wizard scoffed, swung his hand in dismissal at the door, and continued to leave. However, as he was about to place a foot upon the first step of the stairwell, he stopped again and turned to face the door leading into the Lord of Green's room.

The Lord of Blue shrugged and said, "Some tendencies just can't be helped."

The wizard, nearly laughing at himself, walked up to Barlow's door, placed his hand on the knob and flung the door open, exposing the esoteric.

"Rudgaf?" Said a small voice from the other side of the room of where Rudgaf was currently laying.

It had started to get dark after the day's incidents, so the group decided that it would probably be for the best if they prepared for their journey, got a decent night's rest and then departed early in the morning lest they be forced to travel through the swamp in the dark. The decision had been a frustrating one, especially for Rudgaf who desperately wanted to get back to see how his brothers, the Lord of Green in particular, were doing.

The voice woke the Lord of Red up with a start, who quickly fumbled over the lantern that sat on an end table next to his bed and lit it to expose the source.

"What's wrong, Joem?" Asked the red wizard.

Joem smiled, entered the room and shut the door behind him.

"Couldn't sleep." He replied.

Rudgaf sighed and stared back at the ceiling, "I haven't had much luck, either."

"Want to talk?" Asked the yellow wizard hopefully.

The Lord of Red smirked and said, "Sure."

"That conversation," said Joem, "it bothered me for a couple of reasons."

Rudgaf turned to face his companion and said, "Being?"

"I look into Ramona's eyes," the yellow wizard explained, "and I see that I can trust her. However, some things she said didn't make any sense."

"You mean that part about Tatiana." Rudgaf said, frankly.

"Yes. How could she know Tatiana?"

Rudgaf rubbed his beard, "There's been a lot of strange things going on lately."

The Lord of Yellow sighed and said, "You're telling me."

"I think," said the Lord of Red, "that necromancy has a part in that whole thing."

Joem's eyes widened, "You mean that Tatiana…"

The red wizard nodded, "The maximum life for an elf is two hundred years. She's nearly three hundred years past that mark."

The yellow wizard shook his head and said, "That's it, then."

"No." Said Rudgaf.

Joem raised an eyebrow, "No?"

The Lord of Red smiled and said, "It's Ramona, too."

The Lord of Yellow inhaled sharply and said, "Are you quite sure?"

"Quite."

"But, how?"

"All the signs are there," Rudgaf explained, "when I travelled with her, she rarely ever ate anything – I certainly never saw her eat enough to sustain herself. I never saw her rest –

whenever I awoke for the morning, she was already up and about as if she had been awake for quite some time. Whenever I asked her about it, she just said that she had 'trouble sleeping'."

"Maybe she did?"

"No," said the Lord of Red, shaking his head, "I'm afraid she's far more complicated than we gave her credit for."

"So," said Joem, "you mean to tell me that she's...undead?"

Rudgaf nodded and said, "Yes."

The Lord of Yellow found a chair, slumped in it and said, "Wow."

The Lord of Red waved it off and said, "I've really known for some time. I just tried to dismiss it because I didn't want to believe that necromancy had suddenly become a reality."

Joem looked at the red wizard sharply and said, "And you trusted her anyway? I mean, that's quite a big secret to keep from you."

The red wizard sat up, hung his legs over the side of the bed, propped his elbows on his legs, leaned forward and said, "I'm not without my secrets, Joem."

The yellow wizard protested, "Yeah, but..."

Rudgaf shrugged and said, "It was only fair. I couldn't tell her everything and she couldn't tell me everything."

The Lord of Yellow sighed and said, "I guess so, but don't you think that balance has been tipped in her favor now?"

"Hmm," said the red wizard, rubbing his beard, "you're probably right."

Joem nodded his head toward the door, "Should we?"

"I don't know," Rudgaf groaned, "she said she'd talk about it on the way."

"Yeah, but that was before we decided to rest up for the night before leaving."

The Lord of Red sighed and submitted to that point.

"Besides," added Joem, "neither of us can sleep and, as you said, Ramona doesn't even sleep, so now would be a perfect time to talk."

"I suppose so." Rudgaf admitted.

Both wizards hoisted themselves up, straightened their clothes and headed out the door with Joem leading and Rudgaf tailing behind.

It was incredibly dark outside, but Joem seemed to know the way without any source of light, so the Lord of Red continued to follow him until they came upon another hut which Rudgaf knew to be Ramona's.

Joem knocked.

There was no response.

Joem knocked again with more emphasis and also added a, "Hello?", for good measure.

There was no response.

Rudgaf gave Joem a worried look and said, "Open it."

The Lord of Yellow nodded and flung open the straw door. Before he could enter, the Lord of Red immediately ran inside.

"Ramona?" He asked the air.

There was no response.

Joem entered and created a ball of light in front of him which seemed to follow the motion of the forefinger on his right hand. The ball moved from side to side with Joem directing it, illuminating areas of the room as it went. Finally, the Lord of Yellow directed the ball to hang in the middle of the room and commanded its light to expand until the entirety of Ramona's quarters were illuminated.

As he suspected, there was no sign of Ramona. There was no sign that the room had even been disturbed, save for one, small note on the end table next to her bed.

The yellow wizard nodded toward the note and said, "Look at that, Rudgaf."

The Lord of Red followed Joem's eyes until his sights came upon the object in question. He quickly rushed over to the note, picked it up and unfolded it. His eyes scanned it quickly.

"What's it say?" Asked Joem.

The Lord of Red simply let the hand holding the note drop to his side. His hand gently let go of the note, letting it fall to the floor.

"We're too late." Said Rudgaf.

"What do you mean? What did the note say?"

The red wizard turned toward Joem and said, "It said, "I'm sorry."."

"I'm sorry." The Lord of Yellow repeated.

Rudgaf nodded, "Yeah."

"That's it?"

"Yeah."

"Well," said the yellow wizard, "what do you we do now?"

The Lord of Red fell silent.

"Rudgaf?"

The red wizard remained silent while chewing on his lower lip.

"Rudgaf?"

"I'm thinking!" Shouted Rudgaf.

Joem looked startled, but Rudgaf turned to him, winced and then gave him a wink in apology.

"She could be well into the swamp by now." Said the Lord of Red.

"But why would she do that?"

"Didn't you see how guilt ridden she was, Joem? She blames herself for all of this mess."

The Lord of Yellow scratched his head and said, "But what involvement does she have in all of this?"

"That," said Rudgaf, "is what I feel she was going to explain to us. Instead, however, she decided to try to fix the matter herself."

Joem shrugged, "Are you sure she didn't just have a change of heart about divulging her secrets to us?"

The Lord of Red shook his head, "I'm sure. It's more than that. She's been acting strange since we got here."

The yellow wizard protested, "Rudgaf, you haven't known her for very long, have you?"

"Technically," said Rudgaf, "only a few weeks or so."

"Then how could you differentiate her strange behaviors from her normal ones?"

The Lord of Red rubbed his beard and said, "Joem, if I knew Ramona for a very long time, you would tell me, right?"

"Well," said Joem, "I guess I would if you asked. Otherwise, I would just assume that you'd know if you knew someone for a long time or not."

Rudgaf raised an eyebrow, "That might not be a safe practice to continue."

The yellow wizard was about to speak, but then caught himself and instead said, "I see what you mean."

The Lord of Yellow crossed his arms and furrowed his brows in thought, then said, "No, I don't think you've known her for a long time, Rudgaf. But…"

Rudgaf's eyes widened, "But?"

Joem rubbed his chin, "It's probably nothing."

"No," protested the Lord of Red, "in times like these, assume nothing is nothing."

The yellow wizard nodded and said, "She reminded me of Tatiana quite a lot. Not in appearance, necessarily, but in many other ways."

The red wizard said, "Yes! I thought so, too."

"Then," added the Lord of Yellow, "that boy…what was his name?"

"Mendax."

"Right," said Joem, "Mendax referred to her as, 'mother'."

Rudgaf folded his arms, "Mendax is a human name."

Both wizards contemplated for a moment, then Joem suddenly exclaimed, "Tatiana!"

"Hmm?" Asked Rudgaf, snapping out of his state of mind.

"Danagan!" Shouted the Lord of Yellow.

Rudgaf scoffed, "No, don't be ridiculous."

"You said it yourself, Rudgaf – assume nothing is nothing. Tatiana was pregnant with Danagan's child!"

"But both Tatiana and the child died while she was giving birth to him." Interjected Rudgaf.

"Then again," the red wizard continued, stroking his beard, "Mendax told me that his mother died in child birth."

"Don't you see?" Asked Joem with bright eyes.

"It can't be coincidence," said the Lord of Red, "Tatiana is Ramona. Ramona is Tatiana."

The Lord of Yellow nodded in approval, "I agree. Now the question is – how?"

"I believe," said Rudgaf, "that our necromancer isn't quite as good at necromancy as he wishes to believe."

"Ah, yes," said Joem with a smile, "that would probably mean…"

Rudgaf finished the sentence for him, "He doesn't possess the black, lesser stone. Not yet."

The Lord of Yellow scratched his head, "Then how would he have acquired the power of necromancy?"

The Lord of Red whirred around and started walking in the direction of the swamp, the faint rays of light coming from the just rising Sun guiding his path.

"Where are you going?" Shouted Joem.

"Ramona!" Shouted the Lord of Red. "We *need* to find Ramona!"

King Nolan gave a smug smile at the approaching wizard cloaked in grey.

"I don't have time for you or anyone of your order for that matter." Said the king with a canyon's worth of arrogance as he waved the approaching wizard away.

Danagan stopped a few paces away from the throne, laughed out loud and said, "You'd better make time."

The king raised an eyebrow and said, "Or what? You'll kill me?"

The Lord of Grey smiled and said, "That's the rumor."

"Oh, please." Said the king, rolling his eyes.

The grey wizard patiently waited for the king to continue with a look of pure amusement glued upon his face.

Nolan continued, "The Behun Guard would have you killed before you even stepped foot out of my throne room."

Danagan took another step forward, his look of amusement now turned into a lion's snarl, "Don't you think that I've already considered that?"

The Lord of Grey went to take another step forward, but the king interjected and said, "Ah-ah."

The grey wizard stopped and King Nolan continued to speak, "You have two options, Danagan. The first option is quite simple – you can turn around, go back to that hovel you call home on the beach and contemplate on the fact that, much like you can't do anything to change the rising tide, you can't do anything to stop what I've set in motion."

Danagan smiled and said, "And my second option?"

Nolan folded his arms, "You can see what kind of mess that you and your friends have landed yourselves in and then you can die."

The Lord of Grey snorted and took another step forward.

At this, Nolan stood up from his throne and screamed, "I warned you, wizard!"

Before Danagan could react, the double doors of the throne room burst open and a hulking figure, standing over seven feet tall and wearing jet, black armor with sharp points on the shoulder pads came rushing through in a whirling dervish. The Lord of Grey barely had enough time to perform a backflip maneuver before a battle-axe came crashing down over his head.

Quickly, the grey wizard landed on his feet and focused his eyes on his enemy.

"Ah, yes," said King Nolan, "the both of you haven't been properly introduced..."

"Can it, elf." Said the figure in a brash, uniquely disrespectful tone. Presently, King Nolan did so.

The figure then turned his masked visage to the king and said, "Leave us."

To Danagan's surprise, the king merely nodded and began to make his way out of the throne room to the outside.

"Wait." Said the Lord of Grey.

Nolan stopped to face the wizard and said, "What?"

Danagan glared at him and smiled, "How does it feel to be a dog? You were barking quite a bit just a moment ago, but now I see who truly bears the leash."

The king inhaled sharply, straightened his robe and exited through the double doors without protest.

"Now," said the masked figure, his voice sounding as if the room were filled with bees, "we can get down to, 'brass tacks', as you humans would say."

Danagan shrugged, "No need for introductions, I suppose. I already know who you are."

"Do you? How is this so?"

"Tatiana told me."

The figure paused a moment as if in thought, then laughed a laugh that sounded more like a rock tumbler and said, "Ah, the elf!"

"If I were you," added the figure, "I wouldn't make a habit of trusting her."

Danagan spat, "I trust her with my life."

"How is it," said the figure while removing his mask, "that one so old and so powerful can be so stupid?"

"It takes all kinds." Replied the wizard.

The figure threw his mask down, a plain steel structure with two holes to see through and another hole for air, allowing himself to be exposed.

His face was green and scarred well beyond anything that Danagan had ever beheld before. The wizard not only got the impression that the figure had seen more battle than he, himself, would ever dream of seeing, but also that the figure used to look quite different before swords, knives and other pointy things got to him. He had no eyebrows and giant, red eyes that seemed to observe everything. His nose was mangled and in great disrepair, he had no facial hair and when he smiled, Danagan could see that his teeth were in surprisingly good health for an orc.

"Taarok." Said Danagan bluntly.

The Mad One quickly tilted his head to one side, cracking his neck in several places.

"Don't you know," said the orc, "that elves are only good for a fuck?"

"Is that so?" Said Danagan, unsheathing his daggers. "I wonder what your elf, 'buddy', would think of that?"

Taarok chortled, readied his axe and said, "Who cares?"

The Lord of Grey shrugged, "I certainly don't."

Taarok gave a toothy grin, "You're a bad liar, Lord of Shadows. You act coldly, but inside you stupidly care for these vermin."

The orc spat and continued, "You're soft. You don't have the heart to kill me here."

Danagan, while still holding his knives, brushed a hand through his hair coolly and said, "Good thing my knives are heartless."

Taarok frowned, "I wonder at that."

The Lord of Grey readied himself in a stance that saw him point his left foot forward with his right foot back. He ducked down low and held one dagger in his left hand low to the ground while another dagger, placed in his right hand, he held high.

The Mad One waved the wizard on and in a flash of steel they engaged. The orc immediately attempted to finish the wizard off with a brutal blow of the axe by swinging it over his head and down toward the ground with all of his might. To counter this, Danagan leapt up in the air and when the axe was in midswing, he stepped off of the head and lunged with a dagger toward Taarok's face, to which the orc swiftly took one hand off of his weapon and swatted at the wizard, connecting with his back hand. To the orc's surprise, however, his target disappeared in a puff of smoke. Quickly turning around, he saw Danagan standing in front of him with a smug countenance.

Taarok chuckled and said, "You're good, wizard."

The Lord of Grey sheathed his daggers, crossed his arms and said, "I simply wanted to demonstrate the futility of this fight. There are many paths that we may take from this point forward and all possible paths, save for one, will result in your death."

The orc hefted his axe again and said, "And what is the one path that doesn't lead to my death?"

Danagan smiled, "You running away like the chicken-shit, half-baked failure of a warrior that you are."

Taarok slowly lowered his axe at that remark and then dropped it entirely when he lost himself to laughter. Just as suddenly as he burst out into laughter, he quickly put his head in his hands and tugged at his face as if in severe pain, all while still laughing uncontrollably.

"I…" Said the orc.

The grey wizard unfolded his arms and said, "What are you going on about?"

The orc instantly stood up straight, stopped laughing, frowned and said, "I'm looking forward to drinking your blood at my table. I'm going to tear off your testicles and send them to your unborn child. I'm going to cut out your heart and send it to your whore of a wife. I'm going to lob off your head and send it to the rest of your order so that they can shit themselves in fear for what I'm going to do them."

The Lord of Grey's eyes widened, his face flushed, his brow perspired, his heart raced, his hand reached for one of the daggers that he had put away, his arm threw with deadly precision, his dagger cleaved through the air, the orc's head shot back, the loosed dagger buried itself, the orc smacked the ground, Danagan relaxed his muscles.

The Lord of Grey looked up what he wrought, gritted his teeth and began to make his leave.

Taarok was dead.

Danagan cursed himself for allowing the orc to get him that angry. He had hoped to defeat him in combat and then seek answers about Wilfrey's supposed involvement in everything that had been happening and also, perhaps, get some details on, "Mazuumanesh". That possibility was now gone as he looked back, again, to see the lifeless body of the legendary Taarok simply laying in the throne room, the blood from the blade wound dripping down onto the floor, staining the carpet.

The wizard exhaled sharply. There was no sense dwelling on it, he thought. What's done cannot be undone, he said to himself. Once more, he took in a deep breath and exhaled loudly, then turned to leave. However, just as soon as he made his first step toward the double doors, he heard a small, plucking sound from behind him and almost immediately felt a sharp, stabbing pain through his right leg that caused him to fall to the ground.

Quickly, without thinking about it, he rolled around and drew two more daggers out of his cloak, ready to fire back at whatever had just hit him. He couldn't immediately see what it was, all he noticed was Taarok lying on the ground at first. After a moment, however, he saw a figure immerge from behind the throne, approaching him slowly with a bow drawn.

"Tecza, you son-of-a-bitch." The wizard muttered.

The lizard licked an eyeball and said, "Weren't expecting me, were you Danagan?"

The grey wizard didn't deign to respond, so the lizard continued, "It's payback time, Danagan."

Danagan grunted, "You have an un-readied bow and I have two daggers drawn. You know who I am, right?"

Tecza chortled, "I have insurance this time, wizard."

The Lord of Grey went to move, but had to clutch his leg in pain. He observed that the wound had already left a considerable amount of blood on the ground and he started to feel faint.

"What's given you such confidence, lizard?" Said Danagan through gritted teeth.

Tecza pointed toward Taarok's body and said, "Just look."

The grey wizard looked over to the orc's body.

It moved.

The Lord of Grey swallowed hard and said, "That's impossible..."

The body continued to move and even started to produce noise. Before Danagan could even comprehend what was happening, Taarok was already up on his feet. Promptly, he removed the dagger from his head as if it were simply some sort of benign growth and threw it at Danagan, scoring a hit on his shoulder that sent the upper half of the wizard's body reeling toward the ground.

Danagan screamed in pain and clutched his shoulder.

Taarok laughed and said, "Did you really think it would be so easy?"

The lizard, too, began to chuckle until Taarok turned toward him and said, "You were supposed to kill him."

Tecza looked at the orc with widened eyes, licked the left one, then bowed and said, "My apologies."

The orc grunted and turned his sights back to the wizard whom he noticed had managed to sit up again. He barred his teeth and said, "There are many paths..."

~

"What is this?" Said Thome out loud.

The blue wizard swiftly ran through the doorway and into the Lord of Green's room. Unlike the other two rooms, Barlow's room had not been destroyed at all – if you can call something that seemed to be conquered by pure chaos and madness undestroyed.

Thome looked around the room. The walls were covered in red paper with scribbles all over them. He took one off the wall and read, "Dearest Rudgaf – Fajruakrb."

"What nonsense is this?" The Lord of Blue asked himself.

He crumbled up the paper and threw it down to the ground, then randomly selected another off of the wall and read, "Why? Why? Why? Why must I? Why must? Why must I find it? I must find it! STOP!"

He picked up another and read, "Wilfrey. Wilfrey. Wilfrey. Wilfrey. Wilfrey. Wilfrey."

Still another read, "I hate, hate, hate, hate, hate, *hate* them!"

The Lord of Blue shook his head and let the paper fall to the ground. He looked around some more and noticed that another piece of red paper was pinned to Barlow's pillow. He paced over to the bed, unpinned the note and read it.

Dearest Rudgaf – Lord of Red,

The eastern elven city of Behnon has been besieged and reduced to cinders! I desperately need your wisdom regarding this matter. I urge you to, as quickly as you find possible, investigate this horrifying tragedy. Thank you for your time, which I know to be precious.

Warm Regards,

Moldof – King of the Northern Dwarves

The wizard's brow furrowed, "Behnon? Cinders? Why would Moldof send Rudgaf? What's going on here?"

Thome gently set the letter down on the bed and put a hand through his beard. He simply didn't know what to make of what he found that day. The scratches in the stairwell, the destroyed library, two burned rooms and now this – all of these strange, mostly nonsensical notes splattered all over Barlow's room on red paper, of all things. He looked around some more, peering at this note and that, but the vast majority of the writing was undiscernible. In fact, most of it was just scribblings, save for one that managed to catch the wizard's eye.

The Lord of Blue reached over the bed, snatched the letter from the wall and read, "The plan is in motion. Thome is gone. Now Rudgaf…did they really think they were better than me? Did they really think they could keep it from me? It's *mine*. But…wait, they're my friends. I am the law giver. I am the servant of…*power*. I know where it is, hehe. I know. A king sits atop it. Alas, alas, I only have some of Brown. Brown was strong! Very, very strong! But if I have some of Brown and some of Green…no, I can't, I musn't…kill the rest, they'll just get in the way. They disappointed the master. The trap is set."

Thome dropped the note and his eyes glazed over as the pieces of the puzzle came together in his head. Swiftly, he ran out of the room, down the stairs to the second floor, up to the bookcase where he placed the book that he tripped on earlier and displaced the book again.

"The North Country." He read out loud.

The blue wizard opened up the cover and flipped through page after page of text. After a few moments, he shut the tome and threw the book to the ground after he realized that every, single page read, "Kill Moldof."

The wizard rushed down the stairs to the first floor, grabbed his hat, placed it on his head, flew out the door and headed toward the northern dwarven capital city of Moldof.

Even though he knew that he was already too late.

Ramona sunk into the ground in disbelief.

It was one thing to hear the wizard's talking about the "madness" and the power of second stage phenomenon. It was another thing to fully recognize it as something real and tangible. Something that couldn't be ignored – something that had to be dealt with. With burning eyes, she stared out into the empty swamp – with only dark water, lily pads, and methane to greet her. They hydra was gone…no, she thought. They hydra never existed.

As the elf blankly stared out into the vastness of the swamp, hoping that she remembered the jumping order required to make it to the other side, a cloaked, bearded figure approached her from behind. She heard it coming almost immediately and whipped her head around to gaze at the figure, marveling at how close it had been able to come to her without hearing it. In fact, she reckoned, it was as if the figure had simply come into existence in that state.

She glanced upon the mysterious figure dressed in grey and said, "Who are you?"

The figure slowly approached. Smiling, it said, "Don't you recognize an old lover when you see one, Ramona?"

Ramona's eyes widened. She replied, "How do you know my name?"

The figure looked shocked and said, "How could you ask such a thing? I've known your mind, your soul and your body. You're the mother of our child. How could I not know your name? I know far more than just your name."

The elf scoffed and turned away, "I've never had a child, nor have I ever had a lover. You clearly have the wrong elf."

The shadow slowly approached closer and placed a hand on the elf's shoulder.

"You don't have to face this alone." It said.

Carefully, the figure reached over and placed a finger underneath Ramona's chin, lifting her head up ever so slightly so that her steely, grey eyes met his.

"I can give you the life that you never had." It said.

The elf didn't respond, but just kept staring at the shadow's piercing, blue eyes as if transfixed by a vision of terror.

"The life that was stolen from you." The shadow added.

"I…" Said Ramona, her tongue heavy.

"Forget the others," said the figure, "they would've abandoned you as soon as you told them the truth."

The elf felt a tear stream down her cheek. After a pause, she uttered the question, "Rudgaf?"

The shadow nodded, "Especially Rudgaf. After how much trust he put in you?"

Ramona attempted to turn away from the soul destroying eyes of the figure, but they kept her locked on tightly. It then said, "You were going to betray him, weren't you?"

"N…no!" Ramona protested.

The figure shook its head, "You were."

"Stop it!"

"You already have."

The elf clamped her eyes shut and cried, "No more!"

"Had enough?" It asked, then added, "Was it enough for Rudgaf that you planned to stab him in the back when he needed you the most?"

Ramona shook her head violently and said, "You don't know what you're talking about!"

"Oh, yes I do." Laughed the figure.

The shadow breathed in the heavy air, slowly, then continued, "Save Tatiana, save yourself, right? All it takes is a little favor for Mazuumanesh and then you find out that, oh! Oh!"

"Shut up!"

The figure cackled, "He's the Lord of Black!"

Ramona opened her eyes again to stare into the abyss, "I didn't know. How could I have known?"

The shadow tsk'd and said, "That's right, dear Ramona. How could you have known? But…"

"But?"

Smiling, the shadow said, "Will the others see it that way?"

The elf became crestfallen as the shadow continued, "I doubt it. Don't you?"

Lifting her head up again, the shadow whispered, "But I see it that way, my love."

Ramona, with tears in her eyes, said, "You do?"

"Of course."

There was a pause, then, until the mysterious figure gestured back the way that Ramona came and said, "Come with me."

A look of confusion and almost panic came over Ramona's features as she said, "But, why?"

The shadow ignored the question, "Abandon this foolish quest and come home with me."

The elf looked away while the shadow continued, "Our son needs his mother."

"I told you," said Ramona sharply, "I don't have a son."

"Ah, but that's where you're wrong."

Ramona turned her back on the shadow and said, "I think I'd know if I had a son."

The figure tsk'd again and said, "Tatiana had a son."

"I'm happy for her." Replied the elf with folded arms.

"Come, now. You can't keep secrets from your lover."

Ramona snapped back with fury, "My name is Ramona! I'm more than just a piece of her!"

The shadow shook its head, "No, you're not."

The elf fell silent while the shadow continued, "You're far less than that, even. You're just a shadow, a phantom, an error that shouldn't have been made. You have no reason for being, no purpose in life. You're a mistake."

Ramona, having heard enough from the mysterious shadow, said, "Who the hell are you and what do you want?"

The figure frowned and said, "Stop asking stupid questions."

"You're right," said Ramona, smiling, "it doesn't matter what a dead man wants."

The shadow chortled, "Try me, elf."

"That was my intention!" Screamed Ramona as she drew her bow, readied an arrow, aimed and fired at the figment before it could even blink.

The arrow soared through the air with pin-point precision and hit its target dead-on. However, the target vanished in a puff of smoke. Before Ramona could react, the figure reappeared to her left side and delivered a swift kick to her head which sent her sailing toward the edge of the swamp.

"You stupid, elven bitch." Spat the shadow like a venomous serpent as it slithered its way over to Ramona's body which laid in a heap upon itself.

When the shadow approached close to the elf, she surprised him with a powerful upkick that landed square on his jaw and sent him toppling backwards. She then stood up, threw a knife at her enemy and then drew two daggers. The knife flew at the shadow and stuck in the dirt, harmlessly, as the figure quickly rolled out of the way and jumped back to its feet. That was ok with Ramona, though, because she hadn't expected the knife to hit in the first place.

The shadow wiped blood away from his lip and then with narrowed eyes he charged at Ramona. The elf readied herself for a counterattack. The figure quickly drew a dagger from its cloak and lunged at the elf carelessly. Ramona swiftly side-stepped the attack and then stabbed at her opponent's exposed side, which vanished before her eyes. She suddenly felt a sharp pain in her upper back as she realized that her enemy wasn't actually in front of her, but behind her.

The shadow grunted and twisted the knife as Ramona fell to the ground.

Her opponent had gotten a clear shot into her right lung. She tried to scream out in pain, but could only manage to cough up blood.

The shadow relaxed, sheathed his daggers, walked up to Ramona and shook his head.

"I didn't want to do this to you." It said.

The elf's eyes began to glaze over as she stared blankly at the sky.

The shadow, suddenly filled with rage, knelt over the elf and wrapped his hands around her throat, "You! I didn't want to do it! You *made* me do it!"

Ramona gurgled and spat as the shadow continued to choke her. It then began slamming her head into the ground and shouting, "You're nothing! You're nothing!"

It was then that the shadow was suddenly flung off of the elf's body and landed in the waters of the swamp. The elf couldn't see it, then, but the figment had been hit in the back with a ball of fire.

Rudgaf and Joem had arrived.

"Good heavens! She's dying, Rudgaf!" Exclaimed Joem.

"Tend to her wounds, Joem!" Said Rudgaf.

The Lord of Yellow looked at Rudgaf with concern and said, "But what of the spirit?"

"Nevermind that," said the Lord of Red, "you can't even see it. It's best if I fight it alone. I'm…familiar with it."

Joem stared at Rudgaf, stunned, but after a moment he simply nodded his head and ran to tend to the elf.

The shadow jumped out of the water, then, ready for a showdown with its attacker.

"Now, Lord of the Flame," said the spirit, "is that any way to treat an old friend?"

"Hah," scoffed Rudgaf, "it doesn't matter how you mask yourself. I'll always know that it's you."

The spirit looked itself up and down and said, "Don't you think I sported a good image this time around?"

"Danagan doesn't have a beard, you idiot."

"Ah," said the spirit in surprise, "you thought I was trying to be Danagan?"

Rudgaf shrugged, "Seemed pretty obvious."

"You should know better than to think that I'd be that obvious." The spirit retorted, then added, "How long have we known each other?"

"Too long." Remarked the red wizard with disgust.

The spirit bit its lip and said, "You're beginning to hurt my feelings."

The Lord of Red drew his sword and said, "And you're beginning to bore me."

The phantom tsk'd and said, "You don't even want to hazard a guess as to what I am?"

The red wizard shook his head in response, so the spirit continued, "I'm what Danagan would have been if you hadn't…ruined him."

Rudgaf furrowed his brows and said, "Ruined?"

The spirit spread his arms out and said, "Look at what you've robbed me of, Lord of Fire. A wife, a child, a home, a people. All for your stupid order."

"That was Danagan's decision."

The spirit smirked, "Was it? Can you truly say that it was his decision and his decision alone? Can you say that you and the others didn't put any pressure on him at all?"

Rudgaf shook his head, "Every man is responsible for his own decisions."

The figure laughed, "Look at how you deflect! Deflect away, wizard! But the truth still stands – you ruined his life."

"Enough from you, Spirit of Doubt!" Shouted the Lord of Red.

"Very well. Shall we?"

"Let's." Said the red wizard as he lifted his left hand and shot a ball of flame at the Spirit of Doubt, landing the first blow of the battle and sending the spirit back into the water.

Rudgaf quickly ran toward the water's edge and stabbed at the air with his sword just as the spirit was emerging. However, the spirit failed to be caught by surprise and quickly teleported a few feet to Rudgaf's left side. The Lord of Red turned to face his opponent, but the spirit had already thrown a dagger in the red wizard's direction, which Rudgaf was barely able to deflect with his sword, causing the dagger to fly harmlessly through the air and land with a plopping sound in the swamp water.

The Lord of Red charged at the spirit again, except this time the spirit split into two forms, stopping Rudgaf in his tracks. The split second delay in Rudgaf's attack allowed the spirit to strike the red wizard with a swift knee to the chin, toppling the wizard over onto the ground. The Spirit of Doubt then moved in closer to Rudgaf's body, ready to make the kill until, much to the surprise of the spirit, the red wizard quickly shot his head up and fired two flames from his eyes that burned the spirit's face, allowing the wizard to get back to his feet.

Doubt screeched and frantically patted away the flames that burned his face. It then used its robe to cover its shame.

Rudgaf, breathing heavily, paused his attack for a moment and said, "Is Doubt afraid of exposing its face?"

The spirit snarled and with one hand still covering its face it lunged toward the wizard. Rudgaf, in response, swung at the specter with his sword toward its busy hand, forcing the spirit to block with same said hand and expose its face to the world.

The face was Rudgaf's.

The wizard, startled, erred in his advance and swung wildly, missing the spirit completely when it disappeared and, cackling, reappeared a few paces closer and poked at the wizard with a dagger which, thankfully for Rudgaf, the wizard saw coming and was able to side step so that the blade merely grazed his side. The blow still cut flesh, but at least it didn't result in the Lord of Red's untimely death. Rudgaf, ignoring the pain, leapt back a few paces to distance himself from the spirit and make full use of the range of his sword.

The spirit spoke then and said, "What's wrong, red wizard? Afraid to stare yourself in the face?"

Meanwhile, the Lord of Yellow tended to Ramona's wounds. Joem, holding a ball of light, waved his hand over the elf's body from top to bottom.

"I hope this works…" He said, then added, "I've never tried this on the undead!"

The yellow wizard, when he was satisfied, rolled the elf's body over.

"This is going to hurt a lot, Ramona." He said, then removed the dagger from the elf's lung and watched her shoot up in pain.

The elf coughed up more blood in response and the wound streamed forth a crimson tide – the magnitude of which surprised the wizard.

Quickly holding the ball of light over the wound, Joem shouted, "Don't die on me, Ramona!"

Rudgaf's glare burned through Doubt, but Doubt continued to press his verbal attack, "Can't stand it, can you? Everyone has doubt, Lord of Flames, but out of all the members of your order, you, by far, have the most."

"That's why," the spirit added, laughing, "I get to toy with you so much."

The Lord of Red brushed the hair away from his face and said, "Make your next move, Spirit of Doubt. Whatever it may be, it will be your last."

The spirit raised an eyebrow, "Do you truly believe that?"

"It matters not," said Rudgaf, "if I don't believe that the Sun rises in the east and sets in the west, does that make it untrue? If I don't believe that the sky is blue, does that make it a falsehood? Facts are facts – you're going to die this day."

"Oh," said the spirit with a smile, "is all lost? Should I just step into the methane clouds that hang over the swamp and let you finish me off?"

"Won't you?"

The Spirit of Doubt scoffed, "You wouldn't have the nerve to finish me off anyway."

"Oh?" Asked Rudgaf, amused.

"Doubt is a part of you," explained the spirit, "if you kill me, you kill a piece of yourself."

"Maybe that would be for the best."

"Why don't you try it, then?"

The wizard waved the spirit in and said, "Your move."

The spirit frowned, then instantly disappeared. Rudgaf hefted his sword – he knew that he'd only have one chance to strike and that he'd better make it count. He was ready to execute his final stroke, however when the spirit reappeared it had split its form into six images and surrounded the wizard.

Rudgaf frantically looked around, trying to discern which spirit was the true spirit and which ones were false. Before he could really observe them, however, an image rushed him from behind and slashed at him, drawing more blood. The Lord of Red cried out in pain as the spirit chortled and another image struck, this time on Rudgaf's right thigh, which the wizard promptly held in pain.

It was evident that Doubt was torturing the Lord of Red.

Another image came flashing by, another cut was scored, this time on Rudgaf's face.

The Lord of Red knew that he had to act quickly. The wizard mustered his strength, hefted his sword, and swung it horizontally, creating an arc of fire that split through three of the false images, making them vanish in a puff of smoke. Rudgaf then turned his attention to the final three images. He heard the spirit laugh once more as all three illusions came rushing at him one by one. It was at this time that the Lord of Red simply didn't know what to do – he didn't have time to perform the maneuver that he'd just performed. He could let the spirit strike him and finish him off, which seemed like the most likely thing that was going to happen, or he could take a gamble and hope beyond all hope that he hit the correct one.

But, he thought, there was a third option. The red wizard felt the rush of displaced air as the third image came at him, went through him and dissolved. He closed his eyes and felt the wave of fear and tension leave him. A moment of clarity befell him and he suddenly saw the unseen. The Lord of Red smiled and waited.

Now!

Rudgaf, seemingly without cause, took his sword in one hand and stabbed at the air behind him.

He heard a groan and then, just a moment later, he heard the spirit slump to the ground.

The Lord of Red turned around and stared at Doubt, the sword wound right to the spirit's liver being quite evident. The spirit coughed and spat.

"You fool," said the spirit antagonistically, "you really think that this is over?"

"Maybe not," said Rudgaf, shrugging, "but your power over me is fading. You'll never be the same."

Doubt clutched its midsection and said, "I *hate* you."

Rudgaf sighed and said, "I know."

"I'll," muttered the spirit, "be back."

Doubt then drew his final breath and exploded in a burst of energy, leaving wisps of it behind, floating in the air and then dissipating. Not to any surprise of Rudgaf, the spirit left behind a crystalline object which the Lord of Red quickly picked up and then smashed on the ground, destroying it. Grasping at his side and his leg, he made his way over to Joem and Ramona as quickly as could be expected.

The Lord of Yellow shot the red wizard a look of concern and said with teary eyes, "I think we're going to lose her."

~

The Lord of Green took a step back in fear of the undead army that marched before him. Lines of dwarves – dwarf after dwarf, slain by his own hands, marched toward him, arms ready, prepared to take his life.

The green wizard shouted, "Wilfrey, do something!"

The Lord of Brown shot him a look of horror, "What do you expect me to do, command that the Earth swallow them whole with the castle and us along with them?"

Barlow spat and said, "Damn."

"Well," cracked the Lord of Black, "what do you plan on doing, now?"

Barlow remained silent, so the black wizard continued, "I had thought that the Lord of Green and the Lord of Brown were a little more powerful than this. Are you really giving up so soon?"

"Barlow," said the brown wizard, "isn't there anything you can do?"

The Lord of Green looked at Wilfrey, at the army that was advancing ever closer, then at the Lord of Brown again and said, "I don't know what to do."

The brown wizard shook his head and said, "Then we have lost. If only Rudgaf were here."

"Rudgaf!" Shouted Barlow, feeling a rage build up inside of him.

"Yes," said Wilfrey, "if only Rudgaf were here, he'd know what to do."

"Oh, would he?" Asked the Lord of Green through gritted teeth.

The Lord of Brown nodded, "He was a great leader."

At this, the Lord of Green exploded and said, "That bumbling idiot? A great leader? I'll show you how to lead!"

Wilfrey looked surprised and said, "Have I offended you somehow?"

Barlow ignored the question and continued, "You want to see power? I'll show you *power*!"

The Lord of Green promptly dropped his staff and stared down at the ground, grinding his jaw and clenching his fists.

"They always think that Rudgaf is better." He said to himself.

The army approached closer.

The Lord of Black laughed, "You truly are giving up, aren't you?"

"Shut the hell up." Said Barlow.

The army approached even closer.

"Maybe Wilfrey was right," said the Lord of Black, "maybe the both of you are nothing. Maybe it's Rudgaf I should be fighting right now."

Barlow's rage boiled over like an overfilled pot over too much heat. He felt a burning within his heart and realized that he recognized the feeling from somewhere before. That being the case, he knew what to do with it.

"Shut up!" Screamed the green wizard as he expectorated a stream of flames from his mouth that burned everything they touched asunder.

Row by row, dwarf by dwarf, they all fell – rather, turned to ash – at the might of the wizard's newly acquired weapon. Their own weapons melted under the intense heat of the flames into molten steel and iron. Wilfrey, himself, had to quickly jump out of the way, lest he be burned along with the rest.

When Barlow was finished, he stood up straight and looked at what his anger wrought. The Lord of Brown was in too much shock over the ordeal to say anything. Even the Lord of Black had a look of terror come across his visage.

The Lord of Green snarled and then fired the flames at the black wizard, who barely managed to get a magical ward up before the flames took him.

With great effort, the Lord of Black maintained the ward. Sweat dripped off of his brow at both the intensity of the effort that he had to put into the spell as well as the fact that some of the heat from the flames was seeping through. When Barlow saw that the black wizard had put up a ward, it simply served to enrage him further as he lurched his body forward and intensified the flames.

As Moldof felt his spell slipping, he shouted, "It's *not possible*!"

Wilfrey shouted words of encouragement as Barlow increased the magnitude of the heat even further.

The Lord of Black felt his spell cracking and protested, "But I am the most powerful wizard in existence!"

When he had finished uttering those words, the spell broke and the wizard made the hasty decision to use some of the dispelled energy from the failed spell to launch himself into the ground as opposed to be burned to ashes. The Lord of Black landed with a hard thud and found himself unable to move. Unfortunately for him, he had miscalculated the massive amount of effort that it took to keep the ward up against such a force for as long as he did and now he found himself helpless before the might of the Lord of Justice.

"You did it," shouted Wilfrey, "I can't believe it!"

Barlow grinned, "Believe it. I am the Lord of Justice – the greatest of all wizards!"

The Lord of Brown nodded, "I concede to that point wholeheartedly."

The Lord of Green snorted and walked up to the Lord of Black with an arrogant stride. When he got near to the black wizard, however, he not only saw the paralyzed face of the black wizard, the mastermind behind a thwarted, evil plot, but he also saw the face of a friend. A friend, in fact, that he'd known for a little over a half a century. At this, Barlow lost sense of what was happening and found himself unknowing of what to do, so he simply stared at the helpless being, the helpless friend that happened to also be the Lord of Power.

After a few moments, Wilfrey walked up to the Lord of Green, placed a hand on his shoulder and said, "What are you waiting for?"

Barlow turned his head away and said, "Let him alone. He's no threat to us."

"No," said the Lord of Brown, "you know what you have to do."

"I can't."

"You must!" The brown wizard insisted.

"You ask too much."

"Does justice ask too much, Barlow?"

The green wizard turned around and locked eyes with the Lord of Brown. Wilfrey smiled at him and said, "Will you fail your lady again?"

Barlow shook his head and said, "But he can't defend himself."

The brown wizard shrugged, "After all he's done, justice should begrudge him an honorable death."

The Lord of Brown unsheathed a dagger, placed it in the hand of the Lord of Green and said, "Do it."

Barlow stared at the blade in his hand for a moment, then back at the brown wizard and said, "But, he's a friend."

"He's a murderer!" Protested Wilfrey.

The Lord of Green swallowed bile, "This is too close to me. I can't do it."

"Don't you remember what you said on the day that you judged me?"

"No," protested the green wizard, "don't bring that up now."

"Why shouldn't I? Has it somehow become irrelevant?"

"Don't." Said Barlow, almost begging.

"Did you not say that justice visits the iniquities of the stranger and the neighbor, alike?"

"Wilfrey, stop it."

The brown wizard frowned and said, "It's easy to serve justice until she strikes your own home, correct?"

Barlow stared past Wilfrey's shoulder with vacancy for a moment, then turned back toward the Lord of Black.

"You're right," said the Lord of Green, raising the quivering hand that held death's dagger, "I must serve justice no matter what the cost."

Wilfrey smiled and said, "Good, Barlow. Good. You know what to do."

Barlow nodded and knelt over the helpless body of the king of the northern dwarves. Still holding the dagger in hand, he hesitated once more and said to no one in particular, "He's just lying there."

The green wizard swallowed hard and looked back at Wilfrey with eyes that nearly pleaded with the Lord of Brown to save him from having to do what he knew needed to be done. The Lord of Brown, however, simply nodded, forcing Barlow to turn his attention back to the Lord of Black.

The Lord of Green felt himself perspire, so he patted his brow with his cloak.

"No more delay, Barlow." Said Wilfrey, sternly.

"Right." Said Barlow as he hoisted the dagger in the air.

One more pause, just for a moment to look upon the face of his former friend for one last time, and then he sent the dagger sailing toward and through the king's chest, burying the blade and their friendship in one, violent stroke of malice.

The Lord of Black laid on the floor, lifeless. The moment froze in time in the eyes of the Lord of Green. Stillness and silence mixed together in a noxious brew too hard to intake and, then…laughter.

Laughter?

Barlow turned around to see his companion losing himself in a frenzy of hysterics. The Lord of Green, with half a mind to backhand his fellow wizard, asked, "What the hell are you laughing at?"

The Lord of Brown continued to laugh in same said manner, so Barlow protested further, "Wilfrey, stop it!"

The laughter continued to persist and the Lord of Green had quite enough at that point, so he motioned to stand in order to silence the maddening noise, but found himself unable to move.

"What's going on?" Barlow asked.

Finally, Wilfrey stopped laughing and said, "You've done a great job, law giver. Well done!"

Before the green wizard could inquire as to what the Lord of Brown was talking about, Wilfrey waved his hand through the air and disappeared along with the throne room, the castle, and the remnants of battle, leaving only Barlow and the deceased body of the Lord of Black. Just as suddenly as it all vanished, different scenery replaced it – a bed chamber, a large bed, a shocked audience at the nearby doorway.

Barlow looked around in confusion and said, "What's going on?"

A servant, aroused by the sounds coming from the bedroom, gasped in horror and screamed, "Murderer!"

The Lord of Green didn't react. It took a few moments for him to realize that she was even referring to him. He looked at the body, now dressed in sleeping garb and certainly without any signs of battle, save for the dagger that Barlow, himself, had left in his chest, then looked back at the servant, who was now joined by a few guards.

"But," Barlow protested, "he was the Lord of Black!"

"You treacherous filth!" Shouted one of the guards as he stepped in front of the crying servant, who ran away from the wretchedness of it all.

The other guard followed him into the room and said, "Why have you betrayed us?"

"You, you, you!" The Lord of Green protested, pointing at the guards in an accusatory fashion. "You betrayed me first!"

The first guard scoffed and said, "How have we done this?"

"You!" Shouted the green wizard. "You attacked me! You tried to kill me! You burned down my tower!"

"Your tower?" Asked the second guard. "You mean that one, there?"

The second guard pointed toward a nearby window. Following his finger, Barlow stared at the window, then jumped down, walked over to it and peered outside.

In the distance, beyond the vastness of the forest that he had made with his own hands, tucked away in several trees and beautiful gardens, stood his tower – intact, untouched, unblemished. The wizard blinked twice and slowly opened and closed his eyelids a few more times as if trying to unsee the truth staring back at him in a cold, undeterred manner.

"But," said the wizard, "I swear…"

The first guard said, "You've lost your mind, wizard."

The second guard chimed in, "Let's be done with it. Come with us, Barlow, and we'll make sure that you have a quick execution."

Barlow twirled around to face the guards and said, "Execution?!"

The first guard nodded and said, "For the assassination of the king."

"Assassination?" Asked the Lord of Green, pointing at the corpse in question. "You don't understand. I was in the throne room. Wilfrey was there with me."

The second guard shook his head and said, "The Lord of Brown is dead, wizard. He's been dead for hundreds of years! Are you daft?"

"No!" Screamed Barlow.

"Enough of this!" Shouted the first guard as he stepped closer. Barlow backed up a step and the guards placed their hands on the hilts of their swords.

The first guard spoke again and said, "Don't make this difficult, Barlow."

"Yeah," interjected the second guard, "don't you think that enough blood has been spilled here tonight?"

"Hear me out!" Protested the Lord of Green. "The king was the Lord of Black. He commanded an undead army and tried to kill me. I defeated him in fair combat."

The wizard shook his head fervently and continued, "I'm not an assassin!"

The guards looked at each other, then back at the wizard. The first one said, "And where did he get this undead army?"

"Hah," said Barlow, "I can answer that! He summoned them from the dead bodies of…"

The second guard spoke up, "The dead bodies of…?"

The green wizard gave the guards a blank look and said, "But, how did they die?"

The guards went to ask another question, but Barlow cut them off and shouted, "Oh, yeah! We routed them! Me and Wilfrey and the Behun Guard and…"

The first guard turned toward the second and asked, "What the hell is he prattling on about?"

The second guard merely shrugged in response as the wizard continued, "But, how did Wilfrey command the Behun Guard?"

The Lord of Green paused for a moment, giving the guards another blank stare, before exclaiming, "Oh, yeah! He was King Nolan! But, wait…how?"

The wizard shook his head violently and asked, "How was he the king?"

The first guard stepped forward with an outstretched hand and said, "Barlow, come on. You're just making this harder on yourself."

Barlow, now infuriated with unanswerable questions, began to furiously tear out the hairs from his beard.

"Stop him!" Said the second guard.

The first guard turned to face him and said, "What do you want me to do? He's nuts!"

Mired in his own grief, drowning in a sea of self-inflicted guilt, the Lord of Green tore his robes in twain and said, "What have I done?"

The first guard reached out for him again, but Barlow swatted his hand away and snapped at him, "Don't touch me!"

"Barlow," said the first guard, "don't make us kill you here. Let us give you, at least, an honorable death."

"Honorable?" Asked the wizard.

The first guard nodded.

The green wizard lost it at the word. 'Honorable', he thought. What a ridiculous notion. What was honor? He began to laugh uncontrollably at the mere mention of it. He went into hysterics at the very idea of it all.

The second guard said, "Come on, just cuff him and be done with it."

"Honorable?" Asked the wizard again.

The guards didn't deign to respond, so the wizard continued, "Honor hasn't graced me with his presence in some time, it would seem."

"Just come with us," said the first guard, "and we can change all of that."

"And what will you say of me after I'm gone?"

"We'll say…" started the first guard.

The second guard finished the sentence for him, "We'll say that Barlow gave his services to king and country with a purity of heart that was unequaled by any dwarf that ever lived. He was a good man and a faithful servant until an evil force overtook him."

The corner of Barlow's mouth twitched, "Until an evil force overtook him?"

The second guard nodded in response. The Lord of Green continued, "Do you really think me that weak?"

The first guard interceded, "Something had to take hold of you. Something had to drive you to do...this."

The Lord of Green raised an eyebrow, "Is that so? For I tell the both of you this – this thing that I have done, I have done of my own will and within my own power."

The second guard said, "Then what do you want us to do?"

The green wizard laughed again and said, "I want you to say that I am the murderer of kings. The destroyer of dynasties. I want you to place the blood on my hands where it rightfully belongs."

The first guard shook his head, "You were a hero to our people. Don't make us do that."

"A hero, was I?" Said Barlow with a smile. "From now on, I'm a hero unto myself. And you know what the one thing that I care about is, hmm?"

The guards shook their heads.

Barlow resumed speaking, "Power."

The green wizard laughed again and then, without warning, turned around and jumped out the window, leaving the shattered remnants of his former life behind him and letting the tree tops carry him away into the distance.

Come morning, Barlow was back in an old, familiar place, staring directly at the very tree that he had left a marking on during a time that seemed like centuries ago.

The green wizard snorted out loud, hefted his staff into the air and smacked the tree. A resounding thud echoed throughout the forest, disturbing birds and other wildlife as they fled away from the epicenter of the strike.

Suddenly, a figure with an open, brown robe and a short, thick, brown beard emerged from the tree with a look of glee on his face.

Without hesitation, the Lord of Green fell down to one knee before the Spirit of Want.

"Make me powerful." Said the wizard.

The spirit smiled and covered the wizard in his robes, smothering the piercing green of Barlow's garments.

A visible rot started to overtake the area.

~CHAPTER SEVEN – MASTERSTROKE~

I will not speak of what we found there. I will not tell you exactly what it was. I will not tell you how to access it. I will tell you that you lack the skill required to do it. I will tell you that you lack the willpower required to even get near to it. I will finally tell you that, after Mazuun was finished with it, our treasure changed form into something that was...incompatible with life. We had no choice but to let it be. You have no choice but to do the same.

With the power of the object that we had been seeking for so long, Mazuun became exceedingly strong.

I failed to stop him in time...

The lesser stones were already created.

A pale man dressed in a black, hooded robe narrowed his dark eyes as if sensitive to candlelight and stared at the golden haired elf sitting across from him.

The pale man frowned and said, "The plan is in motion."

Tatiana coolly flipped a dagger in the air, caught it and said, "Is that so?"

The man laughed dryly, "Is that so? Centuries of planning coming to fruition and that's all you can say?"

The elf gave a smarmy grin, "I've seen you fail too many times to express excitement."

"Not this time." The man protested.

"Oh? And just how far along are we?"

"The invasion is about to begin."

Tatiana leaned back and propped her feet up on the nearby table, "How do you expect to pull that off?"

The man tilted his head, "Whatever do you mean, love?"

Tatiana flipped a dagger again and said, "Three wizards. That's a lot to take on during a full scale invasion – even for you, Mazuumanesh."

Mazuumanesh brushed away the statement, "It's already been handled."

"Oh?" Asked Tatiana with a cruel smirk. "Has Barlow turned?"

The necromancer nodded and said, "Oh, yes. It couldn't have worked out better."

"Do tell."

The necromancer gave a throaty laugh, "He murdered Moldof right in his own bedchamber."

"Uh-huh," said Tatiana leaning forward with interest, "and then what?"

"He succumbed to the Spirit of Want."

"Huh." Replied the elf, leaning back into her chair.

Mazuumanesh shot her a look of inquiry, "Is there something wrong, love?"

The elf shrugged and played with the point of her dagger, "It's nothing."

She sighed then and continued, "I just didn't expect him to fall so easily."

"Oh, he was strong," said the necromancer, "but he was blinded with zeal to the point of idiocy."

"So it would seem." Replied Tatiana coolly.

The elf flipped her dagger a few more times and then threw it into the wall directly behind Mazuumanesh. The necromancer didn't flinch.

She played with her nails, then and said, "And what of the others?"

"The others?" Scoffed Mazuumanesh. "They were even easier to dispose of."

Tatiana stared at the necromancer with widened eyes, "You mean you've already taken care of them?"

"Of course."

"What happened?"

The necromancer grinned, "I'm not quite the failure that you think I am, love."

Tatiana waved off the comment, "Never mind that. Tell me what you did."

Mazuumanesh shrugged and said, "Rudgaf was sent to the south to investigate the siege on Behnon and promptly killed by the spirit…"

"Which one?" Interrupted Tatiana.

"Doubt."

The elf nodded her head and motioned for the necromancer to continue.

"And Thome, well, I didn't even have to do anything to him."

The elf looked surprised, "No?"

The necromancer laughed, "He was so mad, already, that he just went off on his own to die in the desert somewhere."

The elf continued to fiddle with her nails and after a moment's peace, the necromancer asked, "What of Danagan?"

Tatiana sprang up and said, "What of him?"

"You took care of him as I instructed, correct?"

"Of course," she replied, "Taarok should be on that right now."

The elf chuckled to herself and said, "If he can handle it, that is."

Mazuumanesh scoffed, "You know the wizard is no match for my creations."

Tatiana quit playing with her nails and turned her head away from the necromancer.

The necromancer sighed and said, "You're going to have to abandon these feelings you have for the Lord of Grey, love."

"What feelings?"

"Oh!" Exclaimed the necromancer.

The elf turned to face him again and said, "What?"

"I just thought of this," he said, "what if he, as in Danagan, ends up falling in love with Ramona?"

Tatiana turned away again, "Don't even joke about that."

The necromancer chortled, "She really is better than you, isn't she?"

The elf waved the dark one away, "Enough of your games."

"Have I touched a nerve?"

Tatiana shrugged, "Not really."

"No?"

The elf shook her head, stood up, grabbed her dagger from the wall, sat back down and began flipping it again before responding, "That 'doubt' garbage might work on a plebian like Ramona, but not me."

"Or...", the elf continued, "did you forget that we're not the same?"

"That thought hadn't escaped my mind."

"And what else?" Asked the elf. "Did it escape your mind that she's a product of your bungled necromancy?"

Mazuumanesh fell silent while Tatiana continued, "For you to even mention her is an affront to your supposed skill and simply shows that you're nothing but a walking mountain of ineptitude."

Mazuumanesh became crestfallen, but Tatiana quickly interjected and said, "There. How was that?"

The necromancer looked up with widened eyes and said, "Oh...yes. You pulled off 'doubt' very well."

The elf turned smarmy mouthed, "Why use all these spirits when you have me?"

"I don't know, love. I suppose it's because I don't want to busy you with such trivial matters."

The elf pouted, "But I'm bored."

"Not to worry," said Mazuumanesh assuringly, "once the plan is complete and I finally join with the Master, you'll have plenty of fun being the Queen of the World."

Tatiana seemed satisfied with the answer and nodded her head. After a moment, the necromancer spoke again, "Getting back to Ramona..."

"What of her?"

"Do you know what she's doing right now?"

The elf shrugged, "I haven't the faintest idea."

The necromancer laughed, "We only had one more loose end in all of this – the Lord of Yellow."

Tatiana flipped her dagger again, "Yeah? So what're you doing about him?"

Smiling, the necromancer said, "I told your counterpart that if she killed Joem for me, I'd let her know about her...well...your past."

"And she agreed?"

"Without hesitation."

The elf shook her head in mock sadness, "I forget how such meaningless drivel somehow manages to amount to something in the minds of certain...lesser beings."

"Still," said the necromancer, "you seem surprised that she agreed."

Tatiana turned in her seat and folded her hands over her midsection, "I'm just surprised that she didn't stall due to some sort of moral dilemma."

"Moral dilemma? She doesn't even know Joem."

"But I do."

Mazuumanesh shrugged, "Why should that matter?"

"You arrogant snoot," protested the elf, "you still fail to understand how this works."

"Please," said the necromancer, "explain it to me."

The elf sighed, "There's memories and there's soul links – things, people, places that you just intrinsically know. It won't be long before she remembers him. Sure, she won't remember anything in detail for lack of physical memories, but she'll know that she doesn't want to kill him."

"Besides," continued Tatiana, "you forget that the lesser ones often take issue killing, no matter the relationship that they have with the target."

"Well," said Mazuumanesh, "she failed to make protest."

"And that surprises me, is all."

The elf folded her arms and, after a moment or two, she said, "You know what she told me the last time I saw her?"

"What did she tell you?"

The elf chuckled, "This one's going to kill you."

Mazuumanesh leaned forward with interest and said, "Please, go on."

"She actually told me that she was going to 'save' me."

The necromancer tittered, "Save you? From what?"

The elf shrugged, "Myself, of course."

Mazuumanesh simpered, "I lack a term slanderous enough to accurately describe how much of a fool she is."

Tatiana began to laugh, but then stopped herself and thought for a moment.

The necromancer gave a look of concern, "What's wrong, love?"

"Hmm," said the elf, pondering, "probably nothing, but…"

"But what?"

"Well," explained Tatiana, brushing back her golden hair, "not long before then, she was inquiring about the central tower."

"Really?" Replied the necromancer in astonishment. "Whatever for?"

"How should I know?"

"Didn't you ask her?"

The elf gave a motion of dismissal, "I honestly didn't care enough to ask her, then."

Mazuumanesh felt his brow corrugate, "Perhaps you should have."

"Perhaps."

"In any case," said the necromancer, "what did you tell her?"

"I tried to wave her off," said Tatiana, "but she's as annoying as a gnat."

"What did you tell her?" The necromancer repeated.

"What's there to tell? I told her the same thing I'm telling you – it's evenly between the eastern and western mountains and that there's nothing there of great import – the wizard's made sure of that."

"I wonder," pondered the dark one, "how she even thought to ask you about it in the first place?"

"The soul links, probably."

"Probably."

"But, then," continued the elf, "shortly after she asked me about it, she came to me and started prattling on about how she was going to 'save' me and that she was convinced that I wasn't 'lost' yet."

Mazuumanesh shook his head, "She must have found something."

The elf shrugged, "Maybe. Who cares?"

The necromancer rubbed his chin for a moment, then suddenly got up and turned to leave. The elf looked up at him and said, "And just where are you going?"

"It's time." The necromancer replied.

"I see," said the elf with a smile, "are you going to contact Taarok?"

Mazuumanesh nodded and left the elf to her machinations.

The Lord of Red was not looking forward to hopping over the lily pads again. For one, he was carrying upon him an extra burden. For another, it had taken quite a lot out of him the first time and for yet another, he didn't know if he could remember the correct combination backwards.

"I should've written it down." He said to himself.

Joem ignored his comment and after a few moments Rudgaf said, "I *really* should've written it down."

Both wizards pressed on toward Barrier Lake with the red wizard mustering as much enthusiasm as he possibly could. He had a friend in immediate danger and his brothers…well, he didn't even want to think of what might have become of them. Still, as their destination loomed on in his mind, he grew more and more nervous – what good would it do, after all, to rush headlong to the rescue if Rudgaf simply blew the steps required to cross the lake and sent Joem, Ramona and himself all to their deaths? Rudgaf sighed at the thought of his upcoming test and listened to his footfall. The fall of his feet, he noted, sounded like the dropping of lead.

The red wizard gazed upon his elven companion who was now half-dead and, unable to move, found herself slung upon the wizard's shoulder.

"It's ok, Ramona," said Rudgaf, "I'll remember the combination and make sure you're taken care of."

"You don't have to know the correct combination for the lily pads." Explained the Lord of Yellow, finally breaking his silence.

The Lord of Red mopped his brow, "What are you talking about?"

"Don't you remember, Rudgaf?"

Rudgaf adjusted himself while his elven companion groaned, "Obviously not, but that shouldn't come as any surprise to you."

Joem folded his arms, "I guess not."

After a moment, the yellow wizard chuckled.

"What's so funny?" Asked Rudgaf.

"Well," explained Joem, "I know that it's not very funny in all actuality, but I just kind of find it to be...ironic that you somehow remembered Thome's ridiculous jumping combination, but you didn't remember the simple passphrase that can get us across the lake without the danger of drowning."

Rudgaf made a half-hearted attempt at a shrug, "I like to live dangerously."

Ramona groaned again, louder this time around.

"Is she ok?" Asked Joem.

Rudgaf sighed, "I hope so. It's imperative that we get her somewhere safe."

"Where are you thinking of taking her?"

"The north tower," explained the Lord of Red, "I know that she'll be safe there."

Joem scratched his head, "Are you certain?"

Rudgaf nodded, "Yes. I'll ask Barlow to look after her while we try to sort all of this out."

"I'm sure that he'll be most interested in hearing about our encounters with necromantic beings."

Rudgaf put a free hand through his beard, "I'm certain that he will."

"By the way..." Added Joem.

The Lord of Red raised an eyebrow, "Yes?"

"Ramona told me about a sniper that tried to do you in up north."

"What of him?"

"Was that him? I mean, the...thing that you just fought."

Rudgaf nodded, "Yes. That's how I was able to catch his arrow in that dwarven mining town. Did she tell you about that?"

"Yes." Said the Lord of Yellow, rubbing his chin. "It's all very interesting...and incredible, you know, the nature of these hallucinations."

"Right," said Rudgaf, "if you have a moment of time and can relax your mind enough to allow yourself to take a look inside your own thoughts, you can predict what will happen next in the hallucination. Fortunately enough for me, at that moment, I had enough time to obtain a state of clarity."

"How about when you were fighting the thing?"

The red wizard shook his head, "Not until the very end."

Joem smiled, "Thanks. I'm sorry to bother you with all of this, Rudgaf. I know that we need to press on in a hurry, but any bit of information about second stage phenomenon is incredibly helpful to me. After all, it's only a matter of time before I start experiencing it myself. I wouldn't want to jeopardize our mission by being unprepared."

"Unfortunately," explained Rudgaf, "when it comes to matters such as these, there is no such thing as sufficient preparation. However, I'll do my best to help you through it one step at a time when it happens."

A sudden squishing sound caused an immediate, yet brief halt to their conversation as Rudgaf realized that he had just stepped in a large pile of softened earth, muddying his boot. He looked down at his foot ware, disgusted with it all as if a fly had just landed in his soup, shook his foot in an attempt to clean his boot as best as he possibly could and then pressed on.

Joem turned his attention to the elf after the small disruption, shook his head and sighed, "I really did my best with her."

"At least you were able to stop the bleeding." Said Rudgaf.

The Lord of Yellow nodded, "That was some sort of…wicked blade the spirit was using."

The mention of the blade caused Rudgaf to manducate on his thought for a moment before speaking.

"What is it?" Asked Joem.

"I believe," said Rudgaf, "that the spirit somehow possesses an anti-magic weapon."

Joem's eyes widened, "That shouldn't be possible."

"None of this should be possible," said the red wizard, "but it would seem that the opposite is quite true. I'm starting to wonder if we should throw out the word entirely."

The Lord of Yellow's countenance fell in thought and after a few moments he said, "That's why I had so much trouble healing her…and you, for that matter."

"Speaking of which," added Joem, "how are you getting along?"

Rudgaf, with his free hand, felt along his side and winced in pain, "I've been better, Joem. But I'll be ok."

"You're lucky that he didn't pierce any vital organs."

"Luckier than Ramona." Said the Lord of Red, crestfallen.

"Hey," said Joem, reassuringly, "it'll be alright."

Rudgaf looked hopeful, "You think so?"

The Lord of Yellow nodded, "Yeah. She's really tough, Rudgaf. She'll pull through."

"I know her time isn't done," Joem added, "because ever since the first day that I met her I got a strange sense that there was something different about her…that she had some sort of special purpose."

Rudgaf looked upon his elven companion and smiled, "You're right. What I mean is, I got that feeling too."

"Rudgaf," said Joem with a concerned brow, "are you…?"

"It's beyond that. It's…deeper than that."

The yellow wizard smiled, "Alright, then. We'll have to put this conversation on hold for now."

"What do you mean?"

"We're at the lake." Replied Joem, stopping in his tracks.

It took a moment for the Lord of Red to process Joem's statement and he noticed that he nearly walked right into the large, murky body of water, being so entranced by the conversation and so worried about Ramona that he hadn't been paying any attention to his surroundings. He quickly negated his forward motion by taking a few steps backward instead. The Lord of Yellow stepped forward a few paces, then, until he was as near to the edge of the lake as could be without actually stepping in it himself. He raised his hands up in the air and said, "Try to remember this for the future, Rudgaf."

The Lord of Red nodded and with great effort concentrated on what Joem was about to say.

The yellow wizard took in a large breath of air and with a casual calm unbefitting of a spell that can disappear the entirety of the epic that comes naturally ensconced in such a large volume of water, uttered the words, "Bifahl, aquam abyssi."

Rudgaf looked upon his childlike companion, then upon the waters before him. They shimmered like steam over a hot pot of boiling water, distorting the land above, below and beyond. The Lord of Red turned his right ear forward, toward the lake, for he could've sworn that he heard a faint whistling sound in the distance. He then quickly was forced to turn back his inquisitive ear when a resounding crack flooded the airspace as nature bit back at having its laws broken in such a manner.

The lake was gone and in its place was safe, dry land that welcomed Rudgaf and his companions with open arms.

"Well," said Rudgaf with a sigh of relief, "that was rather useful."

Joem nodded, "Do you remember the passphrase?"

The Lord of Red thought a moment, then said, "Bifahl, aquam abyssi."

"Be gone, deep water." Interpreted the Lord of Yellow.

"Ancient human tongue," said Rudgaf with a grin, "before the days of the common language."

"Two different dialects mashed together, I might add." Said Joem, impressed with himself.

"Really? I was actually quite unaware of that. Might I ask which two?"

"Certainly," said Joem, "southwestern coastal and northeastern plain."

"Ancient tongue, two different and completely opposite dialects...that was quite clever of you to come up with."

"Us." Corrected the Lord of Yellow.

"Oh, right", said Rudgaf, scratching his head, "I forgot that I was there when we came up with it."

The yellow wizard laughed and bade Rudgaf take the lead, "After you."

"I press on with far more alacrity than I had a moment ago, I assure you."

"I should hope so," said Joem, "for a moment I was beginning to think that you were going to cement yourself to the ground."

Rudgaf scoffed, "Well, you didn't have to jump across the breadth of the lake, earlier."

"This is true."

Rudgaf gave a half smile and stared off in the distance with quaked eyes.

Joem spoke up, "You're worried about her, aren't you?"

"I don't have many friends in this world, Joem." Said the Lord of Red, still staring off into the distance.

"I know."

Rudgaf continued, "I have even less family."

"I know." Joem repeated.

"Ramona...she's like the sister I never had. Or maybe it's different than that."

The Lord of Yellow gave Rudgaf an inquisitive look, "Different?"

The red wizard swallowed, "Yeah, different. Like I said, my feelings for her are deeper than what you were originally thinking. It's not like with Danagan and Tatiana."

"That doesn't mean that it's different from what they had, Rudgaf."

The Lord of Red sighed, "I know, I know. I just don't know what I'm feeling right now. She makes me feel things that I haven't felt in a long time. Things that I thought I could never feel again."

"You sound very confused, old friend."

"I am," said Rudgaf, smiling, "but there's one thing that I'm not confused about – I don't want to lose her. We need to go – now."

"Like I said," said Joem, once again gesturing the wizard to move in front of him, "after you."

This time the red wizard moved forward without delay, doing as best as he could to walk with an elf that was considerably taller than himself slung over his right shoulder. The first few steps into the area where Barrier Lake was just a moment ago were ones that Rudgaf took very gingerly, as if the ground were a falsehood that baited him to step on it so that he could sink into the swamp water to his doom. However, when the soft, squishy ground held itself in check against his first, few footfalls, the Lord of Red simply nodded to himself and continued walking at his normal pace.

"The area where the lake sat seems much smaller when the land is exposed, don't you think?" Asked Rudgaf as he walked.

"Oh, very much so."

"I wonder how big it is, really?"

Joem shrugged, "I've never bothered to measure, but between the junglies outside both sides of the swamp and this lake, no one that King Duhan didn't want in his kingdom has made it in. So I suppose that means it's big enough."

Rudgaf shrugged, "Good thing I had an excuse to come in here."

Joem raised an eyebrow, "The sniper, you mean?"

The Lord of Red nodded, "Suffice it to say that the junglies at the border weren't incredibly elated that someone got passed them without even being noticed."

"Speaking of which," added Rudgaf, "I wonder how Danagan fared?"

Joem's face lit up like an instantaneously appearing full moon on a dark, starless night, "Danagan?!"

"Ah, I didn't tell you about that, did I?"

The Lord of Yellow shook his head, "Nope."

"When I was in Behnon," Rudgaf explained, "I encountered Danagan there. When we parted ways he told me that he was going to be headed south to speak with King Duhan about the trade embargo and follow up on a hunch of some grand conspiracy that we thought might have been underway."

Joem scratched his head, "What trade embargo?"

"So which one of you sons-a-bitches gets to die first?" Asked the Lord of Grey while clutching his wounded leg.

Tecza sniveled while Taarok gave a haughty laugh and said, "You talk big for a dead man."

"I hope you like the view from the ground," said the lizard to Danagan, "because you're going to be spending a lot of time there."

Danagan gritted his teeth and then spat on the ground, "So what's stopping ya?"

The orc sneered and approached the wizard, "You're right. I hate waiting."

The Lord of Grey readied a dagger in his right hand. Relaxing his mind and his body, he prepared himself to attempt a saving throw that he knew would only buy him a little more time to escape. He didn't know how, but the wizard realized that whatever he threw at the orc, even if fatal, would only temporarily stop his advance. The wizard, quaking from pain, turned his thoughts to his friends.

"What will Rudgaf think," he thought, "when I tell him about Taarok?"

The wizard chuckled to himself and thought, "Maybe we can discuss it over another bowl of dread eagle stew."

The more he thought, the more that he realized that his attempt at calm wasn't working. The wizard's mind started to turn to morbid thoughts, "I'm sorry that it's come down to this."

Taarok approached slowly with his axe hefted while Danagan's mind continued to speak to itself, "I'm sorry that I won't be able to help you guys out."

It was at that moment that Danagan heard himself think, "What kind of talk is that?"

The Lord of Grey smiled and said out loud, "Joem." Taarok ignored his comment and continued to approach, slowly, being well aware that, although severely injured, Danagan was a walking bag of tricks.

"Come on, Danagan," said Joem's voice to his mind, "you can pull yourself out of this!"

The grey wizard felt a tear form at the corner of his eye as he said, "That's what you would say, isn't it? You were always so positive. I miss you, little guy."

The orc stopped his approach within striking range of his axe, hefted it and said, "Any last words?"

"Yeah," said Danagan with a grin, "fuck you."

Taarok's face flushed red with anger at the comment and he roared mightily. The room seemed to shake from the force of the sound produced from the orc's mouth. Danagan couldn't help but wince, despite really not wanting to give the orc the satisfaction. The lizard had a much more violent reaction, however, as the sound forced him to let his bow fall to the ground as his hands became preoccupied with covering his ears. Even this wasn't enough for him, so he knelt down to the ground and cowered before the power of the mad one. When Taarok was finished, Tecza looked around the room like a frightened rodent then stood and straightened himself out in a vain attempt at saving face.

The orc barred his teeth at the wizard, hoisted his axe up into the air and swung in a downward arc with all of his strength. In an instant, the Lord of Grey lifted up his arm to throw a blade in the orc's direction. With the reflexes of a tiger, he started to flip the dagger, but to Taarok's surprise, the wizard suddenly performed a hard roll to his right and threw the dagger with as much accuracy as could be expected of a cross-body throw in motion in the direction of the lizard who, with widened eyes, felt the blade sink into his right kidney. A shrill scream echoed off the walls of the throne room as the lizard clutched at the blade embedded in his midsection and toppled over.

Taarok turned away from the wizard and observed Tecza who, still screeching in pain, had begun to squirm left and right as he bled upon the ground. The orc snorted and said, "Useless."

The mad one turned his attention back to Danagan, but to his dismay, the wizard had managed to vanish. A visible panic overcame the orc's features as he grunted, gripped his axe until his knuckles turned white and frantically looked around the room. First left, then right, then left and right, up and down, everywhere as if his head moved independently from the rest of his body.

"Where are you, coward?!" The orc screamed in frustration.

"Interesting." Said a voice from nowhere.

The orc continued his descent into madness as he stubbornly attempted to find the wizard. With extra grit in his voice he said, "Who said that?"

Taarok received nothing but silence.

In anger, the orc bellowed, "I know that was you, wizard! Where are you?"

Again, Taarok received nothing but silence.

In a fit, the orc threw down his axe, stomped his foot and yelled, "I'll crush you, wizard! You can't hide forever!"

This time, the voice spoke, "How is it that an immortal knows fear?"

Taarok opened his mouth to protest, but felt himself succumb to shock when he choked on his own words.

"What's the matter?" Asked the Lord of Grey. "You were so talkative just a moment ago and now you've clammed up. Did I hit a nerve?"

Tecza squealed into the air, "He's got to be around here somewhere, Taarok! He can only teleport as fast as that bum leg will take him."

The orc laughed, "Is that it, wizard? Is that your secret?"

"Believe what you will." Said the voice.

The mad one chortled and snorted, "That's it! You're probably wriggling around on the floor somewhere like fish bait."

"Why don't you come hook me, then?" Replied the voice.

Taarok grimaced, picked up his axe from the ground and then started to run about, swinging it low to the ground in order to attempt to catch the wizard and lob off some body parts. In his estimation, any body part would do.

The wizard began to laugh at the orc who pathetically attempted to do him in by insanely swinging his weapon at nothingness. After a few moments of observation and fun at the orc's expense, Danagan said, "What're you doing? Cutting grass?"

At that moment, Danagan knew that he was getting to the orc. Taarok, enraged, started to bite at the head of his axe and jump up and down in a furious fit like a caged baboon. His vexation started to become more than even the lizard could bear. In frustration, Tecza squawked at his partner, "Don't listen to him, Taarok! He's just trying to anger you so that you can't see straight!" The lizard, wracked with pain, then swallowed and grew silent for a time.

The mad one spat here and there and seemingly began to foam at the mouth. He howled his determination to kill. An incoherent sentence passed between his lips as he made a vain attempt at speaking which only resulted in him uttering gibberish. His eyes, glancing here and burning there, were both crimson red with irritation – the result of Taarok being so indignant that his mind couldn't possibly spare any resources to tell his eyelids to blink.

The voice spoke again, "You know, I think that you can die, 'mad one'."

The orc simply growled in response, so Danagan continued, "I think that there's a limit to your little resurrecting trick."

Taarok, in reply, swung his axe all about his person and returned to the whirling dervish that the Lord of Grey had first met up with. Although Taarok couldn't see it, the grey wizard grinned and said, "How about it, Taarok? Should I test those limits? What will we discover if I push the envelope a bit, hmm? Will you fail the test?"

The orc continued to tirelessly run about the room, cleaving the air with his axe in every direction. Danagan dispensed yet more antagonistic remarks, "What's wrong, Taarok? Feeling nervous? Scared? Are you feeling the rug being pulled out from under you?"

The Lord of Grey added, "Is this the legendary orc that placed fear into the hearts of the goblins? The same orc that was so bad that goblin warriors quake in fear at the very mention of his name? The same orc that was so evil that dwarven mothers used to threaten misbehaving children with wives tales about having to meet the end of his mighty blade in the nether as punishment for their transgressions? Tecza nearly wet his knickers at the mere thought of you. Is all of that fear and worry surrounding you all for nothing? Are you nothing more than a boogeyman – the monster underneath my bed?"

The orc quickly stopped his advance and thundered, "*Where are you?!*"

The wizard took a turn for the serious, "I'm going to make you pay for what you did to Tatiana."

Abruptly, Danagan quit his chatter and sprang upon his enemy like a night cat that blends in with covert backdrops until pouncing on its prey. The moment was incredibly important – for much as the predator must keep the prey unsuspecting and unaware, the wizard, too, had to keep Taarok from knowing exactly when and where he would strike. A rustle of the grass, a snap of a twig, the gentle turning of a pebble and it would be all over; the hunt – ruined. His blade, readied, would have to be quick and decisive. His victim, unwise to what waited for him, would have to remain unilluminated. But this is what Danagan was known for – it was how he had made a living even before receiving his power, before touching the lesser stone, before even knowing what magic was. Stealth was his area of expertise in a time when he was a hardened criminal – a past that saw him working with, not against, the very lizard that he immobilized just moments ago. He always found it ironic, did Danagan, that he would be the one chosen to be the Lord of Shadow. Unlike the others, who really didn't have any experience or alignment with the power that their stones represented, Danagan always felt as if, upon coming into contact with his lesser stone, he had become a part of the power, the shadows, as much as the same said power and shadows had become a part of him. While the others were in no doubt powerful and had become masters at wielding their gifts, the grey wizard lived through what he wielded and what he wielded lived through him.

As he struck a blow into the right lung of the orc, he was convinced that these very facts that flashed through his mind in the midst of his attempt to maintain his position on the proverbial food chain would consume the very soul of this apex predator.

Taarok, the mad one, lurched forward after being stuck in the back with a dagger. After hitting the ground and rolling over to face the wizard, he began to cough up blood. The Lord of Grey, who was wounded himself, limped forward as best as his injured leg would allow him.

Taarok gazed upon Danagan, smiled and spoke in between interruptions by expectorants, "You got me."

"You can only die twice."

The orc reluctantly nodded and said, "Yes."

"I figured, by the way you were acting."

The orc coughed, "You're very perceptive for a filthy human."

Danagan ignored the comment and continued along his line of questioning, "But why can you only die twice?"

"A limitation of my master's powers, I'm afraid."

"Who is your master?"

"A dark and powerful necromancer."

"Who? What is his name?"

The orc smirked, "I'm not an idiot."

Danagan shrugged, "You're going to die anyway."

"That fact is true, but another fact remains."

"And what's that?"

Taarok shifted uncomfortably, "I hate your kind. I hate humans, elves, dwarves, goblins and anyone who works with them."

"Pfft," protested the Lord of Grey, "I just saw you working with an elf."

"Oh, him?" Asked Taarok, laughing. "He's just a pawn for my master."

"Ok, another question."

"Go ahead, but you better make it fast." Said the orc, coughing. "I'm dying and what not."

"Where did your master get this power?"

The orc scoffed, "What a moronic question."

Danagan felt the corner of his mouth twitch, "Why is it moronic?"

"You already know that there's only one person that can wield the power of necromancy."

The Lord of Grey's eyes widened, "And how do you know that?"

"The master lets Taarok know of many things." Said the orc, proudly.

"Why do you refer to yourself in the third person?"

"Sorry," explained the orc, "as Tar...as my life goes, so, too, does my speechcraft."

Danagan sighed, "Did your master tell you that the only person that can wield the power of necromancy is dead and that the only way of obtaining his power is lost?"

Taarok replied, "Kro nach bif wahal."

The grey wizard raised an eyebrow, "What does that mean?"

"Not familiar with the language of my people, are you?"

"I'm afraid not."

"Typical for such a self-centered race."

Danagan crossed his arms, "I'm willing to learn a bit now."

"In the common tongue it most easily translates to, 'Your ignorance is painful'."

"I don't understand what you mean."

"What Taarok means is this – the one who wielded the power of necromancy in ages past did not get his power from where you think he got it."

"Where did he get it from, then, if not the black, lesser stone?"

The orc snorted, "Didn't Danagan ever read the words of Zaan?"

The wizard was stunned by the revelation given to him by such an unlikely source. Was the orc telling the truth? Was his master truly privy to this knowledge? If so, then how did he find out? Danagan, himself, saw to the covering up of such sensitive information on the day that both him and Joem decided to leave the central tower and embark on their own quests. How was it that anyone, let alone Taarok's master, found out about this?

After a moment, the wizard replied, "I've read the words of Zaan, but I clearly misinterpreted them. I had thought that the thing that both he and Mazuun had sought was the black, lesser stone."

"No, no, no." Protested the orc. "Danagan is wrong. The Master, that is, my master's master made all of the lesser stones, even the black one."

Danagan grew silent while the orc continued, "The Master, that is, my master's master found the black, greater stone."

The wizard worked his jaw, "How is it that you know so much that I don't?"

Taarok coughed and spewed up more life onto the floor. He was starting to look pale as he said, "Danagan...Danagan doesn't listen. But master...master is wise. He knows much. He tells Taarok many things. Zaan tried to tell Danagan, but Danagan does not listen. No wizard listens."

"Answer me this, then," said Danagan, now more inquisitive than ever, "Zaan said that the object they sought turned into something else. What did it turn into?"

The orc squirmed, "Taarok knows not. But Taarok's master told Taarok that not even his master could wield it. It nearly killed the Master, that is, Taarok's master's master."

Taarok continued, "Tar...I hate the way I am sounding. Please finish your questioning and let me die."

"I have just one more."

"Taarok will answer."

"Mazuun gave your master some of his necromantic ability. However, Mazuun has been dead for hundreds of years. How was he able to pull it off and why did he even bother?"

The orc laughed, however painfully, "Danagan treats death as such a...tinikh thing."

"Tinikh?"

"Sorry," said the orc, "in the common tongue that means, 'finite'."

Danagan smirked, "From my experience, death has always been pretty finite. I mean, if I killed someone, they weren't out having drinks with a mistress the next night."

"Ho, ho, ho." Laughed the orc. "Perception lies to Danagan."

"Oh, does it now?"

"Danagan is stupid. Death is not the end. Look at Taarok. Is Taarok not enough proof?"

The wizard shrugged, "I guess you have a point."

"No," said the orc, "there are two...two pieces. There is Taarok and then no Taarok. When Taarok body dies, Taarok and no Taarok go different ways."

Danagan scratched his head, "What are you going on about?"

Taarok sighed and pointed to his head, "This...this is Taarok."

The wizard nodded in understanding, "Your mind, your thoughts, your consciousness. Right?"

The orc smiled, "Maybe Danagan not so dumb."

The Lord of Grey ignored the jab and said, "Then what is no Taarok?"

"The thing that make Taarok body breathe. It make Taarok body run and eat and sleep and fight. When Taarok body die, Taarok and no Taarok go different ways and Taarok body no longer breathe and run and eat and sleep and fight, but Taarok and no Taarok still go on. Taarok run and eat and sleep and fight somewhere else, but not here. No Taarok waits."

The wizard rubbed his chin, "Waits for what?"

"To make baby body breathe and run and eat and sleep and fight. It become no baby until baby and no baby go different ways."

Danagan muddled on his thoughts for a moment, then said, "I get it. The soul and the consciousness are two separate things. The consciousness goes somewhere and continues to live on while the soul goes somewhere else and waits to be reused."

"Danagan right!" The orc exclaimed. "But no Taarok keep chains with Taarok so if Taarok and no Taarok meet again, Taarok body remember time when Taarok body breathe, run, eat, sleep and fight. Taarok body remember old life in new life."

"And your master has the power to do this? That is, he has the power to make Taarok and no Taarok meet again?"

Taarok gave a half nod, "Taarok's master can do what Danagan say, but Taarok's master not very good at it. The Master was much better. Taarok's master can only do it sometimes."

"Why is that? Is your master incompetent?"

The orc furiously shook his head, "No, it just hard! The Master is where Taarok was and ought to still be. The Master can only give Taarok's master little power. Taarok's master needs the little, black rock to make better."

"And why would Mazuun bother helping out your master?"

"Idiot Danagan!" The orc yelled. "The Master want new body here! When Taarok's master gets little, black rock, Taarok's master will have power to make Master and no Master meet again."

"And what's in it for your master?"

"Taarok's master becomes new body for the Master."

"And why wouldn't your master just take the black, lesser stone and run off with it? Why help Mazuun when he'd already be the most powerful wizard in the world?"

"No, no, no," protested Taarok, "shadow man wrong again!"

Danagan girded himself up, "How am I wrong? Black represents power. I was there on the day that we had to wrestle that stone from its inheritor. I've seen its power first hand."

"Danagan quiet. Taarok use some of last words to explain."

The Lord of Grey bit his lower lip and said, "Fine, go on."

Taarok coughed, "Taarok's mouth dry."

The Lord of Grey couldn't help but feel pity toward the orc and the state that he had been left in. Despite his hatred for Taarok and his knowledge of all of the foul deeds that the orc had committed in this life and the former, Danagan still respected the orc for being a great warrior. It is sometimes difficult, Danagan decided, to see the mighty fall – no matter who the mighty may be.

"Hold on." Said the grey wizard as he reached into his cloak and pulled out a flask. He promptly tossed it at the orc who didn't bother attempting to catch it and just simply let it bounce off his chest before grabbing it, popping the top and drinking from it.

"I'm sorry that it's not water." Said the wizard.

The orc laughed, "Taarok not mind. Humans make strong drink."

"Yes," said Danagan, "we make it with potatoes."

"What potato?"

The wizard smiled, "Something you like, apparently."

The mad one took another swig of the liquid and said, "Taarok feel like hypocrite for drinking human wine, but Taarok be dead soon anyway."

The orc put the stopper back into the flask and let it fall to his side before speaking further, "The Master go crazy when he get power, but the Master not koikmel."

"What does koikmel mean?"

"Koikmel mean clean...err...more clean than clean."

"Pure?"

The orc nodded, "Yes. The Master not pure, so the Master go crazy."

Taarok paused to laugh and then said, "Danagan go crazy, too."

The grey wizard sneered and said, "Just go on."

The orc swallowed then said, "The Master different now. The Master pure...lucbelra."

"Pure of heart?"

"The Master now is, but that not what word mean. Lucbelra mean...he always do bad thing."

"He's evil? He's pure evil?"

"Koikmel lucbelra!" Exclaimed the orc. "But Taarok's master is not Koikmel lucbelra. Taarok's master is not Koikmel."

The wizard nodded slowly, "So he'd get the 'madness'."

"Is that what Danagan calls it? Taarok calls it fun."

Danagan ignored the orc's obviously uninsightful comment and said, "So the plan is for your master to get the black, lesser stone which contains enough power within it to bring Mazuun back from the dead who will then use your master's body to fully take the power from the black, lesser stone and become the Lord of Black once more."

"Danagan understands."

The orc relaxed his head, exhaled loudly and closed his eyes, "Taarok good teacher. Maybe Taarok be teacher and not warrior next time."

The wizard limped closer to the orc and then sat down next to him and said, "So now what?"

The orc coughed and said, "Taarok no more answer question."

"What should I do?"

Taarok opened his eyes and gazed upon the wizard, "Why ask Taarok this?"

Danagan shrugged, "Do you see anyone else around?"

The orc laughed, "Danagan is a funny human."

"So, how about my question? What happens now?"

"Danagan not stupid. Danagan know that Danagan live on and Taarok die."

The orc coughed up yet more blood. For some reason unknown to the wizard, he felt as if he should help the orc or at least attempt to comfort him during his final moments. He knew, however, that this would only serve to insult Taarok and dishonor him, so he fought back at his feelings.

"What should I do, Taarok? I've been lost for so long. For hundreds of years I've wandered around, attempting to help a people that didn't even want me around. I walk aimlessly in life. Sometimes, I don't talk to anyone for weeks. Sometimes it's even longer than that. Sometimes I go so long without uttering a word that I fear I'll forget how to do it."

"Danagan sounds lonely."

The wizard nodded, "I have been since I lost her."

"The elf with the golden hair." Said the orc, nearly whispering out of respect.

"I know that you were fighting for your people," said the wizard, "but why did you have to be such a bastard about it?"

Taarok looked away, "Taarok does what Taarok needs to do."

Danagan's face flushed with anger and with great control he reserved any disparaging remarks, but did say, "What does forcing elven women to sleep with you have to do with defeating the goblins? Where is the honor in that? What sense of pride can you really extract from that?"

Taarok looked back at the wizard and said, "What does Danagan talk about?"

"You know," said the Lord of Grey, "you conquered some town that the eastern elves were helping the goblins defend and, as per your custom, you selected a number of female elves to accompany you to bed. Tatiana, pregnant, with *my* child…"

The Lord of Grey felt himself start to become angry again, so he stopped talking for a moment, collected his thoughts and continued, "Pregnant with my child, killed herself rather than be your plaything for the rest of her life."

The orc stared at Danagan hard and said, "Taarok never did that."

"Oh, come on," protested Danagan while throwing his arms up into the air, "you said it yourself – 'elves are only good for a fuck', remember?"

"Taarok just wanted to make Danagan mad. Taarok knows that Danagan has elf for a wife. Taarok hates elves."

"I can't believe that's the only reason why you said that. I believe that you have experience with the subject."

With severe lack of comfort, the orc hoisted himself up a bit and with his remaining strength he reached out, snatched Danagan's robe, pulled him in and glared at him.

"Danagan…no…"

The orc scrunched up his face and grimaced as he attempted to focus on what he was saying, "You listen to Tar…to me. I have never touched an elf in that way. The thought repulses me. Taarok…I mean, some of my fellow warriors did, though. I wasn't allowed to do anything about it. Taarok only follows orders."

The orc slumped back down into his prior position and stared at the ceiling, "Taarok does what Taarok needs to do."

Now it was Danagan's turn to glare, "Are you calling Tatiana a liar?"

"Tatiana," whispered Taarok, "is with my master now. My master is Danagan's enemy. Danagan should not trust Tatiana."

"No," bit back the wizard, "Tatiana would never make a cohort of someone like your master. I know her better than to believe something like that."

"Danagan, do you not listen to Taarok?"

"Frankly, I don't know if I should."

"Taarok tell truth. Taarok also say that Taarok's master not very good at necromancy. When Taarok's master brought Tatiana and no Tatiana back together, Taarok's master goofed."

The wizard gave a skeptical look, "He goofed?"

"What Taarok says is what happened. Tatiana not the same. Tatiana no longer one elf – Tatiana is two elves now."

Danagan inhaled sharply, "What do you mean, 'two elves'?"

The orc continued, "Both have not Tatiana. But one has most Tatiana and the other has little bit."

"The soul and the consciousness were split by accident?"

Taarok nodded, "It was Taarok's master's first try. Taarok's master not very good, like Taarok say."

Danagan put his head in his hands and wondered what to think. A few moments ago, he was calling the orc his worst enemy. 'What happened?', he thought. He pondered on how it was possible for two fighters to go from slinging blades at each other to suddenly confiding personal feelings and dark secrets with one another. Should he believe the orc? Did he want to? He tried to blow off what Taarok was telling him as either lies or nonsense, but he couldn't shake the feeling that his one-time enemy was right and not just about Tatiana, but about everything else, even hidden knowledge that Danagan, himself, hadn't known. The wizard knew that the orc couldn't be making this stuff up. He simply had to have some sort of insight into the inner workings of not only necromancy but his master's plans. But what did that mean? Had Tatiana betrayed him? For what reason? Was she simply trying to set him up? Was she convinced that Taarok would be able to do him in? Or maybe she was doing the bidding of someone else who was convinced of it. Danagan didn't know and couldn't care – the thought of being betrayed by Tatiana, his deceased wife who, until recently, he had thought he had lost forever, was too painful for him to think upon.

The wizard lifted his head and asked, "What should I do now, Taarok?"

A peaceful look came upon the orc's features. He closed his eyes and said, "Live."

The orc's life ceased then.

Danagan smiled upon the orc and said, "Fos furta, gais mora."

"That means," continued the wizard, "in the ancient tongue of my people, 'Rest easy, great warrior.'."

The wizard sat up slowly and painfully. Dusting himself off, he made a heading for the doorway until he heard a squeaking sound coming from behind him. He turned around to face the source of the sound and noticed that the lizard, Tecza, was reaching out to him in an attempt to garner his attention.

"Help me, please." Said the lizard.

Danagan scoffed at the notion and turned about to head for the double doors again.

"Please." Begged Tecza.

The Lord of Grey stopped, turned around and said, "Why should I help such scum?"

The lizard crawled closer to Danagan and said, "You're right, I am scum. I'm no leader at all, am I?"

The grey wizard turned his head away and said, "Come on, Tecza. Don't do this."

"No," protested the lizard, "it's true. I lied when I said that I've led the guild to prosperity. I couldn't fill your boots, Danagan. The guild fell apart – it doesn't even exist anymore."

"I don't care about the guild anymore, Tecza. That's why I left."

"I know, but listen. I've been a follower all my life. Someone says, 'go do that', and I do it. Another person says, 'go do this', and I do it. I was tired of the abuse. I wanted to be my own boss, but I failed. The humiliation was too much for me to deal with."

"So you allied yourself with Taarok's master? What did he promise you? Probably a large sum of coin, no doubt."

"No, much more than gold, old friend." Explained the lizard. "He promised me the power to be a great leader."

Danagan lifted his brow, "I can see that worked out well for you."

The lizard spat, "I know, he lied to me. He tricked me and used me just so Taarok could take a shot at you. I was a fool. I'm nothing but a weak, pathetic fool."

The wizard sighed and pondered for a moment. He didn't know if the lizard had finally come to his senses and was being sincere about all of this or not, but, at the very least, Danagan knew that he couldn't pass up an opportunity at squeezing some information out of him. Taarok had been loyal and not given up the name of his master, but he had a strong hunch that Tecza wouldn't be as morally opposed to the idea. After a moment, the wizard finally said, "I don't know why I'm saying this, but, if you're really sincere about all of this, how about turning over a new leaf and helping me do some good?"

Tecza's eyes widened, "Really? Do you really mean it Danagan?"

"It'll be just like the old days."

The lizard sniffed, nearly coming to tears, "Oh, Danagan! You're so merciful! What did I ever do to deserve a friend like you?"

Before the Lord of Grey could answer, he heard the sound of clanking metal come from Taarok's direction. He quickly readied a dagger to fight and when he turned to face Taarok, he noticed that the orc was hanging limp in the air.

"What the hell is going on, Tecza?"

The lizard gulped, "I...I'm not sure!"

"This is the work of your master, I'm sure."

The lizard gulped again, "I wouldn't doubt it."

As abruptly as it rose, the body sailed across the throne room, through the double doors and off into the distance, fading into the light of the setting Sun. Danagan and Tecza both watched helplessly until their vision no longer afforded them the opportunity to see the target of their attention.

Danagan turned toward the lizard in anger, "Your master is robbing Taarok of a warrior's death. A great fighter like him doesn't deserve to be treated like a pawn in some sort of twisted mockery of an afterlife – no matter what he did or didn't do."

Tecza nervously nodded his head, "I agree, Danagan! I agree!"

"Taarok refused to give me your master's name. If you want to prove yourself to me, you'll tell it to me now."

Without even the remotest hint of hesitation, the lizard said, "Mazuumanesh."

"I should've figured."

The Lord of Grey spat on the ground next to him and asked, "Do you know what Mazuumanesh means in the ancient tongue of my people?"

Tecza shook his head, "No, Danagan. I'm afraid I don't."

"It's so obviously ridiculous that I thought you had just made it up or heard it from someone with a small bit of insider knowledge and a large bit of jocularity."

The lizard, weak from the loss of blood, still managed to seem interested and said, "What does the name mean?"

"It means, 'Son of Mazuun'."

"Clever." Said the lizard, turning over and groaning in pain.

With some hesitation, Danagan said, "I could...possibly take care of that wound for you."

With surprise, Tecza turned his body back to face the wizard and said, "You could? Where did you learn to do that?"

The wizard shrugged, "A friend taught me. He's much better at it than I am, but I can at least stop you from bleeding out."

Tecza smiled, exposing his cuspidated teeth, "I would be most appreciative."

Danagan began to limp toward the lizard until the lizard said, "Maybe you ought to do it on yourself first. You might be a bit more...focused then."

"What're you afraid I'll bungle it?"

Tecza licked an eyeball, "Incredibly."

The wizard scoffed, "I'm not going to bungle it and besides, I can't do it on myself."

"Why not?"

"It just doesn't work like that."

"Why not?"

Danagan worked his jaw, "Do you want healing or not?"

The lizard swallowed and reluctantly agreed.

The Lord of Grey continued to limp forward, but after a few steps he stopped and said, "Wait a minute."

The lizard looked dismayed, "What is it?"

"Why should I heal you, anyway?"

"Because I've promised my services to you." Bleated the lizard.

"And your word is as good as gold, right?"

"Come on, Danagan," said the lizard, "I'm dying, here. If you don't hurry up, you'll never know if I was telling the truth or not."

The grey wizard rubbed his chin, "I want more information first."

Tecza screeched, "Come on! I gave you the name you wanted!"

"Yeah, but I want to know where Mazuumanesh is taking Taarok."

The lizard groaned again and said, "Back to his hideout to prepare him for the invasion, probably."

Danagan held a hand up and said, "Wait a minute, what invasion?"

The lizard grunted, "Telling you this could get me killed, you know."

"You're going to die without my help, anyway."

"I'm well aware of that, wizard." Hissed Tecza.

"You were saying?"

"Mazuumanesh plans to use Taarok and a band of orcs to invade the northern dwarven territories."

The Lord of Grey laughed, "A bit outclassed for that, isn't he?"

"You forget," said the lizard, "King Nolan is going to be helping him. Meaning he has the entirety of the eastern elven army behind him and, to make matters worse, they've contracted dread eagles and death hawks."

The wizard seemed shocked at first, but then everything started to make sense to him. Mazuumanesh's ultimate goal combined with King Nolan's ambition, the sudden bounty on King Colibrim's head which would ultimately be chalked up to the elves miraculously gaining intelligence that the goblins were up to something with enough time to react to it, but not enough time to ultimately save Behnon, the reactionary trade embargo that King Nolan absolutely knew King Duhan would enforce, sparking the need for expansion, the actual siege on Behnon…everything. It was all orchestrated to send his people into a frenzied support for his expansion to the North Country. Danagan knew, then, that it wouldn't stop with the dwarven territories. Why else would Taarok be involved? No, Taarok was involved simply as a measure of revenge against the goblins. The elves would support the attack on the goblins because of their supposed involvement with Behnon. They would also support the attack on the dwarves because they've been allies with the goblins for centuries and also because of Rudgaf's report of dread eagles in the area.

The Lord of Grey felt his jaw drop, "The bastards. The clever, clever bastards."

"What is it, Danagan?" Asked Tecza.

Danagan frowned, "I need to stop the invasion as quickly as possible. Where is Mazuumanesh's hideout located?"

"Nuh-uh," protested Tecza, "not before you heal my wounds."

The Lord of Grey clenched his fists, "I don't have time to barter with you, you green-blooded son of a snake."

"Well how am I supposed to know that you're not just going to run off and leave me here to die right after I tell you?"

"You'll just have to trust me."

"No," said the lizard, "I've given you enough information. What I've shared with you can get me killed ten times over so I think that the least you can do is heed my request and free me from this pain before I divulge anymore. A true partnership is give and take, you know."

The wizard sighed. He didn't like it, but he knew Tecza had a point. He also knew that even Tecza couldn't be stupid enough to sell his master down the river and not seek the wizard's protection afterwards – especially since the master in question was a necromancer and death wouldn't exactly save the lizard from his wrath. In any case, he was still feeling guilty for how he beat the snot out of the poor creature during their last encounter. Sure, Tecza got in a sneak attack as a matter of revenge, but he could hardly blame the lizard for being upset with him. So, with that, Danagan slowly sauntered across the room to where Tecza was laying and gently knelt down next to him.

Placing his hands on the lizard's body, he said, "Hold still. This will only take a moment."

Tecza let his mouth go agape as the healing calm washed over him and he dropped much like a droplet of water does into a sea of peace. He immediately felt stronger. A twinge of discomfort came over him as he felt the wizard remove the dagger from his right kidney, but it only lasted a moment before it was gone along with most of the pain that he was feeling before the healing process had begun.

Danagan finished and removed his hands. Tecza looked down at his side – it was still a bit red and sore, but it was a lot better. It was nowhere near completely healed, just as

Danagan had warned, but the lizard definitely felt like he could walk out of the place and live.

"Thank you." Said Tecza as he carefully stood up.

"Feeling better?" Asked Danagan.

The lizard adjusted his clothes and felt his limbs in near disbelief that he was actually standing again, "Remarkably so."

"Just make sure to take it easy for a while."

"Yeah." Agreed the lizard.

"So, about that hideout."

Tecza stared down at the Lord of Grey and said, "Yes, the hideout. You held up your end of the partnership, so now it's time for me to hold up mine."

Danagan smiled, "I'm glad you see it that w…"

To the surprise of the grey wizard, he had apparently underestimated Tecza's supposed stupidity. Danagan's sentence was abruptly put to a halt when the lizard quickly whipped his body around and smacked him in the face with a stiff tail. The wizard's head immediately went sailing to the ground and cracked off of the marble floor. All that Danagan was able to see was a quick flash of light which disappeared and snapped into darkest darkness.

"You'll never learn, will you?" Sniggered the lizard.

Even though the Lord of Grey was lying on the floor unconscious thanks to the treachery of the lizard, Tecza was no fool and made no qualms about making a hasty retreat out of the throne room. Without sparing a moment, he forced his feet to beat marble as quickly as they could in order to put as much distance between Danagan and himself before the wizard woke up from his day nap – most likely in a foul mood.

Two wizards, knee deep in mud, stared at each other as time had stopped functioning around them. One simply had an inquisitive look about him – the innocence of a child, forever captured in the spectator's mind, wondering, questioning what his friend might be thinking. The other – overcome with disbelief, doubting the former, questioning everything, searching for the truth with great difficulty as if it were a shiny bauble dropped and then forever lost in murky waters deep.

Rudgaf attempted to swallow, but felt his mouth turn dry. His heart raced. His stomach churned. Bile shot up and down his midsection. He knew what was happening and what was still to happen, but he also knew that he had to ask anyway. Straining his senses, his hands barely able to grasp the reigns of his fear, he asked Joem, "What do you mean, 'what trade embargo'?"

The yellow wizard smiled and stepped closer, "Rudgaf, what's wrong?"

The Lord of Red matched Joem's step forward with a step backwards. The Lord of Yellow's eyes widened. Softly, he said, "Rudgaf, are you ok? Are you experiencing second stage phenomenon?"

Rudgaf took another step backwards and said, "You're damn right I am."

Joem reached out a hand to the red wizard and said, "Don't be afraid, Rudgaf. I can help you."

The Lord of Red swiped his hand through the air and shouted, "I don't want your help!"

A look of grief came over the features of the yellow wizard as he said, "Don't you see what's happening, Rudgaf? The hallucination is trying to tear us apart!"

"No," said Rudgaf in a stern tone, "We've already been torn apart."

Joem took another step closer and said, "What do you mean by that? You're really starting to scare me."

"How could you not know about the trade embargo?"

Joem hesitated, "I don't know. I must not have heard about it."

"Explain to me," attacked Rudgaf, "how the elder, the leader of a jungle elf village doesn't hear about an unprecedented event involving the very people that he's supposed to be leading."

The yellow wizard furrowed his brow, "I really don't know, Rudgaf. Maybe I just forgot about it."

"You mean *I* forgot about it."

Joem tilted his head, "Your logic bends me."

Rudgaf snarled at the fellow wizard and this time it was Joem that backpedaled. The Lord of Red, while observing his surroundings as if looking for inconsistencies, said, "Somehow, somewhere deep in my memory, I forgot. But I remembered."

The red wizard stopped glancing around and shot arrows at Joem from his eyes, "But I wasn't supposed to remember, right Joem?"

In fear, the Lord of Yellow took another step backwards. The red wizard clenched his fist and determinedly stepped toward Joem in a hostile fashion. The yellow wizard quivered and said, "Rudgaf, please. I'm your friend. I love you, Rudgaf. Don't let it do this to you."

Rudgaf ignored the pleading of his companion and said, "You were right earlier, Joem. It is kind of ironic how I remembered a long, jumping pattern but couldn't remember a simple passphrase that I helped invent in the first place."

Joem remained silent, so Rudgaf continued, "So I asked myself this – why would Thome create such a passphrase to begin with when the existence of such a simple manner of crossing a purposefully placed protective barrier would, no doubt, defeat the purpose of the creation of said barrier in the first place?"

The Lord of Yellow shook his head, "You're not making any sense, Rudgaf. Of course we'd make the passphrase – who could remember such a ridiculous pattern?"

"That was the point, damn it!" Screamed Rudgaf.

The yellow wizard stepped back in fear again, but this time he tripped over a large stick which sent him tumbling to the ground where he landed on his bottom, dirtying his robes.

The Lord of Red spread his arms out and said, "All of this that surrounds us is nothing but a product of my mind, isn't it?"

"No!" Shouted Joem. "You're wrong! This is real, Rudgaf! We have to save the others!"

"Save the others?" Asked the red wizard. "If that's the case, then where is Ramona?"

Joem studdered, "W-what?"

The red wizard looked around and said, "Do you see her anywhere? A moment ago she was flung over my shoulder. Now she's gone. Should I just chalk that up to a miracle?"

Rudgaf stomped forward and continued, "Or should I just kill you now?"

Joem raised his hands and used them to hide his face. Whimpering, he said, "No, Rudgaf! Please don't make me fight you!"

"It was so convenient, wasn't it?"

"I don't know what you're talking about!"

"No?" Asked the wizard. "How can an entire lake just disappear? Tell me that."

"Thome. You'd have to ask Thome!"

Rudgaf shook his head, "Not even the Lord of Water can disappear the entirety of a lake in an instant. Can I vanish the flames of the Sun? Can Barlow make his own forest cease to exist at the blink of an eye? The answer to these questions is no, Joem. You should know this. The *real* Joem would know this."

"The truth is," continued Rudgaf, "that I forgot Thome's jumping combination. So in order to continue this charade, my mind had to come up with a convenient trick that would make the combination a non-issue."

Joem threw his hands down and screamed, "And what if you're wrong, Rudgaf?! Are you really prepared to kill me on a guess? A hunch? I'm your friend! Can't you see the pain that you're causing me?"

Rudgaf smiled, raised his hand and said, "I don't give a damn."

The Lord of Red's eyes shot open wide and from his hand he released a fireball aimed straight at the childlike wizard. The Lord of Light immediately panicked and rolled out of the way, hearing the searing fire burn into the ground next to him. The heat, even though the fireball hadn't touched him, was unbearable.

Joem quickly sprang up and, much to Rudgaf's discomfort, but not his surprise, began to laugh. The Lord of Red grunted and lowered his hand, "You didn't really think this would work, did you?"

The Lord of Yellow, whose head had been glaring at the ground, blasted his glare at Rudgaf. The Lord of Fire braced himself against the haunting vision for when he stared back at the yellow wizard, there were no eyes there to meet him.

The Spirit of Doubt sneered and said, "You stupid, stubborn, bootless son of a whore."

The Lord of Red, with a severe lack of anything but the desire to destroy plastered upon his face, drew his sword. However, before he could even think to use it, the Spirit of Doubt flung his hand in the air and Rudgaf was blinded by a brilliant flash of light.

Where Rudgaf would be at the end of it all was anyone's guess.

~

Where am I?

...

I can't see anything.

...

What have you done to me?

!

I don't have time for this! I have to save Ramona!

?

What is that in the distance that I see?

...

Oh, spirit. Release me from this hell you've made!

Rudgaf squinted his eyes in an attempt to filter out as much of the bright light that he could. He saw a faint object in the far distance, but couldn't make out what it was. Desperate to be released from his prison of light, the Lord of Red ran toward the only object that he could see in the vast infinity of the new world that he had forcefully become a part of. When the object appeared to come closer, his resolve strengthened and he found himself running faster and faster, ever onwards toward his only hope for salvation.

The Lord of Red was shocked by his stamina. While he ran, he continued to test the boundaries of his strength. When he thought that he was running as fast as he possibly should be able to, he found that he could press on ever more aggressively. He couldn't tell how long this process went on for – time meant nothing in that place – but to him it felt as long as the breadth of the world. Rudgaf considered resting toward the start of the process, but found that he was filled with boundless energy. It was as if, he thought, running was his natural state of being or, perhaps, even more basic than that, perhaps comparable to a restful sleep. He felt young. He felt alive. Most of all, he knew that this illusion couldn't have been a product of the Spirit of Doubt – the entirety of the experience was having the opposite effect on the wizard than the one that he was sure that the spirit would intend. Something or someone had interceded on his behalf.

All the while this was going on, the wizard's distant hope started to grow larger. With every step it grew grander. With every second step it seemed more illustrious. Every stride brought it into greater detail. Before Rudgaf even knew it, yet after he was convinced that he had spent so much time in his new world that all of the troubles in the old world surely must've resolved without his assistance, thus eliminating his need to run in the first place, he was face to face with the object of his desire.

The light dimmed and Rudgaf stood on a large, grassy hill overlooking the central tower.

Home.

The Lord of Red scurried down the hill, being careful not to trip over his feet, and across the breezy plain that slowly faded into the wizard's garden. Although he badly wanted to, he didn't take the time to stop and observe the growth – for something much greater drew him into the tower. Determined, he scampered through the garden, then through the courtyard, the order of which he was certain was backwards for some strange reason, but nice nonetheless. Finally, after navigating through a lengthy and annoying hedge maze, he arrived at the front door and without knocking pushed his way through to the greeting room.

The red wizard peered around the room until his eyes met a rack on which rested his old, red cloak and his favorite hat. Without even thinking, as if out of instinct, he replaced his current garments with what laid before him and then ran up the winding staircase and into the second floor.

The second floor contained a mysteriously untouched library – something that Rudgaf knew to be destroyed long ago. Again, almost as if out of instinct, he walked up to a bookcase and withdrew a book. Without reading the title, he started to flip through the pages. Thinking for a moment, he found his current course of action to be foolhardy, so he replaced the book by setting it back in the bookcase. Rudgaf wanted to turn away and see other parts of the tower, but his hands almost immediately gravitated to another book, opened it up and started flipping. Once more, Rudgaf shut the tome and replaced it. Once more, his hands picked up another volume and started turning the pages. The wizard couldn't help but feel his frustration rise in this futile battle with himself. One more book replaced, another picked up and rummaged through. Another book stored, one more disturbed and deciphered. A useless, mundane activity had become the bane of Rudgaf's existence. He found himself gritting his teeth, grinding them until his jaw ached. His forehead perspired. When the wizard went to address the issue, his hands took on a life of their own and nabbed another text from a different bookcase. When the Lord of Red attempted to shut his eyes, one of his hands forced them open against his will. When Rudgaf tried to turn his head away, one of his hands covered his mouth and the other plugged his nose until he submitted and turned his head to its former position lest he run out of air.

From bookcase to bookcase did Rudgaf run, his hands searching for only they knew what…at least he hoped. Finally after he was convinced that they had investigated nearly every book in the entirety of the library, a strong voice rang throughout the room, causing the wizard's hands to drop the book that they were holding and return to Rudgaf's control.

It's not here, Rudgaf.

Where is it, then?

Where your heart is, there your treasure is also.

...Wilfrey?

Search your heart, Rudgaf.

Rudgaf gasped and nodded his head at a thought. Back in control of all of his limbs, he returned to the staircase and climbed it up to the third floor. Once he had arrived, he paced around to the third door and opened it.

Inside was a small room. To the right was a desk that had some parchment and a quill and inkwell combination sitting atop of it. To the left was a small bed, suitable for only one person. It had been made neatly. A large, mahogany chest sat at the foot of the bed, close to the doorway. A dresser rested at the front of the room in front of a large window.

Intuition being as sharp as a razor, Rudgaf walked over to the large chest and opened it. Inside of it was a pile of torn parchment, all with etchings on them of some form. Some of them were rather good, while others appeared to be drawn by more of a novice than anyone else. Most of the drawings were of flowers and shrubberies – these Rudgaf discarded in his process of filtering through them. He then came across some drawings of trees – all sorts made up the subject matter for these pieces. Some were short, others were tall. Some had grey trunks, others brown, still others were red. Some had needles, others had leaves. Some were drawn during Spring, others during Fall. To Rudgaf, they were all beautiful in their own right. However, the wizard was looking for something in specific, so he threw most of the drawings in an ever growing pile behind him. That was until he came across a drawing of a giant conifer...

~

...As of the trees, Rudgaf encountered a gigantic conifer whose roots must've spread out over a mile in all directions. The tree was very gnarly and quite old...and the Lord of Red knew that he saw it before somewhere in a distant memory.

The Lord of Red took a glance at his surroundings. Somehow, he found himself transported to Barlow's Forest, as if the drawing of the conifer had managed to defy nature's laws and pull him into the scene. After a few moments, he took a deep breath of freshly familiar air and returned his attention back to the tree.

I hadn't thought that I drew this.

You did...with me. Don't you remember?

Rudgaf turned his head toward the sound of the voice. A tall elf with long, black hair and steely, grey eyes stood next to the tree, leaning against it. She looked at the

red wizard with near enough intensity to stoke flame, yet Rudgaf found himself to be unafraid.

I was supposed to meet you here.

Yes, but you never came. Why didn't you come, Rudgaf?

Why...didn't I draw you in this picture? Why just the tree?

Our love had to remain a secret.

Wh...oh, yeah. I remember now.

He was jealous.

Yes, he was. I didn't want him to be in pain.

The forest would have told him our secret, but this conifer didn't like the trees of the forest, so it always remained silent.

I'm sorry that I didn't come.

Why didn't you?

Believe me, I wanted to. I wanted to come so bad.

Then why didn't you?

I made a choice.

The elf turned away.

Are you happy with your choice?

I don't remember the last time I was truly happy.

Do I make you happy, Rudgaf?

You always made me happier, but...

There was someone missing.

Now it was Rudgaf who turned away and stared off into the distance.

I still can't believe that he was killed.

It's ok, Rudgaf. It's ok to grieve.

I couldn't in front of him. Does he feel nothing at all?

You always clashed. You're both so different.

I sacrificed so much for him. It makes me angry. If I could just do it all over again...

You would make the exact same choice.

The Lord of Red turned to face the elf. She was staring at him again with a fiery stare of adoration.

That's why I love you, Rudgaf.

You don't hate me?

How could I hate you? I will love you forever, Lord of Red.

Curse that name. Curse the day I ever found that stone. Curse the day that stone was even made.

No, Rudgaf.

No? But look what it's done to us.

There are things in this world that are more important than us, Rudgaf.

I don't want there to be.

Nor do I, but as long as you're destined to be the flame of the world, we cannot be together.

When can we be?

Someday, my love.

…But not today.

Not today.

Rudgaf nodded and somberly turned his attention back to the tree. My, was it huge – the largest tree that the red wizard had ever beheld. It was no wonder why he wanted to sketch it, although his drawing wasn't really able to capture its majesty. The wizard stared for a few moments, examining the entirety of the behemoth from the top of its twisty branches all the way to the bottom of its curly, extensive roots. It wasn't until the elf spoke that he stopped marveling at it.

It's time for you to leave, Rudgaf.

Really? But I just got here.

I know, but you must go.

…I don't want to leave. I want to stay here with you.

Nothing would make me happier, but you know you can't stay.

Next time, I'll stay.

Next time.

Rudgaf glanced around.

How do I leave?

Just walk away.

Walk away?

Yes, Rudgaf. Walk away until you've returned to where you came from.

I love you.

You don't know how happy it makes me to hear you say that after all of this time.

Love never dies.

I know mine never will.

Rudgaf nodded and reluctantly started to walk away.

Wait, Rudgaf.

Yes?

I have something for you. I was going to give it to you…that day.

The elf came close to Rudgaf, then, until he could feel her warm breath on his forehead. She put a hand in the pocket of her cloak, pulled out a folded up piece of parchment and handed it to the red wizard who promptly stored it away.

Promise me that you won't look at it until you're back.

I promise.

The elf smiled and gently kissed Rudgaf on the head, just below the brim of his hat.

Go now.

The Lord of Red stared at the elf and ignored the painful burning building in his eyes. He then swallowed, nodded and walked away. Every now and then, he would look back at the conifer to see if she was still watching him.

She didn't look away until Rudgaf couldn't physically see her in the distance any longer.

~

The red wizard found himself back in the room that he was in a few moments ago. He stared at the drawing of the conifer in his hand. Staring at it intently, he tried to will it to bring him back to his lover, but try as he might, the tree wouldn't yield to his will. In defeat, he folded up the parchment and placed it back in the chest. He then restored the pile of discarded drawings to where he had found them and then closed the lid and stood.

Turning to leave, he remembered the parchment that he had brought with him from the other world. He felt through the inner pocket in his cloak and pulled it out. Unfolding it, he beheld a beautiful drawing of a young man in his forties, dressed in brown from head to toe. The sketch smiled at him warmly.

Wilfrey…she drew a picture of Wilfrey for me.

Below the sketch was a small note which Rudgaf read.

To My Love –

Words cannot fully express the fullness of my adoration for you, my love. Our deep, heartfelt conversations culminated to intimacy's zenith last night when you put your hands in mine and let me peer into your mind, your heart and your feelings. This was the strongest image that I found. I hope that you can someday be at peace with his passing. To that end, I have drawn this sketch for you. May it help you to remember him always just as I will remember you always. I write this note to you on the eve of a decision that will impact the rest of our lives. Whatever decision you choose to make, my love, do not have doubts about the purity of its intent. Never doubt your love for me. Never doubt my love for you.

Forever Yours – Ramona

The Lord of Red looked taken aback by the note and gave it a stiff eyebrow.

Ramona? That wasn't her name…what's going on here?

Before Rudgaf could ruminate on the issue any longer, the booming voice returned.

Doubt cannot be defeated through might alone, Rudgaf.

Then what will you have me do?

On that fateful day, Rudgaf, doubt sunk itself in me. I failed to trust the judgment of my brothers and the integrity of the dwarves. I failed to defeat the wicked spirit on that day.

I'm sorry, Wilfrey. I had no idea.

Please, Rudgaf...let me avenge myself. Let me help you defeat what I could not defeat on that cursed day. Then and only then will my spirit finally be at rest and the necromancer, the one with the gall to reach out and grasp what should not be grasped, to try to control what cannot be controlled, will not be able to use my soul for his nefarious deeds any longer.

I'd do anything for you, Wilfrey. You know that. Just tell me what you need me to do and consider it done.

Reach out to me, Rudgaf. Reach out to me and grasp me and don't let go.

I...think I know what you mean.

The Lord of Red, knowing what to do, but confused on the mechanics behind it, held the drawing straight up in the air over his head and then with a free hand he reached at it. Much to his surprise, the paper gave way and allowed his hand to fly clean through it without actually tearing a hole into it to the opposite side. He waved his hand about in the picture until he felt something soft and then, gripping it as hard as he could possibly grip it, he tugged and tugged until a body fell out of the parchment and landed on top of him, sending both bodies to the ground in a heap.

Both wizard and fallen body rose and brushed each other off. When they were finished, they stared at each other in amazement.

Wilfrey!

Rudgaf!

The wizards embraced, finally united after hundreds of years of pain, suffering, grief and regret. He didn't know for certain, but Rudgaf thought that he squeezed Wilfrey tighter than he's ever squeezed someone before on that day. The Lord of Red tried to hold back, but a few tears escaped him and soaked into the brown wizard's cloak.

I never thought that I'd see you again, Wilfrey.

Nor I you, Rudgaf.

What happened? Who did it? Who assassinated you?

The Lord of Brown pushed Rudgaf away and stared at him strongly.

The same bastard that you've all been fighting for centuries, but haven't known it.

Who, Wilfrey? Who?

He calls himself, 'Mazuumanesh'. A name of ancient human origin that translates to, 'Son of Mazuun'."

Arrogance made manifest.

He's very strong, Rudgaf, but he's not indestructible. At least not yet.

Not yet?

No, but the Dark Lord, the true Dark Lord is at his side.

Mazuun himself? But how, Wilfrey?

He commands the necromancer from beyond the grave and with great power wills him to find the black, lesser stone. With the power of the stone, Mazuun will have enough strength to join with Mazuumanesh and once again plague our world.

What should we do?

You need to get back to the others, Rudgaf. They're in grave danger.

The only way to do that is to defeat the evil spirit.

That's right, Rudgaf. I'm going to help you.

You are?

Yes. I owe him one and I owe Mazuumanesh more than one.

Where did these evil spirits come from, Wilfrey?

The spirits have always existed, Rudgaf. They've simply laid dormant in the hearts of men, elves, dwarves...all races, to come up and rage war with the mind and the heart of the bearer every now and again.

But how did they manifest themselves in a physical sense?

Mazuumanesh.

He commands them?

He killed me and used me as an experiment for his necromancy. He sought to reverse the spell that keeps the black, lesser stone banished from the world, but he failed to capture the entirety of my being. When my soul and my consciousness reunited, they split into several pieces, some of which he captured in crystalline objects and used to power his machinations.

Rudgaf clenched his fist, digging his fingernails into his hand until they nearly pierced the skin.

The son-of-a-bitch! He's made you suffer for centuries, Wilfrey!

I know, but it's my fault as well.

Your fault? How?

Because I was weak, Rudgaf. Because I gave into doubt. Because I am responsible for the deaths of millions. I should've had faith in you.

The wizards stared at each other, not knowing what to say. After a few moments, Wilfrey shook his head and spoke.

That's why I need this, Rudgaf. I've been reaching out to all of you – Barlow, Joem, Danagan, Thome and yourself – to try to get one of you to find me and allow me to make up for my failures in life.

That's why I've been having those dreams...

That's also why Thome ventured off into the desert. He came to visit my tomb. Now he knows himself again.

Knows himself?

He has purified himself of the spirit that was haunting him and is now cured of his madness.

There's a cure?

Yes, there is a cure, Rudgaf. All of you can be cured, but it takes time and the right opportunity. I can't tell you any more than that – each one of you has his own demons to contend with. Only you know how to defeat them.

But what of doubt? Isn't doubt the spirit that haunts me?

He haunts you only because of your link to me. Once I help you defeat him, he will be gone forever and the madness will be cured for me, but not for you. You must find your own path.

I see...

Something else.

Yes?

What Thome also discovered is that my lesser stone has been stolen from the tomb.

What? Why would anyone want your lesser stone? They can't do anything with it.

Don't you see, Rudgaf? Mazuumanesh has it. I know this because if he didn't have it, he couldn't have caused my soul and consciousness to reunite.

I'm confused, Wilfrey.

Each person has a soul and a consciousness. The soul gets reused, but the consciousness is unique to a person for forever. When I died, my consciousness went to another world, but my soul, instead of also going to another world to be reused, stayed linked with the stone. This is a protective measure so that no one can assassinate one of us and simply take our power by force. However, as you can see, my soul and consciousness have been reunited in some form, meaning that Mazuumanesh has been able to at least partially strip my soul from the brown, lesser stone and has, in all likelihood, either taken the power into himself or given it to someone else. I'm thinking that the former is most likely.

But why?

His original goal was to completely strip the stone of my soul, but like I said, when my soul and consciousness reunited they split into several pieces. He was able to get some of my power, but not most of it. More likely than not, he'll be looking to take someone else's power now.

I get it...the combined power, at least he hopes, will be enough to reverse your spell and expose the black, lesser stone.

That's why he's been intent on killing you all. It was easier to kill me because I was alone. He's had trouble with the rest of you because, save for Danagan, you're not usually alone until recent events have caused you to be. Even so, you've been with your elf friend and Joem, when not with the jungle elves, has also been with you. Thome, well, I had my ways of keeping him safe and regardless, Mazuumanesh probably assumed that he'd die on his own. And Danagan, well…he's something else.

His power is incredible. He never ceases to amaze me.

I feel the same way.

But what of Barlow? He's been by himself for a while.

Rudgaf, I didn't want to say this, but I haven't felt Barlow's presence for some time.

The Lord of Red turned pale at the news. He certainly hoped that his absence didn't leave an opening for the necromancer to attack one of his friends. For that, he could never forgive himself.

When was the last time you felt it?

Since before both you and Thome even left.

Well, he was fine when I left. It must be for another reason.

Let's hope so.

Rudgaf grew silent for a moment. Sensing his friend's distress, Wilfrey placed a reassuring hand on the Lord of Red's shoulder.

Everything will be ok, Rudgaf. You have to have faith. Just like I had faith that you'd save me.

Thank you, Wilfrey. I promise I won't let you down.

Let's get to it, then. We have a demon to kill.

Right, but…how do we get out of here?

Just take my hand and leave it to me.

The Lord of Red nodded and grabbed Wilfrey's hand. With a smile, the Lord of Brown stared up at the ceiling and outstretched his arm. Inexplicably, Rudgaf felt lighter than air. It was then that he noticed that both wizards were levitating and he almost let go of Wilfrey's hand out of shock.

Are you ok, Rudgaf?

Yeah, it just startled me.

Make sure to hang on tight, ok?

Alright.

Both wizards started to elevate to a greater altitude. Higher and higher did they soar until Wilfrey touched the ceiling. In much the same way that Rudgaf was able to place his hand through the sketch that Ramona had remarkably drawn for him, both the Lord of Red and the Lord of Brown, reunited for one, final battle, vanished into the ceiling and left the world of Wilfrey's imagination behind forever.

Spacetime is a funny thing. One moment it seems an unfathomable thing, even when, comparatively speaking, dealing with a small portion of the whole. A wizard can look at a distant mountain and marvel at the space between himself and the peak. A dwarf can set his heart on writing a volume and then wonder at the massive amount of time that it takes to jot down a few pages worth of information, let alone an entire tome's worth. Yet, at some point, what seems unfathomable becomes easily measurable. The wizard discovers that from his grassy knoll a space of one hundred miles is all that stands between him and the summit and then it takes a ten thousand foot hike from the summit to reach the peak. He never thought that he could accomplish the feat until he stood on the peak of the mountain in triumph. However, when he looks back at the knoll where he once stood, the distance, again, seems unfathomable even though he knows the precise measurement. The dwarf, although ten tomes into his illustrious writing career, when setting his sights on an eleventh, will throw his quill down in frustration. "How will I ever make time for this," he says to himself, "the task is simply impossible!" Then, when all is said and done and the quill writes its last letter and then is retired to its inkpot to rest and wait to write another day, the dwarf can most easily recount all of the days between when he started his work until when he finished and that time, as a whole, never seems unreasonable or immeasurable to him at all. That is, of course, until he seeks to write his twelfth novel and repeats the aforementioned process all over again – this was and is the same for all novels that the dwarf has written and will write prior to and after the eleventh…as silly as that may seem to someone observing from the outside.

What is space? What is time? If one is looking to take a measurement of the space between one landmark and the next and finds that the distance is non-existent, does that make the measurement insignificant for the smallness of its size? If so, does this make an immeasurable distance more or less significant to the measurer? Unlike the first example, there is a significant distance to measure, but it simply cannot be measured. If the first distance is immeasurable by means of its tininess and the second distance is immeasurable by means of its grandness then how is one more significant to the measurer than the other? Furthermore, if the measurer can't measure everything, should anything be measured at all or is measuring for measuring's sake a good enough reason to continue the practice? The same may be said of time. Should a measurer that calculates time give up by reason of the fact that he simply will not live long enough to count every second of eternity? Also, why are seconds measured at all? Should the second be split into smaller units? How small does a unit have to be before the measurer deems it to be insignificant? What if one were to go in the opposite direction and expand the second into larger and larger units? How large does the new unit have to be before it becomes insignificant by way of its immeasurability?

As one can well see – the boundaries are fuzzy at best. The greatness of spacetime is simply a product of one's perspective. If the casual observer observes with a broadened mind, very little will escape that observer's understanding. However, if that same observer gazes upon the world with narrowed thoughts, even a stone's throw seems an infinity and a tick of the clock passes like an eternity. Given all of this, what is the space between a reality and a fantasy? How long does it take to cross the gap between the two? Is the reality truly a reality? Is the fantasy truly a fantasy? Should these concepts exist at all?

Could one tell both Rudgaf and Wilfrey that what they observed wasn't reality, but fantasy instead? As they both soared through the air, visiting world upon world, the fantasy, as so deemed by the majority of the majorly agreed upon reality, no other being existed that couldn't see, touch, hear, smell, taste and feel the same things that they did. How could one say that what they experienced wasn't real? Was it because they saw large, furry mammals with elongated snouts that stretched out as far as a redwood tree does from earth to sky? Was it because, on the subject of trees, they observed pines with pink trunks and purple needles as well as the apple trees with fruit that was already candied? What of the rivers filled with flowing red wine that splished and splashed on the river banks and tumbled over rocks? Or was the wine actually blood that the wizard's saw? No matter, because one moment they were observing the red filled river and the next they were whooshed off to a desert where such things had no meaning. Then after experiencing the searing heat of the desert they were transported to the freezing cold mountaintops and when they stuck out their tongues to catch the rogue snowflakes that drifted too close to them, they both could've sworn that the snow was made of pure sugar. At one point the inhabitants of one world seemed to be nothing more than tiny, horned imps that delighted at tugging at Rudgaf's beard until they were fully grown – an event that both wizards, to their amazement, found themselves with time enough to watch. Rudgaf feared that he would have to fend off one of the adult imps, a giant by comparison to even an elf, until both him and his companion were again swished off to another world – this time a barren, deserted, rocky wasteland with little atmosphere, allowing them to gaze fully at the majesty of the heavens above them and, surprisingly, not have trouble breathing. Finally after what felt like an endless lapse of time, yet a blink of an eye, a bright light surrounded them, blinding the wizards until it shattered like glass and the truth, at least the truth for them, what Joem would call a semi-reality, appeared before them. They both traveled through worlds unknown – unseen by mortal eyes. They wandered through oddities, saw zounds of strange creatures that any person in the world that they were used to inhabiting would say were impossible to exist and even, if just for a fraction of a second, understood the true meaning of existence. Then, when all was said and done, they both stood side by side in a swamp, knee deep in mud, with death in all of its terror and all of its glory at their heels. They had no choice but to meet it head on and the only solace that the both of them could take in that fact was that they came to the swamp looking to do just that very thing – as if the process of agreeing to do it and convincing themselves that it should be done somehow made it less insane. In conclusion, Rudgaf truly didn't know if he'd ever be able to convince anyone in his world that the other worlds he visited were part of reality and not fantasy. He did know, however, as he was sure Wilfrey did, that whatever the Spirit of Doubt did to them in that place, whether theologians deemed the entire experience to be real or unreal, would be very, very real and, in all likelihood, just as permanent.

When the light started to die down, the wicked spirit lowered its arm, which it was using to shield its eyes from the intensity that was too much for even it to bear. When its sense of sight fully returned to it, which took a moment or two, it looked upon the sight in front of it with amazement. Gobsmacked, the only words that it could manage to utter in response to the situation were, "What the hell?"

"It's good to finally see you again, old friend." Said Wilfrey cockily.

The spirit squinted its eyes for a pinch of time, then smiled and said, "Oh, yes. I remember you. We met when I was but an infant. No, that's not true. I wasn't even an infant...more like a thought."

"A thought that I'm personally going to erase."

Doubt smirked, "Is that a fact?"

"You better believe it you contemptuous waste of existence."

The spirit tsk'd and said, "My, my, such harsh words. Last I checked, we worked fairly well together."

Doubt laughed to itself, drooling over the mouthwatering thought before making it vocal, "How many millions did *we* kill *together*, Wilfrey? Oh, just thinking about it is so...tantalizing."

Rudgaf turned toward his brother, "Don't listen to it, Wilfrey."

"Shut up, red wizard!" Shouted the spirit. "This doesn't even concern you. He's the one I want, so stay out of my way."

The Lord of Red drew his sword and assumed a fighting stance, "That's not going to happen, spirit. If you want him, you also have to contend with me. While we're taking trips down memory lane, here's a memory I'd like to share with you – last time we fought, you lost. How do you plan to contend with both of us at once if you cannot even handle me?"

"Arrogant fool. Do you truly believe you won our last engagement?"

The Spirit of Doubt chortled haughtily, "If that's the case, then why am I still standing here? Why are you trapped in my web of illusion?"

"Enough of this!" Shouted the Lord of Brown through tightened teeth. "No more talk. We fight and we fight now."

The spirit shrugged, "It's your death wish, weakling." Then in such a speedy manner that even a mouse couldn't fit in between the space between the spirit's action and the end of his sentence, it managed to throw a dagger at the brown wizard and watch as Wilfrey jerked to his left in a vain attempt to dodge the attack. The Lord of Brown managed to avoid a fatal injury, however the blade sunk deep into the flesh of his right shoulder which exploded in a fury of blood.

Wilfrey cried out in pain and gripped his would tightly. The distraction of pain served to give the spirit another opening. In a flash, Doubt sped forward, disappearing in mid-run and then reappearing in front of its victim, attempting to finish the brown wizard quickly by shoving a dagger into his midsection. However, Rudgaf was able to intercede on his friend's behalf and land a headbutt onto the spirit's jaw which sent it toppling over and backwards, away from Wilfrey.

While Doubt was on the ground and stunned, the Lord of Red turned toward Wilfrey and asked, "Are you alright?"

The Lord of Brown nodded, "It's fine. Don't worry about me."

Rudgaf nodded and returned his attention to the Spirit of Doubt who was just starting to stand. The spirit sent a piercing stare at both of the wizards with as much contempt and disdain as it could possibly show for another, living being and said, "I *hate* you filthy wizards."

The Lord of Red spat at the spirit and said, "Are you going to attack or are you going to run away? Either way, get it over with already." The red wizard then raised his hand and shot a fireball at the spirit in an attempt to persuade it to action. However, the attack proved to be ineffective against the nimbleness of Doubt who dodged it and set out to make an attack of its own.

Rudgaf braced himself against the approaching assailant then, to his astonishment, found that the spirit had managed to get himself stuck in some of the stickiest, goopiest mud that he'd ever beheld. The spirit, with a look of pure dismay splattered across its features, attempted to fight the soft, iron grip of the exceedingly wet earth, but the more it struggled, the more it sunk as if it were truly digging its own grave.

The red wizard looked at the Lord of Brown, who smiled at him and said, "I got him."

Before the wizard's had time to celebrate, however, they both took a sharp elbow the face which sent them crashing down to the ground. Rudgaf quickly gripped his face in pain and then rolled over to see the spirit hovering over the space between where he and Wilfrey were just standing.

The spirit scoffed and said, "You didn't really think that little trick would stop me, did you?"

In response, Rudgaf fired upon the spirit, which actually served to catch Doubt by surprise. Searing flames soared through the air like a dread eagle in flight and connected directly with the spirit's side who quickly found himself igniting from the blast. In a panic, it frantically threw off its robes and displaced the burning flames. Enraged, the spirit vanished again and when it reappeared, it greeted the red wizard by stomping on his ribs, causing Rudgaf to scream out in pain. The wizard's cries only served to entice the spirit to continuously stomp harder. The Lord of Red gritted his teeth clenched his fists and heard his ribs crack under the pressure that the spirit was putting him under. It was exactly when he was certain that the spirit had broken at least one of his ribs that Wilfrey weighed in on the situation.

Seemingly from out of nowhere, a rock cleaved through the wind and pelted the Spirit of Doubt in the back of the head. Out of reflex, the spirit grabbed its skull and felt blood. Angrily turning about to face its opponent, it found that instead of being greeted by the sight of the brown wizard, it was simply met with another rock – this one hitting its right eye, shattering the socket.

In great suffering, the spirit dropped down to its knees and held its face. The attack, however, displayed no mercy to the spirit. Rock after rock, stone upon stone, hurled through the air and smacked the spirit all over its body – cracking bones and cutting, bruising and swelling flesh. Doubt screamed at the top of its voice in both pain and rage and then with great travail it pressed its attack on the Lord of Brown.

As the spirit held up its arms to defend itself against the rocks while it came ever closer to the brown wizard, Wilfrey realized that his assault wouldn't keep the spirit at bay forever. It was then that he devised a quick plan. He knew that the spirit couldn't be thinking straight and because of this fact its reflexes would suffer. He was sure of it. He was willing to bet his life on it.

Smiling, the Lord of Brown lifted a finger and said, "Eat it." It was then that a thunderous noise came over the area – the sound of rocks sorting and shifting, breaking and grinding. A rumbling overcame the area and only the Lord of Brown was able to remain standing. The spirit, unable to withstand the power of the quaking, stopped in mid-run and fell over on its back. However, the Spirit of Doubt quickly found that, when it fell, there was no solid ground there to meet it. Instead, the softened earth was replaced with a gaping ravine. In a panic, but ultimately unable to escape the massiveness of the newly formed foramen, the spirit swiftly grabbed on to one of its rocky sides and gripped it as tightly as could be gripped. Doubt's only saving grace was that it hadn't fallen so far as to make stopping itself an impossibility.

Wilfrey slowly paced over to the edge of his creation and peered down at the spirit with disgust, "You've lost."

The spirit, desperate to fight the suggestion, attempted to climb out of the mess that it had found itself in. It placed a hand on a piece of rock above its head in order to scale the rock wall that had saved its life, but at that moment the stone betrayed it, broke off and nearly took the spirit with it in its descent into the void.

The brown wizard, ignoring his enemy's frenzied scamper, said, "When we first met, I made the mistake of fighting you alone. However, I don't ever make the same mistake twice."

A visible perspiration overcame the spirit's countenance, the drippings of which fell to the earth like molten steel. The wizard continued, "Faith. Faith in friendship, in brotherhood…that's why I beat you today."

The spirit snarled, "Spare me the pathetic diatribe."

Wilfrey laughed, "Yes, I should've suspected that you'd find my statement to be derogatory."

"So, how about it, Lord of Earth? Are you going to finish me? Are you going to close up this wound that you have created in the earth and have it swallow me up for all eternity?"

The Lord of Brown shook his head, "No. You're going to burn."

"Rudgaf?" Asked the spirit with scorn. "What do you need him for? Just finish me."

"I'd love to be the one who kills you."

The spirit smiled, "Then do it, wizard! I'm done for! All you have to do is loose the proverbial arrow and I'll be nothing more than a distant memory."

Wilfrey turned away, "Stop tempting me."

"So, what're you going to do? Are you really going to deliver me to the hands of the red wizard? You're more than capable of doing this without him, Lord of Earth!"

"Stop it."

The spirit continued to shout, "He'll just bungle it! He's too merciful, you know that. He'd let me get away and deny you the peace that you so rightfully deserve. Are you really prepared to let him do that to you?"

The brown wizard gnashed his teeth at the spirit, "Rudgaf would never do that. He knows how important all of this is to me."

"No!" Insisted the spirit. "He can't help but have his own interests at heart. Can you truly say that he's never hurt you before?"

Wilfrey hesitated, but begrudgingly answered, "No."

"Then how do you know he won't hurt you again? I say he will! You don't need to take that risk, brown wizard. You're powerful enough to defeat me yourself."

The Lord of Brown turned his back on the ravine. His thoughts, combined with the spirit's words, had brought him to an impasse. He badly wanted to destroy the spirit himself to guarantee his freedom – the freedom that he's sought for centuries. How could he possibly pass up such an offer? How could he deny his own salvation? Besides, he thought, Rudgaf was badly injured. At that point, he was pretty sure that the red wizard didn't have enough strength to finish the job. And maybe the spirit was right – maybe Rudgaf wouldn't finish the job at all and let the spirit escape either through merciful tendencies or through incompetence. No, he just couldn't let that happen.

Wilfrey lifted his hand in the air and felt the split in the earth start to close behind him. Had he made the right decision? Was this just some kind of trick? No, it couldn't be. There was no way for the spirit to escape death at this point. Its destruction was all but assured. Yet, he thought, it was so insistent that Rudgaf not be the one to finish the job. The Lord of Brown, just realizing that he had been grinding his teeth, worked his jaw while he thought. Would Rudgaf really bungle the job? Why, all of the sudden, was Rudgaf so incompetent?

After all, thought the brown wizard, out of all of his brothers it was none other than Rudgaf that broke into his machinations, navigated his imagination and brought him to the one place where he may obtain his salvation. Furthermore, why would Rudgaf not destroy the Spirit of Doubt? Didn't Rudgaf say that he would help? Is the Lord of Red, all of the sudden, not to be trusted?

The brown wizard violently shook his head.

When couldn't Rudgaf be trusted?

"But...I really can do it myself!" Shouted the Lord of Brown.

Wilfrey paused and thought for a moment. Finally, after a deep breath he said, "But that's not the point."

The Lord of Brown waved his hand in a downward arc, stopping the movement of the gigantic hole that laid behind him. He then turned around and quickly ran over to Rudgaf's side. Kneeling down, he lifted the Lord of Red's head up, pointed toward his creation and said, "Look, Rudgaf. I have it trapped in there."

The red wizard, with a great deal of effort, stared at the aperture, then at Wilfrey and said, "Do it, Wilfrey. Destroy him and be free."

Wilfrey smiled and shook his head, "I can't, my brother. You have to be the one to do it."

The Lord of Brown expected his statement to be confusing to Rudgaf, but as the Lord of Red stared at him in the eyes with a stern expression and nodded his head, he knew that somehow, some way, Rudgaf understood what his trials and tribulations were all about. What took Wilfrey centuries to comprehend and atone for, the red wizard understood in mere seconds. Indeed, thought the brown wizard, he was wrong to ever have doubt in his friend.

The Lord of Red stared at the ravine and said out loud, "The fires below."

Wilfrey nodded, "Yes. Only the heat from the fires below will be enough to cleanse the world of this evil."

Rudgaf swallowed hard. To summon the fires below the earth was no simple task. As a matter of fact, he'd only managed to do it one time and that was when he was in far better condition than what he was in at that moment. Attempting to concentrate, the red wizard breathed in slowly and exhaled slowly. It was only then that he realized the true extent of the damage to his ribcage. Every breath he took felt like the Spirit of Doubt was stabbing him in random parts of his midsection. The pain was almost too much for him to handle and this thought, as well as the mere thought of the complexity of the spell, quaked Rudgaf's mind and caused him to feverishly shiver.

"What's wrong, Rudgaf?" Asked Wilfrey.

"I'm...too weak right now, Wilfrey. I can't do it."

"Yes you can and you will."

The Lord of Red shut his eyes tightly, "No, you're wrong. I don't have the power. I'm too injured!"

Wilfrey gave the red wizard an austere stare and said, "Look at me, Rudgaf."

Rudgaf hesitated, but the Lord of Brown insisted, "Look at me."

The red wizard opened his eyes to find the definition of serious staring back at him, locking eyes with him, gazing into his soul. Yet, despite the severity of Wilfrey's face, there was also something...calming about it. It was reassuring, thought Rudgaf. On that day, at that moment, the red wizard saw something in Wilfrey that he had never beheld in him before. It was something admirable, something that Rudgaf couldn't help but respect. It was a strength of character and a burning of the soul. It was as if the Lord of Red was beholding an entirely different person or as if Wilfrey had been a puzzle with a missing piece the entire time that Rudgaf had known him and it was only now, on the battlefield, that the missing piece had been found.

Still locking eyes with the red wizard, Wilfrey said, "I believe in you, Rudgaf. I wouldn't have asked you to do this if I didn't have faith in you. Now you just have to have faith in yourself."

The Lord of Brown stood then and said, "Finish it."

The Lord of Red grinned at the brown wizard and then painfully concentrated. It wasn't long before sweat poured off of him like the rains of a spring storm. A sense of fear and calm battled one another in the wizard's psyche. Inhaling and exhaling...slowly...precisely. Breathing in...and...breathing out. He felt the calm overtaking the fear. Now the fear could be harnessed. It burned like a flame that sat heavily in his belly – intent on burning him up. He could use that to his advantage and he would. The wizard licked his lips and focused even harder. What was beneath the earth again? Oh, that's right, roaring flames...intense...burning...heat. Energy. He could use that energy. He felt along its surface. It was so vast, so powerful, the most powerful thing he'd ever felt. If he could just take a little bit...yes. That was it. Now for the final push.

Wilfrey observed as his companion slowly opened his eyes. Out of impulse, he took a step back when a feeling of trepidation came over him for, before him, sat his friend – his once lifelike visage now replaced with pure concentration. His beautiful blue eyes were now completely white. Instead of the friendly face, filled with a childlike sense of adventure, that Wilfrey was used to, Rudgaf became as a night terror that haunts the dreams of man. He was now as a conduit of death – an eater of worlds.

The earth shook, even more so than it did when Wilfrey created the gaping hole that had become the center of Rudgaf's destruction. The crack grew wider, then wider still, breaking under immense pressure. The world cracked and snarled and bit back at the abuse. Flames from unsullied depths spewed forth from the elongated wound. First, it came slowly and oozed out like a thick paste, burning everything in its path, but then it exploded out in a fiery blast of slaughterous heat and obliterating anger. A shriek filled the air during the magnificent discharge, but was promptly muffled. A bubbling inferno sailed toward the sky and no force that could be mustered at that point could halt its advance until it, nearly having sentience of its own, decided that it should stop.

And stop it did when Rudgaf stopped commanding it and let nature take the reins back from him. In its destructive wake, change had been effected. Vegetation was burned beyond recognition. The fires of the earth eventually cooled and formed deposits of hard, jet black rock that were splattered throughout the area. And as a lonesome wind howled through the area, the most noticeable difference came to light.

Doubt had perished.

Wilfrey ran over to the cavernous channel of his own doing and stared into the void, confirming that the spirit was no more. He then turned back to Rudgaf with a smile and shouted, "You did it!"

Rudgaf's face, wracked with both pain and joy, grinned from ear to ear and, slowly laying back down, he uttered the words, "Finally."

The Lord of Brown walked back to his companion and asked, "Can you stand on your own?"

"I don't think so."

"I'd best help you then."

Wilfrey knelt down next to the red wizard and carefully took his hand. With a free hand, the brown wizard supported the red wizard's back and hoisted him up into a sitting position. He then slung Rudgaf's arm around his shoulders and together they stood up slowly.

"Are you ok?" Asked Wilfrey.

"It hurts."

"Can you walk?"

The Lord of Red grimaced, "Maybe."

"You should try."

Wilfrey slowly let Rudgaf's arm go and the Lord of Red began to walk under his own power, albeit under immense duress.

"Every step feels like a highway mugging." Said Rudgaf.

Wilfrey smiled out of pity, "I'll bet."

The Lord of Brown turned away and looked at the horizon, "I'm finally free, thanks to you."

"It took both of us."

Wilfrey nodded, "You're right. Neither of us could've done it alone. It was the strength of our bond that defeated the evil spirit and banished him from our minds for forever."

Rudgaf paused for a moment and then said, "What will you do now, Wilfrey?"

The Lord of Brown looked back at the red wizard with loving eyes and said, "I finally rest."

The Lord of Red nodded somberly, "I bet you're tired."

"I've been waiting for this sleep for centuries."

The red wizard, nearly choking on his words, barely managed to say, "Will I ever see you again?"

Wilfrey shook his head slowly, "I'm afraid not, my red friend. My time in your world has come to an end."

Rudgaf wept.

The Lord of Brown placed an arm around the red wizard's shoulders, squeezed him a little bit and said, "I know it's hard, brother, but try to be happy for me. I have finally obtained the freedom that I've been robbed of for so long and I have you to thank for it all."

The Lord of Red stopped crying, sniffed and said, "I know, but you have no idea how much I've missed you all of these years."

Wilfrey rubbed Rudgaf's back and said, "Rudgaf, do you remember those days where you and I would walk out into the garden by ourselves and sit there amongst all of the flowers and vines, talking for hours on end?"

"We always had the best conversations, didn't we?"

Wilfrey nodded, "I always felt as if I could talk with you about things that I couldn't talk about with others. You know, really personal things – like our childhoods and our hopes, dreams and even our theories on the workings of the Universe."

"I remember," said Rudgaf, "when we'd go out there at night and stare out the stars, wondering if there were any worlds out there like ours."

"Back then...you told me that you thought there were. Do you still think that?"

"More so now than ever, Wilfrey."

The Lord of Brown smiled and said, "I do, too. In fact, I know that there are and you know what else I know?"

Rudgaf gave his companion a look of inquiry, "What?"

"I know that when I leave this place, I'm going to be on one of those other worlds."

The Lord of Red stared up at the grey sky and said, "Yeah...yeah, I bet you will be."

"And do you know what I'm going to be doing on that world, Rudgaf?"

"What are you going to be doing?"

Wilfrey joined the red wizard in staring at the sky, "I'm going to be in my garden, amongst all of the flowers and the vines. At night, I'll venture out into the midst of it and stare up at the stars. I know I'll be alone, but I'll never feel lonely, Rudgaf. Do you know why I'll never feel lonely?"

Rudgaf began to tear up again and said, "Wilfrey..."

"Because I know that you'll be staring with me. And because we both do this, my brother, it's like we're together – no matter the distance between us. I can sit there and know that you're on one of those stars out there and that you'll be looking up at me and I you."

The Lord of Red began to feel knots growing in his stomach. An indescribable, burning sensation at the pit of his stomach that knew not mercy. It was more than he could stand. He drove his head into Wilfrey's shoulder and wept, soaking the brown wizard's robe with dolor. Wilfrey, in turn, let Rudgaf have all the time that he needed to grieve.

After a long while, once the red wizard had been drained of all of his tears, the Lord of Brown pointed out into the distance and said, "My ride is here."

The Lord of Red collected himself as best as he could and looked where Wilfrey was pointing, "The hole in the ground that you made?"

"I am the Lord of the Earth," said the brown wizard, "so now I go to rejoin it. To give back what it has given me all of these years."

Rudgaf nodded, "I wish that there was another solution."

"So do I," chuckled the Lord of Brown, "because I really miss the world of the living. I'd much rather go home with you, but trust me – this is the best and only way."

"I'll try to understand." Said Rudgaf reluctantly.

Wilfrey touched the red wizard's chin with his fist and said, "You're a great friend...and an even better brother. I'll never forget you."

"I'll never forget you, Wilfrey."

"Well," said Wilfrey, girding himself up, "I'd best get to it."

The Lord of Brown took a few steps forward toward earth's wound, then stopped, turned around and walked back.

"I nearly forgot something important, Rudgaf!"

Rudgaf looked surprised, "What is it, Wilfrey?"

"Hold out your hand."

The Lord of Red complied with the request. The Lord of Brown then placed a small, smooth, oval shaped stone in his hand. Rudgaf observed it in its brown splendor and recognized it immediately for what it was.

"The brown, lesser stone." Commented Rudgaf.

"That's right," said Wilfrey, "I don't really need it anymore. I figured that you could make better use of it than I can. I mean, I know that it's not the real stone, but this is the manifestation of all of my remaining power. Everything that wasn't stolen is in the stone that you hold in your hand."

"What are you doing?" Asked the red wizard angrily. "Are you asking me to replace you?"

Wilfrey shrugged, "No one can ever truly replace me, Rudgaf. We're more than our powers – remember that."

Rudgaf calmed down and nodded, "I'm just a bit upset right now."

"I understand that, Rudgaf. But I would be remiss if I didn't give you that stone. You have to reunite my powers with the real stone and then you must find someone worthy of commanding the power of the earth in my stead. You'll need that person's strength to stop Mazuumanesh."

The Lord of Red stopped observing the stone and shot up in horror, "Mazuumanesh…Ramona! Joem!"

"Yes," said Wilfrey, "now you see the importance of what I'm asking you to do. Do it for me as my last wish, alright? Then my spirit can truly be at peace knowing that I did everything that I absolutely could do to help you save the world."

The red wizard nodded and gripped the stone tightly, "Alright. You can count on me."

The brown wizard beamed and then embraced Rudgaf for one last time. He then turned around and headed back toward the gateway to his freedom. The Lord of Red watched silently as his companion slowly approached the end of the opening.

Once Wilfrey had reached the edge of the opening, he turned to face the red wizard, waved and said, "I love you, Rudgaf! Thank you for all of your help!" Then, without delay, The Lord of Brown, the brown wizard, and the Lord of the Earth dove into the crevice and exited our story forever.

The Lord of Red contained himself by focusing on what had to be done. He had to save Joem. He had to save Ramona. He had to stop Mazuumanesh from obtaining the black, lesser stone at all costs. If Mazuun returned, the end of the world would be nigh. He knew that even the combined might of all of the wizards couldn't stand up to the power of the Lord of Black. No, he thought, he had to nip the problem in the bud.

The Lord of Red carefully placed the brown, lesser stone in his pocket and observed as his illusion melted around him.

Rudgaf awoke with blurred vision and in severe pain, which wasn't much different than how he had felt just moments ago. This, he decided, was probably significant of something greater, but he hadn't had time to ponder on it further then.

He blinked a few times, which served to help clear his sight a bit. At first he noted that he was on his knees for some reason. Then he observed that there were several trees in the area. When they came into better focus, he noted that they weren't ordinary trees – they were Barlow's trees. Somehow he had gotten from the swamp all the way to Barlow's forest, meaning that he had been under the spirit's illusion for quite a long time. This was not a comforting realization.

The Lord of Red looked to his left and gasped. Ramona was on the ground with a visible puncture wound in one of her lungs. That, much to Rudgaf's chagrin, had not been completely illusory. Her breathing was incredibly shallow and the Lord of Red feared that he had snapped out of his trance too late. He then looked to his right and beheld, much to his horror, both Joem and Thome tied up in the air by tree branches, desperately clutching at freedom but lacking the strength to obtain it.

The red wizard attempted to stand then. Sitting still was driving him crazy as his friends were obviously in grave danger. However, when he made the attempt, he quickly found out that it was a futile effort because both his hands and his feet were bound, causing him to fall flat on his face. He stayed in that position for a bit, not really having the energy to do anything else at that time.

After a moment or two, he heard a rustling of leaves in the distance straight ahead of him. As Rudgaf laid with his face in the dirt, helpless, the rustling of the leaves became louder, then even louder, then loud enough to sound as if the leaves that were being disturbed were right next to his head. It was at that point, however, that they stopped.

A familiar voice spoke then and said, "Ah, so I see that you've awakened from your hallucinogenic slumber."

A pair of hands then picked up the red wizard by his head and forced him into the sitting position. When Rudgaf was finally able to focus on what was in front of him, he immediately smiled and said, "Barlow! I'm sure glad that you're here! You won't believe the things I have to tell you."

The Lord of Green glowered, lifted up his wooden staff and shoved the bottom end as hard as he could into Rudgaf's face.

The Lord of Red's vision faded into nothingness.

~INTERLUDE TWO~

When was the inn destroyed?

No one really knows.

There are a couple of things for certain, however, these being – who did it and how they did it. Even the why is a bit fuzzy, being that it was such an out-of-the-way location. Historians studying the massacre often debate on the topic of why, but most agree that it was simply out of malice – even most elves, which is saying quite a lot. And for what other reason would there be? The inn housed no enemy more than it did an ally. The inn was owned by a dwarf whom, after inheriting the place of business from his father's, father's, father's, father, had kept his nose so low to the ground while running the place that you'd be surprised that he managed to keep the thing stuck to his face at all. Furthermore, as I've said before, it was out of the way – meaning that the eastern elven army would've had to have strayed far from the war path, delaying their march to locales of greater import, just to raze the town and the tavern along with it. So, to you I raise the question again – for what other reason, other than malice, would there be for the eastern elves to destroy such a place? That's the question that I bring to this inquiry as I boldly defy the common opinion. Instead, I choose to do away with the very ideals of good and evil – for the word, 'malice', implies the will to do evil – and opine that it was the intention of King Nolan to commit an act of genocide. Whether this intention was born of ill will or not should not make a difference to the inquiry – this isn't about the moral fiber of the king, but rather an historical analysis as pertains to lost culture. He willed an act of genocide because, for some reason, good and evil aside, he sought the, 'purification', of the world. I intend to present you with some of our findings on the very reasoning behind this course of action a bit later. For now, however, let us turn our attention to the inn…

It has been written that this very inn, although not of great significance or fame for anything in particular, had housed a few, signal individuals while they were on their chosen paths to make their marks on the annals of history. In fact, one noteworthy individual, other than myself, of course, was that very person that has been dominating our conversations as of late – The Lord of Red – who has found himself in quite a messy predicament as we near to the close of this chapter of our story, which I will also return to at a later time.

As I was saying, history records that Rudgaf, the Lord of Red, frequented this establishment on three separate occasions (this number is probably incorrect as my primary source admits that he had been afflicted with numerous memory problems at the time and the only other primary source that could've been interviewed on the subject was, unfortunately, killed by the eastern elves). Now, although three separate visits might not seem, at least in the eyes of this inquest, to be enough for any source of information to fully capture the beauty of a culture that has since been largely irretrievable and I, myself, must admit a bit of wanting, I present to you what I have found in the hopes to, at the very least, build a foundation for more discoveries to come. It is with pride and a simultaneous heavy heart that I present you with some of the lost art of a once, great civilization.

In front of you, at this time, you will find Exhibit A – lyrics to a fairly rambunctious, dwarven drinking tune that is anything but politically correct and may come off to some of you as offensive – for this, I apologize, but art is art and must be appreciated nonetheless. The song is entitled, "King Narvis' Washtub". I have also included some musical notation to accompany the lyrics and it is imperative that it be noted that the musical notation written here is not official by any means, but is merely my interpretation of the butchered tune given to me by my primary source who, unfortunately, has a singing voice more akin to that of a crocodile than a bird.

Laughter

As you can plainly see from the lyrics, this song, if not having its origins from the First Age, was, at the very least, written about events pertaining to that very age. In the song, King Narvis, a hero to the northern dwarves, bathes in the blood of his goblin enemies in the days before the, "War of the Mountain", where, even after atrocities had been committed by both races toward one another, the northern dwarves found themselves strangely allied with their former, goblin enemy. My primary source, at the time of his visit, had the prestigious privilege of seeing this tune performed live and as I'm sure you can all imagine it must have been a captivatingly breathtaking experience. I, myself, having witnessed art from all throughout the continent with every sense of my being, cannot help but find myself filled with a bit of jealousy over the affair.

Exhibit B, which is now being placed in front of all of you by my assistant, is a cup of herbal tea that was served frequently at the inn. Fortunately enough for me, my primary source wasn't the only one who had this wonderful brew pass between his lips. When I visited the establishment on my way to the dense jungle toward the south of the continent, I was lucky enough to be served this fragrant drink. Being of the inquisitive sort, I asked the innkeeper for the recipe, however he refused to give it to me saying that it was a, "family affair", and that the recipe would, "die", with him – alas, he was correct on that point. So, in order to recreate it for your sampling pleasure, my primary source and I wracked our brains for several days – adding this ingredient and taking away that until it was mutually agreed upon that the tea tasted as close to how we remembered it as possible. It's not perfect, but art never is. Please, do drink.

Slurping

How does it taste? Notice the bitter, earthy undertones that are counterbalanced by the sweetness of the duku fruit...

~CHAPTER EIGHT – FAREWELL~

...I know that someone will be inquisitive enough to find this letter. You must find your brother – the one who will surely have received his power from the black, lesser stone just as you have received yours from one of the others. Your brother may be very dangerous. Do not hesitate to kill him. His power will recede back to the stone from which he received it. You must locate this stone and dispose of it any way that you can. Do not try to draw power from it. Do not let your brothers attempt to draw power from it.

I know that this may be difficult, but these are sensitive matters.

Trust no one.

Do not seek me. I go into exile because of my aforementioned failures to stop the betrayer. Perhaps...to the west? I have felt a strange urge to travel there for many weeks, now.

I'll have long been dead by the time that you read this letter, anyway.

Warm regards,

Zaan

"Rudgaf?"

The Lord of Red gave a long groan.

"Are you awake?"

The red wizard inhaled heavily through his mouth and with blurry eyes said, "I don't want to be."

"How are you feeling?"

"My nose is broken."

"I saw."

Rudgaf shifted uncomfortably. He noticed that he was still on the ground and that his hands and feet had remained bound. A throbbing pain in his face dominated his senses. After a moment, he said, "What happened, Thome?"

The Lord of Blue replied, "He's gone nuts."

"Can you move?"

"No. Can you?"

"No."

"...And so it is." Said Thome with disappointment.

"How did you get here?"

"That's a long story, Rudgaf."

"We've got time, apparently."

"Isn't that the truth?"

"Well?"

"Well," explained the blue wizard, "I returned to the north tower after my trip to the desert and found the place abandoned."

"Barlow wasn't there?"

"No and to add to the oddity of it all, the place was in great disarray."

"What happened?"

"As near as I can tell," said Thome, "Barlow went into a wild fit of rage. He wrecked the library and destroyed our rooms with fire."

Rudgaf inhaled sharply, "He...what?"

"That's not all, Rudgaf."

"What else happened?"

"His room...Barlow's room...that was the craziest of all."

"Was that burned, too?"

"If only."

"Then, what?"

"Rudgaf...did you get a letter from King Moldof asking you to go to Behnon to investigate reports of the city being destroyed?"

Rudgaf hesitated at the painful memory, but finally said, "Yes. Why?"

Thome sighed, "Moldof didn't write that letter, Rudgaf."

The Lord of Red swallowed hard, "Then who did?"

"Barlow."

"But why would..."

The Lord of Red thought for a moment as the pieces of the puzzle fell into place, one right after the other. He shook his head in sadness, "He was trying to set me up."

"What did you find there, Rudgaf?"

"Some orcs, dread eagles and death. Lots of death."

"I'm shocked that you survived."

"I probably wouldn't have made it out if not for Danagan."

"Danagan?" Asked Thome with surprise. "What was Danagan doing there?"

"He was following up on a rumor involving King Nolan offering money for the head of King Colibrim and just happened to stumble upon the situation."

"Hmm," said Thome, "he does have a way of doing that, doesn't he?"

"Yes, but back to the topic at hand."

"Right, well, after I discovered the letter and other vain scribblings that Barlow had all over his room, I went back to the library and picked up a previously displaced volume about the North Country."

"And?"

"Inside I found that his aim was to kill King Moldof all along in order to try to retrieve the black, lesser stone."

Rudgaf fell silent.

"Are you ok, Rudgaf?" Asked the blue wizard.

"He has fully turned, Thome."

"What do you mean by that?"

"His goals are now one with the Master's."

"Surely you're not suggesting…"

"I'm not suggesting anything," said Rudgaf, "I'm saying with certainty that Barlow is now a slave to the will of Mazuun."

"I don't want to believe it," said the Lord of Blue, "but it certainly would explain all of this."

"How did you find yourself here anyway?"

"Well," explained Thome, "after I found that book, I ran out of the tower and headed toward the capital city of Moldof. But when I was running through Barlow's forest, something knocked me in the back of the noggin and when I woke up, I was here."

"That's odd…this is nowhere near the capital city of Moldof. This place is closer to Behnon than anything."

"That observation hadn't escaped me."

"You were dragged a long way. I'm glad that you're ok enough for us to talk one last time."

Thome smiled, "It's good to see you, by the way."

"It's been a long time – longer than our parting may suggest."

"So you know?"

"Wilfrey told me."

"Wilfrey? Ah, yes…that makes sense. How is he?"

"He's resting now…finally."

The Lord of Blue inhaled deeply and felt a tension leave him, "I knew you'd be the one."

"How did you know?"

"Because," explained Thome, "you always have been, Rudgaf."

Rudgaf fell silent for a moment and then said, "I'm not sure what you mean."

A small voice whispered and crackled, interrupting the conversation, "Hello, Rudgaf."

The Lord of Red turned his attention to the source as best as he could, "Ramona?"

The elf coughed, "Yeah, it's me."

"Ramona," said Rudgaf, nearly crying, "I'm so glad to hear your voice again."

"Rudgaf…I'm sorry."

"Shh, none of that now, Ramona."

"But, it's…" The elf paused briefly while she choked on the air that sustained her life, but caused her so much pain to intake. She clenched her hands in pain and with great effort said, "We're all going to die…and it's all my fault. I shouldn't have run off by myself."

"This is no time to cast blame."

"But…"

"Look," said the red wizard, "we have no future. All we have is the here and now. All we have left are these last, few moments together. Let's just enjoy being together so that we may march forward unto death laughing and smiling and filled with life, despite it all."

"Rudgaf…"

"Save your strength, Ramona. Save it for the good things. Save it for everything that is true, honest, just and pure. Save it so that you may think on the things that are lovely – like this great adventure that we've been on, the conversations that we've shared and the memories that we've created together. Regret has no virtue, Ramona. But love does. Think about love instead."

"You've changed, Rudgaf." Said a childish voice from the trees.

"Joem? Is that you?" Asked the red wizard.

"You've changed for the better, I'd say." Said the Lord of Yellow.

"I'd make that claim, too." Added Thome.

"What better time to change than now?" Asked Rudgaf, chuckling.

"Indeed," said Joem, "it's not like we've anything left to lose."

"Today is a good day to die." Added the Lord of Blue.

The wizards took a moment to let imminence sink in. Silence reigned until Joem said, "I wish I could've seen Danagan one, last time."

Both wizards concurred and were quiet again.

"Rudgaf?" Asked Ramona, weakly.

"Yes, Ramona?" Replied the Lord of Red.

"I thought…of a mem…ory."

"That's…that's good, Ramona. What did you think of?"

Laboriously, the elf said, "Re…mem…ber…the hydra?"

Rudgaf tittered a bit, "Yeah, I remember."

"That's…a memory that we…only we have."

"That's right," said the red wizard, "nothing can take that away from us."

"Rudgaf…do you…do you know why…that mem…memory is so…so special…to me?"

The Lord of Red remained silent and let Ramona continue, "It's be…because y…you saved m…me."

"I'd do it again, Ramona. I'd do it anytime."

The elf coughed, "I…I know. But…no one…no one had ev…ever done that…for me."

"Ramona…"

"I…I'll nev…never forget…that."

The Lord of Red heard the elf audibly slump over.

"Ramona?"

There was no response.

"Ramona!" Screamed the red wizard.

There was still no response.

Teary eyed, Rudgaf said, "Don't worry, Ramona. We'll be together again soon."

"We'll all be together again soon." Said Thome.

"Oh, you don't know how correct you are, my inferior counterpart." Said a voice in the distance.

"Great." Said Rudgaf, exhausted.

"That must be him." Said Joem.

"Yeah." Thome agreed.

Disturbing and cracking leaves as he walked, the Lord of Green said, "I've been listening to the lot of you."

"Oh?" Asked Thome. "Hear anything tantalizing?"

Barlow snarled at the blue wizard, "Of course not. What knowledge could you fools possibly have to offer me?"

"Barlow..." said Joem, "what has come over you?"

"Silence!" Screamed the green wizard. "I've no time for the weak and you, Joem, are the weakest of the bunch."

"Oh, and I suppose you're the strongest." Said Thome, sardonically.

Barlow smirked, "You have a point, Thome. Rather, you would have, but all you remember is the old Barlow. I am now much improved. Attempt to undermine my authority over you now and you will find your power to be sorely insufficient for the task."

"What do you want from us?" Asked Rudgaf.

"Ah, Rudgaf...how delightful it is to see you gravelling at my feet. The dirt suits you well."

The Lord of Green laughed to himself and continued, "What do I want? Nothing much. All that I've ever truly wanted is already in my possession. However, I couldn't help but notice that your situations have left you all lacking a certain...something."

"Get to the damned point." Spat Thome.

"Very well, then," said Barlow with a frown, "let's get to it. You want to save your worthless hides, correct? I'll let you all go right now, but you have to do something for me in return."

"What do you want us to do?" Asked the Lord of Yellow.

"It's simple – I want you to join me...not for me, but for our Master. Then I want you to use your powers to help our Master recover what is rightfully his."

"Bah! Forget it!" Protested Thome.

"I could never do such a thing, Barlow." Said Joem.

The Lord of Green shook his head and then looked at Rudgaf, "And what about you, Rudgaf? After all, I'm going to take your powers one way or another so you might as well just do as I tell you. Will you not join me?"

"No," said Rudgaf in defiance, "I'll not join you."

Barlow scowled and then with a flick of his hand, vines came and wrapped up the Lord of Red, slamming him harshly into a nearby tree and causing him to cry out in pain. With rage, the green wizard walked up to him and said, "Even now you provoke my anger? Even now, when I am clearly your superior?"

When Rudgaf had recovered, he said, "You're not superior to anyone – not even the Barlow of old."

Barlow laughed, "You truly have gone mad, haven't you? Can you not see the truth that's right in front of your eyes? I have three wizards bowing before me – three supposed equals at my mercy – and you want to tell me that I'm not superior?"

"You're wrong, Barlow!" Rudgaf screamed.

Sarcastically, Barlow said, "How? How am I wrong? Do tell! I need a good laugh before I destroy you."

The Lord of Red grimaced in anguish and said, "You're nothing but a pawn. In your quest for power you've sold your free will to the Lord of Black – the very thing that we all swore we would never do, the very thing that he created us for in the first place – to be a slave for as long as you live until he decides he doesn't need you anymore."

Barlow went to protest, but Rudgaf cut him off, "No. Shut up. You're just wrong. The Barlow that I once knew realized just as I do that there is more to being strong than just being powerful. What good does it do for a king to have the power to defend his kingdom if he willfully walks away from it for fear of ruling it? What good does it do for a man with the physical strength of ten strong men to have all of that strength if he lacks the desire to make change in the world? What good does it do for a man with all of the talent in the world to have that talent if he is too lazy to actually do something with it? Strength is more than power, Barlow. Strength is the fortitude of character, the will and the desire to be something better than what you are. To build strength one must constantly strive for perfection, not take a shortcut through nefarious means. You may, indeed, be more powerful than you once were, Lord of Green, but in all reality you're far weaker. All that you've obtained is nothingness – a kind of emptiness that forms a gaping hole in the middle of your soul that will eat away at you for the rest of your life."

The corner of Barlow's mouth twitched, "You insolent little bootlicker…how dare you talk to me that way? Ever since we met, I've felt inferior to you. So I trained and I trained. Night and day I honed my craft. Some nights, I would cry myself to sleep due to my ineptitude. I would spend weeks in my forest, not talking to another living soul, just practicing and expanding myself…all to be more powerful than you, Rudgaf. And now you dare to tell me that it's all for nothing? All of my struggle, all of my effort, all of my desire is for nothing?"

"It's your own fault that all of your sacrifices were in vain, not mine."

The Lord of Green barred his teeth, "In vain were they? How about I show you, Lord of Flames?"

The green wizard went to lift his hand, but then stopped and said, "No…I have a better idea."

Rudgaf raised an eyebrow, "What are you going to do?"

Barlow smirked, "I'm going to beat you at your own game. The forest never gave me the power to defeat you, but what about your power?"

"My power?"

"You see," shouted Barlow, "you're not the only one that can command the flames! I can ascend! I can be like the Lord of Fire!"

"What are you talking about?"

"I, too, can command the fires of Mount Shuun!"

"You've lost your mind."

"Have I? Do you know where you go, Rudgaf? Where demons rest on burning coals. Where you will look out beyond the ashen shores and, lo, an ocean of flames shall welcome you home."

Rudgaf snapped, "How dare you mock the flame?!"

"Mock?" Asked Barlow. "Nay, I am merely a follower of its path. I am a student just like you, but our common teacher has a favorite. You're about to see which one of us that is."

"Rudgaf," shouted Thome, "be careful! He's lost it!"

The Lord of Green laughed menacingly, took in a deep breath and then lurched his body forward. As he did so, torrid flames expectorated from his mouth, engulfing Rudgaf in their destructive heat.

"Rudgaf!" Shouted Joem.

"No…this isn't possible." Said Thome.

But then, as suddenly as the Lord of Red was taken by the flame, he re-emerged unburned, willing the flames away from his body with his mere thoughts.

"Way to go, Rudgaf!" Yelled the Lord of Blue.

"You can do it! Hang on, Rudgaf!" Cheered the Lord of Yellow.

Overcome with anger, the Lord of Green intensified the severity of the flame and Rudgaf quickly found himself being assailed again. However, as hard as Barlow worked the spell, Rudgaf worked equally as hard at countering it. A true master of his craft, the Lord of Red willed the flames away from him once more. This time, the hatred in Barlow's heart boiled over and represented itself in the flame, which turned bright white with heat. The red wizard, mustering the remainder of his strength, which had been severely drained from the day's events, again ordained that the flames should leave him and thus they did, forming a giant, white hot burning wall in between both of the wizards. Barlow pushed the wall forward, Rudgaf pushed it back. The Lord of Green hammered on the wall, demanding that it collapse on his enemy's head while the Lord of Red built up the wall's foundations, commanding it to stay strong. On and on the wizards went until Barlow, unable to even stand from lack of strength, collapsed on the ground, sending the wall of flame firing off into the sky and exploding in a brilliant spectacle of sparkling reds, yellows and blues.

Rudgaf exhaled from exhaustion. Barlow slammed his fists into the ground in frustration. Thome and Joem cheered Rudgaf's victory.

The Lord of Green slowly stood up and with disdain gave Rudgaf a swift backhand, then said, "You bastard."

The Lord of Red couldn't help but laugh at the green wizard's plight, "What's wrong? I thought you were the favorite."

"Hrmph," said Barlow, "it's obvious that I still need practice. No matter. Now that you're completely drained of energy, I can command the forest to finish you."

With a serpent's smile, the Lord of Green waved his hand.

And nothing happened.

Nearly asphyxiating at the inaction, the green wizard waved his hand again.

Still, nothing happened.

The Lord of Green gasped and with widened eyes he stared at his hands and said, "What's going on?"

Suddenly, the vines let go of their stranglehold on the red wizard, who fell to the ground in a heap. Barlow then whirred around when he heard two more thudding sounds nearby and realized that the trees had also let go of both Joem and Thome.

"No!" Screamed the green wizard while waving his hands. "I command you to seize them at once!"

Abruptly, a rumbling shot through the forest. The leaves in the trees rustled in a deafening manner, as if constantly being blown by a ferocious wind. Branches cracked and snapped. Finally, a low grumbling was heard. It was difficult for the wizards to make out the sound at first, but then it got louder and louder until it was almost on par with the sound of the leaves. Barlow had to cover his ears at the severity of the volume. It was then that the trees of the forest spoke.

"Barlow, thou doest dare calleth thyself, "The Lord of Green". Many a day hast thou spent amongst the greatness of the trees. When we were but saplings, thou nurtured us until the day that we were fully grown. In return, we hath given thee everything that we can give until we could not give thee anything more. We presented unto you our beauty and splendor, but thou didst desire more. We lent you our strength, but with it thou still couldst not lifteth the gnat. We yielded our fruits to thee, but thou wast sorely lacking. We gave thee our firstborn saplings, yet still thou criest into the night until thou finally criest unto the burning embers of Mount Shuun, of which we hatest with an untempered hatred. And now, Lord of Green, as our father didst turneth his back on his children, so too doest the children unto their father. No more shall the forests of the world lend thee their might. No more are thee the Lord of Green, nor are ye the keeper of the law for the atrocities that thou hast committed hath caused your children great pain and hast also caused justice to cry out in mourning. Now tis thou who shall weep bitter tears. We bid thee farewell from this day hence."

As soon as the forest stopped speaking, the leaves seized their rustling, the branches stopped cracking and the rumbling halted. Barlow looked off into the distance in utter disbelief. Then, girding himself up, he glowered and snatched Rudgaf's sword from its sheath.

"To hell with the forest and to hell with you, Lord of Red!" Cried the deposed wizard as he hefted the sword in the air, ready to strike.

With the remainder of his energy, Barlow swung the sword in a downward arc. However, halfway through the swing, a sharp, stabbing pain overcame the entirety of his being. In shock, he dropped Rudgaf's sword and stared down at a blade protruding out of his midsection. Attached to it was a hand that twisted the blade into the wizard, causing even more pain and shock. Barlow followed the hand with his eyes, up to the arm, then the shoulder, the long, black hair and finally locked eyes with Ramona.

Through gritted teeth, she said, "Die, you son-of-a-bitch."

The elf let go of the dagger and collapsed backward, landing next to Rudgaf. Barlow clutched at his solar plexus and staggered backward until his back collided with a tree and he slumped down to the ground in a sitting position.

"How could this have happened?" Barlow said to himself in dismay.

Rudgaf painstakingly crawled over to his former brother who, in disgust, smacked the red wizard away and said, "Get away from me."

"But..." protested Rudgaf, "you're dying."

Daggers shot from Barlow's eyes, "I don't want your pity, nor do I need it."

Joem ran up next to Barlow and said, "Barlow! Let me heal you!"

"I'd rather you put a knife in me," said the wizard, "but, of course, your friend over there already did that, didn't she?"

Barlow spat on Joem's boot, "And where were you, then? If you all truly loved me, you would've stopped her."

Thome stepped forward and said, "This wasn't anyone's fault but your own, green wizard."

"Don't say these things," cried the Lord of Yellow, "is this really how you want to spend your last moments? You're finally together with all of us. Doesn't that fact bring any semblance of joy to your heart?"

"You're such a sentimental dope, Joem." Said Barlow. "The time that I spent alone, away from the lot of you, were the happiest moments of my life."

"…And so it is." Said Thome.

The green wizard hawked and then said, "My powers…are returning to the stone."

The Lord of Red slithered as best as he could over to Ramona, who was laying lifeless on the ground. Gently shaking her, he said, "Ramona, are you ok?"

It was then that something unexpected by all of the wizards started to happen. As Barlow was breathing heavily, giving up the last portions of his air to the world, a faint, green glow began to surround the elf. The trees then began to move about, much as they had done before. Instead of a booming voice making a proclamation, however, a faint whisper overtook the area and before it faded back into silence it uttered the words, "She is chosen."

Suddenly, Ramona was hoisted up into the air by an unseen force while the wizards looked on in amazement. Large, luminescent green orbs began to appear out of thin air and shoot into the elf, causing her to glow ever more. Her eyes sprang open and she inhaled in revelation.

"Impossible!" Shouted Barlow. "I would never give my power to an elf!"

"It wasn't yours to give anymore, Barlow." Said Thome, dryly. "You threw it away."

"I…I knew it. I knew there was something different about her." Remarked Joem in astonishment.

The invisible force gently placed Ramona's feet onto the ground. She stared at her surroundings as if viewing them for the first time. In one hand she held a long, gnarled wooden staff. In her other hand she clutched onto a small, round stone. Her elven garb had been replaced with the green robes donned by the chosen one of the forest.

Barlow swallowed bile, "B…but…the elf?"

Ramona, the Lord of Green, looked around until her eyes met the sight of Rudgaf, whose hands and feet were still bound as he laid on the earth. Her eyes widened and while running to his side she shouted, "Rudgaf!"

The Lord of Red smiled at the elf while she knelt beside him. To him she asked, "Are you ok?"

"Look at you." Said Rudgaf while grinning ear to ear. "Just look at you."

He then passed out from fatigue.

~

Two weeks later, Rudgaf and Ramona stood at a site containing two grave markers that were placed just outside of the northern tower. Out of impulse, the Lord of Red knelt down, grabbed a clump of dirt, and somberly spread it over the markers.

"I've lost two brothers…two brothers lost to these powers." Said the Lord of Red.

Sighing, he turned toward the Lord of Green and said, "I start to wonder whether they're a blessing or a curse."

"Only time can tell, I suppose."

Silence crept in as both wizards stared at the grave markers placed for both Wilfrey and Barlow. Ramona then asked, "Rudgaf, do you trust me?"

The red wizard turned his attention back to Ramona and said, "Of course I do."

"Even after everything that I told all of you last week? Being undead, working for Mazuumanesh…all of that?"

"Well," said Rudgaf, "you're not truly undead."

The green wizard shrugged, "I was dead and now I'm not, I don't see what the difference is."

"The difference is that Mazuumanesh doesn't own your soul."

"Yeah," said Ramona, "thank heavens for that."

"Yes," continued Rudgaf, "I trust you. You've saved my hide twice now."

Ramona smiled, "Thank you, Rudgaf."

The Lord of Red nodded, collected himself for a new line of thought and said, "I'm leaving soon."

"Are you going to the central tower with the others? We're all rebuilding the place."

Rudgaf shook his head, "No, Ramona."

Ramona's eyes widened, "Why not? Where the hell do you think you're going all alone? Have you forgotten that Mazuumanesh is after our heads?"

"I'm sorry, Ramona. I need to leave."

"But why?"

The Lord of Red stared up into the sky and said, "To find out the meaning of what I am. To find out the meaning of my powers. To find the meaning in all of this death."

Rudgaf continued, "I've lost two brothers, Ramona. You know what one of those brothers said as he passed away? He said, 'I'll be back. I'll seek my vengeance from beyond the grave.'."

Ramona nodded, "I remember, Rudgaf."

"Wilfrey told me that each of us has to battle our own demons. I fear that Barlow will end up being my demon. I have to face him alone, Ramona, as each man must face his demons alone. Whether it be my undoing or not, whether it waxes me or wanes me, this is what I must do."

The green wizard crossed her arms, "I don't agree with this at all, Rudgaf."

Rudgaf smiled, "I know, Ramona." He then embraced the elf who, due to her anger at the red wizard's decision, was reluctant to return the embrace at first, but did eventually.

"Please be careful." Pleaded Ramona.

The Lord of Red pulled away and said, "I will return to you soon."

Both wizards smiled at each other and then, with no more delay, Rudgaf turned away from his companion and headed south.

When the Lord of Red was a few paces away, Ramona whispered, "I know that you will...this time."

Solemnly, she watched as Rudgaf walked off into the sunset of the age.

The End